ONE HELL OF A
CANDIDATE

ONE HELL OF A
CANDIDATE
WILLIAM F.
GAVIN

THOMAS
DUNNE
BOOKS

ST. MARTIN'S PRESS
NEW YORK

THOMAS DUNNE BOOKS.
An imprint of St. Martin's Press.

www.stmartins.com

Book design by Jonathan Bennett

Library of Congress Cataloging-in-Publication Data

Gavin, William F.
One hell of a candidate / William F. Gavin. — 1st ed.
p. cm.
ISBN 0-312-31283-0
1. Legislators' spouses—Fiction. 2. Coma—Patients—Fiction. 3. Southern States—Fiction. 4. Legislators—Fiction. I. Title.

PS3607.A985O54 2003
813'.6—dc21

2003046843

First Edition: November 2003

10 9 8 7 6 5 4 3 2 1

To American politics:
"With all your faults, I love you still. . . ."

ACKNOWLEDGMENTS

Thanks to Nina Graybill, for taking a look and then taking me on as a client; to Sean Desmond, for taking the trouble to make the manuscript better; and to Mary Alice Erickson, for taking the time to share her unique knowledge of congressional campaigns.

ONE HELL OF A
CANDIDATE

SIXTH DISTRICT

Pop. 520,677 . . . 14% black, 1% Spanish origin . . .

For many years the Sixth Congressional District belonged to the late, legendary Big Ed Kingsbury ("I'm a boy from the river counties and I never wore shoes till I got drafted"), the undisputed political boss of the state Democratic Party and the Sixth's representative in Congress for thirty-two years.

But after Big Ed's death, the district (following political and economic changes in the region) started to vote Republican. Six years ago, in a major upset, Republican T. Claude "Buzzer" LeBrand, sheriff of Grange County, upset the incumbent Democrat. LeBrand has increasingly disappointed his supporters by his lackluster performance and erratic behavior. With an outsize ego (even by congressional standards), he made an initially bad impression on his colleagues. Democrats have targeted him for political oblivion, but until now he has managed to keep the seat, each time with a smaller margin of victory.

—from Volume XXI of the *Register of Congressional Districts*

7:18 A.M. MONDAY, DECEMBER 28, WASHINGTON, D.C.

The day began badly for Congressman T. Claude "Buzzer" LeBrand and went straight to hell from there.

He awoke hungover (as he usually did these days), to find it was snowing—unpredicted by the damned TV so-called weathermen. If that wasn't bad enough, he seemed to have a touch of the flu. And, of course, his left knee, permanently damaged in the Big Shootout, hurt bad. It always did on a wet day. He limped over to the bathroom and, wincing as he bent over the sink, began to shave.

The mirror showed a forty-two-year-old man, just a bit over six feet two, the once-hard, sharp edges of his ruggedly handsome face now blurred from too much good liquor and fast food. His brown curly hair, cut short, was graying around the temples, and he had a paunch edging over the top of his boxer shorts. *But,* he thought, *I still look pretty good.*

Of course, he had looked much better just a few years ago—damned good, in fact—in his sheriff's uniform, boots shining, belt buckle gleaming, dark glasses giving him that mysterious, dangerous, Hollywood tough-guy look.

Usually a shave worked wonders for him, and woke him up, especially after he splashed on some of that expensive, bracing cologne. But this morning the aftershave magic wasn't there. He still felt lousy as he got dressed. Worst of all, there was no one in his Connecticut Avenue apartment to get angry with or blame. A week before Christmas, Georgie, his wife, had stormed back home to Grange City, taking Buzzer Jr. with her.

Now, driving to work, with the snow falling harder, Buzzer got caught in one of the inevitable traffic backups that even a hint of precipitation brings to Washington. Damn it, he was a United States congressman, just reelected. *Why don't they have a special lane for congressmen on a day like this, even if we aren't in session, instead of being tied up with a bunch of idiot bureaucrats?* When he finally arrived at his Cannon Building third-floor office (with its awful view of the ugly inner courtyard—no Capitol view for poor ol' Buzzer, with his lack of seniority), he was looking for someone to dump on. His secretary, who had long since learned the danger signals, knew he was in a special mood this morning.

"Well, what do I have to do first?" he growled, slumping into his blue, high-backed leather desk chair and kneading his aching kneecap.

She gingerly handed him a schedule card.

"Lottie, damn it, you got me overscheduled, as usual," he snarled, throwing the card on the rug. "Call Al Long's office and tell him I can't make the meeting."

"But you promised Mr. Long you'd—"

"Promised? I said I'd *try* to be there. Did you hear me use the word *promise*?"

Knowing better than to argue, Lottie left the office, quietly closing the door behind her.

Personally and politically, things were going badly for Buzzer and had been since his razor-thin reelection. Two weeks ago, WGMR's *Action News*, Grange City's most popular local news show, did a rotten, lying exposé on the Eudora Rhett Finchley Senior Care Facility, the nursing home where he had placed his mother a few years ago. *Damn it, the rats weren't that big. And Momma never liked to eat very much anyhow, so why the big fuss about some spoiled food? Besides, she didn't die of the food, did she? It was a heart attack that finally got her.*

Buzzer had only made things worse when the same station—they sure had it in for him—reported that staff members at the Finchley place swore Buzzer hadn't visited his mother in three years. In a news conference, he heatedly denied this charge of maternal neglect. His political enemies were conspiring against him, and even if this rumor was true—and he wasn't saying it was, no sir—his momma, God bless her, had always told him to take care of America first. That was the kind of mom she was.

"Let me tell you about these charges, in my own words, let me speak from my heart," he had said, reading from a statement written for him by his administrative assistant. "I fought the drug dealers back home, I bear in my body the lead those scum shot at me on that day not too many years ago. I have sacrificed a lot to serve the good folks who sent me here, and to serve our great state and this wonderful country. The folks back home just reelected me, so I must be doing something right. I know my dear mom, if she were here, would support my efforts. Family is first with me. Always has been. So I say, God bless my mom, God bless all moms—and God bless the United States of America."

Well, wouldn't you know it, WGMR, in a special investigative report on Buzzer, ran the audio track of him talking about serving constituents while showing a newly acquired home video, taken last year, of Buzzer frolicking with two bikini-clad young women on the beach at St. Kitts. Damned unfair it was, because he had been on an exhausting congressional delegation visit to the island nations—democracies, all of them—of the Caribbean, to foster goodwill between Americans and all those good black folks down there. And while he had in fact slept with both of the beach bunnies, he had not done so at the same time. Whatever else Buzzer might be, he was no pervert.

Well, one good thing, WGMR hadn't run those pieces during the last election, but only because they didn't have the facts. It would have given his Democratic opponent, the former NFL all-pro running back Bobby Ricky Diddie, just the edge he needed.

To make matters worse, things still weren't going well in the Sixth. The fat, happy economic prosperity of only a few years before was forgotten. Folks were hurting, and they were taking their pain out on poor ol' Buzzer. Well, to hell with them—he had squeaked through in November, and he'd be sworn in next week. They couldn't touch him for two years, by which time they'd forget.

Buzzer had a simple philosophy: politics is motion. Just keep on moving, shuffling and skipping. Never give them a sitting target, because if you do, they draw a bead on you. When you're in trouble, blame other people, change the subject, and then just boogie on down the road.

He looked at the wall opposite his desk, filled with framed photographs, all autographed, of practically everyone of importance he had ever met. A President, four movie stars, three governors, various state and county celebrities, and about a dozen photos of Buzzer, in full Grange County sheriff regalia, standing proudly with state and local law enforcement officials. He liked looking at his pictures—they reminded him of how very far he had come from his days of poverty. Folks used to think he was just trash, but he had shown them all.

He had a sudden sharp pain in his chest. He felt gassy, as if something was down there, heavy, maybe the two medium pizzas and the half a bottle of scotch he'd had last night. He was drinking too much, sure, but it was lonely in the apartment. He wished he could go back to Grange City and see little Buzzer. But Georgie had told him, quite emphatically, she didn't want to see him, even for Christmas. So here he was, wandering around a deserted House of Representatives, most of his colleagues back home. They'd be here next week to get sworn in, but for now he was almost the Lone Ranger, or at least the lone sheriff.

He went back to his desk, signed some letters, returned phone calls, and then picked up his schedule card from the rug. His first meeting of the day—right now, in fact—was with Carl Racksley, a former high-school classmate. The Racksley family was in Washington on a little holiday visit.

In high school Buzzer had not paid much attention to Carl except to occasionally extort lunch money from him. But since those days Carl had made a lot of money speculating in real estate and had bribed his way into the Barview Country Club, so Buzzer, during his first race for the House seat, had asked Carl for a campaign donation. Carl, like so many other people who are shrewd about business but clueless about politics, was easily seduced by a grin and a shoulder squeeze from a celebrity and dazzled by the sudden attention from the Fighting Sheriff, a genuine folk hero. Carl was as starstruck as a teenager in the presence of a rock star, and from that moment on, he couldn't do enough for Buzzer. He became his biggest fan and an indefatigable fund-raiser.

"Carl, great to see you," Buzzer said, leaping up from the chair and giving him a manly handshake, his right hand crushing Carl's right, his left hand clenching Carl's forearm—plus a big, dazzling Buzzer smile.

Carl, five inches shorter than Buzzer, pudgy and balding, had brought his two children with him. Jodie, whom Buzzer called Sugar (he could barely remember adult names, never mind these little brats), was wearing a Girl Scout uniform. Buzzer picked up the eight-year-old and whirled her around.

"Why, here's the prettiest little girl in Grange County. And look at that nice uniform. Sugar, the Girl Scouts are my favorite organization."

He put her down and tousled the hair of Carl Jr., age eleven.

"Hey, big fella," Buzzer said, putting his arm around the boy's shoulders, "am I wrong, or are you the guy who scored ten points in the school league basketball tournament last week? Ain't that right, Junior?"

"Yeah, Uncle Buzzer," Junior said sullenly, "and I woulda had twenty if it wasn't for that damn blind referee. He called four bad fouls on me, cramped my style, the bastard."

"Now, boy, watch your language," Carl said, smiling with pride.

"Well, that's what you called him, Dad. I heard you yelling at him. Blind and stupid, too, you said."

"Referees and umpires and folks like that are mostly stupid, and a lot of them are crooked, too, always remember that, son," Buzzer said, smiling and leading the three visitors to the couch. He liked constituents to sit on the couch because it faced his pictures. Let the idiots see who they're dealing with. He sat at his desk and gave the Racksleys another big Buzzer smile. Carl was about to speak when Buzzer suddenly said, "Hey, wait a minute, pardner. Isn't somebody missing here? Where's the prettiest gal in the district? Where's Marge? Didn't she come up with you?"

"Oh, you know women," Carl said. He loved being able to talk man talk to good ol' Buzzer, the Fighting Sheriff. "She wanted to go shopping by herself while I take the kids to the Air and Space Museum. She needs air and space of her own, she said. But she sends her love, like always. Marge is a big fan of yours."

"Glad to hear it. God only knows I need fans these days."

"We believe in you, Buzzer. Marge was just saying that the TV news, they never give ol' Buzzer a break. Just the other night she was saying how big a man you are. Those were her exact words, a big man."

"I'm going through tough times with that lying television news. They forget that ol' Buzzer put his life on the line for the community."

"Reporters are scum," Carl said.

"They sure are, pardner."

Buzzer stretched out his leg and tapped his knee.

"See this, Junior?" he said. "Still got a piece of bullet in there. Know how I got that, son?"

"Yeah, Uncle Buzzer, Dad already told me," Junior replied with the whining, bored tone of an eleven-year-old wiseass. "You whacked three goddamn drug-dealing spics."

"Now, Junior, watch your mouth," Carl said, smiling benevolently at his son. "I told you—you got to say Hispanic or Latino or something. They got rights these days."

"Well, that's what *you* call them," Junior whined. "You said ol' Buzzer just mowed down those goddamn spics."

Buzzer disliked Junior. The kid needed a slap across the mouth if any brat ever did, but Buzzer was glad to know the legend of his Big Shootout was still able to thrill kids.

"Let me tell you how it happened," Buzzer said. "I just did my duty, nothing more. I got a tip about these drug dealers out at an abandoned farm just off Route 61, near the county line. They fired at me first and I fired back. And when it was over, I was the last one standing. It was worth getting one in the knee, just so I could keep all those drugs from little kids like you."

He had told the same story so many times, he had just about forgotten that most of it was untrue and that the parts that were true were deliberately misleading. And he had not been sheriff when the Big Shootout happened, so the "Fighting Sheriff" nickname was also not exactly accurate. But it sounded great and, to Buzzer, that was all that mattered.

"Just like in the movies," Junior said, showing something close to enthusiasm. "I wish I could kill spic drug dealers."

"Well, maybe someday you will," Buzzer said amiably. "And you, too, Jodie, honey. The way they got girls on the police force these days, you might get your chance to shoot some drug lord. Equal rights for girls, it's only fair."

"Yuck, I don't want to shoot anybody. It's gross."

"It takes getting used to, is all," Carl Racksley said in a tone that conveyed that he, too, had looked death in the face. "Am I right, Buzzer? Just point and shoot."

"Right, Carl," Buzzer said, smiling, thinking, *You pussy, you couldn't hit the side of a goddamn Trailways bus with a shotgun if you were standing next to it.* After some chitchat, Carl shooed the kids out of the office, telling them to wait with the secretary while he talked to Uncle Buzzer. When they had gone he pulled a chair close to the desk. Buzzer could smell his cheap aftershave lotion, which Carl probably bought by the gallon. Buzzer had learned, long ago, even when he was dirt-poor, that the expensive stuff was worth it, women could tell the difference. But that was Carl, no class.

"So what's the big secret?" Buzzer said, moving his chair back a few inches.

"Buzzer, I got big problems."

"Don't we all, pardner?"

"Well, see, the thing is, lately I been borrowing a lot of money I can't pay back. I'm in a bind. I'm so strapped, I can't make my payments to the banks on the new shopping center I'm building out on the Western Pike. A few of my plans fell through and, well, I borrowed a lot of money from the Little Guy."

"Jasper Huggins? You borrowed from *him?* The Little Guy's a damned criminal. What the hell were you thinking?"

"Yeah, I know, it's risky. But what was I going to do? I was strapped. But now I can't see how I can pay him back."

Carl sighed, got up, and walked to the window. In the courtyard the snow was now coming down heavily, in great big wet, fat flakes. Buzzer waited, expecting to hear some kind of plea. *Buzzer, can you speak to some people at the bank, please. Or maybe introduce me to some big shot, ready to invest.* Fat chance. Pardner, you dug the hole with the Little Guy; get out of it yourself.

Carl, turning back to the desk, said, "This is none of my business, but I thought you'd want to know, Marge had lunch with Georgie out at the club, and she tells me you two got some serious problems."

Buzzer was surprised and pleased by the sudden change of topic. Carl is getting smart; he knows there's no way I'll help him with money problems, especially with Jasper Huggins.

"Nothing I can't handle," Buzzer said with the self-satisfied smile of a man in complete control. "Georgie'll settle down. She just got all crazy when she heard about those tapes of me down in St. Kitts. She'll come around."

"Women. They always cause you grief," Carl said with a big, one-of-the-boys, world-weary grin. "But what can we do? Can't live with them, can't live without them. I don't know what I'd do without Marge. Still crazy about her. We got problems, I won't lie about that. She's been distant recently."

"Sorry to hear that," Buzzer said, and yawned. He got up from the chair and walked, limping, toward the door. "Tell you the truth, ol' buddy, I got another meeting scheduled. Very important, top-secret national-security stuff. Please say hello to Marge and tell her I hope to see you all back home soon. They're keeping me busy up here, even though we're not in session."

When they left, Buzzer poured himself a stiff drink from one of the bottles of scotch he kept in his desk. Then he poured another one, and belted it down. He cleared his throat and shook his head. Good stuff. But he wasn't feeling any better. Damned flu or whatever it was made him weak, sweating, feeling a bit nauseous. He put a mint in his mouth and then picked up the phone and hit the intercom button. There were only two cures for the flu, he thought, and smiled. One was liquor. And the other was sex.

"Lottie, I'll be back around one-thirty, two, thereabouts."

Three-quarters of an hour later, in a downtown hotel room, Buzzer lay naked in bed, next to Marge Racksley, who wore only black lace bikini panties. She turned to him and put her hand on his stomach.

At thirty-seven, Marge was a damned good-looking woman, in a big, blond, generously proportioned way, maybe just a bit overweight, but Buzzer didn't mind that. Once, during his second term, Buzzer had been dragged to the National Gallery of Art (his first and only visit) by some important constituent and his wife. He was bored silly listening to them oohing and aahing over a bunch of stupid pictures. But then they came to a painting of a plump naked woman, her flesh all rosy and white and sexy looking, you wanted to touch it. She was looking right at Buzzer, the way women do when they want it, and it got to him. He remembered the woman in the picture the first time he saw Marge naked. She had that same pink, rosy, sexy glow about her. Some women had it, others didn't. It had nothing to do with beauty. It was a kind of bold, look-you-in-the-eyes sexiness, as if she were thinking, *Take a good look, big boy, I'm driving you crazy; I know it and I love it.*

Buzzer had been banging Marge ever since the night last June when Carl threw him a big birthday party at the Barview Country Club back home. Buzzer, just drunk enough to feel hornier than usual, had taken Marge for a walk in the soft air of the early-summer night, along the golf course. He screwed her near senseless on the grass near the fifteenth, par four hole, where he had taken a goddamn seven that afternoon. Not his fault, the damned green wasn't properly taken care of.

The quick hump amid the fairways had started something. It turned out that Marge was just crazy about ol' Buzzer, always had been. So, since that night in June, they had been meeting, back in Grange City and, less frequently, in Washington. Maybe her daddy had been one of the founders of the country club while his momma was washing other people's floors, but when ol' Buzzer was using his driver on her fairway that night, she didn't seem to mind the class differences at all, moaning and whimpering and begging him the way she was.

The last time they met, in a motel back home, she had told him she wanted more than sex—she wanted companionship, attention, the usual things women want, even love. She and Carl, it seemed, now had separate bedrooms as well as separate bank accounts (Marge had her own successful real estate office). She had Carl wrapped around her little finger, but it no longer mattered to her. She had married him at the height of his financial success. He had seemed almost glamorous, a buccaneer of high finance. Carl, surprised by the attention from such a socially prominent, good-looking girl, had done everything but wag his tail, roll over, and play dead to please her, so eager was he to marry the daughter of Dr. Lambert Hennings. But after the big wedding, she soon found that Carl didn't live up to her expectations. He was always talking about money, which bored her. Worse, he made love the way he made business deals—he was fast, clumsy, and selfish.

Marge tended to talk in a kind of psychobabble she had picked up on *Oprah,* and Buzzer was beginning to get tired of listening to her rattle on about "connecting" and "sharing." But he didn't know how to get rid of her, and he needed Carl as a fund-raiser. Besides, the sex was great—usually. Not today, however.

"It's okay, Buzzer, honey, it happens," she said in that damned chirpy little-girl voice she used when they were alone. "Don't make a big thing out of it, darlin'."

He could feel her hand slowly, gently moving on him. He brushed it away.

"Easy for you to say. Never happened to me before. Not once. It's this damn flu."

"It don't matter. It used to happen to Carl all the time when we were, you know, still doing it."

"Let's not talk about Carl, okay?"

"Okay."

"He tells me he can't pay back his loans."

"I guess he expects me to give him the money. But he's not getting it. That's my *daddy's* money."

"And by the way, while we're talking about Carl, use your brains. You told him I was a *big* man. Even Carl ain't that stupid; he's going to catch on to what you mean."

"Buzzer, I swear I didn't mean it that way, I just meant—"

"Forget it," he said, sulking. "Now I'm not in the mood, anyway."

"Sure, hon. We could just, you know, cuddle."

"Marge, sometimes you say the dumbest things."

"Well, at least we had some time together," she whispered, moving closer to him. "When Carl said last week we were going up to Washington, gonna see ol' Buzzer, I thought I was going to bust. I called you as soon as I found out. Honey, can I ask you something?"

"Yeah."

"You won't get mad? Promise?"

"Woman, do me a favor: say what you're going to say."

"Okay. Well, I just wanted to know, well, have you talked to Georgie about a divorce? You know, hon, you did kind of promise as soon as the divorce comes through, you know, then I'll get my divorce, and I just can't wait to be Mrs. Buzzer."

He was silent. There would have to be a windchill factor of minus 275 degrees in the deepest part of the blackest pit of the subbasement of the parking garage of hell before he'd marry Marge Racksley. To be fair, he had sort of said things along those lines, but all's fair in politics and sex, don't let anybody ever tell you different, and she should have known it. And he never once used the word *promise*.

She tried to kiss him on the lips, but he turned his head away.

"Buzzer, don't be mad, baby."

"Marge, shut up for once in your life."

He got up from the bed, his bones creaking, limped over to the chair near the window, and began searching through his clothes for his underwear. When he bent over to tie his shoes, he suddenly felt momentarily dizzy and had to steady himself on the chair. Damned flu had him short of breath, hurting all over. Maybe he'd get a shot from the doc at the Capitol.

Marge was chattering away. Since Georgie was back home for a while, Marge had thought, Gee, wouldn't it be romantic to just send a little love letter to Buzzer's Washington apartment and that's just what she did, yesterday, when the Racksleys had arrived in Washington.

"Wait until you read it, Buzzer! I'm blushing to think of some of the things I said."

He had been half listening, as usual, when he suddenly realized what she had been saying. He took three quick steps to the bed and grabbed her by the arm, pushing her down.

"Did I just hear you right? You sent me a *love letter?* To my apartment?"

"Buzzer, you're hurting me," she whimpered, frightened. "Please let go."

"Listen to me. Never, *never* send me anything, not even a goddamn Christmas card, unless Carl's name is on it, too. Goddamn it, woman, what do you use to think with? Letters like that have a way of winding up on the front page of the goddamn *Bugle* back home or the *Washington Post* even. Don't ever do that again. You got me?"

"Y-y-yes, Buzzer, I'm sorry."

"Sorry don't cut it. Writing me a love letter and sending it to my *apartment?* Are you crazy, woman?"

Riding down in the elevator, Buzzer thought, *She's so stupid, she drives me crazy, but she's so damned easy.* Yet, even considering her willingness to do anything he wanted in bed, he hadn't been able to do anything at all today. Nothing. It was scary, a stud like him, not being able to perform. He felt lousy.

Back in the office, now totally depressed, his muscles aching, he spent most of the afternoon stretched out on the couch, slowly sipping scotch, emptying one bottle. Occasionally he'd get up, walk into the staff rooms, and yell at his people. He locked the door and fell asleep on the couch but had bad dreams. About five o'clock it stopped snowing. No use going back to the apartment right now.

Nobody there. He drank a little more, watched the local TV news, all about the storm, the damned weathermen just smiling sheepishly and making jokes, as if they hadn't missed calling it. He thought of walking up Pennsylvania Avenue to one of the restaurants, see if there were any women, but this damned flu made him feel eighty years old.

He remembered thinking about Momma earlier in the day. She had been a tough old bird, not easy to live with, drank too much, her mind going at the end. But he could always depend on her; she had protected him from Daddy's rages, took a few punches that were meant for Buzzer. Now he had nobody. Georgie was ready to divorce him, little Buzzer would forget him. . . .

Ah, to hell with it. He'd think of something. Always had. Maybe he'd pull a sneak attack on Georgie. After all, she'd been hitting the bottle herself, maybe he'd hold a news conference, say he apologized for all the stuff on the TV news—people loved apologies from politicians—and then blame Georgie for the "pressures" (good word) in their marriage. Don't exactly say she's a drunk or to blame, but hint at it. Sounded good. Always keep moving and blame somebody else if you can get away with it. And finally, he'd say he was "seeking closure." He liked that phrase, it had class.

It was time to go back to the apartment. He decided to leave his car in the House garage. The roads were bad, plus the fact he had had some close calls with drunk driving charges and right now he didn't need the heartache. He'd take the Metro home, probably the only congressman in history to do that. He got up and put on his raincoat. All that scotch had at least taken the pain away from his knee, small blessing.

When Buzzer reached First Street, he pulled his raincoat collar close around his neck. He couldn't catch his breath. His chest felt as though someone were sitting on it. He leaned against the fence of a House outdoor parking lot and tried to stop the world from spinning. When he was a few steps from the Capitol South station's steep moving stairway, across the street from the Capitol Hill Club, the Republican Party hangout, he reached into his inside pocket to get money for a Metro card. He had the wallet in his hand, ready to take out a bill and . . .

His chest and his left arm were one great white hot pain. Buzzer let forth a deep, guttural, animal growl. He stumbled, lurching this way and that as he clutched his throat because he couldn't get any air. He was all pain, radiating from a deep, hot, bottomless hole right in the middle of his chest and down his left arm. He slipped and fell forward when he reached the top step of the Metro escalator and flew through the air a short way, hitting his forehead on the edge of one of the steps. His body turned over, he hit his head again, and he landed with a thud, banging the back of his head on another step.

Buzzer LeBrand lay sprawled, face up, bleeding, on the moving escalator, which, with the confident calmness of efficient machinery, took his unconscious body smoothly down and down and down.

Grange City, fifty miles southeast of Capital City, on the Little Pinellas River, has long been the financial, if not geographic, heart of the district, starting with its founding in 1826 as a trading post. The river counties to the east of the city, where the Little Pinellas flows into the Big Pinellas, are among the most productive agricultural areas in the state, rich in soybeans, cotton, and rice. But west of the city, the middle counties of the district have suffered from chronic economic underdevelopment

The district now has two claims to fame: Grange City is the headquarters of the BigBo stores, the regional discount chain founded by Republican political power broker Beauregard "Bo" Beaumont (who is Congressman LeBrand's father-in-law), and in the hills of the western part of the district is the Little Brown Church in the Wood, headed by nationally syndicated TV evangelist Reverend Herman Throe. The struggle between Throe—a rock-solid religious conservative—and Beaumont—a political pragmatist—for primacy in the Republican Party has often weakened the party's chances in statewide elections.

—from the *Register*

8:06 A.M. TUESDAY, DECEMBER 29, U.S. CAPITOL, WASHINGTON, D.C.

Morris "Never Ever Call Me Moe" Lansdale, Speaker of the House of Representatives, grunted. He was sitting at the head of the long table in Room H-227, part of the Speaker's suite on the second floor of the Capitol. Behind him was a marble mantel and a large mirror with a two-tiered gold-leaf frame. On the walls of the room were portraits of former Republican leaders.

Speaker Lansdale was a tall, thin, near-cadaverous, ill-tempered man in his early sixties. His most prominent feature was what he liked to think of as an aristocratic Roman nose. His many enemies preferred to call it a real honker. He grunted again. He was, in fact, an amazingly articulate grunter, able to evoke a range of emotions with one abrupt, throaty sound.

Gus Gorham of Arizona, a five-term member of the House and head of the National Republican Congressional Committee, a tall, slim, boyishly good-looking forty-year-old, sat at the Speaker's left. Gus was one of those rich, handsome, ravenously ambitious political golden boys who look as if they were turned out on the assembly line of the JFK-Lookalike Wannabe Political Manufacturing Corporation. An enemy had once said that all Gus's brains were in his hair—thick, curly, lustrous, and blow-dried to perfection. Occasionally he was mentioned by columnists as a prospective presidential candidate, for no discernible reason other than that he looked so . . . Kennedyesque.

Attending many meetings with the Speaker, Gus had gained a hard-earned expertise in Speaker Gruntology. He knew this last grunt had meant "Damn it, I am the Speaker, and I am annoyed."

The Speaker and Gorham hated each other. But each had been properly schooled in the small, useful civilities of congressional courtesy. So there they sat, in the ornate trappings of H-227, like figures in one of those allegorical paintings that graced the Capitol: *Ambition Achieved Condescends to Speak to Just Plain Ambition.*

"What's the latest on Buzzer, Gus?"

"He had a heart attack and he has head injuries. He's still in a coma."

"That's too bad," the Speaker said, with no great degree of enthusiasm.

"Yes, it is," Gus said in the same bland tone. "A tragedy."

There was a brief silence while the Speaker caressed his nose. Then he grunted and said, "Let me talk a little politics here. If Buzzer dies, we'll have a special election down there. Bobby Ricky Diddie will run again for the Democrats, that's for sure. Who do we have?"

"Joe Wholey, one of Herman Throe's people."

"Hellfire Herman? Jesus."

"There's another problem. Bo Beaumont, Buzzer's father-in-law, hates Herman's guts. If Wholey runs, Bo will run somebody in the primary."

"Gus, we need to keep that seat," the Speaker said with a little forced smile and a certain familiar nasty edge to his voice. "Let me paint the picture for you."

I know what the picture is, Gus thought, *it's my business to know. But if you want to pontificate, be my guest.*

"We didn't do well in November, Gus, as you know. We did lousy, in fact. We'll have a six-vote majority in the new Congress," the Speaker said. "Amos Collingswood in Texas is eighty. It's no secret Amos is no longer on the same planet as the rest of us. So we'll probably lose that seat next time unless they allow space aliens to vote in Texas. Jamie Donovan in New Jersey has cancer and I think we have to kiss that seat good-bye. Susan Degnan is making sounds she's not going to run next time and she's the only one who can hold that seat for us in Pennsylvania. And there are at least three other seats we barely kept in the last election."

He paused for a grunt (which Gus interpreted as *There! I stuck it to you because you did such lousy work as head of the Committee*), and then continued.

"I need to retain Buzzer's seat to build party morale, after what happened in November. And it's no secret there's people in the House Republican Conference—I name no names—who would like nothing better than to spread the word I'm losing my grip if we lose this seat."

"Well, thanks for that capsule summary, Mr. Speaker," Gus Gorham said, thinking, *You son of bitch, thanks for putting the needle in about the last election. It wasn't my fault. It was yours. We didn't get one important bill passed in the last Congress. That's you. Not me. I can't perform miracles.*

The Speaker shook his head and smiled ruefully.

"Buzzer couldn't do anything right when he was conscious, and now he's still messing up everything when he's a vegetable," he said wearily. "But let me see if I have this straight. Let's say Buzzer recovers and takes his seat."

"Then Bobby Ricky will almost certainly beat him next time. Anything can happen, of course. But I don't see Buzzer getting any stronger in the next two years. And I don't see Bobby Ricky getting any weaker. We can't exactly say it out loud, but the only thing we got going for us is if the, er, black thing works against Bobby Ricky. I'm not saying we say or do anything along those lines. . . ."

"Hell no, of course not," the Speaker said. "Here's what I want you to do. Go down to the Sixth as soon as you can. Meet with Herman Throe and Bo Beaumont. Tell them I want—no, no, put it this way, the party needs—one strong Republican candidate to run if Buzzer dies. We don't need a primary battle. Work it out and get it done."

"Sure thing, Mr. Speaker," Gus said, thinking, *Yeah, right, and after that easy job, I'll come back, jump off the Washington Monument, flap my arms, fly around the Capitol, and land on your nose.*

10:21 A.M. GEORGE WASHINGTON UNIVERSITY HOSPITAL, WASHINGTON, D.C.

A young doctor was telling Georgie LeBrand what she had already been told by another doctor earlier. But she had learned long ago that there are no instinctual drives—not lust, not hunger, not power, nothing—more basic to men than explaining things to women. She had spent her whole life listening to men—Daddy Bo, teachers, doctors, lawyers, preachers, and, of course, Buzzer.

Georgie and the doctor sat in the hospital visitor's room, furnished in hideous, uncomfortable institutional chairs and tables. A television set was mounted and bolted high on the wall facing her. Some talk show was on. Fat, homely people with bad skin were screaming at one another—but mercifully the sound had been muted.

"There are two problems, Mrs. LeBrand. First, the congressman suffered a heart attack caused by a single area of a coronary artery narrowing, specifically the left anterior descending. We can correct this by angioplasty . . . are you familiar with—"

"The balloon? You put the balloon in and expand it? Is that it?"

"Yes, yes, the balloon," he said with a delighted expression, as if he had just heard a chimp discourse on nuclear energy. "The second problem is, when he fell, he hit his head on the Metro escalator."

She nodded, indicating she knew what an escalator is. Suddenly she felt very tired. The flight up, the anxiety . . .

"Aside from the deep lacerations and abrasions, what he has is an epidural hematoma, which can be evacuated and repaired surgically," he continued. "But he is in a comatose state."

"Is he going to live?"

"His condition is critical, but . . ."

"I want to see him."

"I should warn you that it might come as a shock seeing him this way. You should prepare yourself."

When Georgie got to the room, there was Buzzer, his head bandaged, his face bloodless, his eyes closed. She suddenly began sobbing, which surprised her. She went into the bathroom and tried to get her face together. She looked into the mirror over the sink.

Most of her life people had used one word to describe Georgie—*cute*. She had been a cute child with her blond Buster Brown haircut and her quick intelligence and vivaciousness. She had been a cute teenager, with a cute little nose and a cute little figure, a particularly cute little backside, and a cute little laugh. And then there were her light brown eyes, lively and filled with intelligence and openness. She was the girl next door, full of pep and ginger, perky and passionate and capable of great enthusiasm, qualities that had made inevitable her rise to the position of captain of the Grange City High School cheerleading team, turning cartwheels with the best of them.

But that was eons ago, and now she was thirty-six. When she worked at it—which she really wasn't doing much these days—she could still look good, a former cheerleader who had turned into an attractive soccer mom. But after eleven years of Buzzer, something had happened to her eyes. The great zest for life that had once defined her had at some undetermined point simply faded away.

And, of course, a small but very smart part of her heart knew—although the other part vehemently denied—she drank too much. She was a woman who, ever since childhood, had wanted to be with people. Now all of that had changed, and these days, what she wanted above all was to be left alone, in peace, with a bottle of Merlot.

She sniffled, blotted her tears with a tissue, and walked back to the bed. Here was Buzzer, lying there like a corpse, and all she could think of was having a glass of wine, maybe two. Just to sit alone and think of nothing, have the TV on, letting the healing rays of inanity bathe her in soporific calm, deadening everything. A sitcom, a cop show, a movie of the week and a bottle of Merlot, maybe two bottles, the other just in case she got through the first. She did that a lot these days, or rather, nights. Back home it was great being with Buzzer Jr., he was a handful, and she loved him so much and he loved her. But when he went to sleep it was wonderful being alone, curled up before the TV with a bottle of Merlot and a box of Cheez-Its. It was like being on a spaceship, leaving the world behind.

At first she didn't know what it was about Buzzer that made her so sad, but then she realized it wasn't all the tubes and medical equipment—it was that he was motionless. Buzzer was always on the move, but now here he was, the whole world spinning around him and he was lying there, helpless. It was the saddest thing she had ever seen. She was surprised at her emotion because for a long time she had hated him, more than she had ever thought it possible for her to hate anyone.

Georgie knew he had been seeing someone new, but did not know who. The news story about the two girls in St. Kitts had hurt her, but she had become used to his quickie escapades. No, it was something different this time. All the usual signs of infidelity were there: his too hearty displays of attention to her and the look in his eyes as he listened to her, as if he were playing the role of a man with nothing to hide. After all of his women, it should not have bothered her so much, but for some reason, this latest one drove her crazy. She had become furious, questioning him. *Who is she? I know you're seeing somebody. Do you think I'm a fool?* But he had denied everything, telling her she was drinking too much. Buzzer lecturing *her* about drinking! And so she had left him.

Then a strange thing had happened. Being away from Buzzer had given her time to think. And the more she thought about it, the less she hated him. In fact, she could almost look at him objectively. He had told her—not much, but enough—about his sad childhood and she almost—almost—felt sorry for him. Maybe he really couldn't help being the way he was.

Back in Grange City she had told Marge Racksley all about the situation at lunch. Marge, who since last June had become her closest friend, might not be too bright, but she was a good listener. She didn't give one of those disapproving looks if Georgie had a second—or even a third or fourth—glass of wine with lunch. In fact, she encouraged Georgie to have another, just to relax. After Georgie had explained her mixed feelings about Buzzer—she certainly didn't love him, but no longer hated him—Marge had said to her, Georgie, sweetie, just get a divorce. You really should. It was comforting to have Marge to talk to.

Georgie knew she should get in touch with her brother, Russell, and find out how Buzzer Jr. was doing. She hadn't told the boy about what had happened to his father. He worshiped Buzzer, and she couldn't find it in her heart to hurt him with the news.

Suddenly Georgie was smiling—it happened so rarely these days that it came as another surprise—and then realized it was because she was thinking about Russell. Dear, sweet Russell was always ready to listen, her lifelong ally in trying to stop Daddy Bo from running her life. But she couldn't find the strength to make the telephone call. All she wanted to do now was to go back to the hotel—she could not bear to be alone in the Connecticut Avenue apartment—take a shower, and slowly drink a bottle of wine, seeking not forgetfulness or peace but something she had no name for but had long since learned to settle for. It was not happiness. Happiness was beyond hope. No, what she sought now was only some momentary sense of contentment.

12:06 P.M., KINGSBURY MEMORIAL PARK, GRANGE CITY

Robert Richard Diddier became Bobby Ricky Diddie when a high-school football coach mangled his name. At the time Bobby Ricky was fourteen and already the best player on the Grange City High football team. Since then, people had been staring at him. Over the years, as an all-American running back at State and then during his all-pro career in the NFL, he took for granted the adoration in everyone's eyes. He was, after all, worth staring at, with his good looks, light brown skin, irresistible big smile with just a touch of mischief in it, and, of course, as so many women could attest to, the seductive power of those shrewd, sexy dark brown eyes.

Now, in the late afternoon, in the third mile of his regular five-mile run around Kingsbury Park, near Grange Square, he saw other runners stare and smile in recognition. He gave each of them a nod of the head and a tight little smile, which, as a matter of fact, was about all he could muster, since he was having a hard time running. A few years ago, five miles would have been a warm-up. But now, at thirty-seven and out of shape from too little exercise, the pressures of his sports talk radio show, too many speaking engagements ("non-political" talks about motivation and teamwork), and too little sleep, his body, which had always responded to and often led his brain, was sullen and rebellious.

In November he had narrowly lost the election to Buzzer, but with Buzzer in critical condition, here he was ready to start again. It was all crazy. Now he had to call Kalya, his wife, and beg her to come back and campaign with him.

During the last election, Kalya had been of enormous help. She made appearances with him, dazzling everybody with her super-model looks (those cheekbones! those legs! that perfect deep brown skin!) and her charm and her brains. But Bobby Ricky and Kalya were in fact—if not yet legally—separated. Throughout the marriage, too many women could not resist his smile, his eyes, and his lean, supple, hard-muscled body. And he could not resist good-looking women. So two years ago Kalya had moved back to New York while Bobby Ricky continued to live and work in Grange City, setting the stage for his race against Buzzer.

He had flown to New York and begged Kalya to come back, just for this campaign, no more. He had promised her he would be faithful if only she would play the role of supporting spouse throughout the campaign. To his surprise, she agreed. To her surprise—and even more to his—he had been faithful throughout the campaign. But when it was over, he strayed again, with a secretary who worked at the radio station in Cap City. Kalya had moved back to New York, where she had her own public-relations firm. They agreed that there'd be no divorce, not right now. They'd just live their own lives. When asked, each of them said they had a commuter marriage. A lot of celebrities had commuter marriages. But in fact there was little commuting, and less marriage.

During the the last half mile of his run, Bobby Ricky tried to push it up a few notches but felt his knees start to burn. He slowed down. He'd get on the phone to Kalya this afternoon. She would not fail him. He knew she would come back, if only for the campaign, whenever that would be.

12:45 P.M., BEAUMONT BUILDING, GRANGE SQUARE, GRANGE CITY

"You know what politics is, Russell?" Bo Beaumont announced to his only son. Other people just said things—Bo, in his imperious mode, often announced. "Politics is always about *something else*. That's a fact. The stupid media and the League of Women Voters think it's about issues, policies, programs, and money. That's not true. The best thing in politics is to be loose. Don't get tied down to one idea or one candidate or one policy. Once you're sure you know what an election is all about, something comes along and suddenly it's about something else. You get the concept, Russell? Russell, damn it, I'm speaking to you."

"Oh, sorry. Yes, Dad, I'm listening. Something else, that's what politics is."

"Do me a favor, Russell, bark like a seal from time to time or send up a flare to show you're not daydreaming as usual."

For many years folks had told Bo he looked like Harry Truman. He was not a Truman admirer and did not believe all the Truman revisionism by the historians. To Bo, Truman had been a New Dealing, Fair Dealing son of a bitch, the knowing tool of the corrupt Kansas City Pendergast machine. Still, it is good in business and politics to have the "feisty" label, so Bo wore the glasses and the bow tie like Truman's. In fact, Bo dressed and looked like someone who had stepped out of a time machine directly from the Potsdam Conference (another damned Democrat giveaway to the Commies, in Bo's opinion).

Bo was seated in a BoPlastic chair ($14.95, on sale) behind a desk that was built like a checkout counter in one of his BigBo stores, with an electronic cash register at one end, a rack of women's magazines and sleazy tabloids at the other, and a scanner in the middle. In fact, his entire office was furnished or decorated with objects from, or concerning, his business. To Bo, the worst thing a business leader could do was surround himself with executive suite luxury and fancy doodads, and forget where his money came from. To his right was a shopping cart containing stacks of plastic and paper bags, which he used to carry documents to meetings. Around the walls of the room were framed full-page newspaper ads for BigBo store sales, each page from a different year of his company's thirty two year existence. To his left were six scaled-down aisles, modeled on those in BigBo (and, recently, BigJumBo) stores all across the region. The shelves along the aisles were filled with the items found in the stores, ranging from small bottles of BoHerbs to gigantic MaxiBo ten-gallon mustard jars. The left wall of the room, behind the aisles, was taken up by a huge freezer chest in which Bo-sicles (in fourteen different flavors, including BoBerry and BoCherry) and BoFro frozen dinners were prominently displayed. The right wall was covered by a large refrigerator unit containing BoMooMilk, BoBeer, and six kinds of BoPop soft drinks, including his bestseller, BocaCola.

As was the case in every BigBo store, three signs hung on chains from the ceiling, each one bearing one of Bo's favorite mottoes:

A CLEAN FLOOR MAKES A GREAT STORE

WASTED TIME IS A BIGBO CRIME

DON'T JUST STAND THERE! HELP A CUSTOMER

On the hour, a jazzy bugle call—the sound of BigBo Sales! in his stores—emanated from the BigBo Ol' Grampa Clock near the electronically operated doorway that opened when you approached it. On Bo's desk was a ten-pound plastic jar of his latest brainstorm, JumBo chocolate-covered mints with peanut centers.

Bo glared at his forty-year-old son. Russell was the kind of man no one had ever called handsome—the thinning hair, those chipmunk cheeks—but he could, without stretching things, be thought of as "not unattractive." He had a perpetual golden tan from a life lived mostly on golf courses. He didn't play very well—his long game was short, and his short game was inconsistent—but he loved being out on the course, away from his father. He was good, undemanding company, and businessmen who were afraid of Bo but needed to stay on his good side were always glad to play a round with Bo's affable son.

Russell lived under a peculiar kind of curse. The son of a man who had risen from poverty through ambition, shrewdness, and ruthlessness, Russell was not ambitious or shrewd and, worse, was a thoroughly nice man, polite, helpful, and self-effacing, someone whose happiest moments were spent on a putting green or in the clubhouse bar. He had failed at just about everything he had ever tried (as his father was eager to remind him). He had dropped out of State in his sophomore year after flunking three subjects (he wasn't dumb; in fact, he was quite intelligent but, intent upon golfing, just never showed up for class). He failed in two independent business ventures, failed in running one of his father's stores, and failed in marriage (twice).

Bo stormed through life. Russell sauntered. Bo announced. Russell suggested. Bo marched, ready for a fight. Russell shifted his feet, ready for a putt. Bo made war. Russell made nice.

Russell stood patiently at the side of the counter desk, waiting for Bo to resume talking. As Bo's son and now as senior executive vice president for corporate affairs of BigBo Inc. (a grandiose title for a meaningless position—his job was to do whatever his father said), he had learned to be patient. Bo reached into the jar for some mints and popped one into his mouth. He was addicted to the damned things. They made him feel refreshed. He stared over the top of his glasses at Russell, shook his head, and sighed. He took off the glasses and pinched the flesh at the bridge of his nose.

"Okay!" he finally said abruptly, slapping his hand on the desktop, jolting Russell out of a back-nine daydream ("*Tiger Woods is bending under the intense pressure as Russell Beaumont makes his move*").

"The bad news is, Buzzer is in a coma. But that's the good news, too. At least he can't do any damage for the time being. Now I have to figure out what I do if he dies and there's a special election. I have to think things through."

"Well, I agree, that's good, Dad, thinking things through, and—"

"Quiet, Russell, and you'll learn something. Now suppose Buzzer dies. I don't have anybody ready to run against Holy Joe in a primary if it comes soon, and besides, even if I did, a tough primary will split the party. I'm getting calls from the Republican county chairmen, asking me what we should do. I'm going to meet with some of them later. I want you to be here, just to listen. After the meeting I'm going to fly up to Washington, be with Georgie."

"Are you sure, Dad? If you like, I mean, I can come up with you and—"

"Rus-sell," Bo said, putting into the two syllables all the exasperation he had for his son. "You just take care of little Buzzer, like Georgie asked you. Take him to a movie or something out at the mall. Where is he now?"

"Staying with Mrs. Cummins, Georgie's neighbor. . . ."

"I pity her. That kid is a handful. He has a lot of his father in him. Now just leave me alone for a while so I can think this through."

He sat in silence, letting his mind wander, tapping idly on the keys of the computer cash register. Sometimes he got ideas by not trying to think too hard. He got up from his desk, turned, and looked down on Grange Square.

Main Street, running through the square, was divided into two lanes by the long, narrow plot of ground bearing the bronze monument containing the names of fallen Grange County heroes of World War II. For a while Bo stood at the window, not thinking of anything in particular, watching the traffic flow north and south past the monument.

Every major landmark on the square had played an important part in his life. The Beaumont Building, in which he had his office, was at the north end of the square, facing the courthouse directly to the south. He had deliberately erected his building on this spot to block the courthouse from a beautiful view of the Little Pinellas River, his revenge on the small-minded, greedy politicians. When he had started out, they had tried zoning ordinances and political blackmail to force him to make under-the-table payoffs that went into their own pockets. The excuse they used for their harassment was that discount, high-volume BigBo stores wiped out entire blocks of smaller stores and effectively ruined mom-and-pop retail outlets in the county, as if the good ol' courthouse boys gave a damn about mom and pop. For a while he paid them off, but when some of them demanded a piece of the business, he said to hell with it. Through guts, bribes, blackmail, collaboration with the gangster Jasper Huggins in keeping out unions, and shrewdly made campaign contributions to up-and-coming ambitious, hungry, politicians, Bo got to the point where he was powerful enough to place the Beaumont Building just where he wanted it. He had never forgiven the old courthouse crowd, a self-perpetuating aristocracy of indolence and greed. Knowing that the Beaumont Building spoiled their view was a great source of comfort to him.

To Bo's left—on the east side of the square—was Kingsbury Memorial Park, with its bronze statue of Big Ed. Bo could see, diagonally across the square from the park and down a block, the weathered white steeple (the view of which was partially obscured by an office building) of the First Baptist Church, which his late wife had attended and where Georgie had married the idiot.

Up the west side of the street, past the Grange Hotel, nearer the courthouse, was Fawcett's Diner, where Bo used to hang out in the old days, when Old Man Fawcett owned it. It was still the place to go see and be seen, but it lacked the homey atmosphere Old Man Fawcett had created just by his presence. Some damned corporation in Capital City owned it now.

Grange Square was the economic dividing line of the city. Two-thirds of the city lay to the west of the square, block after block of low-cost housing and rent-subsidized apartments, where most of the black population lived. East of the square were the stately old trees that in the summer shaded stately old homes purchased with stately old money. When you were in Grange Square it was safe to say that, generally speaking, to the west were deep pockets of poverty and to the east were people with deep pockets.

But these days, with the county and the entire district in a big economic downturn, the square no longer seemed to Bo the symbol of hope and success it had been when he had first come to Grange City, a poor boy from a hardscrabble farm in Holmes County. These days there were homeless people in the square, and the whole place just seemed to be lifeless and ugly.

The BigBo Ol' Grampa Clock let loose a bugle call blast, jolting Bo out of his reverie. One o'clock. He turned away from the window. It was time to face the cold facts: *If Buzzer dies soon, there's no way I can beat Herman this time. But if Buzzer lives, in a coma, Bobby Ricky Diddie just gets stronger and stronger.* Bo had nobody, either way.

Stop feeling sorry for yourself, you old man, he thought. *Think. Do something.*

2:45 P.M., THE LITTLE BROWN CHURCH IN THE WOOD, PRITCHARD COUNTY

Reverend Herman Throe, big, sweating, loud, and happy, 318 pounds of shaking, quivering, living praise to the Lord, six feet two of old-time religion incarnate, big in all directions, with a huge belly, hands the size of frying pans, a great squashed-potato Babe Ruth nose, and ears with lobes so big that some folks joked a small child could swing on them, sang out, his booming, rolling, leather-lunged bass-baritone voice raised joyfully, as the audience/congregation (this was being taped for broadcast later) joined in:

Oh, the Little Brown Church,
'Midst the pine and the birch,
The Little Brown Church in the Wood! [repeat]

Once I walked down a path with the devil
Never doing the things that I should.
Now I walk with you, Lord, on the level
To the Little Brown Church in the Wood.

Oh, the Little Brown Church
(Don't be left in the lurch)
The Little Brown Church in the Wood [repeat]

Through his successful television ministry, Herman guided the religious and political thinking of many good Christian folk in this area and in neighboring states. But unlike some of his famous TV evangelist colleagues, Herman had never been connected with any kind of scandal. He was, in fact, exactly what he appeared to be: a dedicated man of God, a childless widower, filled with the spirit of bringing suffering men and women out of the clutches of Satan and Self and Sin and setting them on the path away from hell.

As he sang, raising his arms to heaven, Herman thanked the Lord for providing the wherewithal to build this new church, an imposing modern structure with walls of glass supported by beams of natural wood, so that the congregation seemed to be in the church yet amid the very pines of which they sang. The New Church, as it was known, held eight hundred and stood next to and dwarfed the original Little Brown Church, with its four-window, fifty-sinner capacity. Within whose cramped confines Herman's father and grandfather had hammered the Lord's word into the thick skulls of hill folk. These days, Herman drew sinners from all over the state and the country.

In front of the original building stood the message board telling the mission of the church, then and now:

WE PREACH ETERNAL DAMNATION AND EVERLASTING AGONIZING BURNING TORMENT FOR SINNERS.

WELCOME TO ALL!

Among TV preachers with hundred-dollar haircuts and fashionable suits, slickly offering their consumer-friendly versions of the gospel, Herman Throe proudly and unfashionably preached the horrors of the pit, the unavailing screaming of the damned, and the noxious odors of the inferno. He did so without histrionics, in a conversational tone, and almost never raised his voice. His message was always the same. In today's little sermon, he had said in a quiet, avuncular tone, with a little smile gracing his lips: "Oh, yes, my friends—the agonies of hell are real, real as a tree. A tree grows, it dies. It is here and it is gone. Same thing with mountains, pure granite. Takes time, but the result is the same. Mountain is here—and it is gone. *But hell is forever.* It never dies. Oh, yes! And don't fool yourself about somebody rescuing you, like one of those SWAT teams you see on the TV, come swooping down out of a helicopter and *pluck* you out of the flames. No way, my friends. You're doomed. If that's what you *want,* then there's no accounting for tastes, nothing I can do about it. But the Lord, now He can help you escape, oh yes. . . ."

After the last ringing notes of "The Little Brown Church" were sung, Herman got out of his size XXXXL black robe, rubbed the sweat off his face with a white bath towel handed to him by one of the production assistants, and waddled to his office just as quickly as his enormous frame allowed. He had learned long ago, as a young preacher, that God gives only a certain amount of time, and every second of it should be directed toward His glory.

The first thing that you noticed—you couldn't help but notice—when you came into Herman's office was that the entire back wall, behind his desk, was made of glass, through which could be seen the magnificent green hills with their fir trees, in wave after wave, as far as the eye could see. Hanging above the windows was a huge rectangular piece of wood, roughly hewn, on which appeared the hand-carved words:

I WILL LIFT UP MINE EYES UNTO THE HILLS, FROM WHENCE COMETH MY HELP —PSALM 121

The decor of his office was anything but conservative, including a simple natural wood slab that served as his desk, and a large circular blond-wood table at which meetings of the Religious Coalition were held. On the walls flanking his desk were large color reproductions of two famous works of art. On the left was the scene from Michelangelo's *The Last Judgment*, showing writhing, horror-stricken sinners on their way to hell. Opposite it was a reproduction of Hieronymus Bosch's *The Seven Deadly Sins*, in which every conceivable kind of hellish horror was depicted. Some church members had criticized Herman because there were naked people in the paintings, but he thought the big pictures added a nice touch to his office.

Herman went to his new iMac computer with its futuristic hemispheric base and adjustable flat screen, gradually wriggled and scrunched his way into his oversize desk chair, hit a key, and searched for the file showing the demographic changes in the western part of the Sixth District (his mention of trees in the sermon had started a steam of consciousness flowing, from trees to hills with trees to hill people to voters). He looked at the numbers for a minute. He was right—the retirees were still coming in, but more young couples searching for a simpler lifestyle were coming to the hills from out of state. These folks tended to be more liberal. The western part of the district was changing. If he was to lead his flock politically, he might have to adapt the style, if not the content, of his political message.

An aide was standing in the doorway.

"Reverend Throe, Congressman Gorham would like to talk with you."

"Just tell him I'll call him back, Bob. I got the Lord's work to do here. I'm afraid even a congressman can't come between me and the Lord's work."

Well, it wasn't exactly the Lord's work that he was looking at on the computer. It was politics. But politics can be the Lord's work, if you do it right, he thought.

So Gus Gorham was calling. That meant those people back in Washington wanted peace in the Sixth if Buzzer died and there was a special election. They want Herman and Bo to make a deal. Well, here's the deal: this humble messenger of God's will has Joe Wholey. Bo has nobody.

Of course, Joe Wholey wasn't the easiest man to get along with. Some folks said he was unbalanced. Extreme. There was some truth in that, although Herman would never admit it publicly. A few years back, Joe, a state senator, had an old-fashioned nervous breakdown just before Herman had brought him to Jesus. Joe, roaring drunk, had wandered through the state senate chamber, babbling about the flames of hell. Some people thought he was going to burn down the place. He had told Herman he could not get out of his mind the idea of burning in hell. Joe said he could actually smell the foul odors of the pit.

Herman had counseled him back to some semblance of spiritual and mental health (and sent him to a drying-out facility). But you could look into Joe's eyes and see he was still not secure in the Lord. Joe Wholey—Holy Joe to his detractors—was a nervous, worried sinner who was always ready to talk about hellfire and how he had been singed by it. In his mind, he had one foot in church and the other in hell. But if there was an election, Joe would win. We got the organization. We got enough money. And we got the Lord.

Herman got up from the desk slowly, left his office through a side door, and walked down a short hallway to another door, which opened to the parking lot. Cars were still lined up, waiting to pull onto Route 220, and for a moment he stood there, watching the long line inch its way out of the huge lot. Back in Grampa's day, folks still rode horses to church. He crossed the lot and walked into the original church, which was empty. He went to the back pew and managed to squeeze himself in after much wriggling, puffing, sighing, squirming, and strategic placement of his enormous posterior. He knelt, asking God to do what was best for Buzzer and his family, especially sweet little Georgie and her poor child. He prayed to the Lord to focus his mind, to stop hating Bo. *And while you're at it, Lord, remember: it would be in your interest to have a good Christian in that seat in Washington. But, whatever happens, Thy will be done.*

6:56 P.M., GEORGE WASHINGTON UNIVERSITY HOSPITAL, WASHINGTON, D.C.

When Bo got off the plane at Reagan National, he took a taxi directly to the hospital. When he got to the room, Georgie was sitting by Buzzer's bed, staring straight ahead. She got up slowly, wobbled a bit, and threw her arms around his neck, sobbing. He smelled the wine on his daughter's breath.

"Daddy, thanks for coming."

"I got up here as fast as I could, sugar."

"I know you did. Poor Buzzer. Daddy, just look at him."

He looked in her red-rimmed eyes. She was getting a little bit soft on ol' Buzzer, feeling sorry for the idiot. Bo couldn't feel any sorrow for Buzzer. For Georgie, sure—she was his daughter. He knew women took these things differently. Buzzer was a bastard, but he was her husband.

Bo stayed with her for a while as she talked distractedly. When it was time to go, Georgie asked him to go to the Connecticut Avenue apartment the next day, pick up the mail, and see that everything was all right. She could not bear to look at the place, she said, giving him Buzzer's keys. They embraced.

6:45 A.M. WEDNESDAY, DECEMBER 30, WASHINGTON, D.C.

At Buzzer's place, after getting the mail from the mailbox in the entry hallway downstairs, Bo gave the apartment a quick once-over. He looked through Buzzer's personal papers. He turned on the computer and checked out a few files. He flipped through old checkbooks and just let his eyes wander all around the rooms—pizza cartons, an empty bottle of scotch, the place looked like a wreck. Well, why not? Anything Buzzer touches falls apart. He searched through dresser drawers. Bo liked to have an edge, and you never could tell what you'd find if you just bothered to look. But there was nothing here, nothing that he could use in the unlikely case that Buzzer ever recovered.

In the taxi taking him to the hospital, where he would meet Georgie, he absentmindedly skimmed through the mail. Bills. Advertisements. Junk mail. More bills.

A pink envelope.

A woman's handwriting, not Georgie's. Washington postmark. Addressed to Buzzer. He carefully opened it, trying not to tear the envelope. A letter. Same handwriting as on the envelope. No return address. He checked the last page. No signature.

My Dearest Darling Buzz-Boy,

By the time you read these words, my B-boy, we will have already been together once again. Oh, if you only knew how I look forward to being in your strong arms again, to be totally yours! When I say I love you "deeply" you know just what I mean!!! You are the "strongest" man I've ever known, in "every" way. Ever since that night last June, at Barview, right there in Nature's very own realm, we expressed our eternal love for the first time.

Last June in *Barview?* What the hell, she was from back home! She had been up here, though, when she sent the letter. Traveled this far to get laid by Buzzer? Must be hard up. Last June?

She was at Buzzer's birthday party. Now who the hell was it? Babe Hadley, that little tramp? No, she moved out west, married some idiot. Who then?

It's been almost a half year and ever since then, every time we make love, it is just as glorious and fulfilling. Please don't be mad at your best girl for writing but I feel I have to say what is in my heart and I know you don't like for me to talk "mushy" talk while we are together. Oh lover boy, I look forward to the day when we can be together always. I know it is dangerous to write like this, but I don't care—I just have to tell you what is in my heart.

I had lunch with you-know-who the other day at the club and I feel sorry for her, she just doesn't know what a prize she has in you!!! You are right about her, just as you say, she does not understand you and she drinks too much. (She still drinks Merlot, which is so yesterday!) I guess she thinks I am her best friend, and in a way I am because I know what is best for her (and for us!!!) and that is to let you go. My poor darling, to be stuck with someone like that, who had let herself go, when I could be your girl all the time! I never knew a man could be as exciting as you, oh, I'm spoiling you, I know, but I can't help it, a woman has to say what is in her heart (and other places!!!). Please, please write to me For ever and ever yours, my darling . . .

A friend of Georgie's. I'll be damned. Who? He replaced the letter in the envelope and shoved it in his inside jacket pocket. You never know what you're going to find if you look. He'd read it again later, at his leisure. Who was Georgie's best woman friend back home? Bo had no idea. He realized he really didn't know that much about his daughter these days.

So, two hours later, there they were, Bo and Georgie, sitting in the backseat of a taxi. Bo had maneuvered the conversation around to Georgie's needs. How was she coping, things like that. One thing led to another and she said she had a lot of friends. Bo, looking out the window, seemingly uninterested, casually asked who her best friend was back home, someone she could depend on now. Georgie said, "Well, I guess these days it's Marge." Bo—although now he knew—said, "Marge? Marge who?" Georgie said, "Marge Racksley, Carl's wife. We had lunch just last week at the country club. Marge thinks I ought to divorce Buzzer."

As Georgie got out of the cab, she turned to Bo and said, "I forgot to tell you. I talked to the doctors. I'm having Buzzer moved back home, to Grange Memorial, so little Buzzer can visit and see his daddy."

"That's a great idea, honey," Bo said, thinking, *This way we can all keep an eye on Buzzer, the cheating son of a bitch.*

10:53 A.M. THURSDAY, DECEMBER 31, AIRPORT MARRIOTT, CAPITAL CITY

Ladeeeez an' gennnnel-min . . . in this corner, weighing about half a ton, give or take a few dozen good meals, wearing something that looks like a dark blue circus tent, the undisputed heavy heavyweight political champion of the western part of the Sixth District, fat, faithful, and forthright, Big Herman "God Is My Political Consultant" Throe. And in the opposite corner, wearing a blue suit and bow tie, weighing little more than a good-sized baby killer shark, feisty, fulminating, and furious, Beauregard "Bad Bo" Beaumont. Boys, you know the political rules—no hitting above the belt. . . .

The prizefighting image flashed through Gus Gorham's mind as Bo briskly marched into the center of the hotel suite, and Herman Throe, sipping coffee, slowly arose in sections from the couch, groaning and gasping with effort. Herman covered Bo's extended hand with one great paw (the other was holding a jelly doughnut).

Shake hands, boys, and come out fighting.

"Bo, please tell Georgie she's in our prayers out at the church."

"It's Buzzer needs prayers, the way it looks to me, Herman," Bo said. "Gus, pour me a half a cup, black."

They sat in silence for a moment, Herman in sole occupation of the couch, with Gus and Bo sitting in chairs across the pastry-laden coffee table from him.

"I see you still like your doughnuts, Herman. I thought you preachers always resisted temptation. It relieves me to know you're human. Speaking of relief, how about one of my JumBo mints? They're good for digestion, which should be a concern of yours."

"No, thank you, Bo. You just go ahead and gobble them down. They must keep your stomach calm, with your business in such bad shape."

"Well then, gentlemen, let me get right to the point," Gus said brightly, trying to get things moving. "We all want to keep this seat, if Buzzer dies, that is. Nobody wants to see that, of course."

Silence.

Gus cleared his throat and continued.

"Let's try to work things out so we don't have a primary fight."

"There's not much to work out, far as I can see," Herman said with a big smile. "If Buzzer dies, Joe Wholey is going to run and win. I think I'll indulge in another cup and maybe just one more of those tiny little jelly doughnuts, Gus, if you will."

"But, Herman, with respect," Gus said, pouring, "Joe Wholey has some far-out ideas."

"Like his idea about the Ten Commandments becoming part of the Constitution?"

"That's one of them. Will we have a contested primary? That's what I need to know," Gus said.

"Could be," Bo said. "It's still a free country, more or less."

"Who would deny what a great country this is?" Herman said exuberantly. "Everybody has the right to engage in politics—except maybe for people who believe in God a little too much. They're too extreme, or so I'm told."

"Herman, Bo, can either of you think of a compromise candidate we could agree on? What about Joanne Turner, the state senator, she's—"

"Too liberal for my people," Herman said.

"Well, we agree there," Bo said. "She's a big spender."

"Anyhow, I support Joe Wholey, proud to do so," Herman said. "Join us and support Joe, Bo. We'd love to have you out to the Little Brown Church. We'll hold a unity rally."

"I'd rather get hit in the head every five minutes with a baseball bat."

"We'll just put you down as undecided about Joe Wholey, Bo," Gus said, trying to lighten things up and move this damned thing to some kind of conclusion. *Why did I come here on this fool's errand? Why didn't I tell the Speaker to go to hell? Why . . . forget it, you're here, deal with it.*

"Herman, quite frankly, people I know in Washington, not just in the party, but in the media, feel that if Buzzer dies and it's Wholey versus Bobby Ricky, we lose big."

Herman had his big hands folded across his great belly. The front of his trousers was generously sprinkled with jelly-doughnut sugar. He nodded his great head in agreement.

"Thanks for telling me what folks in Washington are thinking, Gus," Herman said with a mischievous smile. "It helps hicks like me to see the big picture. But I got to disagree with those learned folks. Joe is going to win. My coalition helped elect three congressmen in four states. We helped elect a lot of good people to various local offices, in this state and in neighboring states. I think we have a good track record."

"You're spoilers!" Bo said suddenly, his face red. He leaned forward in his chair. "You'll never elect Joe Wholey to Congress. Never. Can't you see that? The issue is jobs. Not sin. Jobs."

"Now, now, Bo, calm down. We're never going to build one job that matters more than saving this country's soul."

"See," Bo said to Gus, half rising from his seat and then sitting again, his jaw set, "see what I have to put up with? Only Herman's folks have morals. All the rest of us, well, we're *pragmatic* Republicans. We like to win in politics, it's a little peculiarity we have."

"Bo, I can see your point but—" Gus began.

"The hell you can. Those morals of Herman's cost us a state senate seat down in Blaine County. What about state-licensed gambling, lottery, casinos, which people down here need bad to pay for education? Herman's against that. Our state schools are bad, and Herman doesn't have one idea of how to improve them."

"Yes, I do," Herman said pleasantly. "It's just simple arithmetic. Add God to the curriculum and then subtract evolution."

"God don't need to go back to school, Herman, you people do. If we had gambling—"

"Now, now, Bo, use the politically correct term. The gambling industry calls it gaming these days. Let's all go gaming. Just look at Mommy and Daddy, happily gaming away their paychecks. The kiddies can become gaming-addicted."

"You people scare off the independent voters. And to you, all other Republicans are evil."

"Bo, let me jump in here and make a slight correction," Herman said with the same pleasant smile he used when speaking of the unending horrors of hell. "You and the golf-playing, country-club Republican businessmen aren't evil. It's just that in moral matters, you're terminally *flexible*."

Bo, his red face transformed into a mask of pure hate, jumped up, almost knocking over his chair. It was such a sudden move that Gus flinched.

"Well, this has been just *dandy*. This has just been peachy keen," Bo shouted as he walked quickly to the door. "Just a pure pleasure. Let me tell you both something—if Joe Wholey runs, then we can all wish Bobby Ricky happy New Year tonight."

Bo slammed the door. Gus looked at Herman Throe, who shook his head.

"So there we are. I got Joe Wholey. Poor Bo got nothing but temper-management issues. Do me a favor, son, will you? Looks like the jelly doughnuts are gone, so just pass me one of those little prune Danish—and pour me just one more cup. They make great coffee here at the hotel, they certainly do. I wish I could get this kind of coffee at home."

Drink up, Herman, Gus thought. *Now at least I know what I have to do. I have to get in touch with Jay Hollings. Tonight. New Year's Eve or no New Year's Eve.*

As the chauffeur drove him back along the Ed Kingsbury Memorial Highway (Route 61), Bo had time to do some thinking.

Old Herman just cleaned my clock, the fat, psalm-singing son of a bitch. But I deserved it. Lost my temper. Any fool loses his temper, in business or politics, gets what he deserves. Just a few years ago, I would have been like ice. I'm getting old. I let Herman get to me. Ah, well, it will give him a few laughs for a while, until he sends the next batch of sinners to hell. That's what really makes him happy, thinking of sinners sautéing and barbecuing forever, sort of a hobby for him, like bird-watching.

As the car moved south along the highway, Bo became more and more dispirited. There was a time when there were thriving little businesses on this road. But now all he saw were boarded-up storefronts and debris being blown around empty parking lots by the winter wind. The whole area seemed to be buckling and bending and sagging. Seedy. The car passed Tolmann Farm Equipment, and Bo recalled that they had laid off thirty-five more two weeks ago. On the other side of the highway was the King's Manor mini-mall. Carl Racksley had built it, but now all but five stores were empty or boarded up. The whole district was in the dumps.

Bo's thoughts returned to his half-dead halfwit son-in-law. *Buzzer can't talk. He can't vote. He can't do anybody any good. Come to think of it, I don't see much difference between Buzzer awake and Buzzer in a coma. He might die today, but he might die twenty years from now. Comas are tricky things.*

Bo paused in his ruminations and looked out at the BigBo store just off the highway at the junction of Kingsbury Highway and Route 12. The parking lot wasn't exactly crowded, there were shopping carts abandoned in the parking area, and fast-food rubbish was strewn about. *I'll have to pay a sneak visit to the store and shake up the employees, put them on their toes.*

All right, damn it, keep focused, zero in on the problem. Where was I? Oh yeah, waiting for Buzzer to go to the big Sheriffs Association in the Sky. And that's just it, he thought. *I can't do anything until the big dumb bastard has the decency to die.*

8:57 P.M., 1507 WINTER VIEW DRIVE, MCLEAN, VIRGINIA, THE HOME OF GUS GORHAM

"Honey, will you get the door?" Peggy Gorham shouted from the master bedroom. "I'm still doing my hair."

"It's probably for me," Gus said. He was dressed in his tux, and when he opened the door, Jay Hollings, without smiling—he rarely smiled—said, "No need to dress for me, Gus."

"Jay, come on in. Peggy and I are on our way to a party, so this won't take long. Let's go to my study and we'll talk. And thanks for coming on such short notice."

In the study Gus took Jay's overcoat and then turned on the radio so that their conversation could not be heard (even in your own home it was good to remember security). He poured two scotch on the rocks and closed the door. Jay took a sip and put the glass on a coaster.

"So what's the problem this time, Gus?"

Jay Hollings was short and slim, with blond hair that was so light in color that it looked almost white. He was meticulously dressed in a dark blue blazer, light blue shirt open at the collar, gray slacks, and black loafers. He was thirty-two years old, but there was an eerie, preternatural seriousness about him, a pitiless objectivity in his cold affectless blue eyes, and a scary way he had of being very, very still that made him seem much older. Ten years ago, when Gus had first been elected to the House, he had hired Jay as a legislative assistant, fresh out of college. But it soon became apparent that Jay wasn't the usual starry-eyed college grad grateful to have the chance to learn the ropes on the Hill, and with luck, someday become a highly paid lobbyist who plays golf with committee chairmen. Jay was, in fact, that most rare of political specimens, a natural. He had been born with the gifts of an uncanny memory for names, faces, and statistics and the craftiness and cynicism and guile that make a certain kind of brutal politics work.

He had come to the conclusion very early in his life that other people existed to be used. It was an idea so contrary to what he had been taught at home and in Sunday school that for years he believed he must have been wrong. But as he grew older, it became clear to him that it was the rest of the world that was wrong. People not only should be used—most of them secretly *want* to be used by someone slicker and smarter, someone who knows what is really going on beneath the deceptive surface of things.

When he was in the fifth grade he ran for class president and won by giving out Oreo cookies he had stolen from a convenience store. In junior year of high school he played his first successful political dirty trick, spreading a rumor that his opponent in a race for class president, a popular good-looking boy, was gay. In college he won his race for the student government presidency by spreading the rumor that his opponent, a woman running on the Diversity Party ticket, was *not* gay.

Jay had found the Hill boring. Congressmen were dull, stupid, and predictable, and the legislative process was dull, stupid, and slow. He left Gus's office after one term, deciding to strike out for the wilder shores of politics. Now, eight years later he was . . . what?

The closest description was *political operative*. Like *consultant,* the word was too vague to convey exactly what he did, which was to discreetly and at times illegally fix problems for politicians who had the money to pay his exorbitant fees. Over the years he got to know people who knew people who did things good citizens should not do. But he also had a database containing information on hundreds of ordinary people he had met, from his college years onward. He knew that in politics, where there is a premium on good looks, intelligence, and success, there were times when ordinary people—homely, dumb failures, eager to be useful—could provide him with information he couldn't get from other sources. More than once he had gleaned political intelligence from janitors, typists, and washroom attendants, from lonely, plain women and desperate, poor men.

Gus told him what had happened in the meeting that morning.

"Jay, I can't afford getting stuck with the label of a guy who can't get the job done. The media pick up on something like that. One day you wake up and you're a national joke, Letterman is doing routines about you. I made a mistake in the last election. I overpromised. I swore we'd pick up six seats. We lost five. It wasn't my fault, but after what happened in November, my reputation can't afford another setback. Two years from now there'll be a governor's race back home. It'll be tough, but I can win it. Then there's no stopping me. But first I need to get this goddamn loser-image monkey off my back."

Jay took a sip.

"Good scotch, Gus. But I always expect the best from you."

"Obviously I can't determine who the Republican candidate is going to be down there," Jay said.

"And so?"

"Something has to happen to Bobby Ricky's campaign."

"Got anything in mind?"

"In the immortal words of somebody, I don't know and I don't want to know."

"Our arrangement is as usual?"

"Of course."

Jay raised his glass.

"Happy New Year, Gus."

"Happy New Year to you, Jay."

9:07 A.M. WEDNESDAY, JANUARY 6, THE LITTLE BROWN CHURCH

Herman Throe had spent the past five days making calls to members of his coalition, sending e-mails, conferring with pastors and prominent laymen all across the district and the state. There was a genuine enthusiasm about Joe Wholey running and winning if Buzzer passed away. Joe could beat Bobby Ricky if he ran a good race. The coalition was making sure Joe would get off to a running start if the Lord saw fit to call Buzzer home. Until this moment, Herman had been feeling good. But he had just finished a telephone conversation with Joe Wholey that left him shook up:

Herman: All I'm saying is maybe you kind of soft-peddle the Ten Commandments idea.

Joe: Herman, are you asking me to back off making the Ten Commandments part of the U.S. Constitution?

Herman: Not exactly backing off. Just, maybe, put it in context, like they say. Folks you and I trust, they been telling me some voters have problems with your rhetoric, like we saw in the last primary against Buzzer.

Joe: Herman, I got to say I'm a bit surprised. You're talking like a politician.

Herman: Now, Joe, there's no cause for insults. God wants you to win.

Joe: God wants me to speak the truth.

Herman: Just keep in mind the district needs jobs. Remember that.

Joe: All right, Herman. I'll talk about jobs. But the Ten Commandments bill is my top priority.

10:06 A.M., ED KINGSBURY MEMORIAL HIGHWAY

Bo was in the backseat of his limousine, on his way to his office from the Cap City airport. He had been to Memphis on business. He looked out the window and let his mind drift and float, not settling on anything in particular. Buzzer, still in a coma, would arrive at Grange Memorial Hospital later today. *Hard to think of my Georgie as a widow. But that's practically what she is.* Bo leaned his head back and in a while he was in a half-asleep state, aware of his surroundings but detached from immediate reality, his mind drifting, images and mini-dreams popping in and out, and . . .

And then, slowly, in dim, tantalizing outline, from somewhere deep in his memory, out popped something he hadn't thought of in years. He sat upright, trying not to lose the thought. It took him a moment of concentration, getting his mind in gear again, to focus the eye of his mind. Look at the thought sideways, not directly. If you try to force these things . . .

Widow.

No, no, not widow. *Widower.*

That was it. Some woman congressman. Years ago, couldn't remember her name. In Maryland? Delaware? One of those places. She had a heart attack and fell into a coma, just like Buzzer. The House declared the seat vacant. And there was a special election, and the congresswoman's husband, a widower, ran for the seat. He lost.

But he ran.

Suppose . . .

Suppose Georgie told the Speaker that the doctors don't believe Buzzer's coming out of it? Buzzer had never been sworn in as a member of the new Congress. The House could declare the seat vacant. There'd be a special election. And Bo knew for the first time who his candidate was going to be. Why hadn't he thought of it before? Widows of congressmen have run for their deceased husbands' seats and won. Georgie wouldn't technically be a widow, of course. Buzzer was more or less still alive, his tiny brain still functioning at the level of a piece of celery. But she'd be *like* a widow, getting the sympathy vote. The brave little thing, running in her first race, female candidate—we need more women in office. Spunky, that's what she is. She has a cute little boy. She's Bo Beaumont's daughter.

And then there's her husband. Even if he is a son of a bitch, lying there in a hospital like a rutabaga, she's a devoted wife. She's a patriot. She'll make the sacrifice of running, God bless her, a woman who knows what the Sixth District needs, unlike certain religious fanatics or famous former athletes. This brave, spunky little gal has lived among us all her life.

Ladies and gentlemen, I give you the next congresswoman from the Sixth, Georgia "Georgie" LeBrand! No. Georgie *Beaumont* LeBrand.

Bo was on a roll.

I could raise money quickly. I could talk to anybody else who thought of running and convince him not to, one way or the other. Just Georgie against Holy Joe in the thirty-day primary. Head-to-head. Anything can happen.

But she has absolutely no experience, has never run for office.

Neither has Bobby Ricky, except that one race against Buzzer.

But Herman Throe will back Joe Wholey in the primary.

Let him. Let him split the party, hurting the chance of this brave, spunky wife and mother, sacrificing everything for the good folks of this district, God bless her.

But she's feeling all misty with Buzzer near death. She'll never agree to it.

She'll get over it. I'll see to that. Of course, as soon as the process starts, everyone will know. It'll leak out that Georgie wants the seat declared vacant. But I'll know before *the rumors start. I can make plans, maybe even hire some people, do it all below the radar.*

It's true what I told Russell: politics is always about something else. Buzzer barely won last time. Now he's a pet rock, so most folks are asking, How much is Bobby Ricky going to win by, sooner or later? But if we spring an election on Bobby Ricky, on our terms, right now, before Buzzer dies, it just might catch him off balance. Then anything can happen. Georgie, the spunky almost widow. Damn, it was good!

2:37 P.M., GRANGE MEMORIAL HOSPITAL, GRANGE CITY

"Mizz LeBrand?"

Georgie, standing by Buzzer's bed, turned and saw a young nurse—homely, rail-thin, and serious-looking—dressed in hospital greens.

"Mizz LeBrand?" the nurse said again. "I'm Patsy Earlings. From Etons."

"I know Etons, Patsy. It's in Pritchard County, in the hills," Georgie said, giving the automatic smile of a congressman's wife, using the person's first name as soon as possible.

"Well, I just want to tell you how sad I am to see what happened. I thought you'd like to know we're all so glad we'll be taking care of your husband. I admire you so much, you're so pretty and brave and all."

"Thank you, Patsy," Georgie said, "it's nice of you to say that."

Patsy took Georgie's hand, squeezed it, and said, "God provides."

"I used to think so," Georgie said.

"Oh, I *know* so. Reverend Herman Throe always told us God provides."

"Do you attend the Little Brown Church?"

"Oh, no, ma'am. Not anymore, me being a nurse here in Grange City. It's too far for me to travel. But we were members, me and my mom. Reverend Throe saved us both from eternal fire, damnation, and eternal suffering. He's close to God, Reverend Throe is. But now we belong to the TMC."

Seeing the incomprehension on Georgie's face, Nurse Patsy explained: "Tabernacle of the Messenger to Come. The Messenger is coming, Mizz LeBrand. He'll come in secret, so no one will know him, only the brothers and sisters of the TMC. The scales will be lifted from our eyes. Nobody else will know him, only us. And he'll be like unto Joshua with the heathens. And we'll be in his ranks."

"Well," said Georgie, having no idea what Nurse Patsy was talking about, "that must be very comforting for you."

"There's only forty-three of us right now. But we'll know when the Messenger comes back. And when he does, we'll help him smite the heathen the way the Lord smote Pharaoh's army. Vengeance is mine, saith the Lord, and ain't that a fact? Mizz LeBrand, I hope you don't think I'm being too forward but, see, I still got lots of faith in Reverend Herman's powers. Can I just play some of his tapes for your husband, right here on this VCR? They got it hooked up anyhow."

"Patsy, he's in a coma."

"Oh, I know, Mizz LeBrand, but God's got His own ways, and doctors will tell you, people in comas, they can sometimes understand more than we think. Let me just play some of Reverend Throe's videotapes. Maybe Mr. LeBrand can hear him. Reverend Throe speaks God's words, and they can be heard amidst the stormy night."

"Thank you for caring so much, Patsy."

"Oh, I just want to make sure your husband don't suffer no eternal torment. The flames and all."

"That's very thoughtful of you."

When Georgie got home from the hospital that evening, there were two messages on the answering machine. The first was from Bo. He wanted her to meet him at her favorite restaurant, La Salle de Classe in Capital City, tomorrow night. He had something important to discuss with her. Russell would drive her.

Then the other message played:

"Georgie, this is Jack Danzig. I got your number from Nancy Bitterman, I work with her now, in Evans Humphrey in Cap City. I read about Buzzer and I just want you to know . . . if . . . if there's anything I can do. . . . I just want you to know I'm thinking of you. This sounds a bit crazy, but I saw the story about Buzzer being moved to Grange Memorial and . . . I guess I'm not making any sense."

And then there was that self-deprecating, sweet little laugh—she would recognize it anywhere. He left a Cap City number, in case she wanted to talk.

Jack. After eleven years, Jack.

8:47 P.M. THURSDAY, JANUARY 7, LA SALLE DE CLASSE RESTAURANT, CAPITAL CITY

Bo hated Capital City. The snobby people up here looked down on the good folks of Grange City. They were proud and stuck-up because they had the legislature and the governor's mansion and two or three real tall buildings. The presence of the university didn't help things, either. There were all those damned tax-supported left-wing intellectual professors, in love with the sound of their own voices, most of them from out of state, teaching damned foolishness to boys and girls from the hills and small towns. But what he hated most of all was the way Cap City folks thought they were really sophisticated, not like the rubes and rednecks in the rest of the state.

Take this place, La Salle de Classe, a few blocks from the university. Georgie said it was supposed to be just like one of those French bistros, like the kind she dined in when she traveled to Europe, long ago. Bo wasn't sure what a bistro was, but to judge by what he had seen tonight, it was probably French for "a place with a phony chalkboard menu out front, overpriced food, poor service, snotty waiters who looked down their noses at you in three languages, and a chance to be made to look like a fool when they asked you about the wine you wanted, you stupid peasant."

But Georgie was always talking about it, so he had decided this was the place to make his pitch, driving all the way up here in the rain. When they were seated, she made him and Russell notice the darling red and white tiles on the floor and the authentic-looking dark-leather-covered banquettes. Then they looked at the menus, handed to them by a waiter whose bored expression made it clear he would rather be someplace else.

Bo looked at the entrées.

Bouillabaisse Jean-Paul Sartre.

Steak au poivre à la Woody Allen.

Jean-Baptiste Lully Chicken Liver Pâté.

And today's special, Filet Mignon Deconstruction, a tribute, the menu said, to Foucault.

But Georgie seemed to be enjoying herself. Bo waited until she had a few glasses of the outrageously overpriced wine and then, casually, as if it had just occurred to him, told her of his plan to have her run for Buzzer's seat. She kept on drinking as he was talking. For a moment she didn't reply. Then she said, "No."

"Georgie, let me explain this to you—"

"No, Daddy, I don't want *anything* explained to me, ever again," Georgie said quietly but firmly, then took another sip of wine.

"No explanation?" Bo said. "You won't even listen to your old dad explain the situation?"

"I know what the situation is. If I knew this was what you wanted to talk about, I wouldn't have come. Russell, I'll have just a bit more, please."

Russell poured the wine, finishing the bottle. He signaled to the waiter for another. The waiter lifted his eyes toward heaven. He snapped his fingers, and a busboy took away the empty bottle. When the waiter had performed the wine ritual, Russell said (Bo had coached him) pleasantly, "Now don't say no before you think it through, Georgie."

"There's nothing to think about. You're asking me to pull the plug on Buzzer. Then you want me to run for his seat in Congress. That's ridiculous."

"Now, now, hold on, sugar. Nobody's pulling the plug. It's more like you're saying he can't take his House seat. He still gets the best care. Am I right, Russell?"

"Absolutely, Dad."

"Georgie, you told me what the docs at Grange Memorial said, just yesterday. 'Negative prognosis' were the words they used. That means he's not coming out of it. All you have to do is get a judge to attest to what the doctors say, and inform the Speaker. The House declares the seat vacant and the governor has to call an election."

"It's the same as saying he's dead."

"But it's not, sugar," Bo said soothingly, trying not to lose his temper. "We're just facing the facts here. You were the one who told me about this prognosis negative thing."

"They can't be sure. It looks as if it *might* be irreversible. But they didn't say it was."

Bo gave a little snarl-laugh.

"Sugar, those witch doctors are just covering their behinds. They don't want to be sued, so they talk cautious, just like politicians. But you know and I know and they know Buzzer's not coming out of it."

"I guess that would suit some people."

"Now, now, baby, no use in raking up the past. We have to look forward."

"To the future," Russell said.

"That's where the future is, Russell, forward," Bo said.

Georgie had her angry face on, so Bo decided to make a tactical retreat and not take things too quickly.

"I really like this place, Georgie," he lied, trying to get back in her good graces, but she wasn't buying it.

For a few moments all that was heard was the clinking clatter of a busy restaurant and the laughter and low rumble of dinner conversations all around them. At a table nearby, a young woman wearing dark glasses was talking to her dinner companion, a bearded man wearing a denim jacket, torn T-shirt, and a State baseball cap on his head backwards.

Bo caught bits and pieces of the conversation. They were talking about some man named Wittgenstein, and how great he is. Probably one of those damned professors at State.

Bo waited.

"Besides, that's not the worst part," Georgie said finally. "I never ran for anything in my life. Except being captain of the cheerleaders."

"Joe Wholey can be beat, Georgie . . ." Russell began.

Georgie put down her wineglass and said with a little smile, "If he's so easy, why don't you run against him?" looking Russell in the eyes.

He looked away, flustered, and then smiled his sweet, boyish Russell smile.

"Politics isn't my game," he said.

What is? Bo thought, biting his tongue. He couldn't say what he wanted. He needed Russell here as an ally.

"Well, there's the difference between us. I don't see politics as a game," Georgie said. "I'm not saying politics was the cause of . . . what happened between Buzzer and me. I'm just saying it didn't help. So where does that leave us?"

Bo was surprised at her obstinacy. Probably the wine. He had never heard her talk this way. Maybe it was time to play on her emotions. With his fork, he shoved deconstructed pieces of filet mignon around his plate and then slowly looked up—over those Truman glasses—with a pained, defeated look, and said, in a small, whiny voice, "Honey, we don't *have* anybody else who can beat

Bobby Ricky. Joe Wholey can't. And nobody else is out there."

"That's for sure," Russell said, looking at Bo for approval for his remark.

"And we owe it to Buzzer to put up a fight," Bo said, ignoring Russell, pretending to take great interest in the filet mignon, not daring to look at Georgie to see if she was swallowing this. "For the sake of the party."

She laughed. Georgie had a nice, strong laugh, not like some women, Bo thought. But it was so unexpected, Bo looked up and saw that the sudden sound had drawn attention from other tables. How many drinks had she had?

"Daddy, I know what you're up to," she said with a big smile. "You want me to run so I'll split the party. Wholey will lose, either to me in the primary or, once the party is split, to Bobby Ricky. And all of this so you can spoil Herman Throe's chances of being the big man in the Sixth."

He hadn't thought her capable of thinking in that mean-spirited, cynical way. He was very pleased.

"Now, sugar, that might be part true, but that's not all. You've been reading those editorials in the *Bugle,* same as I have. The people need representation, Buzzer being non compos mentis and all. The district is hurting. We need somebody to represent us."

"You could give people hope, Georgie," Russell said.

"How can someone like me give people hope, Russell?"

Russell had not expected the question. Hope was not one of those things he ever thought about. But it had sounded like something he should say.

"Let me handle this, Russell, if it ain't too much trouble," Bo said quietly. "Think of this, honey. You'll just be like a grieving widow, only Buzzer's not really dead. You'll be trying to serve the district. Am I right, Russell?"

"Right, Dad, just like Buzzer," Russell said earnestly.

Bo gave him a withering look and then turned back to Georgie. "You're kind of his widow, see, but you're independent. Folks like independence. They're sick of politicians, believe me. They want real folks in Washington, just like themselves."

"That sounds absolutely stupid to me," Georgie said with a giggle, her voice just a bit loud. "Why do they want someone who knows nothing or cares nothing about politics and government?"

"You're a congressman's wife. You know enough."

"Most congressional spouses know the words. But we don't know the tune."

"What's that supposed to mean?"

"It means I know all the political rituals. I even know some of the issues fairly well. But I don't have politics in my heart. You have to have it in your heart to be any good at politics. Or have no heart at all. If people need to get things done in Washington, why send someone there like me?"

"This is a democracy. If the people want things like that, who are we to object? We could portray you as one of those citizen legislators. Just an ordinary woman, a spunky mom who'll go to Washington and—"

Their waiter approached the table, sneered, and said, not looking at them, "I suppose you'll be wanting dessert of some kind?"

"What do you recommend?" Georgie asked.

"Crepes à la Papillon. Or the Danton-Marat Revolutionary Cherry Tart."

They decided to pass on dessert. The waiter said something under his breath and departed.

"Daddy, if I won, what would I do once I got to Congress?"

"Oh hell, sugar, you could hire staff and there's plenty of people to give you things to talk about, job proposals, extensions of unemployment benefits. I got people who could advise you how to vote. Hell, throw a fork at any of these tables—not a bad idea—

and you'll hit an expert on some damned thing or another. You can imagine how many of those experts are up in Washington. I can buy people like that. Sugar, do your old dad a favor—at least think about it."

"No."

Bo looked at Russell, who had a goofy, happy, fantasizing-about-golf look on his face.

"Russell, I wonder if you'd just go to the cloakroom, get the coats?"

"That's okay, Dad, I can get them when we're ready to go."

"Rus-sell."

"Oh."

Bo watched Russell make his way through the tables. He reached into his pocket, took out a roll of JumBo mints, took one and offered them to Georgie. She shook her head.

"You know, Georgie, your brother, Russell, is a nice boy in his own way—"

"He's a man, Daddy, not a boy."

"Anyhow, I love him just like I love you. But I had hoped, well, he'd kind of continue my work. In business and in politics. But he never did."

"Maybe that's because you never let him think for himself," she said. "Did you ever think of that? He's smarter than you think. And he gets along with people."

"Georgie, what you won't admit to yourself is you're just like me. Russell is just like your mom, God rest her soul, soft and gentle. But you're just like me. You want what you want. You wanted Buzzer. You dropped that nice boy, the Jew lawyer, what's his name, Jack something, dropped him—"

"Daddy," she snapped, anger flashing in her eyes.

Bo knew he had gone far enough. Step back.

"Now, now, now, take it easy, sugar. I'm not bringing up the past.

All I'm saying is, you think you're so put-upon. You think I boss you around. But the fact is you're as pig-headed as I am, just as strong-willed, but you never wanted to admit it. That's all I'm saying."

"Maybe, but you know what?" she said, grinning with drunken slyness. "I'm *still* not going to pull the plug on Buzzer. And I'm *never* running for anything. How do you like them apples?"

"That's your privilege, of course," Bo said coldly, rising from the table. "Let's see if Russell managed to get the coats without causing an international incident. I'll take my car, and he'll drive you back home."

Well, he thought as he watched Georgie unsteadily weave her way to the parking lot, *time for plan B.*

As Russell drove her back to Grange City, Georgie saw a police car pass them on the rain-slick road, lights flashing, siren on. She remembered how handsome Buzzer had looked in his police uniform that day in May long ago, when they met outside the Barview Country Club, at one of Bo's political events. Buzzer was on duty, standing by the main doorway, arms folded over his big chest, wearing his shades, looking great.

She was twenty-four at the time, a couple years out of college. She had made a grand tour of Europe, Bo's little graduation present. She was working in Cap City as an elementary-school teacher in the inner city, but she didn't have to depend on a teacher's salary, being Bo's daughter. She loved Cap City. It was, by her standards, sophisticated and cosmopolitan. More important, Daddy Bo didn't own the town. He owned a handful of state legislators, but he couldn't get his way all the time, as he could in Grange City.

She found the intellectual atmosphere at the university exhilarating. There were some good restaurants and a movie theater near the university that showed classic foreign films (she saw *Umberto D.* for the first time). Then there were the Capital Players, a little theater group that did Beckett and Ionesco and Albee. She had a nice apartment four blocks from the capitol building. She was prepared to go back for her master's in English at State, at night, in the fall.

She had been dating a young lawyer named Jack Danzig. To Georgie, Jack had three things going for him: he was cute, he was funny, and he was a Jew. He had moved to Cap City from New York only a few years before to take part in a civil rights survey paid for by one of the major foundations and had liked the slower pace, so he stayed. The fact that he was a New York Jew, in Georgie's experience at least, made him exotic and even an erotic object of desire. They recently had been making love on a regular, exclusive basis. Jack was a volunteer in a school reading plan—that, in fact, was how they had met. He was nice looking, if not conventionally handsome, prematurely bald ("balding," she liked to think), but he was intelligent, kind, considerate, dependable, and caring. Jack desperately wanted to marry her, but she wasn't sure.

Jack introduced her to the music of Benjamin Britten, Frederick Delius (she came to love Delius), and Miles Davis, promising to let her listen to his Charlie Parker CDs only when she was more spiritually developed. He discoursed on why Jackson Pollock was superior to Mark Rothko. He recommended books. She read stories by Isaac Bashevis Singer, *Call It Sleep* by Henry Roth, *The Red and the Black,* some Hemingway she had missed in college (she didn't like him, too macho), and tried to slog her way through James T. Farrell's Studs Lonigan trilogy, which Jack had recommended highly. She and Jack would walk along the river and talk through the night, about books and music and art, enjoying each other's company. For a while, life was great. She was away from her father, she had a life of her own, and she liked teaching.

Then she had gone back to Grange City at Daddy Bo's request—his requests were still commands—to attend a fund-raising affair with him. Georgie had obeyed, of course, but she was in a bad mood when, about to enter the club from the parking lot, she saw this policeman. He was tall, he had big shoulders and attractive blue eyes (he had slowly removed his glasses when she looked at him, a very sexy move the way he did it; years later he told her he had modeled the gesture on one of Clint Eastwood's), and she thought—or to be precise, felt—he was the sexiest man she had ever seen. She knew he was vain, taking little side peeks at his reflection in the mirror inside the front door of the club. But she had learned long ago that all good-looking men are conceited. She could tell he was interested in her. Interested, hell. He *wanted* her. It was that blatant.

Hadn't he been at Grange City High, she asked, a senior when she was a sophomore? Yeah, that's right, he said, you're Mr. Beaumont's daughter, you was a cheerleader, right, yeah, I sure remember you in your little cheerleader outfit. Real cute.

Of course, she had not really *known* Buzzer in high school. He was not exactly the kind of boy a girl in her position would know, but she had known about him—who hadn't? Buzzer LeBrand had a bad reputation. He had been left back twice in grade school. He was a troublemaker, suspended for a variety of reasons. He was a bully, the kind of dangerous, sexy boy your parents didn't want you to go out with. Not that she would ever have thought of such a thing. Now here he was, a policeman, handsome as the devil, looking her straight in the eyes.

She was, after all, Bo Beaumont's daughter, royalty around these parts, and many young men were afraid to ask her out, but he casually, impudently, held her gaze. Suddenly, without any preliminaries or small talk, he offered to take her out for lunch the next day. Surprising herself, Georgie accepted.

The next day they met for lunch at a little restaurant on the Western Pike, not exactly a high-priced romantic place, but at least they had tablecloths and napkins and real flowers on the tables. The thing was, she knew what he was after. But she thought, *Oh, it's just a game, nothing serious, no danger here,* but as they talked, she *knew,* in a way she had never known with Jack.

As they ate she confirmed her original feeling. Buzzer was exciting. He was also egomaniacal, not too bright, crude but with a kind of blunt, artless charm. He ate too quickly, devouring the steak. But when she went home, she could not get him out of her mind. That night in bed, with Jack, she found herself fantasizing about Buzzer. It made her ashamed. Buzzer was what they used to call forbidden fruit. She wanted to take a big, long, slow, juicy, tantalizing, succulent bite. The feeling scared the hell out of her. What was going on? She had never ever felt this way before. She was melting away, sending out signals no male within thirty miles could miss—except, apparently, Jack. It was quite embarrassing, really. It was as if she were drunk—not that she'd ever been drunk. She didn't drink alcohol in those days.

One night Buzzer called her and said he was coming up to Cap City, had some business up there, and asked her again to lunch. She thought for three seconds and said yes. She lied to Jack, saying she was going to meet a girlfriend. After that, one thing led to another, and soon Bo found out. One day when she was back home in Grange City, having dinner with Bo, he said, with his typical directness, "This LeBrand fella you've been seeing, I had some people look into his background."

"You have no right to do that."

"Don't tell me my rights, sugar. The boy's trash. Nothing wrong with being trash, mind you, but *staying* trash, well, that's different: being trash is what happens to you; staying trash is what you do to yourself."

"You don't even know him. Daddy, this is—"

"And, besides, I hear he does jobs on the side for the Little Guy."

"That's crazy. Jasper Huggins is a criminal; everybody in town knows that. Buzzer is a policeman."

"Don't get me wrong. I like Jasper Huggins. I've had occasion to work with him. He's a vicious psychopath, but a man of his word, up to a point. But, like you say, he's a gangster. And, anyhow, ain't you already got a boyfriend, that Jew fella you talk about? Drop this LeBrand, he's trouble."

That very night, on a blanket on the grass near the river, Georgie and Buzzer made love for the first time. Sex with Buzzer was not sweet, as it was with Jack. But, oh my God, was it ever hot. Although as an English major she knew the image was trite, the worst kind of cliché, making love with Buzzer was like being at the seaside and, unaware, getting hit by a big breaker. There was all that surging, overwhelming, irresistible power. She had read juicy descriptions of this kind of sex, but reading didn't convey the . . . *physicality* of it all.

That night she had her first real, honest-to-God, full-blown orgasm. A while later, after Buzzer had rested a bit, she had her second. Afterward, as she lay in his arms on the blanket on the riverbank, she really wasn't sure if she had wanted him because of the way he made her feel (even before sexual intercourse) or because Daddy Bo didn't want her to see him. But now she knew one thing certainly: she wanted Buzzer LeBrand.

Daddy Bo used his usual tricks to break them up. He put pressure on the sheriff and had Buzzer exiled to a post in the boondocks. Bo even had two county detectives sent to "talk some sense into this idiot," which meant physical threats. Things like that had always worked in the past, scared away boys, but Buzzer wouldn't back off. That made Daddy Bo hate him even more, and made Georgie's love stronger. She finally got up the courage to tell Jack. He was angrier than she'd ever seen him. Who is he? Tell me his name! he yelled, the first time she had ever heard him raise his voice. The next day, while he was asking her questions about Buzzer, he began to cry. He sat on the couch and wept, What did I do? Oh Georgie, Georgie . . .

And then, three months after she had met Buzzer, Georgie had told Daddy Bo they were getting married. No, she wasn't pregnant, they had been careful, but she wanted to get married and so did Buzzer. Daddy Bo hadn't said a word when she told him, but she knew he hated Buzzer more than anyone in the world. So there was the big wedding at First Baptist in October.

For Georgie it was great at first. There was, for one thing, unlimited, glorious sex. But she gradually began to see another side of him, a selfishness, a pettiness, and a general meanness of spirit she hadn't noticed before or, if she had noticed, had attributed to the pressures of his job. Her life began to resemble articles published in women's magazines under headings like "How You Can Tell When the Honeymoon Is Over" or "Fifteen Infallible Ways to Know Your Man Is a Rat." When Buzzer had too much to drink, which was happening more and more, he'd roar on about his momma and how his daddy had hit her, and how Buzzer hated his daddy, how damned angry he was at his daddy, how he would kill the old man if he ever came across him. Then there were his bad moods. He'd come home late, smelling of drink. She'd demand to know where he'd been; she was beginning to suspect he was seeing somebody. But he'd yell at her and then sulk for two or three days, blaming her for things she didn't do. They began to argue about sex. He wanted it when he wanted it, but she wasn't exactly in the mood after two or three days of his sulking and anger.

The tension grew. They began to bicker and then to argue and then to scream at each other. He pushed and shoved her to make his points. Then he began to slap her, first on the arms, then on the face. She was frightened of him, but she hoped he would change. *(It's partly my fault, after all, I'm not patient enough with him.)* Then she became pregnant. Buzzer Jr. was born and things were pretty good for a while. But then came the Big Shootout. He was elected sheriff and then elected to Congress, and just about this time she realized she couldn't close her eyes any longer. The son of a bitch had been unfaithful to her from the git-go, the cheating, lying bastard.

She was startled out of her reverie by something Russell said. She hadn't caught it.

"What I said was, maybe this election could give you something new—in your life, I mean."

"Did Daddy tell you to say that?"

"No, Georgie, honest. I mean it."

"The answer is still no. Tell him that, in case he's got some idea you can get me to change my mind."

4:32 P.M. THURSDAY, JANUARY 14, 235 FRANCIS STREET, GRANGE CITY, THE LEBRAND HOME

Georgie liked to think of her home's decorating scheme as Revenge Modern. Years ago, she had learned that instead of arguing with Buzzer, who could shout her down, she could channel her resentments and energies into expensive redecorating plans. Oriental rugs and Barcelona chairs came in the front door as three-year-old couches and side tables went out the garage door on their way to Goodwill. Just two years ago, she had decided to join the Big Bathroom Revolution, just after she caught Buzzer cheating with a woman who lobbied for Amalgamated Textiles. She consulted with an expensive contractor, haunted flea markets, and drove Buzzer crazy by creating a bathroom that was almost half as large as the ramshackle West Side home in which he was raised. The room contained a huge antique white clawfoot tub, a small but perfect crystal chandelier, two antique chests to hold oversize towels, and lavender-colored sinks, toilet bowl, and bidet.

"God almighty, woman," Buzzer had shouted, "I'll be too damned nervous to do what I gotta do in a place like that! Looks like the john in an eye-talian whorehouse."

This afternoon she was sitting on the living room sofa—a lovely light green and white floral pattern with accent pillows, purchased after Buzzer had pushed her against the (new) kitchen sink. She was watching *Oprah,* nursing one glass of Merlot. Buzzer Jr. was playing at a friend's house and wouldn't be back for an hour, so this was her private time. She had imposed a daytime limit of two, no more than three, glasses of wine at lunch and only one more before dinner. Not that she was drinking too much. It was just that she felt she had to get some order in her life. She did not always observe the limit, but it made her feel responsible to know she had set one.

Through the window looking out on Francis Street, she saw the mail truck pull up to the red wooden mailbox. She slipped into her sneakers, reached into the closet for her coat—it was freezing out—and got the mail. Back on the couch, she began to open the envelopes. Advertisements. A lot of get-well cards for Buzzer. Bills.

There was a plain manila envelope. Inside, there was a single sheet of paper with the typed words *"this was found in your husband's pocket that night. thought you'd want to see this. a friend"* and a handwritten letter—two pages, both sides, on pink stationery.

There was no signature.

She read the letter all the way through. Then again.

Buzzer and Marge. All this time. Since last June. On the *golf course.*

She sat for a while, not thinking of anything, and then called Russell and asked him to pick up little Buzzer at his playmate's and keep him overnight. She didn't feel well, she said; she needed to be alone. For the rest of the day and into the evening and then into the night she watched television, nibbled Cheez-Its, and sipped Merlot. She fell asleep.

When she awoke the next morning, she felt awful. But in her mind everything was clear. She dragged herself out of bed, took a long, hot shower, got dressed, drank a glass of orange juice, went to the bathroom and vomited, brushed her teeth, gargled, and picked up the telephone.

"Marge?" she said in a calm, quiet voice.

"Oh . . . *hi,* Georgie. Gee, I haven't heard from you in it seems like *ages*. I didn't want to call. Might, you know, get you at the wrong time. So, how are you? How's Buzzer? I was thinking, how about the next time you visit him, I give you some moral support, and come along? I think at a time like this, you need a friend."

"That's thoughtful of you, Marge. You always think of me."

"That's the least I can do."

"Yes, but it's still so sweet. Oh, gee, before I forget—the reason I called," Georgie said in the same pleasant voice, "is I just wanted to remind you of something."

"What's that, honey?"

"Just that if I ever see you again, I'll kill you."

"What?"

"I've got the letter, you dumb bitch."

"The letter? Oh. Oh. The *letter.*"

Neither of them said anything for a few seconds.

"I thought, maybe . . . I don't know. I thought it was . . . lost . . ." Marge said. "Georgie, are you drinking?"

"Don't *ever* call me or speak to me or come near me or my child again. Stay away from places that you know I'll be. Or else I'll kill you. This isn't the wine speaking. I swear to God, I'll get one of Buzzer's guns and I'll shoot you with it."

She gently placed the phone down. Her heart was pounding, and she felt a little bit better. She needed a drink. But instead of pouring a glass of wine, she drove to Grange Memorial. When she walked into Buzzer's room, the television screen was showing one of Herman Throe's sermons.

Nurse Patsy Earlings came into the room and smiled.

"See, Mizz LeBrand, I was as good as my word. I play two or three tapes for him every day."

"Yes, I see that. I wonder if he can hear it?"

"Oh, God provides ways, Mizz LeBrand."

"Yes, he does. Do you think I could just be by myself, with my husband, for a few minutes?"

"Why, of course, Mizz LeBrand. You take all the time you want. I got all the members of the TMC praying for him."

Nurse Patsy left the room, and Georgie was alone with Buzzer.

"The Devil wants you," Herman Throe was saying on the tape, in his matter-of-fact, take-it-or-leave-it tone of voice. "The devil wants to be your master. Be greedy. Satisfy your dirty, unspeakable, filthy lusts in unholy ways. That's what he wants. He's in the filthy movies—which means almost all movies these days. He's in Washington, D.C., with its godless political corruption. They got the First Ten Amendments but they forgot the Ten Commandments."

Georgie, mesmerized, had difficulty breaking away from the screen. With effort she concentrated on turning off the television.

What was this crazy fat man talking about? The Devil? We don't need devils, thank you. We have people. They can be bad enough. Oh, yes, Reverend Throe, they can be devils, people can. We each get our little bit of hell right here, more than most of us can handle. If there's a devil, I bet he doesn't beat his wife and cheat on her with her best friend. . . .

She stood by the bed, looking at Buzzer.

"Let's send you straight to hell, Buzzer," she said. "It'll do you good."

She squatted by the wall, reached out, and had one of the plugs in her fingers. And in that gesture, all of the bad times, all of the tears, all of the agony, all of the pain and humiliation he had caused her, all of it seemed to be transferred to her fingertips. She felt that just a willed movement of certain muscles and all of it would leave her and disappear. Pull the plug. Isn't that how they say it? For an instant her fingers tightened on the plug and she began to pull it out of the socket.

But she couldn't do it. She backed away from the wall and she could feel the fierce beating of her heart. It wasn't that she cared about Buzzer. He was already dead to her. Infidelity was one thing. Betrayal with Marge Racksley was something else. As far as she was concerned, they were both dead to her. But she wasn't going to jail just for finishing off Buzzer. And then there was Buzzer Jr. She couldn't murder her son's father. So she pulled her cell phone out of her purse and called Bo at his office.

"Morning, sugar, ain't heard from you in a while. How's Buzzer?"

"Daddy, don't ask me any questions. Just listen."

"Something wrong?"

"Don't grill me. Just listen. I changed my mind. I'm going to tell the Speaker about the negative prognosis. I'll ask him to declare the seat open. Then I'm going to run for his seat, as you want."

Bo didn't say anything for a moment, and then, soothingly, "Well, this *is* a surprise. I'm glad you changed your mind. It's the right thing to do."

Bo, allowing himself a little smile, put down the phone. He got up and grabbed the shopping cart and pushed it around, humming merrily to himself.

"Russell?" he yelled.

"Yes, Dad?" Russell came running into the office.

"Georgie changed her mind. She's going to run."

"Georgie?"

"You got hearing problems, Russell? Get on the phone right now, this minute, and get me Ida Mae Watkins. If anybody can pull this thing off, Ida Mae's the gal. I've got to get Ida Mae."

8:30 A.M. WEDNESDAY, JANUARY 20, THE WESTERN PIKE

Ida Mae Watkins was forty-four, five feet eight, and wore a bare minimum of makeup on her freckled, attractive face. She smoked. She drank shots of bourbon. She loved to play golf. She wore her sandy-colored hair in a short, sensible cut. Unsurprisingly, some people who did not know her thought she was a lesbian. This misconception did not bother her. In fact, she was amused by it, because from her teenage years she had been wholeheartedly in favor of and an enthusiastic participant in heterosexual sex. But the misconceptions about her sexuality, which had begun when she was in high school, had taught her a valuable lesson about politics: people make decisions based on misinterpreted perceptions. It was the primary job of a campaign manager to make certain that first impressions were strong, lasting, and favorable and that nothing the candidate said or did weakened a strong first impression.

Thus, to Ida Mae there were three political virtues a candidate must have: a strong, friendly image; consistency and simplicity of message; and flexibility, the ability to adapt image and message to the swiftly changing circumstances of a campaign. These virtues, in order to be effective throughout the race (consistency!), had to be supported by a strong, flexible, responsive organization. Everything else in politics was an afterthought.

Years ago, after a disastrous marriage (the divorce came exactly two years after the wedding ceremony), Ida Mae, bored with her job as a secretary at the Tolmann plant, had volunteered to work for a candidate running for a council seat in Grange County. She discovered she loved politics and particularly loved campaigns. She also discovered that a woman in politics had to be able to roll with the punches because it was traditionally a man's game. But she—and men who looked down their noses at her—found she could play the game with the best of them. Year by year, campaign after campaign, she gained more firsthand knowledge of how local politics worked. She got to know the Sixth Congressional District better than anyone. She knew every courthouse political boss, every influential clergyman, every PTA chairman, every service club president, and the head of every professional organization. She knew the first names of county chairmen and precinct captains (and of their spouses), she knew the reporters and editors of the *Bugle,* and she knew Capital City lobbyists and legislators—a few of them all too well, the lovable scoundrels.

Bo Beaumont had asked her to handle Buzzer's first congressional campaign. For a while things went well. But eventually, inevitably, Bo and Ida Mae, two strong-minded people, began to clash. One evening after a long, long day campaigning in a chilly October rain, they were sitting in the storefront campaign headquarters and Bo said something about Ida Mae's smoking too much. She snapped back. Bo lost his temper and there was a shouting match, with Ida Mae giving as much as she got. Bo fired her four days before the election. They hadn't spoken since. That was why she was so surprised when she got the phone call.

"Ida Mae, I need you."

"Bo, I'm flattered. But you're not my type."

"Cut it out, Ida Mae. This is pure business. It's something big and you'll be in charge, all the way. No interference from me."

"I bet. What's it about?"

"I'll tell you when I see you. It's big, I promise you that."

"Whatever it is, it's going to cost you, Bo."

"Hell, I know that. You got me over a barrel. You're going to stick it to me. Well, good for you."

So for two weeks Bo and Ida Mae and Georgie (with Russell as all-purpose assistant) had discussed strategy, the message, and money. This morning they were all in Russell's new Bronco, heading west along the Pike toward the hill country. At first, Russell had wanted to use his new Cadillac Escalade, but Ida Mae threw a fit.

"Russell," she had shouted when she saw him drive up in the Escalade, "park that damn thing in your garage until the election is over. We don't want folks seeing the caring candidate driving around in a luxury car. Use your brains!"

So Russell, chastened, drove the Bronco, with Bo next to him. Georgie and Ida Mae sat in the back.

"Georgie," Ida Mae said, puffing on her cigarette as she tapped on the keyboard of her laptop, "let me ask you a simple question: why are you running?"

Georgie had been thinking about Jack's call and had been listening with half an ear. She stared at Ida Mae.

After a long pause, Bo said, "You're going to have to do better than that, sugar. That's the kind of question you should hit out of the park. Now damn it, we can't afford—"

"Easy, Bo, calm down," Ida Mae broke in. "We have time."

"The hell we do. Next week she's going to ask the Speaker to declare the seat vacant. The *Bugle*'s been running those editorials every day about how the district needs to be represented. The Speaker will agree and then everybody will know and we'll be in the news. Those media morons like to ask dumb questions like 'Why are you running?' Everybody knows that. You got to have a quick answer, Georgie. What is it?"

"I'm running because . . . I'm a Republican and . . . I'm Buzzer's wife and I want to, I don't know, continue his work?"

"We can come back to that one later," Ida Mae said, thinking, *Oh, Lordy, this is going to be harder than I thought.* "Georgie, we're taking this little ride just to give you some idea of places other than Grange County where we'll be campaigning. You've seen some of them, campaigning with Buzzer. But a lot of things have changed out here, and you should see it. We'll finish out in Homewell State Forest. I always try to begin my campaigns by going out there by myself, just to look at the scenery. It calms me down, gives me inspiration."

"We need money and votes, not inspiration," Bo said without looking back at Ida Mae. "If you want inspiration, go see Herman Throe. He sells it by the truckload."

"Oh, be still, Bo," Ida Mae said. "It's really beautiful out in the forest this time of year. Georgie, back to you. Quick: What's your basic message?"

"Jobs. I should know that one. You've been drumming it into me every day," Georgie said in a flat, bored tone of voice. "At least it's simple."

"It's not simple, it's just easy to remember."

"Well, one thing we won't have to worry about," Georgie said, trying to get her mind off the fact that what she really wanted was a glass of Merlot.

"What's that?"

"I'm well known all over the district. People recognize me. I'm Daddy's daughter and Buzzer's wife. People will have seen me with Buzzer, on television or at campaign stops or receptions. That's a big part of a campaign, isn't it, Ida Mae? Name and face recognition?"

"It sure is, Georgie. Russell, in about ten minutes or so, we'll be coming to Zellenborn. Just park in the town square and we'll go to Bob's Diner for coffee."

"Good idea. I need a pit stop," Bo said. "My kidneys ain't what they used to be."

"Thanks for that intimate bodily function report, Bo," Ida Mae said. "Keep us informed."

"I guess it's all that cigarette smoke that's getting to me," he said, taking a mint and rolling down his window a crack. "It's eating away my kidneys."

They drove on in silence for a few miles as Ida Mae consulted her laptop. Georgie was lost in her thoughts again: *Why did Jack call?* All these years, she hadn't known if he was alive or dead, married or single, or what had happened to him. And then just like that, a telephone call.

"Bo," Ida Mae said, looking at the laptop screen, "we'll need a scheduler. We need somebody to handle media buys. We'll do a lot of radio ads. We also need a press aide and a field director, as soon as possible. And we need you to raise a lot of money, fast."

"Damned tough to raise money this quick," Bo said. "And now with all these damned stupid new campaign-expenditure laws, things ain't as easy as they used to be. But I'll get the job done."

They passed Zellenborn Regional High School with its bleak, empty sports fields. There was a red and blue GO COUGAR CAGERS! banner hanging across the entrance. Georgie could remember the fierce basketball semifinal state championship game between the Zellenborn Cougars and the Grange City High Rangers when she was a cheerleader. Bobby Ricky, as good at basketball as he was at football, had scored thirty points, but the Rangers still lost.

They passed through a number of small towns that all looked the same to Georgie. One block of stores, a couple of gas stations, maybe a fast-food outlet, a few people walking along the street, head down against the wind.

After a few miles they were in open country. There were farmhouses, a few of them new and well-cared-for and prosperous-looking, but many of them needing a paint job or a new roof.

There were wooden fences in need of repair, and rusting, cannibalized cars up on blocks, without tires, beside tired-looking barns. The mood engendered by those lonely farms was disturbing, like the mysterious atmosphere in one of those paintings by . . . who was it? She once knew these things. Edward Hopper. That was it. He painted city things, like that famous diner picture. But the mood, his special mood, that was what the farms looked like. Jack had introduced her to Hopper's works.

"Here's beautiful, thriving downtown Zellenborn," Ida Mae said, pointing to the grubby, grungy, worn-out-looking row of stores, some of them obviously out of business. Russell pulled the Bronco into a diagonal parking space by Bob's Diner.

There were about a dozen people in Bob's, mostly farmers wearing baseball caps and leather or denim jackets. They sat in booths, talking, looking as if they had nowhere else to go on this cold day. A radio was on, and some country singer was whining about cheating and drinking and losin' you, losin' you.

"I wanted to stop here for two reasons," Ida Mae said as they settled in the booth. (Bo had gone directly to the men's room.) "First, although it may not look like it, they make a great cup of coffee here. Second, Zellenborn is the geographic center of the district. This is the heart of the Sixth. Georgie, I know you must have stopped here with Buzzer during one campaign or another. Russell, have you ever been out here?"

"Years ago, when they had that driving range."

"Green Fairways Driving Range. I'd come out here after I had an argument with my husband. I'd work off my anger hitting a couple of pails of golf balls. I damn well should have hit my husband instead. The range is gone now, of course, along with so much else in the county. The whole central part of the district is an economic disaster area these days."

Bo came back and sat next to Ida Mae.

"Real nice place, Ida Mae. They must have last cleaned that men's room during the Harding administration."

A gray-haired, tired-looking waitress—she could have been anywhere from forty to sixty—in a food-spotted uniform (her black plastic name-tag read HI! I'M JESSIE!) shuffled to their booth from behind the counter, greasy-looking plastic-covered menus in her hand.

Georgie looked at her and thought, *Well, Georgie, you're not in La Salle de Classe now.*

"Mornin', folks. What can I get you?"

"We won't need a menu. Four coffees," Ida Mae said. The waitress began to walk away when Ida Mae said, "Jessie, how would you like a ten-dollar tip?"

"Who do I have to kill, hon?"

"Just answer one question. And no matter how you answer it, you get the ten."

"This a trick? You one of those *Candid Camera* people?"

"No, no, this is on the level. The question is this: Who is the lady sitting across from me?"

"What's this all about, Ida Mae?" Bo asked.

"Quiet, Bo. That's the question, Jessie. Who is this lady?"

Jessie stared at Georgie.

"I don't rightly know. She looks real familiar, though. You from around here, honey?"

"No, I'm from Grange City."

"Oh, well, then I don't know you from Adam. I never go over to Grange. Too many people and too noisy for me. No offense, but folks there are kind of stuck-up, some of them anyway. I still get the ten?"

Ida Mae handed her the bill.

"Easiest ten I ever made. At least since I was young and pretty, if you get my meaning," she said, broadly winking at Russell. "Coffee's coming up."

"What was that all about, Ida Mae?" Georgie asked.

"Just a little lesson in political reality. In Washington, you're Buzzer's wife. In Grange City, you're Bo's daughter and the former cheerleading queen. Political pros know you. The media know you. But out here, you're *nobody*. You're going to have to get yourself known out here, very quickly. And over in Lawrence County where the big auto-parts plant used to be. And all across the district. This is the real world, Georgie. Nobody knows who you are."

"That was just one woman," Georgie said. "That doesn't prove anything."

"Maybe. Let's expand our sampling population."

Ida Mae stood up and yelled out: "Hey, folks, can I have your attention? Please, just for a minute."

Conversations stopped and heads turned.

"Ida Mae, *really!*" Georgie whispered.

"Folks, please do me a favor. I'm going to ask my friend here to stand up. And I'd like to know if any of you recognize her."

"Ida Mae, this is *silly*. This is—"

"Stand up, sugar," Bo said quietly. "Do as Ida Mae says."

Georgie stood and turned so everyone could get a good look at her.

"Anyone recognize her?" Ida Mae asked.

"You related to the Dearborns? Out in West Zellenborn? Otis Dearborn owns that hardware store there," an old man in a Cougars sweatshirt shouted.

"No."

"You look a little like one of those Dearborn girls."

"The hell she does," said one of his companions, turning to look at Georgie. "I know the Dearborns all my life, and she don't look nothing like them."

"Thank you, folks," Ida Mae said. "Have a nice day."

The two women sat. Ida Mae was smiling, but Georgie was fuming, glaring at her. The waitress came with the coffee.

"Honey, *now* I know who you are," she said, beaming. "I plumb forgot."

Georgie gave Ida Mae a triumphant glance.

"You're that newslady on Channel Six. You do those consumer reports, about baby car seats and all. I just knew it was you, but for a minute there, I couldn't remember. You do a real good job."

"Thank you. It's really nothing."

"Don't you be modest, honey. You ought to be on that *Sixty Minutes* with that Barbara Walters."

Back in the car, they drove in silence for a few miles. Georgie was sulking, Bo was dozing, and Ida Mae was tapping away at her laptop.

"Ida Mae," Russell said, "did I miss a turn back there? I think I was supposed to pick up 265 North to the forest."

"Damn it, Russell," Bo said, eyes closed. "Stop daydreaming and keep your mind on your driving."

"No problem, Russell," Ida Mae said. "We can take the Margaret Kingsbury Highway north."

They were entering the hill country. Gradually as they drove upward along a winding road, they saw more trees and suddenly they were in a forest of pines.

"This is Herman's domain," Ida Mae said. "We'll spend our time and money where our votes are, back in Grange, and the river counties, sure. But we'll be making raids into Herman's kingdom. There's a lot of newcomers out here. Things are changing. He can't count on the kind of vote his people used to get out here. Do you think you can pull in any votes here, Georgie?"

"How can I? No one will know who I am, according to you."

"Honey," Ida Mae said, "do you know your voice gets just a tad shrill and whiny when you're tired or annoyed? You have to watch that. Folks pick up on it. Russell, the highway is just coming up. Get off at Exit 32 and drive right to the first overlook."

About fifteen minutes later, they were in Homewell State Forest. Russell pulled up at the overlook. There were no other cars. Before them, spread out from north to south, was a vista of farms and barren winter fields and pine forest.

"Bo, you and Russell just sit here. Georgie and I are just going to stretch our legs."

The two women stood there in silence, wrapped in their winter coats, taking in the big sky and the still, cold, harsh winter beauty of the scene below.

"Georgie, like I said, I wanted you to see those farms around Zellenborn, and those small towns. Talking about people's problems in general terms is one thing. But seeing the places where folks actually live is another. That wasn't the East Side of Grange City out here, or the big agri-monster farms in the river counties east of Grange. It's a different world. Politics in the places we've just seen has to be up close and personal."

For a moment they stood in silence.

"Georgie, I get the distinct idea you have something on your mind. Anything bothering you?"

"No."

"I don't believe you. We have to trust each other. Now, what is it? Why are you so lost in your own thoughts?"

"I'm not."

Ida Mae said, peering through the cigarette smoke, "Have it your way. Now I want to talk some girl talk. Do you have trouble with your periods?"

"No more than usual I guess."

"Good. That's one problem we won't have to worry about. What you need is a complete makeover. Get your hair trimmed, a casual, easy-care cut. And some natural-looking color. You're looking a bit frumpy these days."

"Any other compliments?"

"I'm not here to compliment you. By the time this race is over, you're going to hate my guts. That's okay, I'm used to it. Just listen and do what I say. In politics, men can wear anything and nobody gives a damn. But a woman has to take care. If you have good pantsuits, fine. If not, buy new ones, black, navy blue. Jackets, dressier clothes for the evening events, but not too dressy. Mid-heel shoes. And get your nails done, short, light color. Keep things simple, simple, simple. But not plain. We want you to look good, but not glamorous."

"No fear of that from an old frump."

Still looking eastward, Ida Mae, without turning her head, said, "One more thing, and this is important. Stop drinking. No, don't say anything, just listen. People are talking. Just stop it."

They stood in the silence for a few moments. Then Georgie said, "You asked me if there's anything bothering me. Let me tell you. Maybe we can call this off before it's too late. I found out Buzzer was having an affair with Marge Racksley. Since last June. Or did you know?"

"No, no, I didn't know. I'm sorry. Is that why you're running? Revenge on Buzzer?"

"No. Well, maybe. I don't know. Yes, I guess it's revenge. Part of it at least."

"People have run for Congress for worse reasons. You can still back out."

"No, I'm going through with it. I want . . . I don't know what I want. Let's get back in the car. I'm cold."

Ida Mae put her hands on Georgie's arms, turning her so that they were face-to-face.

"Georgie, listen to me: You're going to win this thing."

"How do you know?"

"Because I'm the best. Because I'm going to outorganize everybody else. Some folks will think you're just another congressional widow—or near-widow—looking for the sympathy vote, boohoo, vote for me, I'm such a poor, troubled woman. I say to hell with that. You're going out there and you are going to kick ass and you are going to win as a good candidate, not as a pitiable woman. You're going to win because I think with hard work you can become one hell of a candidate. You're smart, you can be attractive again if you put your mind to it, and you have a strong motive to run. Maybe not a good motive, but a strong one. You just do your job. Let me do mine. We're going to do it, Georgie."

In the car, watching the two women, Bo said to Russell, "Remember: you're going to be Ida Mae's assistant. But what you'll really be is my eyes and ears. Call me every day, twice a day. I want to know every damned thing Ida Mae is doing. She won't like me looking over her shoulder. But you can keep me in the know. Got that?"

Russell didn't answer.

"Russell, I'm talking to you. Stop this damned daydreaming. Get in the real world."

"Oh, sorry, Dad," Russell said. He had been wondering why, in all the years he had known her, he had never realized how good-looking Ida Mae Watkins was. Tall. He liked that. And those freckles across her nose. Nice trim figure, too, all that golf and exercise. Strange, he never really noticed her before. Funny how you can miss something like that, right under your nose.

"Goddamn it, Russell, I want you to keep an eye on Ida Mae. Stay close to her. You got that? Keep your eye on Ida Mae."

"Got it, Dad," Russell said. "Keep an eye on Ida Mae. And stay close to her. I can do that."

TUESDAY, JANUARY 26

The *Bugle*, front page:

HOUSE DECLARES LEBRAND'S SEAT VACANT; ELECTION TO BE CALLED; WIFE TO RUN

Yesterday the House of Representatives vacated the Sixth Congressional District seat of Rep. T. Claude "Buzzer" LeBrand (R), currently in a comatose state in Grange Memorial Hospital.

The decision, taken by a voice vote in House Resolution 70, will lead to a special election to replace the stricken congressman, who was re-elected for a fourth term in November's election.

Immediately after the vote was taken, LeBrand's wife, Georgie Beaumont LeBrand, announced in Grange City that she will run for her husband's seat.

The resolution was sponsored by Morris Lansdale, Speaker of the House, and other members of the Republican Party leadership. Lansdale praised LeBrand for his "unique style" and "love of country." He said that while he shared the sadness of all House members at LeBrand's "incapacitating condition," the House had to act "in order to give the people of the Sixth District the kind of representation they deserve."

"Given the fact that Mrs. Georgie LeBrand has informed me of the negative prognosis given by all attending doctors, I believe the House must carry out its constitutional duty."

A source close to Governor Tim Curruthers believes he may call for the primary election to begin as early as next week, "in keeping with state custom to fill vacant seats as quickly as possible under state law."

WEDNESDAY, JANUARY 27

The *Bugle*, front page:

GOVERNOR: SPECIAL ELECTION

STATE SEN. WHOLEY TO CHALLENGE "GEORGIE"

DIDDIER: "I'M IN TO WIN" DEMOCRATIC NOD

ACTIVIST WEINSTEIN ANNOUNCES "RADICAL" DEM CANDIDACY

10:06 A.M. SATURDAY, JANUARY 30, FAWCETT'S DINER, GRANGE CITY

Years ago, in an interview with a reporter from the *Bugle,* Ida Mae said, "There are two kinds of political consultants: Technicians and Characters. Technicians are like me, all about demographics, polling data, focus groups, media buys, pie charts, flowcharts, computer graphics, and precinct-by-precinct knowledge of a congressional district. Characters are all about themselves."

Gary Garafolo, sitting across from Bobby Ricky at a booth in Fawcett's, looking out of place among the buttoned-up young executives from BigBo Inc. and the old pols from the courthouse, was a Character. He knew the value of a public persona that made him good copy for reporters and gave him the reputation of being off the wall, which was more important in his business than any particular expertise he might have.

He was forty-seven but affected a younger (and somewhat dated) look with his ponytail held together with a red elastic band, a large silver earring in his left lobe, and his retro clothes. Every two days he had his barber trim his facial hair until there was exactly the one-or-two-days'-growth look he desired. He paid teenagers to scour thrift shops for hopelessly out-of-date shirts and suits and shoes. The torn, dirty leather jacket he was wearing looked as if it had been run over by a truck, which in fact it had. Gary himself had driven a rental truck back and forth over the garment until he satisfied himself it had that retro patina, that look of I-don't-give-a-damn insouciance he knew appealed to clients and the media. It cost Gary plenty, in time, effort, and money, to appear as if he didn't give a damn.

His political consultant's creed was short and clear: Radiate confidence. Absorb the cheers. Deflect the jeers. In victory, cover yourself in glory. In defeat, cover your ass.

There was divided opinion about him. Some of his enemies believed he was a vampire who had figured out some way to crawl out of the coffin and get a day job. Others were convinced he was a cunningly devised humanoid, a golem created out of spare parts pillaged from the still burning wreckage of failed candidacies that had been consigned to the hell of political oblivion.

His career in politics began twenty-five years ago when he was a student at Jersey City State College. He volunteered to be an assistant to the press aide to Senator Harley Jennings of New Jersey, running for his third term. At the end of the first week Gary had wrangled his own little cubicle—with no desk, only a metal folding chair—in the crowded campaign headquarters in Newark. Two weeks later he had a bigger cubicle, a desk, a better chair, and a telephone. By the end of his first month he had ingratiated himself with the senator and became his driver. By the last weeks of the campaign he had long since left the press aide behind and was accompanying the senator to campaign-strategy meetings.

By studying the moves of the senator's political consultant, Gary learned the single most important lesson of his career, one that was to be the foundation of his success: political consulting is a confidence game, not only in the sense that a consultant must scam voters, the media, and his clients, but because nothing matters more in consulting than projecting an air of total, assured, rock-solid infallibility. As a consultant, you can be stupid, venal, ill-informed, and know little about politics. You can lose big races. You can sue and be sued by clients. None of that matters if you can convince others you never have a single doubt. Like a pope, a political consultant who doesn't claim infallibility isn't taken seriously. This attribute is as important in defeat as in victory. "I could see the loss coming *weeks* ago when [insert name of client] started fucking up. I begged him to stop [insert bad campaign practice] but, hey, he's got an ego problem."

Gary had many ways of communicating his absolute freedom from doubt in his own judgment, including the Dismissive Half Sneer when someone else proposed an idea that Gary should have thought of first; the Mad Dog Attack, in which he spewed forth invective, the sheer vulgarity and volume of which convinced others that Gary must be right; and the Condescending Shake of the Head, by which he demolished the pretensions of anyone who had dared to contradict him.

Gary's consulting firm was one of the most successful in the nation, and he was at a point in his career where he didn't handle many House races. But he had managed Bobby Ricky's race against Buzzer—Bobby Ricky was a star—and everyone said he had done a great job, even though Bobby Ricky lost. Gary helped this to become the consensus view by off-the-record lunches with favored columnists and reporters in which he blamed Bobby Ricky for the loss. ("But, hey, don't attribute that to me. I love Bobby Ricky, but he fumbled the ball near the goal line.")

Today, he wanted Bobby Ricky to be seen in the popular diner, just a regular guy eating his grits and eggs. (Bobby Ricky preferred home fries, but he understood the gastronomical/political demands of running for office in the Sixth.) Seated next to Gary was a tall, blond young woman he had introduced as Lee Simmons and then ignored as Bobby Ricky and he talked about the coming campaign.

Bobby Ricky knew Gary liked the company of attractive young women, so he wasn't surprised to see the latest acquisition. But there was something special about this one. Lee Simmons had the clean, scrubbed look you see on gorgeous models in ads for skin-care products, as if the models needed help looking that way. Not a lot of makeup, nothing overdone, nothing to call attention to herself. You had to go to her, she wasn't coming to you. She was in her mid-twenties and wore her blond hair simply, turned under, pulled back and held with a black velvet headband. The beige sweater and expensive jeans didn't accentuate but certainly didn't hide her slim, curvy figure, which he had noticed when she took off her coat.

Lee Simmons was . . . what was the word? *Elegant.* That was it. Elegant. Bobby Ricky liked elegance, style, and class, especially when those virtues were accompanied by a great ass.

For the past few minutes Gary had been doing a Gary rap, telling Bobby Ricky how things were going to go in the campaign. To his visible annoyance, he was interrupted a couple of times while Bobby Ricky graciously signed autographs. But now Gary was in full flight.

"Will you win? *Absolutely. Definitely.* We'll run the same way we did against Buzzer. You'll be postured as a Big Ed Kingsbury kind of guy. . . ."

"Yeah, except I'm black, smart, good-looking, and for civil rights, and Big Ed was white, dumb, ugly, and a nutcase racist. Otherwise, we could be twins."

"*I'm one hundred percent right.* Trust me on this. You're a Kingsbury guy because you'll get things done for the district in Washington, just like him. We don't have to do anything tricky. We'll just tweak a few things, correct some mistakes you made last time."

"*I* made last time?" asked Bobby Ricky with a twinkle in his eye. "Weren't you the genius who sent me to the western part of the district in the last week, when I should have been back here in Grange getting my voters out? I seem to recall that."

"Well, that's one way of looking at what happened, even if it's totally wrong," Gary said, giving Bobby Ricky the Dismissive Half Sneer. "Anyhow, there isn't a political figure in the state who ranks higher in name recognition than you. Bobby Ricky, believe me, we got this won."

"What about Georgie?"

"She'll probably lose to Holy Joe in the primary. Half the people identify her with Buzzer in some way, and the other half haven't got a clue about her. By the way, I've done a quickie poll in the central counties and your favorables are impressive, which is great because we didn't do as well as we should have out there against Buzzer. Is Kalya ready?"

"I've been on the phone with her for a week. It was a hard sell, but I wore her down. She promised to be down here for a few days of campaigning. That's all I could get her to agree to. Gary, here's the thing I want to talk about—I want to debate Susan Weinstein."

Gary smiled, and gave the Condescending Shake of the Head. He turned to Lee Simmons for the first time since they had sat down in the booth.

"Let me tell you about Weinstein, Lee. She's a Jew, a left-wing radical feminist lesbian lawyer from New York. In other words, she's all the things people down here hate. She moved here a few years ago, helping the unions when they tried to organize Bo's places, and decided she had to stay here and try to drag the Sixth out of the Dark Ages. She's like a fucking space alien down here. And now Bobby Ricky wants to debate her."

"A lot of kids who go to State in Cap City live in the Sixth," Lee said. "A radical like Weinstein can probably get some college volunteers and generate some excitement, if nothing else."

"True," Bobby Ricky said, glad he had an excuse to look into those green eyes.

"Negative! Wrong!" Gary said, fingering his earring as he ignored

Lee and talked to Bobby Ricky. "Anyhow, college volunteers make a lot of noise but they don't win elections."

"What about those kids for Gene McCarthy in New Hampshire back in 1968?" Lee asked.

"One, this ain't the 1960s. Most college kids don't give a damn about politics, particularly a congressional race. Two, McCarthy actually lost the New Hampshire primary to LBJ. Three, McCarthy wasn't a Jew lesbian Commie running in a district like this. *Capeesh?*"

Lee smiled and her eyes locked for an instant with Bobby Ricky's.

"Weinstein is a wanna-be Bella Abzug, with a few extra added attractions—or detractions," Gary went on, "an agitator from the old New York lefty school. Let her run if she wants to. But give her publicity by debating her? Never. How much chance do you think she has, Bobby Ricky? Honest, how much?"

"None," Bobby Ricky said. "But she'll demand a debate, and we need something exciting in the primary. Buzzer wouldn't debate me last time. I need to show I've got debating chops."

"No, no, no. Believe me on this. No debate. It's ridiculous. I know about these things. *Trust me.*"

"I just think Weinstein should get the chance to say what she wants to say," Bobby Ricky said. "Lee, will you please pass the cream?"

He touched Lee's fingers when he took the pitcher.

"Hey, I'm all in favor of freedom of speech," Gary said. "But that doesn't mean we give her the chance to stand next to you and call you a rich, out-of-touch, sellout Uncle Tom, which are some of the nicer things she'll say."

"What do you think, Lee?" Bobby Ricky said.

"I say debate her."

"That's crazy," Gary said, giving her the Full-Force Sneer, a formidable weapon in his arsenal of put-downs.

"No, it's not," Lee said quietly, apparently not fazed by Gary's manner. "Mr. Diddier will look like a moderate conservative centrist standing up there next to someone like that. Treat her with respect, let her say what she wants. If you turn her down, you've given her an issue."

Bobby Ricky was impressed. Not once did she look deferentially at Gary. She said what she wanted to say but didn't push it too far. He liked that.

"Hey, Lee, let me give you a little lesson in politics, no charge," Gary said with the same sneer. "Never, ever, give somebody that far down in the polls a chance to shine at your expense. First rule of politics."

"This won't be your typical election," she said. "Everyone will expect Bobby Ricky to back off. Surprise them."

"I think you're right, Lee," Bobby Ricky said. Their eyes met again, briefly.

"I disagree, but who the hell am I? I'm only running this campaign," Gary said, smiling but with just the tiniest don't-piss-me-off tone in his voice. "Anyhow, I'm glad you two see eye to eye since you're going to be spending a lot of time together."

He saw the puzzled look on Bobby Ricky's face and laughed.

"I asked Lee to handle the press and to write for you. She's been doing press and speechwriting for Congressman Gerry Berger. Comes highly recommended. I'm going to leave the two of you to talk things through. I have to see Will Parsons—he's the political reporter at the *Bugle,* Lee—to find out what he's been hearing. Bobby Ricky, if you don't like Lee, she goes back to Washington on the six o'clock plane. Your call, pal."

When Gary had left, Lee laughed.

"What's so funny?" Bobby Ricky asked, puzzled.

"The answer is no," she said.

"What answer?"

"No, I'm not sleeping with Gary. I know you think I am because I know his reputation. So don't worry, I'm not some bimbo he's foisting on you because he doesn't know what else to do with her."

"*Bimbo* isn't the first word that comes to mind when I look at you, so don't worry."

Bobby Ricky had set out the bait—she was supposed to smile in reply and say, Well, what *is* the first word that comes to mind when you look at me? and then he'd say, Beautiful, and she'd smile again and . . . but she wasn't biting.

"I can do the job—I have writing samples for you to look at. All I'm asking for is a chance to help you win this seat."

They sipped coffee and chatted about the district. She knew everything there was to know, from the current unemployment rate in Zellenborn County (12.6 percent) to the score of last month's high-school football championship game (Sedley Ridge 32, Harronsburg 12). She was also aware of the mediocre quality of Bobby Ricky's speeches in the last campaign.

"Your speeches didn't sing. Too bland, too generic. You were trying to show people you're more than just a famous football player and that you know the issues. You were citing statistics, showing how well informed you are, not just some stupid jock. But you forgot to tell the voters who you are. What you stand for. Not just the football stuff, but what your dreams are, for the district and the country."

"That old vision thing?"

"In a way, yes. But I mean a vision that comes from your own background, not some pasted-together slogans."

"You've done your homework on the district," he said. "Done any on me personally?"

"Of course."

"And . . . ?"

"Besides the football stuff, which everyone knows, you're a quick study on the issues. You expect first-class treatment wherever you go because you're a star. You're great on your feet, answering questions. You handle the media with ease. You're not officially separated, but your wife has left you, that's an open secret. You have two children. No big scandals. Some whites down here say you're too arrogant, which means you don't know your place. Some blacks say you're not black enough, although you got ninety percent of the black vote, which almost put you across."

"Ninety-two point six. There just weren't enough of them. I've got to turn them out this time. Well, that's me. What about you?"

"Spoiled rich California girl, or did you guess? My father has his own advertising firm in San Francisco. My mother is a lawyer in Los Angeles. They're divorced. They named me Clelia—I prefer Lee—after a character in a French novel, *The Charterhouse of Parma.* I went to Berkeley and majored in poli sci. My father, a big contributor, pulled strings to get me a job with Gerry. But once I had the job, I did it better than anyone expected, including Gerry. A friend of mine introduced me to Gary, he made me an offer, and here I am."

"Currently attached?"

"I keep my personal life private."

"I respect that. Anything else?"

"Yes, one thing. I don't want to spend the rest of my life writing congressional press releases and somebody else's speeches. I've done that. I want a career, maybe in consulting, maybe in the media. What this job can get me is contact with national political and media types. You're not just a candidate. You're a star, a national celebrity, and this will be the only important political contest in the country. I want you to make certain I meet the media and political stars when they come. I want them to know who I am. Once they do, I can do the rest myself."

"I bet you can."

"I'll be loyal to you but I expect loyalty *from* you. One more thing: when you check up on me, you'll find that some people think I'm ruthless."

"Good. You'll need it to get ahead in this business. Just look at Gary."

They both laughed.

"You've got the job," Bobby Ricky said.

"Don't you want to read my speech drafts?"

"Later. I've always trusted my instincts. And I've been listening to you. You're smart, you know politics, and you aren't afraid to say what you think. You'd better get over to meet Will Parsons. He'll be covering us every minute of the race. He's tough, he's smart, and he's informed."

"So am I, Mr. Diddier," Lee said, getting up from the booth and extending her hand. "It's going to be great working with you."

"I feel the same way, Lee," he said, shaking hands. "And make that Bobby Ricky from now on. Mr. Diddier makes me sound like a high-school principal."

"Okay, Bobby Ricky."

As she walked away, Bobby Ricky noticed heads turn in the booths. In a booth near the door, one man, a courthouse type, red-faced, fifty, and fat, took a long, blatantly lascivious look at Lee, turned to stare at Bobby Ricky, shook his head, and then exchanged a few whispered words with his companions, who nodded in agreement.

You don't like it, do you, gentlemen? Bobby Ricky thought. *A sweet young blond thing like that sitting here talking to the likes of me. Well, you can all kiss my black ass. I never gave a good damn what any of you think, and I'm not starting now.*

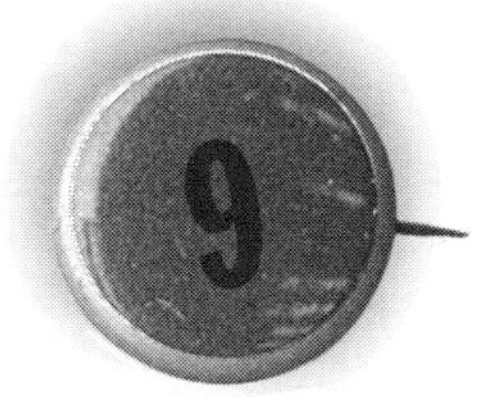

WEEK ONE

7:32 A.M. MONDAY, FEBRUARY 1, GRANGE CITY CEMETERY

It is bone-chilling cold. Susan Weinstein stands among the tombstones and the ornate mausoleums, wearing an old black parka with the hood down. There are a few kids from the college, shivering, holding placards. And two newspaper reporters.

"I'm beginning my campaign here, in a city of the dead, because this place symbolizes what the Sixth District is all about right now: death, decay, loss. The bosses like Bo Beaumont have sucked all the lifeblood out of this district. They've taken all they can out of every last workingman and -woman. They've left the Sixth one huge graveyard of the exploited. Well, listen to me, Bo Beaumont and all the rest: I'm everything you and your lackeys hate—a tough, pushy, Marxist New York Jew lesbo babe—and you can't shut me up."

Weak, sporadic clapping.

"Listen to me, Bobby Ricky, Robert Richard, or whatever your fucking slave name is, *I'm blacker in my heart than you are.* Where were you when workers were beaten by racist cops sent by Bo Beaumont? You were playing a childish game of violence for pay, just so some emasculated white men could get virtual orgasms. Well, Robert Richard, I'm coming after your ass."

With slightly better applause, Susan Weinstein, grim, implacable, one with Che, one with the unemployed everywhere, strides off amid the stones of the dead.

The two reporters present turn to each other and shrug.

9:24 A.M. TUESDAY, FEBRUARY 2, EUDORA RHETT FINCHLEY SENIOR CARE FACILITY, GRANGE CITY

Georgie LeBrand is half an hour late. Butterflies in her stomach. This campaign stop is supposed to show how much she, the caring candidate, the wife and mother, *cares* for our seniors and, by extension, people in general. Now, in the back of the lounge, Georgie is nervous, waiting to be introduced to a small crowd. A woman in a white jacket, the supervisor or something, introduces her, and Georgie starts walking—remember to smile!—through the lounge, toward the portable podium. But someone has her wrist in an iron grasp. She looks down and sees an emaciated old man with missing teeth, slumped in a wheelchair, holding on to her, mumbling something—what?—it's incomprehensible. She tries to move forward as Ida Mae taught her to. But she can't get away from the old man. Now someone else is grabbing her pantsuit jacket from behind; a shrill voice is shouting something. Someone (Russell?) pushes her toward the podium. She stumbles and almost falls.

How many people in front of her? Twenty? Fewer? Where is everybody? Some of them seem to be asleep, some are blankly staring out the window. And just at that instant, Georgie Beaumont LeBrand's mind goes blank.

The room is dead quiet.

Damn it, say something.

"Good morning, everybody. I'm . . . er . . . I'm . . . I guess some of you know me, uh . . ."

The old people who are not asleep stare at her or through her. They're either bored or puzzled or deaf. A fat woman in the back of the lounge, in a wheelchair, shouts in a loud, screeching voice, "Your husband let his own momma die in this place, honey. What are you going to do about that?"

There is scattered applause and a few hoots of laughter.

"Don't mind her, darlin'," a white-haired, gap-toothed woman, all bent over like a question mark, leaning on a walker, says with a cackle, "she's off her nut."

Ida Mae, in the back of the room, is discreetly signaling with her hand. *Is she pointing at my feet? No, no, the podium, the signal means look down.*

Georgie looks down and sees remarks Ida Mae prepared and placed there. Thank God, something to say. Just read the brief remarks, all about caring for our most vulnerable citizens, helping their children and grandchildren by creating jobs. Remember to look up from the text, smile, and make eye contact.

Georgie looks up and makes eye contact with another old man, drooling and smiling, but his left eye is covered with some kind of horrible film. She is hypnotized by this evil eye and loses her place in the text. Her mouth has gone dry. Like a robot, she drones out the words on the paper. She races through them without looking up, eager to get through and get out of there.

There. Done. Now the question period.

The fat lady shouts, "Why didn't you pull the plug on that bum?" and there's a flurry of activity as facility staff try to get her out of the room, but she won't go quietly. As the fat lady argues loudly with the staff, a man wearing a ratty-looking bathrobe talks on and on about World War II and its role in plaguing him with a bad back. What do you think of that landing at Anzio? he wants to know.

Georgie smiles, a sad, tight little Pat Nixon smile, and says, "Well, that's ancient history. I'm not much for looking back."

Immediately she realizes she has said exactly the wrong thing—the people in this room have nothing but history, nowhere to look but back. There is silence. She sees Russell and Ida Mae in the back of the room. Russell looks concerned. Ida Mae has the frozen, cheerless smile of someone who wants to scream. She looks as if she needs a cigarette. Oh, God.

1:30 P.M. WEDNESDAY, FEBRUARY 3, EUDORA RHETT FINCHLEY SENIOR CARE FACILITY, GRANGE CITY

Bobby Ricky Diddie glides through the crowd—about fifty or sixty people—with ease and grace, pausing—barely—to grab a hand, point and wink to someone in a wheelchair, squeeze a shoulder. When he stands at the podium there is loud applause even from the staff and administrators. He doesn't wait to be introduced.

"Hey, this looks like my team," he says. "Is this my team?" There is laughter and applause.

"This is my starting team that's going to help me bring this district back. During the last campaign I visited with you and I said I'd return. Well, maybe some of you thought that was just a politician talking. But I came back just before the election and I did it because you're part of my team. I needed your help then—I need your help now."

Applause.

"That's what I call Team Concept. Working together. Taking care of each other. Looking out for each other. Some folks say, Bobby Ricky, drop the word *concept*. Folks don't know what that means. When they tell me that, I say, hey, I know the people of the Sixth. I was born right here, grew up here. Hey, the folks I know can handle a word like *concept*. Am I right?"

Applause.

The fat lady in the wheelchair yells out, in a surprisingly lusty voice, "God bless you, Bobby Ricky. You're the best damned colored boy this town ever seen."

"Thank you, ma'am," he says with a frozen, practiced smile. "I guess I consider that a compliment."

Reporters look at one another. They are smiling. Standing with them is Lee Simmons and she is smiling, too. This guy is one hell of a candidate, a natural. And for a moment their eyes lock across the room.

2:05 P.M. THURSDAY, FEBRUARY 4, HELEN GRACE JUNKETT THOMAS CHRISTIAN DAY SCHOOL, FREEMAN COUNTY

The large crowd of parents, teachers, administrators, and a busload of folks from the Little Brown Church are in the school's gymnasium, eager to hear what their candidate has to say. Joe Wholey stands alone on the stage. He is a tall, thin, pasty-faced man in his fifties whose eyes have a strange fiery quality to them, like someone with a high fever. He has the drawn, tired, unhealthy look of a man who once weighed a lot and has lost too many pounds too quickly. Joe gets right to the point, because these are his people. They don't need warming up. They don't need jokes. They want red meat, and Joe is eager to throw some their way.

"Every Congress there's debates about taxes. Raise taxes for this, raise taxes for that, so those politicians can spend our money. When I get to Congress, the first thing I will do is walk down Pennsylvania Avenue to the White House. And I'm going to march into the Oval Office and I'm going to say to the President, 'Mr. President, let's pray, let's get down on our knees and pray. Even though this is government property, we can pray, can't we?' "

Great applause.

"And after we're finished praying I'm going to ask him to repeat the following words: 'I swear before Almighty God I will never ask

Congress to raise taxes for any purpose, under any circumstances, and if I do, I should be impeached and found guilty.' And then I'm going to walk right back up Pennsylvania Avenue to Congress and march to the second floor of the Capitol and say to the Speaker, 'Mr. Speaker, the best way we can get the President to do this is if each member of Congress takes a similar no-tax oath, starting with you, right now.' "

Even greater applause.

"Let me tell you, my friends, we are facing a moral crisis, not just in this district but in the country. My Ten Commandments amendment will fix our shattered godless Constitution"—thundering applause—"plus my No New Taxes Oath idea will bring Washington back to its senses!"

11:30 P.M. FRIDAY, FEBRUARY 5, GRANGE MEMORIAL HOSPITAL, GRANGE CITY

In the peaceful quiet of a hospital at night, Nurse Patsy Earlings stands by Buzzer LeBrand's bed, with a videocassette in her hand. Next to her is Jimmy Tuckerhoe, an elder in the TMC. They speak in whispers.

"I wanted you to see him, Elder Jimmy. Just look at him."

"I don't know," Elder Jimmy says at last. "He just might have the mark of the beast on him. Looks like it to me."

"Oh, no, Elder Jimmy. I can see into his heart. He's different. I can see good in him. I can. And . . . maybe I see more. Much more. Maybe he's the Messenger."

"Quiet, Patsy Earlings. Don't be saying things you don't know nothing about."

He stomps out of the room, irritated.

But I know what I see, thinks Nurse Patsy, feeling Buzzer's cool brow. *There's good in this man, much good. But it is buried beneath Self.*

She inserts the tape into a VCR.

"You need saving, Congressman," she says gently to the big, still body in the bed, smoothing down the blanket around his chest. The TV screen is blank and then suddenly it shows a large crowd of men and women singing. She turns the volume up slightly.

"Don't be left in the lurch," the crowd sings lustily, "come, come to the Little Brown Church, the Little . . ."

There's Herman Throe in his robe, at the pulpit, singing along.

"I taped his show twice a week for three years," Patsy says soothingly. "I had too much Self, see, drinking alcohol, smoking, going out with the wrong type of boy, disrespecting my body. But I got rid of Self and you can, too, if you're still there. The Lord accepts everyone who rejects Self and Satan, even if you only have almost no chance of recovery. I'll just leave this on low so you can hear. I'm just going to play all those tapes for you, one every day, until you come back to us. Doctors don't know everything, any nurse can tell you that. But God can do it."

She quietly leaves the room.

Buzzer lies there, propped up on the pillows, facing the television, not moving.

"Well," Herman says with a smile, holding a glass of water in his right hand and staring at it, "this plain ol' ordinary water we see here would look mighty good if you were in hell. You'd give anything for one-billionth of one-trillionth of a quadrillionth of one ounce of that water. Give up everything. All your money. All your friends. All your pleasures. All your family. All your hopes and dreams, just to come within a hundred billion light-years of one molecule of water. But you know what? When you're in hell, it's too late."

YARD SIGNS

GEORGIE BEAUMONT LEBRAND FOR CONGRESS
GEORGIE! JOBS! GEORGIE!
GEORGIE CARES!

JOE WHOLEY: GOD, FAMILY, JOBS
HOLY MOLEY, I'M FOR WHOLEY

BOBBY RICKY: JOIN HIS TEAM
DO THE DIDDIE!

SUSAN WEINSTEIN TELLS THE TRUTH, THAT'S ALL, FOLKS!
SUE! FOR YOU!

(Somebody wrote in the words A JEW between SUE! and FOR YOU!)

8:06 A.M. MONDAY, FEBRUARY 8, SPEAKER'S OFFICE, UNITED STATES CAPITOL, WASHINGTON, D.C.

Gus Gorham, sitting across the desk from the Speaker, looks at the majestic view of the Mall and the Washington Monument. It is a view he never tires of, so filled with the power and the majesty of—

The Speaker grunts.

Gruntology translation: *Can we please get down to business here?*

His Majesty looks peeved, as usual.

"Does Buzzer's wife have a chance to win this damned thing?"

"She's a disaster so far."

"The other idiot, Holy Joe, wants me to take an oath never to vote for taxes. Ever. For any reason. Are they having debates?"

"Bobby Ricky has agreed to debate that woman down there—"

"The Jew lesbian?"

"Yes. Bo Beaumont is under pressure from the newspapers and even from the party people to have Georgie debate Joe Wholey. I don't know what they'll do."

"How is Bobby Ricky doing?"

"Big crowds, big applause. People are excited. And he's got a new stump speech. I heard they brought in a new writer. She's better than his old one. He's sharper and crisper in his delivery than he was against Buzzer. He talked at a business lunch last week. Those people should be with us, but he knocked them out, standing ovation."

Grunt.

"You got any other bad news to share with me, Gus?"

"No, Mr. Speaker, that's it."

"We got to keep that seat, Gus. Make this a special project. It will not be a good career move for you if we lose this seat. You know what I mean?"

"I know exactly what you mean, Mr. Speaker. Exactly."

5:22 A.M. TUESDAY, FEBRUARY 9, GRANGE CITY

Georgie awoke in the dark, screaming, still half caught in the nightmare. It had been so real, so horrible, she could still feel the terror. Buzzer had been there, in the bedroom of their home in the prestigious, tree-lined East Side neighborhood. He had been raised on the West Side, which he never let anyone forget. And now he was proud to be on the East Side, as if to let everybody know how far he'd come.

In the nightmare, there was Buzzer, in his hospital gown, with the tubes coming out of his nose and his arms. Georgie knew he wanted to have sex, but she was frightened. Yet just beneath the fright was sweet, fierce desire. She could see—you could hardly miss it in that medical gown—that Buzzer was excited, but then he lifted his hand to hit her. That's when she screamed and woke up.

Georgie pulled the covers about her and closed her eyes, hoping she hadn't awakened Buzzer Jr. Russell would be there in twenty minutes or so, to put on the coffee, help her get started, brief her on where they would be going, and then drive her to their first stop of the day.

Russell was wonderful and patient with her, never critical. Ida Mae was the one who criticized, all the time. Russell was so eager to have her succeed that half the time Georgie thought she was putting up with all the horrors of a campaign just to make him happy. God knows there was little enough in his life to make him happy. Bo was mad as hell about the way the campaign was going. He wouldn't take it out on her, so he was taking it out on Ida Mae and especially on Russell. They would be meeting him at eleven o'clock at his office, where he would surely raise hell.

Nothing was going right in the campaign. Georgie flubbed her lines. She couldn't make any connection with the audience. She didn't remember people's names, had bad interviews with reporters, and couldn't speak to the issues, as they say. Worse, the schedule was chaotic. Two days ago they showed up early at Grange Hall in Holmes County, way down there in the farthest southwest corner of the district, and then discovered they were supposed to be in *Plains* County, in the far southeast corner. Ida Mae was livid, fired two people—*boom! boom!*—in the storefront campaign headquarters. Oh, well, there was nothing Georgie could do about it now. She should get as much rest as she could. It would be another long, long day and it was raining. She closed her eyes.

She could see the campaign, a whir of faces, a blur of handshakes, endless talking, jaw-aching smiling, listening with a patient, I've-got-all-day look, when all she wanted to do was scream, *Shut up!* Get in the car. Get out of the car. Shake hands, shake hands, shake hands. Enter the home of someone you didn't know, go to the living room, smiling, meet and greet. Now back in the car, now walking along the street. Hello, I'm Georgie Beaumont LeBrand and I'm running for Congress. Trying to remember names—meet and greet—smile, get back in the car—Ida Mae is saying something about farms—they are going to the eastern part of the district, near the river—remember, low prices, exports, soybeans, even some of these farmers in the river counties are hurting. Russell has made a wrong turn—they are on the Pike going west instead of east. Ida Mae, waving her cigarette at Russell, yells at him. He apologizes. A Styrofoam cup filled with hot coffee spills as Russell makes a sudden turn. Georgie's new blue suit has a big coffee stain. . . .

Every minute of the day, every day of the week, was scheduled, planned, committed to a meeting or event. She had no time to think, except in the back of the car, pretending to be asleep, or in bed, wishing she *could* sleep.

Georgie heard a car pull into the driveway. Russell. She got out of bed in the dark and stepped out of her nightgown, on her way to the shower. She paused at the bureau mirror and stared at the dim reflection of her naked body. Needs work at the waist and thighs, but here, in the dark, not too bad. It would be so very nice to make love, just once. Men liked to say about women who are bitchy, Oh, we know what you need, and the damned thing was, they were—damn them—right every now and then. In the nightmare she had been erotically alive for the first time in a long while, with that special sense of expectancy permeating her body as it used to, long ago, when she was with Buzzer. But now she was empty and didn't expect anything at all.

10:28 A.M., ED KINGSBURY MEMORIAL HIGHWAY–ROUTE 12 BIGBO STORE, CAPITAL COUNTY

"We need somebody here on aisle six," Bo shouted to the hapless store manager, who was cowering behind a display of BocaCola six-packs. "Looks like a pigpen in here, scraps of paper on the floor. A BigBo store is a clean store. You got that, junior?"

"Y-y-yes, Mr. Beaumont. I'll get somebody to sweep, right now and—"

"Get somebody, *hell*. Do it yourself. Get a broom. On the double."

"Y-y-yes, sir," said the manager, and he began to jog toward the rear of the store.

"Hold on, I ain't through with you yet, sonny. I just was on aisle eight. You know what we got on aisle eight?"

"C-c-condiments?"

"You asking me or telling me?"

"Condiments. Sir."

"Then where in the *hell* are the JumBo jars of mustard? Where are the JumBo plastic bottles of ketchup? Folks like bulk! Bulk! That's what makes our stores great. Folks want quality in quantity!"

Bo stalked off, continuing what he liked to think of as a reeducation session for employees, up close and personal, with good old Uncle Bo. He made a lightning raid on the auto supplies department. Where're those twenty-gallon oil cans? Then he swooped down on two female employees in Lil' Girls 'n' Lil' Guys BoPeepClothes. The women just happened to be standing still, talking to each other when he sprang on them.

"Ladies, this ain't no social club! Our customers want action! They see you just standing still, flapping your lips, they start to go to stores where salespeople jump on customers when they get in the door, wrestle them to the ground, and drag them to see all the goodies on sale. Speaking of sales, where's the sign advertising our 'fifty briefs for the price of thirty' special? Boys need underwear. Lots of it!"

In a few minutes he had caused havoc throughout the store, brought the manager to the brink of nervous collapse, and thoroughly demoralized the entire staff, including two Hispanic saleswomen with only passable English who could not follow his harangue and kept on smiling at him as he roared. Satisfied it was a productive visit, he searched for the manager to give one last piece of advice. He found the poor man in the employees' rest room, vomiting his breakfast into the toilet bowl.

"Wasting time is a BigBo crime," Bo shouted. "We ain't got time to get sick! Get finished with what you're doing and make sure that toilet gets scrubbed!"

Bo's driver took him back to the office, where Georgie, Ida Mae, and Russell were waiting.

"How did your commando raid go, Bo?" Ida Mae asked as Bo slid behind his counter desk.

"I think I shaped them up. Speaking of shaping up, what I want to know from you three is what in the hell's going on with the campaign?" Bo said, looking more than ever like Harry Truman in a bad mood, his face pinched and small. Even his polka-dot bow tie looked upset, knotted wrong. "Did you see this?" He picked up the *Bugle* from the magazine and newspaper display rack, touched his glasses, and quoted, " 'A campaign in disarray.' Why are we in disarray?"

"Dad, I think—"

"Russell, there's been too much thinking. I want action. Georgie?"

"It's my fault, not Ida Mae's or Russell's. When I get before an audience, I freeze. And, yes, we're making some mistakes."

"That's why we hired a staff, so we wouldn't make mistakes," Bo said, turning his gaze on Ida Mae. "You're supposed to be the great organizer."

"It's coming together, Bo," Ida Mae said carefully. "We had to start from scratch."

"Coming together? Coming apart's more like it. Bobby Ricky seems to be doing pretty good."

"Bobby Ricky had his campaign people practically in place. A lot of Buzzer's old people think we pulled the— They think we treated him badly and they wouldn't sign on, and my people are stretched thin already."

"Why do we have this scheduling mess?"

"I fired the scheduler," Ida Mae said.

"Thank God for small favors."

"Bo, we're doing the best—"

"Well, your best ain't good enough, Ida Mae. Georgie, I thought you'd learn faster about how to handle the media. Remember this: reporters aren't paid to report. They're paid to *distort,* to trick you into saying something dumb. Never answer their trick questions unless you absolutely have to. Use a question to get out your message. I saw you the other night on WGMR, with Shirley Hevling."

"I thought she did pretty well, Dad," Russell said.

"Oh, is that what you thought, Mr. Media Expert? Well, you thought wrong. She was awful. I want the three of you to follow me."

Bo arose, grabbed the shopping cart, and wheeled it to the mini-aisles. They followed him as he wheeled the cart up and down the aisles, pausing to place items in the cart. BoCherry preserves, BoSoft tissues, and a dozen other items. Then he wheeled the cart back to his desk.

"See what I just did? See the cart? Filled with good things. And do you know how all those products get to my stores? Organization! Planning! Schedules! Getting things done! No excuses! Folks can't eat excuses. They can't wear excuses. They can't put excuses for furniture on their patios and barbecue excuses on the Fourth of July. You have to work to make things work! In business and in politics. Now get out of here and get to work, the three of you! If you was employees of mine, I would have fired you last week."

Bo popped a JumBo mint in his mouth and chewed on it, pouting. After a few seconds of silence, Ida Mae got up, put out her cigarette in the ashtray, and looked at Georgie.

"We have to get going."

"Where to?"

"Republican Women, Foster County. This will be easy."

"Nothing's easy," Georgie said.

"Russell, stay here, I want to talk to you," Bo said.

"We'll meet you in the car, Russell," Ida Mae said. "But hurry up."

When Georgie and Ida Mae left the room, Bo said, "Georgie's got to go on the attack in the debate. She's got to go after Wholey, call him a crazy right-winger."

"But, Dad—"

"Don't 'but, Dad' me. Yeah, I know, it's the one thing I didn't want to do, attack Holy Joe. Herman and his people will be mad as hell, and the split in the party will be deeper. But there's no other way. If Georgie can't learn the basics, then she's just going to have to go after Wholey and try to hurt him."

"Dad, Georgie doesn't have the killer instinct."

"No. Neither do you. But I do. Enough for ten people. That's why I got all this money. Tell her what I said. Attack Holy Joe. He was a drunk. Spread some rumors that he's back on the sauce. The campaign's in trouble, boy. And let me remind you—I put you in this campaign to keep an eye on Ida Mae. And I'm not getting any information from you. Is she doing the job?"

"Yes. Yes, she is. I've learned so much, just watching how she operates. She's asked me to kind of manage the campaign office. She knows everybody and—"

"You sound like you got a schoolboy crush on that woman, damn it. Tell me what she's doing, and I mean doing wrong. Something's wrong. You ain't to blame and Georgie ain't to blame, because neither of you knows any better. Ida Mae's to blame for all these mix-ups, and I want to know why. You got that?"

"Yes, Dad."

"Then do as I say. Light a fire under those campaign so-called workers. People need motivation. If pride don't motivate them, fear will. That's the way the world runs, Russell, like it or not."

3:15 P.M. THURSDAY, FEBRUARY 11, THE LEBRAND HOME, GRANGE CITY

Last summer, after a shouting match with Buzzer in which he had pushed her against the door to the garage, badly bruising her arm, Georgie had decided she would work out her anger by doing a Revenge Modern renovation of the kitchen, from cabinets to floors. She had an extension built with a cathedral ceiling and a skylight, opening up the kitchen to the trees and flowers of the backyard. Then she replaced the old fixtures with a stainless-steel Sub-Zero refrigerator, a state-of-the-art glass-cooktop oven, and a sensor-controlled dishwasher. The new kitchen counters were granite. In the extension she placed her most prized purchase: a harvest table with inlaid blue and white tiles.

Buzzer had screamed at the cost.

"Damn it, Georgie, a kitchen's for cookin'. This looks like the spaceship control room on *Star Trek*."

The only problem was that since the renovations, Georgie hadn't had time to enjoy the room. She either had been in Washington or, when back home, was not really interested in cooking, preferring the comforts of Merlot to those of Julia Child. But in wintertime the big room was pleasant and filled with light, so Ida Mae, Georgie, and Russell were sitting around the harvest table, going though a dry run before their full-scale rehearsal for the debate. Russell was playing the role of moderator, and Georgie was trying to give back the right sound bite.

Employment policy?

"Mr. Wholey says the first thing he'd do as congressman is march up Pennsylvania Avenue to see the President. But the first thing I'm going to do is march to the floor of the House and I'm going to . . ."

Silence.

"Fight," Ida Mae said.

"I'm going to fight for . . . this district?"

"No, no, it's fight for jobs and families."

"Oh, right," Georgie said, looking at the list of one-liners typed on a paper in front of her. "Jobs and families."

The Ten Commandments?

"The Ten Commandments have a place in our hearts and our community, but they have no place in the Constitution."

"No," Ida Mae said, "make that 'hearts and community, and that is where they help us most.' We don't want Herman's people to be claiming we said the Ten Commandments have no place in government."

Taxes?

"Mr. Wholey says Washington politicians have to swear not to raise taxes. What we need from our leaders is . . . is . . ."

Silence.

"Jobs?" Georgie said tentatively, looking at Russell.

"Not more *swearing* . . ." Russell prompted.

"Not more swearing . . . I'm sorry, I'm drawing a blank here."

"Not more swearing of oaths but more hard work to build jobs," Russell said.

"I don't like that. Swearing of oaths sounds clumsy," Ida Mae said, lighting up a cigarette. "How about something like, let's say, 'less swearing and more work'?"

Long silence.

"How about 'less swearing and more caring,' " Georgie said.

Ida Mae, grinning for the first time that day, said, "Hey, Georgie, that's not bad. Less swearing and more caring. And then you say, caring about jobs, caring about education, caring about our people—or something like that. Build on the word *caring*. That's good."

"It's very good," Russell said, glad for Georgie. "It really is."

"That's what I got from all the reading I used to do," Georgie said. "I can rhyme two simple words."

"Honey," Ida Mae said, "political rhetoric doesn't need a college degree. Just catch their attention."

"Okay, what about religion, Georgie?" Russell said.

"I believe religion is too important to become a political football to kick around."

"I don't know," Ida Mae said, frowning. "Football? It sounds, I don't know, not like Georgie. More like Bobby Ricky."

Suddenly Buzzer Jr., back from school, came rushing into the room, breathless, red-checked from the cold, his nose running. He gave Georgie a big hug and a kiss.

"Mom, can I go to the movie tonight with Tommy and Brent? Please, please?"

"No, it's a school night."

"Ah, Mom," Buzzer Jr. whined, the *mom* sounding like *maa-mmm*, with much despair and soul-wrenching anguish packed into the final rising syllable. "Tommy and Brent are going and all, it's Brent's real birthday even though the party will be on Saturday, and Tommy's mom will go with us."

"I said no," George said wearily. "I don't want you going to a movie on a school night, and that's it."

"Mom, it's not even R-rated. It's *Space Aliens from Hell*, all the kids seen it. Tommy and Brent seen it twice."

"*Saw* it. There's violence in it. I read about it someplace. No, stay here and watch television with the sitter."

"I *hate* the stupid sitter. And I hate you, you never let me do nothing," he said, eyes brimming with tears of rage. He stormed out of the room, slamming the door, yelling, "Shit, shit, *shit*."

"Watch your mouth, young man," Georgie said, but her heart wasn't in it.

Buzzer Jr. opened the door and stood there, defiant, a malevolent Buzzer look on his face.

"Maybe if you'd stay *home* once in a while, Tommy's mom wouldn't *have* to drive us, anyway," he said, and slammed the door again.

"Kids," Georgie said, smiling weakly.

"Georgie, listen to me," Ida Mae said. "I've been thinking about this attack on Joe Wholey that Bo wants. I don't think attacking is your thing."

"Daddy thinks things are desperate and we have to attack," Georgie said. "He might be right. It's my fault. If I had only been better and—"

"No, damn it," Ida Mae said, her voice rising just a bit. "Attacking isn't your way of doing things."

"That's what I told Dad," Russell said. "But he wouldn't listen."

"Well, I'm running this campaign," Ida Mae said, "and I say we just present our message. We don't back off from disagreements with Joe. But no attack."

6:07 P.M., BOBBY RICKY DIDDIE CAMPAIGN HEADQUARTERS, EAST ELEVENTH STREET, JUST OFF GRANGE SQUARE, GRANGE CITY

Gary was in a Mad Dog Attack mode. He walked through the big room of the storefront campaign office, shouting (at no one in particular) and punctuating his remarks by throwing empty Coke cans, kicking over trash baskets, and pounding on desks with his fists.

"You do it *my way* or you get out! You don't like the way I do things, *get out!* You don't want to work, *get out!* I'm sick and tired of hearing how you people *can't* do things. I want to hear you tell me, *Gary, it's done!* There's going to be some sorry asses fired if this sloppy work doesn't stop and *stop now!* Now get back to work, answer the phones *before* they ring for the third time, have your reports ready on time, have Bobby Ricky's schedule up to date, and *do your fucking job!* And I want to see the senior staff in the conference room at seven sharp tonight. *Be there, or be gone!*"

He marched back to his office, slammed the door, and smiled. The point of a Mad Dog Attack was not to correct errors or improve campaign office efficiency, but to show that Gary was a character and that he was in charge. He carefully calculated every attack, blending a minimum of informative content with a maximum amount of noise, using expletives sparingly so each one would have maximum effect. On talk-fast-and-shout-loud cable talk shows with names like *Political Street Brawl* and *In Your Face the Nation* he rationed his use of the rage, shouting down critics and sputtering in anger when it suited his purposes. Now he put his feet up on his desk, closed his eyes, and thought about which one of the volunteers he would hit on.

Five minutes after the Mad Dog Attack was over, Bobby Ricky entered the office, wearing his sweatsuit and a stocking cap. He was just back from jogging and feeling good, so he decided to talk to some of the women volunteers. He knew their names—Kay, Melissa, Candace, Jackie, Barb, and Sandy—but he didn't know which name went with which face. These young women—and a couple of them were cute—were the first to come in in the morning and the last to leave at night. They did everything: answered phones, typed, emptied trash baskets, got coffee, and even drove Bobby Ricky to events. They were among the tireless true believers every political office must have, people always ready to do a job.

Bobby Ricky laughed with one of them, a plain-looking girl. What was her name? Candy something? Candace? Or was this Barb?

Or Melissa? The girl was looking up into Bobby Ricky's face, smiling, obviously thrilled to have the great man talk to her. Bobby Ricky smiled, put his hand on the girl's shoulder, and moved on to the next desk, smiled at Sandy or somebody, and gave her a quick shoulder squeeze. He said a few words to an older woman who was answering phones.

Three conquests in less than a minute, Lee Simmons surmised as she watched Bobby Ricky's royal progress through the office. He saw Lee and double-timed to her cubicle.

"I didn't get my run in this morning," he said, "so I squeezed in a few miles over in the park just now. What's happening?" he said, sitting in a metal folding chair next to hers.

"What's happening?" she said, grinning and picking up a pile of telephone messages. "NBC and CBS today. CNBC and Fox yesterday. I'm working on all those. Cap City TV, two call-in shows, and WGMR—Shirley Hevling wants you on her face-to-face show. That's what's happening. My God, I can't believe it."

"Well, that's what you wanted, to meet the media. How're the remarks going?"

"I'm plugging away. Listen: 'The issue in this race is more than jobs. The issue is justice. Justice for working families. Justice for the elderly. Justice for our children in schools. The working people of this district need someone in Washington who is not only *from* this district but *for* this district.' "

"Good," Bobby Ricky said, "but change that first part. Don't say the issue is *more than* jobs. Say *not only* jobs. Say 'not only our first priority, which is jobs. It's *also* justice.' And then just keep what you have after that."

"Sounds good," she said. "I think you're in good shape for the debate."

"Yeah, just some fine-tuning. We can do that tomorrow. So why don't we relax and discuss the whole thing over dinner tonight?" he said.

Bobby Ricky flashed his most reassuring, most boyish smile.

"Sorry," Lee said. "Gary just threw a temper tantrum and called a senior staff meeting for seven tonight. Mandatory. I think he needs to kick ass. He can't kick yours, so he'll settle for staff. I guess you know he isn't too pleased that you're debating. You overruled him. He's not taking it too well."

"Oh, hell, that's just Gary, showing he's boss. But he doesn't call the plays. I do. I listen to him. He's smart, but I make the final decision. He knew it when I ran against Buzzer. Nothing's changed."

The bustle and chatter and movement of the campaign office provided background sounds to Bobby Ricky and Lee's conversation. Volunteers on phones read their scripts to potential voters; three television sets blared, each tuned to a different news show; Gary stood in the doorway to his office, bellowing across the room to one of his assistants; gofers distributed fast-food orders—"Who gets this Big Mac? Didn't somebody order a Big Mac?"—and phones rang.

"Gary believes I talked you into debating."

"Like hell you did," Bobby Ricky said. "Nobody talks me into anything, not even someone who looks like you. I *want* to debate. Hell, let's have some fun, get a little action going. The damned campaign is stalling. Even the *Bugle* says so. Nobody's paying attention."

"Will Kalya be here in time for the debate?"

"No chance, unless she catches an early plane, but she can't. She's got meetings all day. Hey, can't you get out of Gary's meeting? Just skip it. I'll cover for you. We can go someplace, act civilized, drink wine, like regular people?"

"I just don't think that's a good idea, Bobby Ricky, the two of us going out, not during the campaign," Lee said. "And not with your wife here tomorrow night."

So now it isn't exactly no, I don't want to go out with you, he thought. *It's just that this is bad timing.*

"Then I'll see you tomorrow afternoon, at the dry run?" he said, trying to sound casual.

"Unless Gary fires me between now and then."

They both laughed. As he walked away, his heart was beating fast and it wasn't from the jogging.

6:21 P.M., GRANGE MEMORIAL HOSPITAL, GRANGE CITY

Nurse Patsy Earlings stood there watching the tape on the TV in Buzzer's room. She turned down the volume slightly. Dr. Gordon, one of the new young doctors who had come on last month, strode importantly into the room and stood still, looking as if he were waiting for Patsy to curtsy to him. He was so stuck on himself, Patsy thought, full of Self, like so many doctors. He took Buzzer's chart out of her hands, flipped through the pages, looked at Buzzer, and then at the TV screen.

"What's this?"

"That's the Reverend Herman Throe at the Little Brown Church in the Wood."

"Some kind of faith healer? What do you have that on for? Mr. LeBrand can't hear anything. Shut it off, now."

Can you imagine that? Never heard of Reverend Herman. And this young puppy needed Reverend Herman just about as bad as anyone Patsy had ever seen. You could practically see the big letters S-E-L-F written across this young man's brow.

"Miz LeBrand insisted on it. I can't go against her."

Dr. Gordon frowned and walked out of the room. Nurse Patsy could just feel the aura of Self he left behind.

11:26 P.M., THE RACKSLEY RESIDENCE, GRANGE CITY

Marge Racksley lay in bed, sleepless. In the room across the hall, Carl was snoring. He had been drinking. She had smelled it on him when he came stumbling in earlier in the evening. They had had a terrible scene. Carl begged her to lend him money and then cried like a baby when she said no. But she refused to give him a nickel of her father's money. Finally he dried his eyes and stumbled off to the other bedroom.

Carl was falling apart, nervous as a cat. Well, just *forget* about sex, mister, even if she could imagine herself doing it with him anymore. She thought of Buzzer and said a little prayer that he would recover. She wasn't sure if God was listening to her prayers these days, but you never could tell, so it was worth a try. She lay there, twisting and turning, trying to sleep. But lustful thoughts of Buzzer kept her awake and excited. Finally she couldn't bear it anymore and she kind of . . . well, she wasn't proud of it, but what was a woman to do?

6:54 A.M. FRIDAY, FEBRUARY 12, BOBBY RICKY DIDDIE CAMPAIGN HEADQUARTERS, GRANGE CITY
Bobby Ricky, on his way out for a run, saw Lee coming through the door.

"Do me a favor. I left my apartment key with one of the volunteers, Sandy or Candace or Jackie or whatever her name is. Tell her to go to my apartment later, I'll be out running. Have her drop off a clean text of the opening statement. I left it on your desk. I made some changes last night."

He drove to his apartment, changed into his running outfit, jogged to the park, and began his five-mile run. He recalled how it used to be with Kalya during the off-season, when he had been playing pro football. They would run in the early morning. There were times he couldn't keep up with her long-distance, she was such a good runner. And then they would come home, strip, and shower together—long, hot showers. Then they'd towel off each other and make love.

He hadn't had a woman in weeks. Trying to be good. Damn it, I *am* being good. Lee was gorgeous, but he hadn't really pushed it. A black man with a white—no, worse, blond—woman. Not here, not in the Sixth. *We're enlightened these days, boy, but we got long memories.* He ran on, waving and nodding to well-wishers. Maybe it was wrong to debate Susan Weinstein. Maybe Gary was right. Maybe . . . damn it, how in the hell had he gotten himself into this mess?

And then, inside his head, he heard a familiar voice: *Dammit, colored boy, stop feeling sorry for yourself. Just* do.

It was his grandmother's voice. He couldn't help laughing, so he had to stop, bend over, hands on knees, and, wheezing and puffing, laugh. Dammit, colored boy, just *do.*

Colored boy. When he was a kid, that would make him so angry, because he was such a bad little dude, at least he thought so, full of attitude even then. He was nobody's *colored* boy. It was only when he got older that he realized it was her way of getting him to *do.* That was her favorite word. *Do. Doing* meant getting done what you were supposed to get done in life, your duty, whatever it was. She would not tolerate whining or making excuses or—the worst of all sins—feeling sorry for yourself. Just *do.*

Grandma. He hadn't thought of her in a long time. But there was her voice inside his head, just when he needed her to set him straight, as she always had, telling him to take hold of his own destiny.

Bobby Ricky ran back to the apartment, feeling much better. The girl from the campaign office hadn't delivered the speech yet, but spread out on his bed in neat rows were his folders with briefing papers and Q and A's dealing with major issues. He'd shower and then do some studying.

He stripped, went into the shower, reached for the shampoo, and lathered up. For a while he let the needles of hot water pound him, washing away some of the tension, soothing him, making him forget everything. He heard something. Someone was in the apartment. What the hell was going on? Was it the girl with the speech? Or did Kalya catch an early plane? Seconds afterward, the door to the shower stall began to open and he was about to say, *Kalya!*

But it was Lee Simmons: blond, elegant, smiling, long-legged—

and, oh yes, naked. She slid the door closed behind her, put her arms around his neck, and kissed him gently on the lips.

"I came by to drop off the final draft. The girl in the office couldn't make it," she said above the noise of the shower. "I heard the shower running and I thought you might like company."

He stared at her, not daring to move. It had happened so quickly, so unexpectedly, he couldn't get his mind—or anything else—functioning properly. Lee Simmons, naked and smiling, was right *here,* with him, *now*. It wasn't a fantasy. He had seen many beautiful women in his life, but nobody like Lee.

"Look, Bobby Ricky," she said in a matter-of-fact voice, her arms around his neck. "We both know this is going to happen sooner or later, so we may as well get it out of the way because you want me and I sure as hell want you."

They were not the most romantic words Bobby Ricky had ever heard from a woman, clothed or unclothed, but their very bluntness had an erotic quality. He was suddenly functioning. He stared at her, the water teeming down her beautiful body. Despite the businesslike words, Lee had a soft, yielding look in her eyes. She moved her long, lovely body against his, insinuatingly, just brushing his chest with her perfect, hard-nippled breasts. She kissed him on the tip of the nose.

"I just called Kalya's office, to check if she was on schedule," Lee said, embracing him. "She's still in New York. So we have plenty of time."

Three-quarters of an hour later they lay on the bed. All of the briefing papers, so carefully compiled, had been scattered on the floor when they had come, stumbling and entwined, out of the shower. She said, "I have wanted to do that from the first instant I saw you in the diner."

"You sure hid your feelings pretty good."

"That's centuries of WASP inbreeding. We know how to hide emotions. Except when appropriate, of course."

He laughed and thought, *When was the last time I laughed with a woman?*

"Hey," he said, "it was . . . just . . . great."

"Great? Mr. Diddier, sir, you're going to have to be more articulate than that if you want to go to Congress."

"Spectacular. What about *spectacular?*"

"Trite, but you said it with the right degree of enthusiasm. You're a quick learner."

"So are you."

"Believe me, it wasn't too hard to follow you," she whispered, nuzzling him. "You're gorgeous, but you already know that. Ever since you first got laid—in the third grade, I bet—girls and women have been telling you that."

She arose from the bed, and got on her hands and knees.

"Don't get any ideas," she said as she crawled around the rug, "I'm looking for the speech text."

She found the speech among the other papers and came back to bed. He reached for her, but she gently moved his hand away.

"Uh-uh," she said, giving him the text, "business first. Read it aloud to me."

" 'For many years, I was fortunate to play the game I love,' " he read. " 'I made a good living doing what I loved to do. I am very fortunate. I know that. But I also know others—good friends and close neighbors, old classmates—in the Sixth District have not been so fortunate. Through no fault of their own, they are hurting. When I was playing and I saw members of my team in trouble, I helped the team by what we call "stepping up," doing a little bit more, working a little bit harder, reaching down deeper. I believed then and I believe now in what I call Team Concept. Work together.

Help each other. Lend a hand. Step up! When your friend is hurting, remember—you're on the same team.' "

"Great!" she said.

He put down the text and looked at her.

"It's very good," he said. "You got the Team Concept idea right out there. I'll make some slight changes it in, but basically it's good."

"Read the rest of it," she said. "Now."

"I don't think so."

"Oh, no?"

"No," he said, and put his hands gently on the sides of her face, drawing her to him.

3:23 P.M., SUSAN WEINSTEIN CAMPAIGN HEADQUARTERS, THE WEST SIDE, GRANGE CITY

Susan Weinstein stood before members of the Grange City Community College Student Group for Jobs and Justice, all eight of them. Her campaign office consisted of one room in a seedy motel on the West Side highway. She told them about her father, a labor lawyer, and how proud he was to have been an associate of William Kunstler. They stared at her, their faces blank with incomprehension. She tried to tell them why Kunstler was important. But none of them had heard of him.

"My father was a charter member of the Emergency Legal Guild," Susan said proudly. "He once shook hands with Che Guevara."

"Was he the dude with the beret? Or was he the one with the big beard and the fatigues?" one skinny goateed young man asked.

"Susan, are you going to make pot legal? I mean, like what's the use of *doing* all this unless we can get something out of it?" said a fat young woman wearing a State sweatshirt. There were murmurs of agreement.

"Yeah," said the goateed radical, "and what about the environment? Like, I'm against capital punishment and all, but we should, like, just *take out* twenty or thirty of these global economy dudes and, like, just *waste* them. That's the only language they understand."

Susan was from the old New York school of hard-core leftist radicalism. She had been warned by her father against infantile leftism. But now all she had supporting her were infantile leftists. She would have to make do. She would have to improvise tactics for the sake of strategy, the way Lenin himself had.

"Yes," she shouted. "Legalize pot! Down with capital punishment! Shoot the fascist polluters!"

"Peace now!" some shouted.

"That too!" shouted Susan. "I'm queer! I'm here! And I have no fear!"

"This is just too *cool!*" yelled the fat girl in delight and the other members of GCCCSGJJ cheered.

6:04 P.M., RAYBURN BUILDING, WASHINGTON, D.C.

Gus Gorham, alone in his office, sitting at his desk with just the desktop light on, stared at the polling data he had received earlier. Polling in a primary is always difficult—the results are always suspect, but at least it was something he could hold in his hand. Georgie wasn't catching on, Wholey was far ahead. But Bobby Ricky, although comfortably ahead in his race, wasn't exactly a house on fire. One week to go. And it looked as though nobody was interested in the race except the participants, their families, and a few dozen politicians. The initial show of interest by the national media had died down. Anything could happen. He wondered what Jay was doing. He really didn't want to know what Jay was doing, but he wondered all the same.

10:07 P.M., GEORGE WASHINGTON PARKWAY, NEAR ALEXANDRIA, VIRGINIA

Jay Hollings slowed down his plain-as-white-bread Saturn (he never liked automobiles that called attention to him). No use getting a ticket for speeding. Just take it easy. When he was involved in a project, he liked to be careful about everything he did. He had just spoken—on a public phone outside a 7-Eleven in Alexandria—with his contact in the Sixth. He was pleased by what he heard. Maybe he had caught a break. He would send some people he knew down to the Sixth to check out what his contact had told him. He still had to be cautious. If this thing blew up, he would be the one who got it in the neck. Gus didn't know anything and never would know anything, if it all worked the way it should.

Jay was thoroughly enjoying himself. People talk about a rush. They didn't know what a rush was. Here he was, alone, trying to pull off something that could, if everything worked just right, determine an election. Risky. Dangerous. Always one step away from disaster. It was better than the best sex. Others called it dirty tricks. But he liked to think of it as UPA—unofficial political action.

8:07 P.M. FRIDAY, FEBRUARY 12, GRANGE CITY COMMUNITY COLLEGE AUDITORIUM, GRANGE CITY

"Our opening statement will be from Mr. Diddier."

After reading his opening, with its "the game I love" theme, Bobby Ricky said, "We are here tonight not just to debate the issues but to determine the fate of this district and its families for years to come. I am proud to be a Democrat. I know the Democratic Party has a heart. And I know the Democratic Party is always ready to help folks when they are down on their luck. Big Ed Kingsbury had that spirit. I believe that as your congressman, I can pick up where Big Ed left off. I believe that you have to work together in order to build anything good—a team, a family, or a community."

Loud applause, some whistles.

"And now we'll hear from Ms. Weinstein."

"Let me get right to the point," Susan said. "Notice that my opponent didn't mention his record in helping people in this community? You know why? He *has* no record of community service. As for Big Ed Kingsbury, he was a racist thug. For a black man to be praising an exploiter like that is a disgrace."

Laughter, and a few angry shouts.

"I don't know what Team Concept is, and neither does he. It's typical moderate-liberal, 'please elect me' Democrat bullshit. That's all I've got to say for now."

"Now, to begin the questioning, Troy Roberts of the *Capital City Times* with a question for Mr. Diddier."

"My question has two parts. First, can you name the organizations to which you belong that have helped people in the Sixth District, and second, can you tell us specific ways in which Team Concept will create jobs?"

"Let me answer the second part first. I have already presented a ten-page position paper on what I call the six steps toward new jobs. My Team Concept plan includes tax incentives for new businesses, aggressive marketing of our products overseas, especially our agricultural products, an extension of workers' benefits and—"

"Bullshit!"

"Ms. Weinstein, please."

"No, I'm not standing here and listening to this crap while men and women are out of work, starving—"

Some cheers, some boos.

"Ms. Weinstein, the rules of the debate are—"

"Rules? That's what's wrong with this district. The establishment wants us to play by their rules while families are being destroyed. Talk nice, you might offend somebody. To hell with that. I want results, not rules. Look at my opponent, standing there. You're not even an Uncle Tom, you're a *Nephew* Tom, trying to be the white man's black boy while your black brothers and sisters are starving and dying."

"Ms. Weinstein, we simply aren't being fair to Mr. Diddier—"

"Fair? What's fair about unemployment? What's fair about kids without futures, about women being battered by men who know they can get away with it? I'm not staying here and listening to Bobby Ricky play his little games. Bobby Ricky, you have always played the whites bosses' games, because they bought you off. This so-called debate is a typical media-industrial-racist-sexist theater piece, fooling people that real argument is going on. To hell with you all. I'm taking this fight to the streets."

She walked away from the podium and then downstage so she was facing the audience. Then she shouted, "Who's got the guts to join me and walk out of this farce?"

The eight members of GCCCSGJJ arose and joined Susan in the center aisle. They marched out, trying to sing "We Shall Overcome," but none of them knew the words. A couple of them shouted slogans about marijuana and the environment, but nobody could understand what they were shouting because of the singing.

"Ms. Weinstein, please . . . we still have many more questions . . . Ms. Weinstein . . . well, it seems we have only Mr. Diddier here and . . . quite frankly . . . I don't know what to do."

From the back of the auditorium, Gary watched in disbelief. Susan had no chance before, and now she had less than no chance.

Later he called Shirley Hevling, who had attended the debate.

"Shirley, just for your background, you can use this after Bobby Ricky wins the election—I don't want to embarrass him—but the fact is he was scared shitless of debating. He absolutely did not want to do it. I practically had to drag him to the debate. Honest to God."

11:06 P.M., BOBBY RICKY DIDDIE CAMPAIGN HEADQUARTERS, GRANGE CITY

"Kalya! Baby!"

Over the roaring DJ rock music and the excited talking and loud laughing of the debate-victory celebration party, Bobby Ricky shouted, jumped up from his metal chair in Gary's office, and embraced his wife. Outside, in the big room, the volunteers were partying the night away.

"Baby, how was the trip?"

"Awful," Kalya said. "But I'm here. Judging by all the noise, you must have done pretty well."

Kalya Hunter Diddier, mother of Bobby Ricky's two children, onetime model, and now chief executive of her own public-relations firm in New York, was the kind of tall, beautiful black woman (she made it clear: she was not brown, she was not beige, she was *black*) who got the Furtive but Lustful Stare from men (and from some women, too). Her classic beauty—high cheekbones to kill for, a body just a touch too curvy, too womanly, to be perfect for a modeling career, and a proud way of holding her head that made her look as if she had just been crowned empress—was not the kind that invited leers, ogles, or crude up-and-down assessments. Most men, whether it was for the first or hundredth time they met her, took quick little glances when they thought she wasn't looking. She was so poised, so regal, so . . . *elegant,* they would look away, and then in a moment take another peek.

"I did great, baby. Susan Weinstein just walked out. *Walked out.* I never saw anything like it. Baby, thanks for coming. I'll make it up to you, I promise. Have a drink. I'll try to find Gary, he's out there in the crowd someplace, I know he'll be glad to see you."

"No, actually, I'm tired. I think I'll just go straight to the apartment."

Lee Simmons, smiling broadly, poked her head in the doorway.

"Shirley Hevling's on. She says the race is just about over. Oh, I'm sorry, I didn't know . . ."

"No, no, come on in, Lee. Kalya, this is Lee Simmons, she's doing a great job handling the media, writing my press releases and speeches."

"It's nice to meet you, Mrs. Diddier."

The two women stared at each other and smiled.

"I have to get back to monitoring the television," Lee said quickly, and disappeared into the noisy crowd.

Kalya's eyes followed Lee for a moment and then she turned to Bobby Ricky.

"Good to see you're in such good hands," she said dryly. "Are you coming? Home, I mean?"

"Hell, honey, I want to, you know that, but I can't leave. The volunteers expect me to stay; this is a big night for them."

"Sure," Kalya said. "You wouldn't want to disappoint those great volunteers."

8:09 P.M. SATURDAY, FEBRUARY 13, GRANGE CITY COMMUNITY COLLEGE AUDITORIUM

"Our questioning begins with Shirley Hevling, political correspondent for television station WGMR."

"Mrs. LeBrand, where do you agree and disagree with your husband's voting record?"

Easy one, thought Russell, standing offstage with Bo and Ida Mae.

Georgie stared straight ahead. The silence became uncomfortable, and then she said: "Well, uh, I think my husband's record is, er, generally good. He voted for, er, the Aid to Stressed . . . excuse me, I mean Aid to Distressed Families Bill. That helped families here. I, uh, support his—in a general sense, I mean—his voting record. Take crime, for example, there I agree. But I am running, you see, as myself, and . . ."

Russell turned and saw that Bo had his squinty, mean-eyed look. Ida Mae had a poker face, and she would not meet Russell's gaze.

". . . my position is, uh, jobs. I care. I want to build jobs, offer hope to families, in my own way. I am running as a woman with a child. I care. I have my own ideas. . . ."

Bo muttered something under his breath and grabbed Russell by the sleeve. He moved away until he and Russell were out of sight of the stage.

"What in hell is going on, Russell? She's awful," Bo whispered.

"She's just nervous, Dad. Jitters. Let's see what happens."

Bo frowned, and they returned to Ida Mae.

"Our second questioner is Will Parsons of the Grange City *Bugle* with a few questions for State Senator Wholey."

"Senator Wholey, do you believe the Ten Commandments should be added to the Constitution of the United States as a constitutional amendment?"

"Yes, I do, Will, and as soon as possible."

"Do you believe future presidents and national legislators must take an oath never to raise taxes for any reason?"

"Lower taxes and raise moral standards, that's my motto."

"Do you believe the federal government should give a schoolchild a firearm on his or her twelfth birthday?"

"Yes, that's an idea I've had. I haven't come up with a plan yet. But, yes, I want every American child armed, trained, and ready. That will build a strong nation and solve the crime problem in schools."

A few chuckles and cheers.

"Senator, these views and others you have mentioned have caused some, even in your own party, to label you an extremist. What is your reply?"

"They are absolutely right. I am an extremist. I always have been. I am extremely worried about the lack of moral backbone in Washington. I am extremely concerned that liberals and left-wingers want to take guns out of the hands of law-abiding citizens and their children."

There was a sharp, brief sound of applause.

"Mrs. LeBrand," Will Parsons said, "I want to ask you about your views on unemployment, but first I have to ask you this: Do you, as a fellow Republican, support Senator Wholey's Ten Commandments proposal, his guns-for-kids idea, and his pledge never to raise taxes for any reason?"

"Here's our chance," Bo whispered to Russell. "Hit him hard, Georgie."

Silence.

Coughs in the audience.

"What the hell is she doing?" Bo whispered, grabbing Russell's arm. "Get him, Georgie. Get him *now,* the crazy bastard."

Georgie said, as if repeating a rote lesson, "The Ten Commandments shouldn't be in the Constitution, they should be, er . . ."

"In our hearts, Georgie," Russell said quietly, "in our *hearts*, just like we said."

"I mean," Georgie said, "I think it's just a bad idea to have the Ten Commandments. I'm against the Ten Commandments."

"Let me give you a chance to clarify what you just said. You're not saying you are against the Ten Commandments as such, are you?"

"Only when they're in politics."

Laughter, hoots, cheers, and boos.

"I mean . . . not just in politics. I mean, I think the way Senator Wholey is using politics."

"Christians ain't using politics," Joe said, beaming. "Politics is using us."

Cheers.

"Mrs. LeBrand, what about the senator's guns-for-children idea?"

"Oh, I'm definitely against that one."

"Tell us why."

"Because . . . it's just . . . wrong. It's just not . . . right. It's ridiculous. I'm a mother. I have one child. His father got shot once. In the leg."

Scattered but loud boos.

Joe Wholey answered a couple of questions about unemployment, and then Shirley Hevling asked: "Mrs. LeBrand, let me get this clear, so we know where you stand. Are you saying you are opposed to

Senator Wholey's idea to have the president and Congress swear, as part of their oath, never to raise taxes?"

"Yes. I'm against that idea. Yes. Definitely."

"Are there any conditions under which you would vote to raise taxes?"

"I'm against raising taxes."

"But you just said you are against Senator Wholey's idea. Doesn't this mean there are at least some circumstances that might lead you to vote for higher taxes?"

"Never . . . I mean, I'm against raising taxes but . . ."

Silence.

"Mrs. LeBrand?"

Silence.

Bo turned and quickly walked down the backstage corridor to the double doors, pushed the door bar, and walked out into the night. Russell quickly followed him. After coming out of the warm auditorium, he could feel the cold. There was Bo, leaning against a car.

"Dad, come on back in, you'll catch cold, no overcoat and all."

"Be quiet, Russell. How much longer is this stupid thing going on?" Bo said morosely.

"Another forty minutes or so."

"Well, you and Ida Mae, the brain trust, got her into this thing. You get her out. I'm going on home. You wait and drive Georgie to my place after it's over. You got that right? Can you remember that? My place, not hers. I don't want her to be by herself. She'll be down and she'll want a drink, and where the hell will we be then? At least I can keep an eye on her tonight. Tell Ida Mae to call me first thing in the morning. She's got some explaining to do."

"Dad, we have the post-debate party all planned. They'll be expecting you and Georgie."

"Party? What in hell are we having a *party* for? Because Georgie is making a complete ass of herself?"

"It's just for the campaign workers, Dad, to pump them up."

"Pump them up? Russell, you have the damnedest ideas I ever heard. Well, enjoy your party. And keep an eye on Georgie so she doesn't drink. I got some thinking to do, since nobody else seems to be capable of thinking."

Bo walked toward his car. From the auditorium came sounds of applause and laughter. Russell walked toward the entrance and was about to open the door when he smelled cigarette smoke and, turning, saw Ida Mae, wearing her coat, standing in the shadows, puffing away.

"Russell, come over here."

She had a little smile on her lips as he approached, head down.

"Bo's not pleased, is he? I couldn't hear what he was saying, but he didn't look pleased."

"He wants to see you first thing tomorrow."

"No surprise there."

"Dad is mad as hell. At all of us. What are we going to do?"

Ida Mae stared at him, took a deep puff, and blew out the smoke.

"Russell, listen to me," she said in a low, soothing voice. "Calm down. Take deep breaths. We're going to win this thing. Georgie's absolutely awful tonight, but debates don't win primaries. You win a primary by outorganizing the other guy and getting out your vote."

As she continued to speak, she appeared to be in a trance, unaware of him or the cold.

"Do you know how to win a primary? You figure out how many votes it'll take to win. Identify your supporters, who they are and where they are. Then you line up enough volunteer callers to do a hundred calls each. You call folks on weekdays between seven and nine P.M., on weekends between two and four in the afternoon. The weekend before the election, call your supporters to remind them to vote. Get your poll watchers with lists of people, mark them off as they vote, have your callers start calling at two o'clock to remind people. Leave messages on answering machines. Target radio spots. Recruit area coordinators. Attend all party events. Go to coffees until your kidneys can't take another cup. Meet and greet. Smile and shake hands. Meet with business leaders and county chairmen. And receptions in all key precincts. Winning isn't concerned with ideas or policies, Russell. It's organization and a good candidate and the right timing and a little bit of luck and a hell of a lot of work. That's what it takes. We have a good organization and the time is right and luck might be just around the corner. Georgie isn't a good candidate yet, but she will be, I promise. I can see her doing good little things she doesn't even know she's doing, listening, making eye contact, even her speech delivery is better. Russell, we are going to win. Do you believe me?"

"Yes, I do, Ida Mae."

"Then let's go back in," she said, taking one last drag and then throwing away the cigarette. "After the debate, I'll spin. I know what to say. We're just delighted that Joe Wholey's crazy ideas got exposure. See, Georgie was just confused by trying to reply to Holy Joe's off-the-wall ideas. Georgie wants to talk about real issues. Jobs, not the Ten Commandments. And all the while I'm shoveling all this horseshit, you're going to be smiling, and don't stop smiling as long as people or reporters can see you."

He was about to begin walking toward the auditorium when he felt her hand on his arm. She gently pulled him back into the shadows. She placed her hands on his face and kissed him, smack on the mouth, her tongue quickly flitting in and out.

"Russell," she said, pulling back and looking into his eyes, "when the party's over tonight—it shouldn't take long, no one will want to party—I'd like you to come back to my place. When we get there, we're going to relax and forget about the campaign. You're going to build a fire. I'm going to get out a bottle of Jack Daniel's.

We're going to have a few drinks, talk about golf, about movies, talk about anything but politics. And then we'll just play it by ear. How does that sound?"

Russell's eyes opened in surprise and delight. A big, silly-looking grin suddenly appeared on his face.

"It sounds *great,* Ida Mae," Russell said. "It sounds wonderful."

11:05 P.M., 724 CHURCH STREET, THE EAST SIDE, GRANGE CITY, BO BEAUMONT'S HOME

Russell had driven Georgie to Bo's place from the somber post-debate party. She and Bo were now sitting in his den, a room furnished with BigBo products, including EZ2 Assemble book cases (the shelves of which Bo had filled with books bought for ten dollars a load on the last day of an AAUW book sale), a huge leather BoRecliner, in which Bo sat, legs up, and a couch on which Georgie had curled up, her feet tucked under her. Bo had built a nice, comforting blaze in the fireplace with EZ2 Lite artificial BoLogs.

"So," Bo said, "how did the rest of it go? I missed most of it. The TV news just had the story, didn't say much, just some shots of you and Joe."

"I was a little better toward the end. About jobs. I did pretty good on that, I think. But altogether I was awful," Georgie said.

The thing that struck Bo was the tone of her voice. It wasn't sad or angry or disappointed, but level, just matter-of-fact, as if she had said, I went shopping and bought a pair of shoes. She had no spirit left. She was just going through the motions.

"I saw the first part of it," he said. "Couldn't take any more. It wasn't all your fault. I'm beginning to think maybe Ida Mae's lost a step or two. She should have had you primed for this."

"She did everything she could. I just froze. It's not her fault."

"It's her job to see to it you function right. I'll be talking to her tomorrow."

"Daddy, for God's sake, what's the matter with you? It's me. I'm awful. Not Ida Mae. Not Russell. I'm just not cut out to do this. I thought I could learn, but . . ."

She shrugged, and then said, "Do you have anything to drink?"

"No."

He wondered if she'd bother challenging the blatant lie, but she just sat there, staring ahead, not up for a fight.

"I want a drink."

"I know you do."

"Well, this will all be over soon, drunk or sober. I'm sorry I let you down."

"I'll tell you when it's over," he said. "Now go to bed and get some sleep. You got an early start tomorrow with that pancake breakfast."

1:18 A.M. SUNDAY, FEBRUARY 14, IDA MAE'S RESIDENCE, GRANGE CITY

Russell and Ida Mae had been sitting in her living room for two hours, swapping golf stories and listening to Sinatra CDs. Ida Mae did not spend time worrying about the finer points of interior decoration—she bought most of her furniture at BigBo stores—but her two-bedroom home on East Fifteenth Street, one block east of Main, was cozy and warm on this winter night. Ida Mae was surprised to learn that Russell knew so much about golf—not just its finer points, but its history. She had known—who in Grange County didn't?—that Russell was an inveterate golfer, but she had until now thought it was just a way of doing BigBo business, something to do while Russell placated Bo's many enemies. But it turned out, much to her delight, that when he loosened up a bit, with the help of the Honorable Jack Daniel, he could talk about the game because he loved it for its own sake.

Now he was talking to her earnestly, telling her things he had never told anyone, about how he was ashamed that he always let Bo down and had never amounted to much. He also told her about his two marriages. The way he told the story, apparently his first wife had been second runner-up for Las Vegas Bimbo of the Year, and his second wife had won Honorable Mention in the Grange County Adulterer's Olympics.

She poured him another. He began to talk about BigBo stores, reeling off statistics. He knew the business, he really did, but Bo never gave him a chance. He played golf with a lot of smart people, and he listened. Even though Bo thought golf was a waste of time, Russell had smoothed things over with a lot of business and political people whom Bo had insulted or slighted. He talked about the need to modernize BigBo, to catch up to their competitors. They needed to use the Internet more. He knew about those things because he listened to the younger people in the organization. But Bo would never listen.

"I'm a good listener, Ida Mae, I really am," he said, slurring the words as *lishner.* "I like people. I'm good with people. Dad, if he would, you know what I mean, would just give me the *chance,* I could help him, Ida Mae. Sometimes Dad's not good with people. You ever notice that?"

"Once or twice."

"Yeah, me too. Came up the hard way. Not me, Dad."

"You came up the hard way, too, Russell, only different."

"What? Thinks he always has to be fighting, Dad does. Fight, fight, fight. Alla time. But sometimes people just want to *talk,* Ida Mae. And I listen to them. But when I'm with you, I talk. Only with you."

Ida Mae sat there, listening, nodding in agreement, asking questions now and then. At one point she left him to go to the bathroom. When she returned he was asleep, sitting up on the couch, mouth open, snoring. She placed him into a reclining position and covered him with a blanket. Then she turned out the lights, returned to her chair, and finished her drink in the dark. She listened to his snores and she smiled, looking at sweet, gentle, sad, drunk Russell Beaumont. He was kind of cute for a forty-year-old man, he really was. She had been hoping the evening would have turned out differently. But this was okay, too.

GEORGIE'S WEEK

8:15 A.M. SUNDAY, FEBRUARY 14, FOSTER COUNTY

On the way to the pancake breakfast at the Methodist church in tiny Hellmantown, in Foster County, on the northeast border of the district, Ida Mae told Georgie: "Listen to them, nod your head, don't get too partisan. Be yourself. And eat the pancakes."

"I don't like pancakes."

"Eat them anyway. You look nice, by the way. You don't have your look the way I want it, but it's coming along. I love your hair."

In the church basement, Georgie saw a distinguished-looking, neatly dressed old gentleman with a full head of white hair to whom folks seemed to be deferring. She sat next to him as the pancakes were served.

"These are very good pancakes," she said, barely picking at them with her fork. "Do you have a breakfast like this every month?"

"Blunt? Sarah Blunt? Ol' Red's wife? She's dead," the man said loudly, drowning his pancakes in syrup. "Nice woman, in her own way. Red was never no good. He drank. Sarah got hit by a truck, right out there on Sixty-one. Changing a tire on her semi, she was."

"I see. That's a terrible way to go."

"Snow? We ain't had any snow this winter. Not one drop. It's those space shots. Changed the weather."

"Well, I just want you to know I'll protect Social Security and Medicare."

"What?"

"Medicare."

"My hair? Just like my father. Had a perfect head of hair till the day he died, and he was ninety-eight when he died. You in politics or something, right?"

11:00 A.M. MONDAY, FEBRUARY 15, STANTON COUNTY

Stanton County was just a few miles southeast of Grange, but it might have been in a different world. This was farm country, soybeans mostly, with big, prosperous farms, fat and sassy, spread out between the Little Pinellas and the Big Pinellas, not like the small, poor-soil farms of the central part of the district. Hard times had rarely touched Stanton. Folks here were generally well-off, content, easygoing, and had a reputation for enjoying the good life.

Georgie was here for a lunch with the Stanton County party chairman, his wife, and a few party officials. She probably had met some of them campaigning with Buzzer, but it never hurt to say hello again. Ida Mae told her the first thing she had to do was nail down her base, and if Stanton wasn't for her, she was in big trouble. As Russell parked in front of the big house with its white pillars (modeled, it was said, after Tara in *Gone With the Wind*), Georgie panicked—she had forgotten the chairman's name. She quickly looked at the chairmen's list in the folder Ida Mae had prepared for her.

Harry and Jo Fogleman.

She closed her eyes and memorized the names. Harry and Jo. Harry and Jo. Say each name as you greet them and look them in the eye. Firm handshake. Harry and Jo.

"Harry," she said, smiling and grabbing the small, grinning man's hand firmly, "and Jo! Good to see you."

Nailed it.

"You got the wrong county," the man said, no longer grinning. "Harry and Jo Fogleman live in Stansfield County out on the Pike. This is *Stanton*. I'm Ken McLean and this is my wife, Doris."

"You got to get those things right, honey," his Doris said sweetly. "Most folks are particular about their names."

Georgie had looked on the wrong line of the county chairmen's list. The wrong damned *line*. As they entered the dining room, Doris said, "We got a little surprise for Ken today, being his birthday . . ."

"Yes, I know, Doris," Georgie said, thinking, *Ida Mae, you dropped the ball, you never told me, I should have known it's his damned birthday.*

"Yes, so for lunch we got the girl to make us a batch of old-fashioned home-style pancakes, Ken's favorite."

"Mine, too," Georgie said, smiling. "I can't get enough pancakes."

10:14 A.M. TUESDAY, FEBRUARY 16, LEESVILLE COUNTY

As they drove west along the Pike on their way to Herman Throe's territory, the conversation turned to the *Bugle*'s morning editorial blasting the two recent debates:

> In the immortal words of Casey Stengel, can anybody here play this game? The Democratic debate, with Ms. Susan Weinstein's staged walk-out, was an anticlimax with touches of farce. The Republican debate was a situation comedy. In the Democratic fiasco, Bobby Ricky Diddier talked platitudes and Ms. Weinstein, when she was coherent at all, used vulgarities and rudeness to make her points, although we are still not clear what her points were. Her most vocal supporters, who followed her out of the debate when she announced her unwillingness to continue—

> in language we can't use in a family newspaper—shouted for the legalization of marijuana. This was the level of debate of one of the two major parties at a time when the people of the Sixth District have no representation in Washington.
>
> As for the Republicans, Mrs. LeBrand proved to be just this side of totally inept. She is new to campaigning and clearly has to bone up on the issues and improve her platform style, what little there is of it. Senator Wholey, on the other hand, seems to revel in presenting the voters with one crazy idea after another. Mrs. LeBrand is, in our view, fortunate to have such an opponent when she is still learning the rules of the game. But eventually somebody, in either party, is going to have to talk sense, if that is not too much trouble for all concerned.

"See," Ida Mae said after reading that part of the editorial aloud. "We got out of the debate with no major damage. They were critical, but at least they said that you could improve and that Joe was too much. Didn't I tell you we'd survive, Russell?"

"You sure did, Ida Mae."

In Leesville County, Georgie spoke to thirty-three people at the Leesville Motor Court Lodge. She read her stock speech ("Jobs . . . I'm a mom and I care . . . my little boy . . . schoolteacher . . . jobs . . . I ask for your help . . .") and made only a few mistakes. The applause was polite, and as far as Georgie was concerned, the long trip had been a waste of time.

But Ida Mae had been watching Georgie carefully and liked some of what she saw. Georgie was more "into" the stock speech now, feeling comfortable with it. She was making eye contact and she wasn't stumbling over the words as much as she previously had. There was a small, but real, improvement. Ida Mae didn't tell any of this to Georgie, because she wanted to see if the improvement was a one-day fluke or the beginning of a trend.

9:00 P.M. WEDNESDAY, FEBRUARY 17, STANFORD COUNTY

Stanford County, next to Leesville, was on the western edge of the district, bordering the neighboring state. It was considered Herman Throe country, but Ida Mae's analyses of changing demographics suggested that Georgie make a quick visit, get some publicity, and—who knows?—maybe attract the attention of the newcomers to the county.

At nine o'clock that evening, after a long day of coffees, meetings, a luncheon speech at the Kiwanis, press interviews, and infinite hand shaking, they went to the home of Jack and Nancy Moore, where they'd be staying for the night. The Moores were old friends of Bo's. Jack had retired from BigBo stores six years ago, and they had moved out to Stanford because of the lower cost of living. The Moores had known Georgie since she was a baby.

"Shoot, the day lil' Georgie Beaumont comes out this way and don't stay with us is the day I vote Democrat—and that's not gonna happen," said Jack Moore, plump and jolly and friendly as a big ol' hound dog. "Get ready for a big old-fashioned dinner. You must be famished, out there in the cold all day."

"And after dinner," Nancy, plump and jolly and friendly, said, helping Georgie out of her coat, "we're just going to sit in the living room, turn off that durn TV, and have ourselves a good old-fashioned talk."

They all sat at the dining room table. Georgie was physically, mentally, and spiritually exhausted. She did not want to talk. She did not want to eat a big, old-fashioned meal, or a meal of any kind. It was too late; besides, she had been nibbling junk food all day. What she wanted, desperately, was a bottle of Merlot and then sleep, hours and hours of sleep.

"Now, how 'bout some good old-fashioned bourbon?" Jack said, getting up and searching around in the liquor cabinet. "Doubles for everybody, get the chill out of your bones. What do you say to that?

Or, for the ladies, some of this nice fancy wine our daughter gave us? We don't drink the stuff. It's called"—he looked at the label—'Mer-lot.' Never heard of it, but June, she's up in Cap City, works for Harley Tibbins in the legislature, she drinks the stuff and says it's good. It's real Californian. Georgie and Ida Mae, how's about some of this Mer-lot for you? We got four bottles."

Ida Mae, seeing the look on Georgie's face, said quickly: "Jack, I think we'll all have to pass up a drink, because—"

"Oh, now, come on, Ida Mae," Jack said, holding up a bottle of Old Uncle Dexter's bourbon that he had just found, "you're all off duty for the night and I won't take no for an answer."

Jack poured three shots of bourbon and gave one each to Russell, Nancy, and himself. He then searched through the kitchen for a corkscrew, found one, and opened the Merlot. He poured two water glasses to the brim.

"We don't have any of those fancy wineglasses, but I filled your glasses up because wine ain't as strong as liquor. Kind of a lady's drink. Am I right, Georgie?"

Georgie stared at the deep, dark red wine in the water glass, incredibly lovely looking. She turned to look at Ida Mae, who was looking right into her eyes. Georgie looked back at the wine. She put her hand on the glass and lifted it. But then, before it reached her lips, she slowly put the glass down on the table.

"Maybe I'll have some after we eat," she said to Jack. "I really don't drink that much. Do I, Ida Mae?"

"Maybe at Christmastime you'll have a glass of sherry, Georgie. But that's about all."

"Well," Jack said, "to each his own, like they say."

After a big old-fashioned meal of roast beef and mashed potatoes and string beans, regular coffee, and apple pie à la mode, all of which Georgie dutifully ate, the five of them went to the living room to talk about the old days when Bo didn't have a nickel and the Moores were the Beaumonts' next-door neighbors.

"That was back in 'fifty-one, we moved next door," Jack said. "How about a roast beef sandwich, with a nice cold beer, Georgie, before you turn in?"

"I'm fine, Jack." She closed her eyes, but Ida Mae, sitting next to her on the couch, nudged her.

"Honey," Nancy said to Jack, "you're wrong. It was back in 'fifty-three we moved next to Bo. Reason I know that is Betty Carpenter, she's the one with the one eye, well, her sister—"

"Catherine?" Jack said. "The one who married the Dobson boy?"

"No, no, Catherine ran away with that crippled railroad man. No, the one I'm thinking of was Faye."

The talk of the old days went on and on and on. And on. Every time Georgie would nod off, Ida Mae would poke her. Just before one-thirty, Nancy Moore got to the end of her story about how Bo tried to fix the roof and fell through. His leg went right through, you wouldn't believe the language he used, but you couldn't help but laugh.

"Honey," Nancy said to Georgie, whose willpower had reached its limits since not even Ida Mae's rib-cracking nudges could keep her awake, "if I was you, I'd think about getting my sleep. You probably got places to go tomorrow."

Russell slept on the couch. Georgie and Ida Mae shared a room. Just before she closed her eyes Georgie said, in a zombielike voice: "Tell me the truth, Ida Mae. I can take it. Do I have a chance? Is all this worth it?"

"Just keep on doing what you've been doing this week. Maybe that debate was all for the best. You got all the bad stuff out of your system."

But Georgie was already asleep.

7:30 A.M. THURSDAY, FEBRUARY 18, ERROLL COUNTY

Erroll County was just south of Zellenborn, in the depressed central part of the district. It had gone for Buzzer last time, but barely. Ida Mae wanted to show the flag and keep Republicans reminded of who was running.

Georgie, groggy from lack of sleep, still feeling bloated from the night before's big old-fashioned meal, met with a small group of contributors and party officials at the home of Jimmy T. Carroll, a burly, red-faced, jovial, crushing handshaker and a successful car dealer who had long been one of Buzzer's loyal supporters. He had the most ridiculous comb-over Georgie had ever seen, a full, 100 percent, six-whisps-across-the-entire-dome work of engineering art.

"Georgie, *damn* good to see ya! You know my Betty here, my better half, like they say. You make sure you sit next to me when the grub comes, I'll eat what you don't, ha ha ha."

There were seven round tables set up for coffee and pastries, with folks sitting and chatting, and as Ida Mae had told her to, Georgie walked around the room, making small talk at each table, and then sat next to Jimmy. She was talking to a man on her right when Jimmy placed his hand on her thigh and squeezed.

She removed his hand and turned to him. He winked.

"What are you doing, Jimmy?" she said in a conversational tone, smiling.

"Nothing you can't handle, honey."

"How would you like it if I told your wife?" Keep smiling.

"Betty? Oh, hell, she'll never believe you anyhow," he said in a low voice, his facial expression beaming goodwill and friendship as the other people at the table carried on their own conversations. "You know, Georgie, I always said you was wasted on ol' Buzzer. Don't get me wrong, I love Buzzer, he's my good buddy, but facts are facts. With him a vegetable, I bet you're just a bit, you know, frustrated. You know what I'm saying here? How's about I give you a call? Just to get to know each other. I can do you a lot of good out here."

He gave her thigh another squeeze.

"Despite your irresistible charm, I just don't quite see that happening, Jimmy," she said, still smiling. "Excuse me, I have to mingle."

She picked up her steaming cup of coffee, brought it below the level of the table, and poured the contents onto his crotch.

"Jesus Christ!" he shouted, leaping from the chair, brushing the front of his pants.

"Oh, how *clumsy* of me," she said.

7:35 A.M. FRIDAY, FEBRUARY 19, GRANGE CITY

Russell and Georgie were standing on Main Street in Grange Square, in front of Fawcett's Diner, as Georgie greeted folks on their way to work in the courthouse and the Beaumont Building. They had started at the courthouse steps and then slowly made their way along the square, Georgie shaking hands, Russell handing out flyers. On the east side of the square, they walked past the park and Georgie shook hands as they made their way to the Beaumont Building. Then they recrossed Main to the Grange Hotel, and now here they were at Fawcett's. As Russell moved about, busily distributing the leaflets, Georgie, shaking hands with passersby, couldn't help but smile.

"Russell, you've been in a very good mood recently. Any reason?"

"Sure, we have a good chance, we—"

"Russell, this is Georgie. You can't fool me. Tell me the truth—are you and Ida Mae . . . ?"

"Here comes a bus, get ready," Russell said, but it was too late, he was blushing. "Remember, look them in the eye as they get off."

"I've managed to memorize this drill, Russell," Georgie said with a smile as the bus squeaked to a stop. So it was true. *Russell and Ida Mae!* Who'd ever have thought?

For the next few minutes she was caught up in the rapid-movement dance of voter greeting: step forward, arm extended; grab their hand; give it one pump; look them in the eye—but not for too long, you don't want a big conversation.

"I'm Georgie LeBrand, running for Congress, and I need your vote."

All of this was accompanied by a shuffling of the feet toward the next person, again and again. Some of them just smiled and walked away. Others said things like "I'm with you," and some frowned and walked past, deliberately ignoring her outstretched hand. The important thing was not to get caught up with one voter for too long. Keep shaking hands, meet and greet, repeat your name.

1:35 P.M. MONDAY, FEBRUARY 22, MARGARET P. KINGSBURY ROOM, CAPITAL CITY AIRPORT MOTEL

Georgie, acknowledging the applause after the introduction, walked to the microphone. She stood before about a hundred prominent small-business men and women, participants at the Fifth Annual Jobs! Fair, sponsored by the local service clubs and the chamber of commerce.

She stood there, smiling and looking confident. And why not? She looked terrific. After trying out certain looks on the road, today Georgie finally had it all together. The waitress at Bob's Diner had not been far off the mark: Georgie had that generic news-anchor look. Her highlighted hair had a fashionable wind-swept look. Her smart, well-cut navy blue pinstriped suit was set off with the traditional, demure white blouse. A single strand of pearls and tiny pearl earrings added just the right touch. She was not threatening to women and was attractive to men without being distracting. After the usual intro material about it being an honor to be there, and after mentioning five or six names of club officials, Georgie looked down at her speech text.

"Let me begin by making a confession. That *Bugle* editorial about the debate was right when it said I have a lot to learn. I am here to tell you this afternoon, yes, I'll make mistakes. But I'll learn from my mistakes, because I want to make a difference for the people of this district. I respect my opponent. But we have major differences. My opponent wants to talk about anything but jobs—and I want to talk about jobs more than anything."

For a moment she paused and looked out at the crowd and Ida Mae, standing at the rear of the room, thought it was going to be another one of those Georgie moments. But instead, it was a pause for effect. Ida Mae was impressed. A little thing like a slight pause at the right place, a little hook to focus and hold their attention—that was pretty good.

"My opponent believes in his views very deeply. I respect his right to hold those views. I believe, as he does, we have to have morality in government. I am a mother and I have a deep sense of what it takes to raise a child in today's environment, with what we see on television and in the movies. So I don't disagree on the moral issues my opponent has raised. All I'm saying is that there are other issues, urgent ones, like jobs for families, like economic growth, like bringing this district back to where it should be. And whoever is going to face the Democratic primary winner—as if we don't know who is going to win *that* race . . ."

It got a laugh, even from Ida Mae, who wasn't prepared for it. Georgie had actually ad-libbed.

"Bobby Ricky keeps on talking about Big Ed Kingsbury. But times have changed. We're not going to solve our problems with old-fashioned big-government solutions."

Hearty applause.

"I believe in fewer regulations on business. Democrats believe in taking orders from big-labor bosses who are financing their campaigns. But I believe that our Sixth District workers and their families benefit most when local businesses get the chance to create jobs."

Hearty applause.

"My opponent in this primary just won't talk about these issues. I believe that when we have low-tax policies that favor investment and foster job growth, all families benefit. This is a campaign with differing viewpoints, and my opponents—Republican and Democrat—won't talk about the one thing we must talk about: getting this district back on its feet."

Applause.

"I believe in free enterprise. I have never owned a business—but I am my father's daughter."

Laughter.

"I see Dad has friends in the audience."

More good-natured laughter.

"At least I *hope* they are friends."

Big, room-wide, laugh.

"My father built a business from the bottom up, and I knew what a bottom line was when I was six years old."

Laughter.

"I know how hard it is to run a business because my father's been a good teacher. He can be very persuasive, as many of you may know."

Laughter and applause and a few cheers.

"Very persuasive. And one thing he persuaded me of years ago is this: businessmen and -women—not government—create jobs. Jobs—not big government—build strong families. Strong families—not big government—build strong communities. And strong communities—not big government—build a strong nation."

Ida Mae knew it was a mainstream Republican speech, the same old tired speech Republicans had been giving forever and the same speech she herself had been writing for years. In fact, Ida Mae had written this speech, but Georgie was saying the old words as if they were being said for the first time. She spoke as if she really had a big secret she was bursting to tell the audience: free enterprise works. That was the difference between ordinary speakers and good ones. The good ones made it sound as if this old stuff was a big discovery, something new. Georgie had finally gotten the hang of it.

TUESDAY, FEBRUARY 23

The *Bugle*, headline:

LEBRAND IMPRESSES IN BUSINESS SPEECH

. . . One local Republican political figure, who requested anonymity, said, "I was impressed with her speech. That was an important crowd for her, and they liked what they heard and saw. I think Georgie's turned the corner. She's more confident. She's speaking better. A few days ago, I didn't think she had a chance. Now I think we got ourselves a horse race."

6:32 A.M. TUESDAY, FEBRUARY 23, GRANGE MEMORIAL HOSPITAL, GRANGE CITY

Nurse Patsy Earlings approached Buzzer's bedside and made the usual checks on the machines, fluffed his pillows, and checked his IV. She pulled open the blinds, not that it made any difference to Mr. LeBrand, him being in a coma, but a hospital room bright with winter light wasn't as cold looking. From this room you could see the old courthouse and the Beaumont Building, over there on the square, a few blocks away. Patsy had grown used to Grange City, even though it was so big, with so many people. Sometimes it still scared her. But since she and her mom had joined the TMC, she felt more at home. Her mom had gone back home to Etons to do some conversion work in the hills. Patsy had a two-room apartment on the West Side, out near Gunther Park. It really wasn't a nice neighborhood, but Patsy was confident in the Lord.

She heard a sound. Very brief it was, like someone clearing his throat.

She turned and looked at Mr. LeBrand. Nope, there was no sound coming from that poor man. Elder Jimmy had doubts about Mr. LeBrand, but Patsy was certain there was something unusual about this poor, suffering soul. After all he had gone through, he was still alive. Of course, he never moved. His eyes were shut. But he was still here. Nurse Patsy was inspired by that fact, even though he was not of this world right now. That sound she heard probably came from somebody passing by in the hall.

She was about to insert one of the Herman Throe tapes into the VCR when she remembered she had not swabbed out Mr. LeBrand's mouth. She moistened the swab and walked to the bedside. She was about to put the swab in his mouth when she felt the grip of his hand on her forearm.

"The hell *time* is it?" Buzzer LeBrand asked. His eyes were squinting against the morning light. "The *hell's* goin' on?"

Nurse Patsy screamed and jumped back, staring at him.

"Oh, sweet Lord! Oh, sweet Lord!"

"Stop screamin', woman," Buzzer said, his voice thin and raspy but containing his usual tone of annoyance.

Patsy bolted from the room and ran along the hallway toward the nurses' station, shouting, "It's a miracle, praise the Lord, a miracle. He's alive."

She ran back to Buzzer's room with nurses scurrying after her.

"It's a miracle," she wailed as three nurses ran into the room.

"Woman, will you shut up?" Buzzer growled, closing his eyes against the light.

"When you was in your coma, I played tapes of Reverend Herman Throe, every day. I knew you'd come back. Reverend Throe's brought you back from the dead."

"The hell you talkin' about, woman?"

By that time, a doctor was there, staring in disbelief.

"He's back!" Patsy shouted. "God and Herman Throe did it!"

7:54 A.M., BO BEAUMONT'S OFFICE, GRANGE CITY

"Daddy? This is Russell."

"I recognize your voice after all these years, don't waste my time telling me it's you. What is it? Ida Mae mess up again?"

"No, Daddy. It's Buzzer. He's back."

"Back?"

"Georgie heard from the hospital and she just called me. They told her he woke up this morning, just like that. He can talk, he can answer questions. The news will be on the TV pretty soon. A doctor is holding a news conference this afternoon."

"Listen to me, Russell: put out some kind of news release from campaign headquarters, right away, saying how glad Georgie is. And tell her to call me right away."

9:25 A.M., GRANGE MEMORIAL HOSPITAL, GRANGE CITY

Buzzer, propped up on three pillows, listened to Dr. Stern finish his account of all that had happened: Buzzer's heart attack, his fall, the coma, and Georgie's decision to run for his vacated seat.

"What's all this stuff about Herman Throe? That crazy nurse is saying Herman saved me. Saved me from what?"

"Oh, it's nothing. While you were comatose, Nurse Earlings played his videotapes, hoping, I suppose, that part of your mind was able to comprehend, although I most seriously doubt it."

"She says it's a miracle. Herman brought me back."

"That's hardly a scientific opinion, Mr. LeBrand."

"What else you got to tell me?"

"That's all we know right now," the doctor said. "I must say, Congressman, your recovery is—"

"I'm no congressman," Buzzer said sharply. His voice seemed to grow stronger by the minute. "From what you just said, I'm an ex-congressman. Ain't that right?"

"Mr. LeBrand, consider how fortunate you are. Your heart is better than we could hope to expect. Your memory is spotty, but that's to be expected. Your muscle tone, your strength—remember, I'm speaking comparatively here—are impressive."

"You say you told my wife I'm back? What did she say?"

"She was surprised, that's only natural, I'd say stunned. She kept on asking me if I was absolutely certain. I'm sure she's delighted, as we all are."

For a few moments Buzzer stared at his hands folded across his chest, then said, "Get out of here, Doc. I have to think. Come back later."

When Dr. Stern returned, half an hour later, Buzzer said, "Get me a pen and paper."

"Are you sure you're up to—?"

"Yes, damn it, I'm sure. I want to write something out and I want you to read it at that news conference you're having this afternoon."

"Certainly. But there's no need for you to make any kind of a statement. You can just rest, there's no need—"

"Oh, yes there is," Buzzer said. "I got something important I want to say."

10:07 A.M., WASHINGTON, D.C.

"Mr. Speaker, it's Gus. I hope you're sitting down. We just got word. Buzzer's awake. He's talking. He's alive."

"Just my damned luck."

"I don't know what happens now."

The Speaker slammed down the phone. *What a mess. All Buzzer had to do was die like a man, and he couldn't even do that right. Now I have to put out a news release saying how glad I am he's back, the rotten son of a bitch. And I'll be expected to fly down there and see him. Just what I need, a visit to Buzzer. Why didn't I stay in the insurance business?*

11:09 A.M., BEAUMONT'S OFFICE, GRANGE CITY

"Daddy, it's Rus—Daddy, I can't find Georgie."

"What the hell do you mean you can't find her?"

"She called me just after I spoke with you. She said she wanted to be alone and no one should look for her. She's not home. The car is gone. No one in the campaign has seen her all day. Ida Mae is worried sick."

"Did you get someone to write a news release like I told you?"

"Well, Dad, I thought Georgie would want to use her own words since it's a family thing and—"

"Damn it, Russell, we got to get something out to the press, it don't matter if Georgie sees it. Tell Ida Mae to write how Georgie's thankful that Buzzer has been returned to her and Buzzer Jr., stuff like that. Throw in God a few times, that can't hurt. Tell anyone who asks she's secluded and she's eager to see her husband."

"I think this news has hit her pretty hard, Dad. She thought that Buzzer—"

"Yeah, she thought he was as good as dead. We all did. Well, he ain't. Just do what I tell you while I see how this is going to play. And goddamn it, Russell, get off your rear end and find Georgie."

2:08 P.M., HOMEWELL STATE FOREST

Georgie sat in her car, the heater on, parked at the same overlook where, only a few weeks before, she had walked and talked with Ida Mae. She had an open bottle of Merlot on the seat next to her, a cheap corkscrew, some plastic glasses, and a box of Cheez-Its. There was another, unopened, bottle on the backseat.

Far below, there was a lone car heading east. Where was the driver going, snug, as Georgie was now, inside a car on a cold winter day? She giggled. What difference did it make? What difference did anything make?

From where she sat she could see the mountains covered with pines. The trees just kept on going, no matter what happened, no matter how tough things got, they just kept pouring out green, green, green. When the going gets tough, the pines get green.

The peace and stillness of the scene reminded her of a famous painting. By whom? Jack Danzig would know. Jack knew about such things. If he were there, he would tell her. But he wasn't there. Maybe she should have returned his call. No, to hell with it.

Everything that had happened to her in the past few weeks was gone, lost. There was only this moment, now, just being there, alone, sipping wine, nibbling on Cheez-Its, warm in the car. She felt that if she placed one foot outside the car, something awful would happen. But something awful had already happened. Somewhere, on the trip out there, she had lost all the confidence she had slowly, painfully, built up, bit by bit, since the campaign started. *Where did I lose my confidence? I had it this morning. I must have just put it down and drove off without it. I have to place an ad in the* Bugle: *Lost: one medium-sized confidence. Big reward.*

She rolled down her driver's-side window just a bit, to get some air. It was dangerous sitting in a car with the heater on unless there's some air, or so they said. Just being here like this was nice. There was no one to tell her to do things. She didn't have to make a speech or smile or try to look interested. There was no past, no future, no Buzzer, just herself, here. How perfectly lovely and sweet it was, sitting in comfort, warm and cozy, sipping wine, looking at the whole world spread out before her, the hills and the pines and the little roads crisscrossing in the valley below, all of it there, just for her, in the winter light.

She looked at her fingers. If, weeks before, they had just pulled the plug, if she had had the courage to just will her fingers to make that almost infinitesimal movement . . . But she had let him live. And now he was back. She began to weep.

2:10 P.M., THE LITTLE BROWN CHURCH

When Herman Throe heard the news, he was in the original Little Brown Church, sitting uncomfortably in one of the back pews, his Bible held across his great paunch. He was thinking of nothing, just trying to hear the silence and read the Word, a refresher he needed from time to time, just to be alone with the Lord.

Linc Islington, one of his close aides, was suddenly standing beside him, out of breath.

"Herman, I hate to bother you and all. I know you like your private time. But it's on the TV. Buzzer LeBrand is awake. And that's not all. He wrote out a statement. Herman, you're not going to believe this."

"What is it, Linc?"

"Buzzer's saying you're responsible for his recovery. And he's saved. He's born again."

"Buzzer? Born again?"

"It's the honest truth. It came over the TV. One of the doctors read something Buzzer wrote. Buzzer says when he was in the coma, some nurse up there played your tapes, over and over, while Buzzer was asleep. Somehow he must have, I don't know, in his mind heard them or something, and he's saying now you saved him."

"Find out from the hospital when I can see him, Linc."

As Linc rushed out, Herman thought: *Just when I'm thinking of maybe getting out of politics, what with Joe Wholey driving me crazy, God gives me a great sign like this. The sheep that was lost has been found.*

3:22 P.M., CARL RACKSLEY'S OFFICE, THE WESTERN PIKE, GRANGE CITY

Carl Racksley had just had a not-so-friendly talk with Jasper Huggins. It was difficult to carry on even a normal conversation with Jasper because the Little Guy really was little. In plain fact, Jasper Huggins was a dwarf (but *never* call him that). He was about three feet high, and when he was doing business with people he was angry with, he insisted they look him straight in the eye. This was difficult because Jasper was so small, you had to squat down to look him in the eye because he refused to look up at you.

Jasper and two of his people had come directly into Carl's office, ignoring the secretary's lie that Mr. Racksley wasn't in. The two men with Jasper were very definitely not little people. One of them was the size of an NFL offensive lineman, and the other looked as if he was about a minute or so away from an attack of steroid rage.

Jasper marched in, all business, with his little person's side-to-side stride. He was wearing one of those Russian black fur hats and a beautifully cut black overcoat made especially for him by a tailor in Cap City.

"Where's my money, you fucking pimp?" Jasper yelled in that tiny, whiny voice, not looking up at Carl. Carl quickly assumed the squat position in front of Jasper so they were on eye level. Carl knew that if he put out his hand on the floor to steady himself, one of the goons would slap him across the face and the pain would be horrible. It had happened before. You had to stay in the squat position and hope you didn't fall, because then the goons would kick you in the ribs until you got back in the position. Jasper Huggins had his little rituals and he expected people to either follow them or pay the price.

"Jasper, I'm working on that. In fact, I got a lead. I'm very confident and—"

Jasper swiftly slapped Carl in the face with a gloved hand. Carl fell. One of the goons took two steps and kicked Carl so hard, tears came to Carl's eyes. It was as if someone had stuck him in the side with a red-hot poker. But he reassumed the position, knowing the goon would kick him until he did.

"You know why I call you a pimp?" Jasper asked.

"No, Jasper."

"You probably don't, you stupid fuck. A pimp's a guy gets women for other men. You been doing any of that? You been helping a good friend of yours get laid?"

"Oh, no," Carl said—his legs hurt from the position, his ribs hurt, and his face was still stinging—"oh, I'd never, Jasper, I—"

Jasper said, "You're so fucking dumb, you don't even know what's going on. Well, I won't tell you. Listen to me. Are you listening to me?"

"Yes, Jasper."

"If you don't give me my money in two weeks, all of it, I'm going to put you in a little room I got, out on my place near the river. Just you and my two associates here. In the first thirty seconds you'll start screaming louder than you ever did in your life. And it won't end for twenty-four hours. My associates take twelve-hour shifts. For you that means start-to-finish screaming. First I'll play you tapes I got of other guys who thought they could stiff me. But don't worry about dying. You won't die. But you'll wish you had. And then you'll still have to pay me off."

With that, Jasper, adjusting his big Russian hat, wheeled about and walked out, followed by the goons. Drenched in sweat, trembling, and in desperate need of a drink, Carl got up, wincing, tears in his eyes. He sat at his desk. His secretary showed her head through the open doorway.

"Mr. Racksley? Is everything . . . all right? Those men—"

"Everything's fine, Lorna. Just shut the door. And don't ever mention this to anyone. Far as you're concerned, those gentlemen were never here."

The phone rang, his private number.

"Carl, did you hear?"

"Hear what, Marge?"

"Haven't you been watching it on television?"

"Marge, I got things going on. What are you talking about?"

"Buzzer's alive."

"Buzzer? Out of the coma?"

"Honest to God, Carl."

Carl put down the phone. It was the damnedest thing, Buzzer

back again. Carl had to get the money, somehow. He smiled. Maybe Buzzer would help him get the money. Yes, that was it! This was a break. One minute Jasper was threatening him, and just like that, Marge calls and says that Buzzer is back. With Buzzer back, anything can happen!

10:06 P.M., KINGSBURY MOTEL, JUST OUTSIDE OF CAPITAL CITY

Lee Simmons and Bobby Ricky lay naked in each other's arms in the small, tacky motel room.

"Baby . . ." he whispered.

"Shhhhh. I think I died, about ten minutes ago."

"You seemed alive to me."

"Just rest. We have a big day tomorrow. Home stretch."

"This is crazy, with Kalya right here in town. But I can't get enough of you. I can't help it, I don't care."

"Neither do I. Please remind me to call CBS tomorrow. I was talking to one of Dan Rather's people this morning. Can you believe it?"

WEDNESDAY, FEBRUARY 24

The *Bugle*, front page:

LEBRAND RECOVERS, IS BORN AGAIN

. . . Dr. Stern said the former congressman was in "extraordinary" mental and physical condition considering his ordeal. . . . LeBrand said in a written statement read by Dr. Stern that he was "born again" and that Reverend Herman Throe had saved him from the fires of hell. . . .

From the same page, same day:

MRS. LEBRAND IN DUI INCIDENT

Georgie LeBrand, candidate in a Republican primary race for her husband's congressional seat, was arrested last night in Zellenborn County for driving erratically on the Western Pike. She has been charged with driving under the influence of alcohol.

Police sources say that Mrs. LeBrand's Breathalyzer test was recorded at .07, sufficient for the DUI charge. If guilty, she faces a two-month license suspension and a $500 fine.

Attempts to reach Mrs. LeBrand were unsuccessful, but her brother, Russell Beaumont, who is a campaign adviser, issued a statement:

"On advice of counsel, my sister will have no comment on this unfortunate incident. She has been under extraordinary pressure recently and the wonderful news of her beloved husband's recovery proved to be too much of a shock. She is eager to be with her husband and child and to continue the campaign."

The *Bugle*, page three:

WEINSTEIN ARRESTED

. . . the Democratic primary candidate for the Sixth District congressional seat had chained herself to the main entrance of the BigBo store on the Western Pike, in protest against what she termed "fascist tactics" of BigBo owner Beauregard "Bo" Beaumont, in refusing to unionize.

Commenting on the race as she was dragged to a police car, Ms. Weinstein said, "Some choice. It's me, Nephew Tom, an airhead cheerleader, and one of God's storm troopers. I'm not in this race to debate them, I'm here to denounce them and to destroy the system."

10:06 A.M., THE LITTLE BROWN CHURCH

"It's a damned trick, Herman," Joe Wholey said as they sat on a couch in Herman's office, looking at the hills through the glass wall. "Buzzer's no more born again than the Devil himself. He's up to something."

"You never know, Joe. God don't play by our rules."

"The only rules I care about are the Ten Commandments, which Buzzer never heard of."

"Joe, you got to start talking about jobs."

"My job is to save this country from hell. And God is on my side. You read about Georgie? The DUI? Tell me God's hand's not in that, her getting drunk like that. That DUI means I win."

Herman put his arm around Joe.

"You ever hear the saying, Joe, pray like everything depends on God, and work like everything depends on you? Well, that's what you got to do. Forget about Georgie. Forget about Buzzer. Leave them in the hands of the Lord. Now all you have to do is go to the eastern part of the district and talk jobs, jobs, jobs to Georgie's base. We got a little chance to cut into it, with Georgie getting this bad press over the DUI, or at least make her protect her base, keep her away from undecideds. We got our base secure out here. Just keep on working."

Joe Wholey leaped up from the couch and stared at the Bosch painting hanging on the wall. He pointed at the large scene filled with unimaginable horrors.

"Herman," he shouted, his voice trembling, "I'm telling you, the only way I can lose this is if the Devil himself stops me! The Devil himself! There's no other way."

"Just calm down, Joe. Take a walk in the woods. Breathe the air."

9:30 P.M., GEORGIE LEBRAND CAMPAIGN HEADQUARTERS, GRANGE CITY

Will Parsons from the *Bugle* ambushed Russell just as he was coming out the front door on the way home. Russell was tired, irritable, and despondent. He had been in the office since six-thirty that morning, coordinating the response to the barrage of phone calls about Georgie's "incident" (the word Ida Mae had demanded all campaign workers use in referring to the DUI disaster). Now, fifteen hours later, here was more trouble.

"Russell, you got a minute? I've been trying to get you all day."

"Give me a break, Will. I've been busy all day. I'm on my way home."

"Just give me a minute. What's the real story with Georgie?"

"I gave a statement. We stand by that statement. Georgie's been under a lot of stress and—"

"Russell, for Christ's sake, don't give me press-release garbage. Why hasn't she been to see Buzzer today?"

"We canceled all appearances."

"Appearances? Her husband comes back from the dead, and she has to make an *appearance?* All right, Buzzer's a bastard, but he's her husband."

Russell beeped open the Bronco door and slid in behind the wheel.

"As a matter of fact, Georgie, Dad, and I are going to see Buzzer first thing tomorrow morning. Give me a little break on this, Will. Georgie has been under—"

"Yeah, yeah, I know, I read the statement. But what I think is, when she found out Buzzer was alive, it drove her to drink. Or should I say back to drink? The rumor around town is that Georgie drinks too much. Folks have seen her out at the club, at lunchtime, drinking folks under the table. Somebody saw you and Bo and her at that French place in Cap City a few weeks ago and they say she was loud and drunk."

Russell stared at him stoney-faced.

"Russell, come on. I've been hearing the rumors about Georgie just like everybody else. But before this, it was all private, her drinking too much. Granted, Buzzer would drive anybody to drink. But I just want you to know, I can't sit on this stuff any longer. It's a legitimate question now, her drinking habits."

"Will, do what the hell you have to do. I'm too tired to argue," Russell said, and drove off.

8:32 A.M. THURSDAY, FEBRUARY 25, GRANGE CITY

Russell went into Georgie's house while Bo waited in the car, sulking, still smoldering over Georgie's fiasco. Russell found her in the living room, seated on her floral-print Revenge sofa. She was all dressed up, in a dark green pantsuit with a white, long-sleeve silk turtleneck. She looked very pretty except that she had a lost, haunted look in her eyes, what combat veterans call "the thousand-yard stare."

"You okay, Georgie?"

"I'm fine, Russell, just fine. How's Daddy?"

"He's in a bad mood."

"How can you tell?"

"Georgie, Will Parsons says the *Bugle* knows about your drinking problem. They haven't run anything yet, but they'll use it the first chance they get. Your DUI gives them a chance to make your drinking an issue. I just wanted you to know that might be coming up."

"Be sure to tell Ida Mae."

"I already have."

"Good. Now let's get this over with."

On the drive to the hospital, Bo started in on Georgie.

"It's a wonder you made it as far as Zellenborn without getting pulled over or having an accident. Maybe I can get the charge knocked down from DUI. So, it's going to cost me. You've put us in a hole we can't get out of."

Georgie, silent, stared out the car window.

"I had it all planned," Bo said, reaching into his pocket for a mint. "All you had to do was go around and meet and greet and don't say too much. We could have beaten Holy Joe. But, no, you had to make a fool of yourself and of me, too. I'll say no more, because if I do, I'll say things that can't be taken back. Things about ingratitude. Things about being irresponsible. Things about—"

"Dad," Russell broke in, "I just remembered. Now don't get mad, but Ida Mae said you have to handle Buzzer carefully this morning. We might need him now, she says."

"Oh, is that what the girl genius says? I'm very impressed. She's done so well handling the campaign and keeping an eye on your sister here. Oh, well, we'll get the drunk-driver votes for sure."

"Dad—" Russell began.

"Don't you or Ida Mae dare tell me what to do, Russell. I know we got to deal with the idiot boy this morning and I'm already prepared. So don't deplete your remaining brain cells trying to tell me what to do."

"Well, Dad, you have to admit Buzzer gets under your skin and you lose your temper with him."

"I don't have to admit anything. Now do me a favor and keep quiet."

"Russell is right, Daddy," Georgie said, her first words since she got in the car. "This isn't going to be easy for any of us. So don't make it worse."

"What a lucky old man I am," Bo said. "In my golden years I got two nitwit children telling me what to do. It does my old heart good."

———

Buzzer's room was filled to overflowing with flowers, cards, and get-well balloons.

"My public," Buzzer said with less-than-Buzzer strength, gesturing toward the display. "From all over the state and the country. From Canada, too. They love me."

"Who wouldn't?" Bo said sourly.

"Buzzer, we're glad you're back," Russell said. "Considering what you've been through, you look great."

"It's the Lord's work, Russell."

"Buzzer," Georgie said suddenly, "before we say anything else, let me get this over with."

She paused.

"I know how you must feel about . . . what I did," she said. "But every doctor I talked to said it was a negative prognosis. Every one. And I—"

Buzzer smiled and held up his hand like a cop stopping traffic. He had a strange little smile on his face, not a big fake Buzzer smile, but something different, a sappy look of contentment.

"Georgie, Georgie, Georgie, it's all right. Nurse Patsy Earlings says that God tells us to forgive those who hurt us, like you hurt me. And God told me the same thing while I was in my coma, so I got no grudges against nobody. Forgive and forget, that's me."

"That makes me feel warm all over, Buzzer," Bo said, barely keeping his temper in check. Was it the tone of Buzzer's voice, the little self-satisfied whine of the martyr who now holds all the cards, or that pious smile? Or was it just seeing Buzzer alive?

"Tell me something," Bo continued. "When God told you all this stuff, did he speak English? Or can you understand speaking in tongues? I'm interested because so far as I know, and correct me if I'm wrong here, you and the Lord ain't ever been on speaking terms before. So I wonder how you knew who it was talking to you."

"I don't know how to explain it to you, Bo, but that's no reflection on you," Buzzer said tolerantly. "You've never been much on God because you're so full of Self, like Herman says. Laugh if you want, Bo, but I got the Word."

"Well, just keep the Word to yourself for a little while and let's talk some political business here."

"I got no political business now. The way I see it, I'm unemployed. A *former* congressman. But that's all right. I got God now."

"Well, Buzzer, that's the way it is," Bo said. "You lost a seat in the House and gained a heavenly throne. I'd call that a pretty good swap, if that's the kind of thing you like. I wouldn't be found dead in either place."

"Don't worry, Bo, you won't."

"My loss, I'm sure. Anyhow, Georgie is trying to win your old seat, so it will stay in the family."

"Look, I had a near-death experience. I was declared officially dead by my own wife. My so-called congressional colleagues threw me out of a job, which the people elected me to. So I ain't had much time for current events. But I did manage to hear you had a little trouble with the police, Georgie. Is that so?"

"Yes. I was driving drunk."

"Drunk? You? That's too bad. It sets a bad example for little Buzzer Jr. Mizz Cummins brought him over to see his dad yesterday. I kind of expected to see you, too. But I guess you're busy these days, filling out statements to the police and being interrogated. Well, anyhow, don't blame yourself for disgracing the family and hurting little Buzzer and probably losing the primary. Just learn to forgive yourself. I've forgiven you."

"You're all heart," Bo said. "Now let's get down to business, I ain't got all day. What we want to ask you is this—are you willing to make some kind of statement? An endorsement? We got a draft of a support statement for you right here. All you have to do is sign off on it and we'll send it out."

Georgie began to say something, paused, and then said, "Daddy, Russell, I want to speak to Buzzer alone. Just for a few minutes."

They left the room and she stood by the side of the bed, looking at Buzzer through the strings of the get-well balloons.

"You're looking great, Georgie," Buzzer said. "Do something with your hair? It looks lighter and—"

"Buzzer, I know about you and Marge Racksley."

"Marge?"

"I saw the letter."

"What letter?"

"Have it your way, Buzzer, I'm too tired to argue," she said. "Anyhow, I need your endorsement. People have forgotten what a bastard you are, and you're popular again, at least for the moment. I wish to God I had never gotten into this race, but I'm in it now. And I want to win."

"Georgie, honey—"

"No, let me finish. Number one, don't ever come back to the house. Number two, stay away from me and little Buzzer. And win or lose, I'm going to file for divorce right after the election is over. So there it is. I owe it to you to be honest, even if you've never been honest with me."

She expected him to be on the attack, but he just lay there, propped up on the pillows, and stared out the window. Finally he turned his head and said, "Georgie, honest to God, I don't know what you're talking about. I wish I did; then at least I could repent. But I can't remember anything about Marge."

"Damn it, Buzzer, I saw the letter. It was very explicit. She appears to know a lot about the way you're . . . built."

"Well, honey, if that's true, my best guess is this: Marge is suffering from what they call fantasies and delusions. They talk about them on those TV talk shows. She makes up things. But let me give you some advice. I've learned one thing, lying here in what could have been my deathbed. Forgive those who hurt you. Now you hurt me by deserting me in my hour of need. I guess Bo persuaded you. But that's all over. And I forgive you."

Bo and Russell reentered the room.

"So, Buzzer," Bo said, "are we going to get your endorsement?"

"Bo, me and Georgie been having a nice little family talk. I'm not up to thinking about politics right now. I've been getting these headaches. In fact, one came on just as you arrived. I'll tell you what—give me the endorsement statement, let me take a look. Tomorrow I'm having a little news conference and maybe that'll be the time to address my political plans. Is that okay?"

"We ain't got much time," Bo said. "The damned primary election is next Tuesday."

"I know, Bo, and I wish I could say yes, but in fact I'm feeling a little peaked. Give me a chance to read it and see what I think. I'll get back to you. Is that okay?"

"Sounds good to me," Bo said, which was all he could say because Buzzer, the bastard, had them over a barrel and there was nothing else to do but wait for him to make up his so-called mind.

One hour later, the Speaker and Gus Gorham stood by the side of the bed.

"You're looking great, Buzzer," the Speaker said. "We speak for all the members, on both sides of the aisle really, when we say we're glad you're back with us."

"Well, actually, I'm not back with *you* exactly, if you know what I mean. You took my seat away."

Nurse Patsy Earlings wheeled in a cart loaded with flowers.

"Here's another bunch of them, Mr. LeBrand," she said. "Ain't they the prettiest things you ever seen?"

"They sure are, Nurse Patsy. Mr. Speaker and Gus, if you want any flowers, for the wife or office, it don't matter, feel free to take some. There's more where they came from, I'm sure."

"Oh, I wouldn't want to take away your beautiful flowers, Buzzer," the Speaker said, wondering how much longer he was supposed to take all of this.

"Then I guess I got to send them to the children's ward, like I been doing. Always loved little kids. Nurse Patsy, just send them all downstairs for the little tots."

"Sure thing, Mr. LeBrand. The little kids think you're just the kindest man."

"That's the Lord working through me, is all."

The Speaker grunted.

"Buzzer, I want to talk a little politics here," Gus said. "Is it better that you endorse Georgie or that you don't endorse her? I mean, things being what they are, what's your read on this?"

"Now, ain't that funny? Just a while ago, Bo and Georgie were asking me the same thing. Great minds think alike, or so they say. Well, I'm holding a news conference tomorrow, just to let people know how good the Lord has been to me. I'll probably be saying something about the election at that time."

"We're counting on you to do the right thing for the party, Buzzer. Like always, big guy," the Speaker said. "We need your help because we need to keep your seat. I can't endorse one Republican over another in a primary, so my hands are tied. But we feel Holy Joe can't beat Bobby Ricky. Whichever way you play it, we want you to help Georgie."

"I think you hit it right on the nose, Mr. Speaker," Buzzer said, staring at the big honker. "You can always count on ol' Buzzer to do the right thing. You know that."

"I know how much I can count on you, Buzzer," the Speaker said. "I always have."

Two hours later, Marge Racksley said, "Oh, Buzzer, Buzzer. It's so good to see you. I had to tell them I'm your sister to get in."

"When the nurse told me my sister was here, I knew that wasn't true. None of my real sisters would come to see me, that's for sure. You've always been a loyal supporter, Marge, you and my good friend Carl."

"I've been more than that, more than a supporter," Marge said, her eyes brimming with tears. "Much more. I need to be more than a supporter again."

"Marge, I just can't remember a lot of things, so I'm not sure what you're talking about."

"I'm talking about you and me, Buzzer. You know what I mean."

"No, Marge, I'm afraid I'm not making any connection here. When my head clears, we'll have to have a long talk. Oh, by the way, if I was you, I wouldn't be talking to Georgie. She says she came across some strange letter she says you wrote to me. She's mad as hell. I told her I don't remember any letter."

"Buzzer, don't you remember I told you I sent—"

Buzzer winced and put his hand to his forehead.

"Marge, I got to be honest. I'm not feeling too good. See, I get these stabbing pains in the head and I'm getting one right now."

"Oh, Buzzer, I'm sorry, I didn't know. I just had to see you."

"No, no, it isn't you. It's just that the Lord has left me in considerable pain. He has his ways. But I welcome it. I'm suffering for my sins. I deserve to. So it's been nice to see you, Marge. Please say hello to Carl for me. How's he doing?"

"He still owes money and he looks awful. Thank God I got my own business in my name, not his. Buzzer, don't you remember anything? About us, I mean? Out on the golf course that night?"

"Some things are coming back to me. I got these pictures in my mind. Like, they flash in and out of my mind."

"Pictures?"

"Yeah, about you and me. We're together. We're doing—"

"Doing what, Buzzer? Tell me."

"It's all pretty vague right now, Marge. My mind ain't clear. But the thoughts are pretty good, I can tell you that."

"Buzzer, when it comes back to you—about us, I mean—will you tell me?"

"I sure will, Marge. Now just let me get a little rest."

Two hours later, when he arrived at Buzzer's room, Herman Throe first tried praying with Buzzer. But Buzzer didn't know any prayers. Herman then read from the Bible, the Psalms and Proverbs mostly, but Buzzer said it gave him a headache. He was prone to headaches now, he reported. It was the Lord's will.

"Buzzer, I don't pretend to know what happened to you. But we've gotten more phone calls and messages, and, well, we never got this kind of a response before. Buzzer, the Little Brown Church is on the TV and the front page of the *Bugle*. And it's all because the Lord saw fit to save you. God be praised!"

"I second that motion," Buzzer said. "I'm just thankful, is all."

"Buzzer, one more thing. I know it's asking a lot. But can you see your way clear to be neutral in the race? I know Georgie is your wife, but Joe represents our—your—values now, and from what you've been telling me, you and Georgie aren't exactly close anymore. Maybe just say you're not taking sides."

"Herman, I'm holding a news conference tomorrow. Let me think about it."

"God be praised in all his glory," Herman said. "He that was lost is found! The prodigal returns! Do you remember the story of the prodigal son?"

"Is that the one where one brother kills the other? I always liked that one."

"No, that's Cain and Abel."

"Oh. Well, anyhow, one thing is sure. I'm back."

10:05 A.M. FRIDAY, FEBRUARY 26, GRANGE MEMORIAL HOSPITAL, GRANGE CITY

The small auditorium was packed with media, national and local, and with die-hard Buzzer supporters, hospital staff and administrators, and Nurse Patsy's friends from the TMC.

"Thank you all for coming here this morning," Dr. Stern said. "Mr. LeBrand has asked me to tell you that he is still having memory lapses, which are quite understandable. He just wants you to know so that if he cannot recall things, you'll understand. And now, Mr. LeBrand."

From a door on the left, Buzzer, clean-shaven, with a new haircut, dressed in a new dark blue bathrobe and light blue pajamas, came on in a wheelchair pushed by Nurse Patsy Earlings. There was applause. Nurse Patsy brought him to the microphones and then went to stand with Dr. Stern.

Buzzer grinned.

"My good friends," he said, "I don't have any kind of prepared statement. Don't need any. I got a bad break a few weeks ago. A lot of folks, even some very close to me, expected me to die. But the good Lord had different ideas. I guess he figured if I survived the drug pushers years ago, well, I could survive a little ol' heart attack and some bumps on my head. Let me thank all the good doctors and nurses here at the hospital for their care. And I want to say a special thanks to Nurse Patsy Earlings, that pretty little gal right back there"—he gave Patsy a wave—"who did something more important than save my life—she saved my soul. Thanks, Nurse Patsy. Okay, let's get to the questions."

"Will Parsons from the *Bugle*. There are some in the Sixth District who are questioning the sincerity of your conversion. What do you say to them?"

"I say I saw the light. If they don't believe me, so be it. Next question, from the lady back there."

"Who are you endorsing in the primary race for your old seat?"

Buzzer stared at the questioner and then blinked. He looked down as if gathering his thoughts.

"Let me address a sad, private issue that must be faced in public," he said. "As you know, my wife was just involved in a DUI case."

Pause for a drink of water.

"I feel sorry for Georgie. I pray for her. But I am not endorsing her or anyone in the Republican primary in the Sixth. In fact, today I announce my resignation from the Republican Party. Now let me make it clear: I'm not becoming a Democrat, either. God did not bring me back from the dead, in my opinion, just because he wanted me to go back to the mud-slinging partisanship we have these days. Partisanship divides. I want to unite, bring folks together. I am going beyond bipartisanship. I am for nonpartisanship. *I am weighing my options.*"

Scattered applause for option weighing.

"Congressman, are you saying—"

"Now, now, just let me finish," Buzzer said with that tolerant little smile. "I need to get on with my life. *I am seeking closure.*"

There was loud and prolonged applause and a few cheers for closure seeking.

"God told me, Buzzer, don't go back to politics as usual. So I am now of no party. I am now of the people, by the people and . . . whatever it was that George Washington said, with the people, on the people's side or whatever. I am announcing this morning that I am a write-in candidate for U.S. Representative for the Sixth District. Let me tell you, folks, I am willing to discuss the issues with whoever wins the primaries. I will discuss all of the issues, including character. I take full responsibility for my past actions. I will demand from my opponents, whoever they may be, that they answer questions of character. When I say I have experience, I don't mean just political experience, not just legislative experience. I have the experience of meeting the living God face-to-face."

Big, sustained applause from Nurse Patsy and the TMC members for the face of the living God.

"When I was in that coma, I had a vision of personal and political renewal. I had a vision of an eight-lane superhighway crossing this district, replacing the Pike, creating construction jobs for our folks. A highway built with federal funds I can get for us. I will go back to the House, where I belong, and, in a Christian way, fight for the families of this district. I will bring home the bacon, and the whole pig to boot."

Big applause for the whole pig.

"You want more? In that vision I saw some military bases reopening down here, old Fort Tyler among them, bringing more new jobs. We got enemies in this world, and the Sixth District can play its role in fighting those heathens. And I saw, in this same vision, two, three, maybe five new prisons being built right here in the Sixth, all with federal funds. In that vision I saw Big Ed Kingsbury—yes, I did. And he said to me, Son, these folks in Washington, they take and take and take—ain't it time we got some of that money back? And I saw truckloads of tax dollars leaving Washington, a whole convoy of them, sixty, a hundred semis, loaded with money to create jobs."

"Congressman, isn't this emphasis on federal spending out of character? As a Republican, you were for cutting the budget."

"I was lost and now I'm found. I was blind and now I see. Thank you so much," he said, and waved to the crowd. "Nurse Patsy, it's time to saddle up."

SIX REACTIONS TO BUZZER'S ANNOUNCEMENT

- Bo's secretary could hear strange, muffled sounds coming from his office, like those of a maddened beast howling at the night sky, but she thought it best to pretend she had heard nothing.

- Gary Garafolo laughed and laughed and laughed.

- The Speaker said to Gus Gorham, "That rotten son of a bitch. That goddamn lunatic. That . . . *independent!*"

- Ida Mae said to Georgie, "You're going to beat Holy Joe. And when we face Bobby Ricky, we'll beat him, too. Write-in votes for Buzzer? There's no way he can win. And how many people are going to vote for him? This is just Buzzer trying to get back at you."

- Herman Throe tried to pray. But nothing came. Dry as a bone. "If Joe wins, Buzzer's write-in campaign will take votes from him. Sure, write-in campaigns never amount to much. But maybe he should talk to Buzzer. Tell him that Joe is carrying the flag for them. No, he's made up his mind. He believes the Lord is telling him to run. Who was he to challenge the Lord? Thy will be done. But it would be helpful if it was thy will to keep Buzzer out of the race."

- At 10:06 P.M. Marge Racksley knocked three times on the door of a third-floor apartment in a shabby, weary-looking building on West Seventh. The door opened, but there were no lights on in the room. For a moment she was afraid, but she walked into the darkened room, as she had been told to do. Suddenly she felt strong arms around her and she let out a yelp.

"Damn it, Marge, keep quiet," Buzzer whispered in her ear. "Come on in."

He led her by the hand through the darkened room into another. He closed the door and turned on a lamp. It was a bedroom, sparsely furnished. There was a small, narrow, neatly made bed, a decrepit-looking dresser and mirror, and a night table with a lamp and a Bible on it. On the walls were cheaply framed religious prints, each reproduced in garish, lurid colors: Herod's soldiers wading through blood to slaughter the innocents; David and Goliath, at the very moment when the stone is embedded in the giant's head; Joshua massacring Philistines at Jericho; and Pharaoh's army being drowned by the thousands in the waters of the Red Sea.

Marge noticed the pictures and shuddered.

"Nurse Patsy told me about her pictures," Buzzer said, seeing Marge's expression. "She said they give her comfort in times of need. The Lord's vengeance on the heathen, or something like that."

"Nurse Patsy?"

"Yeah, this is her place," he said with an old-fashioned big Buzzer grin. "I told her I needed a place to be by myself tonight, to get close to the Lord, away from all the distractions, pray and prepare myself for what's to come. She's working the night shift."

"But you can walk. I thought you were in a wheelchair."

"Hell no," he said, moving close to her and putting his big hands around her waist. "That was just a prop for the news conference today."

"When I got your call, I was so surprised. I mean, all you said was drop everything and come to this address. It's such a bad neighborhood. I've never been in the West Side before. It's so . . . awful. This woman is a nurse. Why doesn't she live in a better place?"

"She sends most of her money back home to her mom in the hills. And she gives the rest to this idiot church she belongs to, the TMC."

"Well, this whole area is just terrible. How can people live like this?"

"I was brought up two blocks from this house."

"Oh. But, anyway, you didn't tell me what . . . what this is all about."

"What's it all about?" he said, stepping back and looking serious. "Marge, sit right here on the bed, and I'll explain it to you."

They sat. He placed his hand on her thigh.

"You know I been telling folks the Lord had spoken to me."

"Yes, but—"

"Well, I had another vision. And in it, I saw you."

"Me? In a vision? Oh, Buzzer!"

"You. And me, of course. Just the two of us, buck naked as the day we was born. Like Adam and Eve, we were. In that garden, where they were."

"Oh, Buzzer, I thought since you got God now, you forgot about me."

As he spoke, his hand began to move under her dress, slowly, up her thigh.

"In this vision the Lord said to me, Buzzer, your own wife, cursed by drink she is, has turned against you. There's only one woman in the world you can trust. And that's this lovely woman, Marge. Those were His exact words."

"Oh, Buzzer, I mean . . . is this right? I don't want you to do wrong. You said you were saved."

He unzipped the back of her dress and slipped the top down to her waist and then took down the straps of her bra. He kissed her shoulders. She shuddered and he held her tight.

"Marge, I'm *saved.* That's the best part. That's why this isn't wrong. It was wrong before. That was all Self. But now I'm for others. I'm for you, Marge. It was wrong before. But not now."

The bra came off, and when he repeatedly brushed her erect nipples with the tips of his fingers, she gasped and squirmed, bit her lip, drew in her breath sharply, and put her arms around his neck.

"See," he said, whispering in her ear between kisses along her neck, "this ain't wrong. Georgie left me and Carl's always been full of Self, so what we do is sanctified."

"Oh, Buzzer," she said, and moaned. "Are you sure?"

"Not so loud, Marge," he said softly, but still sounding like the Buzzer of old, in command. He held a hand across her mouth as she made those ecstatic sounds he remembered so well.

"Just like I said, I want to . . . *unite* . . . and . . . bring . . . folks . . . *together.*"

"Oh, *Buzzer* . . ."

"Shut up, woman. We don't . . . want to wake . . . up Nurse Patsy's neighbors, do . . . we?"

9:06 A.M. MONDAY, MARCH 1, KINGSBURY MEMORIAL PARK, GRANGE CITY

The cold air felt good to Georgie as she walked swiftly on the jogging path near the tennis courts. A few hardy joggers passed without noticing her. She had this one free hour before the day's busy schedule resumed, and she wanted to be by herself.

Georgie cares, she thought, *but who else cares?* Not the majority of the people in the Sixth District, if the blank stares and puzzled looks of so many people were any indication. The whole point of her campaign was that she was supposed to give jobless people hope—but most of them didn't seem to want hope. They wanted to be left alone.

Apathy, Ida Mae said, was their worst enemy. So today is the "get out and vote" blitz among known supporters. No message. No Georgie caring. No jobs. Just—get out and vote for me tomorrow. There had been two "get out the vote" breakfasts already this morning. No pancakes, though. The rest of the day she would visit her strongholds in and around Grange County—Dane, Columbia, Gaines, Capital, the eastern part of Zellenborn, then south to Errol and Blaine Counties—a last-minute, whirlwind tour to make certain every last one of her potential voters was going to vote. She would finish up back here in Grange with a rally at the Grange Hotel.

Georgie turned and looked back. There was Russell following her, at a distance, standing in a grove of trees. She knew what he was doing—and Russell knew she knew what he was doing. But the rules of the little game were that they'd both pretend he wasn't there. Russell Beaumont, supersnoop, making sure his errant sister doesn't stop off for a few drinks at nine o'clock in the morning. Daddy's idea, no doubt. *All right, I'm a drunk. There, I said it, and I'm—*

"Hello, Georgie."

The words snapped her back to reality and there, about ten feet from her, smiling broadly, making little clouds in the cold air with his breath, dressed in sweats and a State warm-up jacket, was Jack Danzig. Someone had once said that Jack had the looks of one of those Hollywood character actors who play the star's best friend. He was good-looking enough to be interesting, but not handsome enough to be devastatingly attractive. He had a face that radiated kindness, humor, and intelligence rather than sexual charisma. He had lost some of his once-thick, curly brown hair and he had put on a few pounds. But the brown eyes were still there, lively, bright, intelligent. And he still had the shy little smile.

"My God, Jack . . ."

She didn't know what to do or say. What's the appropriate greeting to give a good man who had once loved you but whom you dumped to marry a maniac?

"I have a confession. I had this all planned," Jack said. "I wanted it to look like a coincidence. My cover story was, here I am, see, in town on business, minding my own business, just jogging along in the park, and, oh my God, could that be *Georgie?* What an amazing coincidence. But the truth is, Georgie, I called Russell early this morning. He told me where you'd be now. I just want to see how you are, just talk, if that's okay with you."

"Yes, Jack, sure, but actually I have very little time."

"Okay, then, let me give you my story in headlines, just to fill you in quickly. Let's see, eleven years ago it was Jack Danzig Leaves Cap City to Conquer Big Apple. Nine years ago it was Jack Marries New York Lawyer. Three years ago, Danzigs Divorced, exclamation point. Last year it was Jack Back in Cap City, Fans Cheer, two exclamation points. That's about it. I read about Buzzer, and when you didn't return my call, I thought, Well, that's that. But I changed my mind. I'm glad I did. It's really good to see you again, Georgie. You look great."

"Thanks. You were always very diplomatic."

"No, I mean it. Are you going to win tomorrow?"

"Not according to the *Bugle* editorial this morning."

"I'm still a rabid Democrat, a Jewish liberal, the absolutely voist kind, dollink, so I can't vote in your primary. I raised some funds for Bobby Ricky when he ran against Buzzer last year. He's attractive, he has charisma to burn, he's smart, and all the rest of it. He has a lot of charm. But I still don't know what he believes in, except himself. I get the feeling that if he thought the Republican Party would give him a better chance to get ahead, he'd become a Republican without giving it a second thought. And I still don't know what Team Concept means."

"Team Concept? Hell, I don't even know what 'Georgie Cares' means."

They laughed, and the sound of their laughter together brought back memories to Georgie of the way it used to be. In all the years of her marriage, Buzzer and she had never laughed together like this. They had laughed simultaneously, but not in this kind of harmony.

"Jack," Georgie said, "I have to get my walk in. We can compromise. I'll walk a little faster and you slow down your jogging so we can talk as we go."

"Sounds good to me."

They started down the path. In a minute they entered the heavily wooded area at the rear of the park. There were no other joggers. It was as if they had the place to themselves.

"Georgie, I know this sounds like a dumb question after all these years, but how have you been?"

"How have I been? I don't know. It's as if I really *haven't* been. Somewhere along the line, I disappeared and a grumpy, bitter old woman took my place."

"I think I know what you mean. When Janice and I divorced, the old me just packed his bags and went off somewhere. No forwarding address. And I was left with this new, dreary, self-pitying Jack. I broke the New York freestyle whining record."

"The strange thing is," Georgie said, "with all the pressures and all the mistakes I've made in the race, I feel like myself again, for the first time in years."

There was silence as they moved along, and for a horrible moment Georgie thought Jack was going to start talking about what she had done to him.

"Do you have any children?" she asked suddenly.

"No. Janice didn't want any. Not right now, she kept saying. But it wasn't that. We just drifted apart."

"Buzzer and I never drifted. We kept on running into each other at full speed, like runaway locomotives in the old movies. Crash, bang. No drifting. I wish we had drifted; it sounds nice, just drifting away."

"I see that Buzzer says he's got God on his side."

"God help God."

They laughed again and then there was an awkward pause.

"Georgie," he said, stopping and turning to her, looking into her eyes, not in a sexy way, just as honest, open Jack would look, "I want you to know I've been thinking about you. If you need someone from the old days to talk to, I'm available. Anytime."

"Thanks, Jack, I'll take you up on that, I promise."

"Good luck tomorrow, Georgie."

He leaned toward her and gave her a peck on the cheek. He hadn't mentioned any woman in his life. Was that good or bad? She watched him jog away and then she turned and walked back toward where Russell would be, practicing his surveillance technique.

Now all she had to do was get out the vote.

6:00 A.M. TUESDAY, MARCH 2, PRIMARY ELECTION DAY

WGMR *Morning News Show,* Nancy Loesser and the Weather:

"If you haven't looked out the window yet, here's a big surprise. Snow. A lot of snow. More snow than we've seen in years. It caught everybody by surprise. The storm is just raging in from the west, a big, brutal, old-fashioned blizzard with sleet, ice, and wind. It's been roaring across the state since about eight o'clock last night. We have scattered reports that the western part of the state is being buried in what some observers are calling a storm of possibly historic proportions. It has been hitting our area with a fury over the past few hours. Our camera crews have been out all night, and as you can see on your screen, snow is piling up in great white drifts along the roads, lines are down in many places, cars are buried, and three have been killed in road accidents. Road crews can't keep up. We're keeping you advised at WGMR all morning, with school closings—you can bet that will be a long list—and traffic reports up to the minute. In fact, there's only one word you have to remember about the driving conditions. That word is *treacherous.* This may not be the storm of the century, but it will do until the real thing comes along. Back to you, Gwen."

7:36 A.M., GEORGIE LE BRAND CAMPAIGN HEADQUARTERS, GRANGE CITY

Ida Mae stood by the window of the campaign office, looking out at the traffic crawling along Main Street. Everywhere she looked, cars were skidding on the iced-over streets. In the west of the district, in the hills, they were buried in snow already. That's good. It will keep the vote down out there. Russell was staying with Georgie at her house to keep an eye on her.

Russell. How had it all happened? A few weeks ago he was nothing more to her than Bo's son, the target of gentle ridicule from most folks she knew. But the morning after he fell asleep on the couch in her living room, they were talking about the campaign, sitting in the kitchen, drinking coffee. She had arisen from the table and put bread in the toaster when, without saying a word, he came behind her and, turning her around, kissed her. From that moment on, she didn't know or care whether the toast was burning.

Russell had turned out to be a surprisingly wonderful lover, very gentle, maybe to a fault, although forceful enough to make the morning very sweet and memorable. He was considerate and, he had made abundantly clear, grateful. Since then they had been making love every chance they got, in her house and his. Was it just campaign sex, fueled by tension, a way of letting off steam? Sure it was. Was it great sex? Yes. But there was something more. The phrase "out of the closet" came nearest to describing the transformation in Russell. He had indeed come out, not as a homosexual (which he definitely was not) but as a man. He was showing people that he was a man on his own terms, not just his father's son. He was managing the campaign office, and Ida Mae was amazed by his organizational skills, his ability to get people to work together with just a smile or a pat on the back. *Russell.*

Her thoughts returned to the business at hand. *Did I do everything,* everything? *I think so. God, just keep it snowing.*

7:54 A.M., BOBBY RICKY DIDDIE CAMPAIGN HEADQUARTERS, GRANGE CITY

Gary Garafolo sat in his little office, door open, drinking coffee out of a mug, munching on his second chocolate doughnut, staring at the snowfall through the storefront window. He felt good. *Where the hell was Bobby Ricky, anyway?*

"Hey," he yelled to one of the girls on the phones—what was her name? Candy something—"get Bobby Ricky on his cell phone and get him over here. And while you're at it, call Lee. Where the hell is she? We got work to do."

3:54 P.M., THE LITTLE BROWN CHURCH

Herman had been getting calls from his people all day. The blizzard was keeping the vote down in the western counties. Joe Wholey had called and was as confident as ever. But Herman was worried.

7:38 P.M., THE RACKSLEY RESIDENCE, GRANGE CITY

Buzzer, out of the hospital, was staying at the Racksleys', taking it easy. Carl had insisted upon it and would not hear another word about staying at a motel.

"Buzzer, we're going to treat you just like a long-lost brother," Carl had said. "Marge is just looking forward to doing everything she can to make you comfortable. You ask for it, you got it. Whatever I got, it's yours."

"I'll keep that in mind."

So there Buzzer was, election night, scotch on the rocks in his hand, in the Racksley living room, alone, TV on, sound off, waiting for the returns. Carl had called earlier. He wouldn't be able to make it home, stuck in the snow up near Cap City. He'd try to be back tomorrow. Marge's sister had called to say she had the kids, who would spend the night with her—she had picked them up from school in her SUV so they wouldn't have to ride that school bus all the way home. Warm and cozy and feeling damned good, Buzzer sipped Carl's scotch—good stuff. Carl was a damned fool, but he didn't skimp on the booze.

This time, Buzzer thought, nothing could stop him. Funny, after the heart attack and the knock on the head, his mind was clearer than ever. When Nurse Patsy Earlings, that lunatic woman, had told him about playing Herman's tapes and he knew what he was facing—Georgie running, his seat gone—the whole born-again idea had come to him instantly. Folks love to forgive repentant sinners, especially politicians who seek closure and want to put the past behind them. And then he had just made it up as he went along, and every damned step he took had been right. All that stuff about an eight-lane highway just came to him. All he had to do was follow his own instincts. That was when he was at his best. When he stopped to think, he always got in trouble.

Take the Big Shootout. He had been on Jasper Huggins's payroll, doing little favors on the side, ever since he had been on the police force. Jasper had asked him—told him, really—to drive out to an old abandoned farm in Gaines County, north of Grange, make the deal, and bring the drugs back to Jasper at his place by the river. Easy enough. Buzzer had done things like that before for Jasper.

So, at five-thirty that morning, while Georgie was still sleeping, Buzzer got up, threw some water on his face, got into his jeans and T-shirt, and had a cup of coffee. Then he went into the garage, where Georgie wouldn't see him if she came downstairs. He put on his shoulder holster and placed the .38 in it. You could never be too careful meeting with scumbags. He put on his shades, a State baseball hat, and his old blue zipper jacket. Finally, using a stepladder, he lifted the little trapdoor to the garage ceiling and took down the small leather bag containing the fifty thousand dollars.

He got in the pickup truck, put a Merle Haggard tape in the cassette player, and drove slowly north on Route 61, headed for

Gaines County. Just a mile or so before he hit the county line, he saw the dirt road with the old Coca-Cola sign by it, just as Jasper had said. He made the right-hand turn and drove along the tree-shaded, bumpy, unpaved road, more like a path, until he came out of the trees, and there, a hundred yards away, was the barn, barely standing, with part of the roof torn off. There was a lot of junk lying around the barnyard, big sheets of rusting corrugated tin, auto parts, and three carcasses of old cars. There was a new black Buick parked near the barn's open entrance. Three men, two of them wearing windbreakers and jeans and the other one in a T-shirt, came out of the barn. The guy in the T-shirt said something to the others. They all laughed and then went back into the dimness of the barn, still looking his way, still laughing.

When he got out of his truck, he adjusted his glasses, and did his John Wayne walk toward them, leaning over to one side like the Duke. When he got inside the barn, he took off his shades, slowly, like Clint Eastwood, and put them in his jacket pocket.

Two of the men were squatting on bales of hay on the broken concrete floor. Next to them was a suitcase. The third man, a short, ugly-looking dude wearing a T-shirt so you could see his muscles and the jailhouse tattoos on his arms, was leaning against what had once been a stall. There were a few stalls still standing, but the barn was otherwise a wreck. Buzzer had never seen these guys before. He didn't like dealing with new people.

"Hey, man," one of them—he had a big gold earring—shouted. "S'bow fuckin' *time*. Where you *been,* man? You keep us waitin' in this place, man. We be late for our Carnival cruise."

The guy was drunk. The others, drunk too, thought what he had said was hilarious and broke out into laughter. Buzzer began to get a queasy feeling in his belly. Something was going on here. He knew the gold-earring guy who had just spoken wasn't the leader. He wasn't the type, too loud, showing off.

"Don't you worry none, Pedro," Buzzer said. They were all Pedro to him. "You just do what you're getting paid to do. Is that the stuff in the suitcase?"

"His fuckin' name's not *Pedro,* man," the tattooed guy said. He was the boss, no doubt about that. "And s'pose we doan *wanna* hand over the stuff? S'pose we got other plans? What you goan do 'bout that? You goan back and tell the fuckin' *midget* we bad boys?"

The midget. That was the biggest joke of all. The three of them howled with laughter, and the third one, much younger than the other two, just a young teenager really, about fourteen or fifteen at the most, jumped up and down laughing. Then they all laughed and jabbered in their spic lingo. The gold-earring drunken one was laughing the hardest, and at the same time he was slowly walking to Buzzer's right, just moseying along, not looking at Buzzer but trying to get behind him. The tattooed guy walked toward Buzzer, grinning.

"That the money, man?"

"Right here in the case."

"Well, then, you jus' give it to me and go home. We got no beef with you."

So there it was. They were going to take the money, keep the drugs, and kill him.

"You don't want to mess with Mr. Huggins, asshole," Buzzer said. "He'll hunt you down and kill your sorry ass if you try to fuck him over. Use your brains."

"Fuck you and your midget, too," the tattooed guy said merrily. "Now give me the money."

The drunken gold-earring one was now out of Buzzer's line of vision. The kid was moving slowly to Buzzer's left. The tattooed guy was moving toward Buzzer.

Buzzer drew his gun from his holster quickly and smoothly. He shot the tattooed guy in the face. Then he wheeled to the rear and shot blindly, not knowing exactly where the gold-earring guy was, except that he was back there someplace. The instant he got off the shot, he saw the gold-earring guy clearly, right in front of him, not ten feet away. He had a gun pointed at Buzzer.

They both fired. Buzzer must have hit him, he didn't know where, but the guy grunted loudly and fell backward and then to the ground as if he'd been pushed. At the same time Buzzer's leg gave from under him and he fell, yelling out in pain. Buzzer looked up and saw the kid holding a gun, his hand shaking so badly, he probably couldn't have hit Buzzer if he took five shots. But Buzzer knew he couldn't take a chance with the kid, who might get off a lucky shot.

"Son," Buzzer said through gritted teeth, the pain in his leg growing, "drop it."

"Hell no, motherfucker," the kid said, trying to look tough and evil, with his baby face, but his eyes were scared.

"Son, don't be foolish. Drop the gun, drive away, and no questions asked."

Buzzer could see in the kid's eyes that he was considering the offer.

"Don't try to fuck with my head, man," the kid said nervously. "I'll kill you, man."

"Just drop the gun. What do I want to shoot you for?"

The kid hesitated. Then he dropped the gun at his feet.

"Atta boy," Buzzer said, and shot him twice. The kid crumpled and fell to the floor.

The pain in Buzzer's knee—in his whole leg—was so great that he began to howl and cry, Oh, God, oh, God. But the pain went from dull blue to white hot and stayed there. He was weeping, trying to make the pain stop, but it wouldn't. He took off his jacket to use as a tourniquet. He lowered his pants as far as his shattered knee and almost fainted with the effort. He tied the sleeves of the jacket around his lower thigh. But even in his agony he remembered the money. It couldn't be found on him or near him. Hell, it couldn't be found at all. But where could he hide it? He had to act fast, before he passed out.

Screaming out in pain as he half crawled along the jagged concrete floor, he managed to get to one of the stalls. He was saturated with sweat and he couldn't see straight with the throbbing pain that now seemed to fill his entire body. He somehow made it to the back wall of the stall, which was filled with rubbish. He cleared away a space and placed the case down. He then buried it under chunks of concrete and pieces of wood and other debris. Then he covered the concrete with hay.

It would have to do. Now he had to get some aid quick, or he might bleed to death. He made the call on his cell phone and while he was waiting, he wept, afraid he was going to die.

He knew he was going to pass out. He needed a story explaining what he was doing in a barn with three dead drug dealers. And without any conscious effort on his part—his mind was just floating and drifting—the Big Shootout idea came to him, whole and entire, simple and heroic. It was untrue and not entirely plausible, but it was a story. If he brazened it through, he knew he'd get away with it. He passed out.

The next day, in Grange Memorial Hospital, he told a *Bugle* reporter what he had told his superiors. He had received an anonymous tip about a big drug buy going down at the old farm. Damn it, no, he didn't follow department policy, and that was wrong. He should have followed procedure. Yes, he was dumb to just go out there by himself, a real dumb cowboy stunt instead of being a team player. But, see, Buzzer had felt there was no time to follow regulations, these drug guys might get away. So he went out all by himself, like a lone wolf. Yes, that was wrong. He was foolish, but God almighty, these were *drug lords,* poisoning our kids. He didn't have time to follow regulations, by God, he had to get out there and do what a man's gotta do.

The *Bugle* and the television news shows played him up as a hero, and he never looked back. Two months later, on a beautiful summer night, he went back, found the spot in the barn, and there was the leather case. Jasper had of course asked about the money, but Buzzer said the other cops must have taken it, the crooks.

All of this was thanks to pure instinct, from the moment he pulled out his gun until the last interview with the press. If he hadn't listened to his instincts and shot first, he'd be dead. Just act. Keep moving. Don't give the bastards a sitting target. Just be yourself, that was the rule that counted.

His memories ended abruptly when he heard the garage door open and a car pull in. Marge, bundled up in a big coat, stumbled into the room in her snow boots, looking exhausted.

"Oh, Buzzer," she said. "Oh, my God, it is so *bad* out there, the roads are awful. Please get me a drink."

"Help yourself. Carl called. He won't be coming home. The kids are with your sister. And the maid can't make it in."

As she came toward him, having dropped her coat on the floor, already beginning to unbutton her sweater, her lips parted, her dreamy-looking eyes telling him all he needed to know about what was on her mind, he saw her not only as Marge but as the world, open for him as it now was, ready to do anything he wanted. Anything and everything.

11:04 P.M., THE GRANGE HOTEL, GRANGE SQUARE, GRANGE CITY

Georgie, dressed in her blue pantsuit, was sitting up in bed, trying to get a little rest. Through the door she could hear the muffled voices of the crowd in the suite. The door opened. Russell and Ida Mae came in. Russell closed the door behind him, and just from the way he did it, carefully, not slamming it, Georgie knew she had lost. She saw tears brimming in Ida Mae's eyes. So that was it. All that work. All the time, all the effort. All the people who had worked for her, and she had let them down. Ida Mae said something, but Georgie, intent on her sorrow, hadn't heard it. What difference did it make now?

"Georgie," Ida Mae said, shaking her on the shoulder, "don't you understand? You won."

"What?"

She got up from the bed and looked at Russell, who was beaming from ear to ear.

"Russell? I won? Honest to God?"

"Honest to God, Georgie. Not by much, but it's over. There won't be a recount. Ida Mae talked to Herman. Joe Wholey is going to call you. And we got the television crews downstairs, remember."

"I won? But how?"

"We got our vote out, honey," Ida Mae said, "just about every last one of them, and with the blizzard, Herman didn't. And I think a lot of the new people out there in the west voted for you. The district is changing. Anyhow, we won."

Ida Mae began to cry, her face streaming with tears. Russell embraced her. Georgie was crying, and then the three of them were embracing. The door opened and Bo stood there, watching them. He said, "Well, the three stooges finally pulled it off, much to my surprise, but now we got real work to do. Bobby Ricky won, of course, and . . ."

The three of them were ignoring him and now were shouting and jumping up and down. Bo, shaking his head in disbelief, closed the door.

WEDNESDAY, MARCH 3

The *Bugle,* front page:

IT'S LEBRAND VS. DIDDIER— VS. LEBRAND!

WEINSTEIN TO LEAVE DISTRICT

. . . Ms. Weinstein, who will return to her native New York City next week, said:

"Bobby Ricky will win the seat—Georgie LeBrand is an airhead, and Buzzer's conversion is so phony even the people in the Sixth will catch on to him. Bobby Ricky is the biggest opportunist and sellout of them all, so he'll win. He's the white man's favorite black boy."

Asked if she was giving up politics, Weinstein laughed and said:

"I'll never give up politics. I breathe politics. I eat politics. I'm returning to the direct politics of the street, honest politics, instead of this kind of farce. My parents taught me everything you do is connected with politics, so either you change politics or politics changes you. There's no middle ground. Besides, what's a New York Jew Commie dyke like me going to do? I'm going home where I belong and raise some hell in a place where they know how to make a sandwich."

6:05 A.M. WEDNESDAY, MARCH 3, THE RACKSLEY RESIDENCE, ORANGE CITY

Buzzer, Carl, and Marge were sitting at the kitchen table, looking at copies of an advisory from the State Board of Elections. Carl had just come in half an hour ago. It had taken him two and a half hours to make the trip from the motel near Cap City. Buzzer informed Carl on his arrival that he was the campaign manager. Carl was delighted. He'd welcome anything to get his mind off his financial troubles with the Little Guy.

"Now, Buzzer," Carl said, putting his finger on a line of type, "here's something, on page three. Sections 23.2-665 and 23.3-668 of the State Code says you have to instruct your supporters to write in some form of your full legal name. Your first name, middle initial, and last name would be preferred, that's what it says here."

"Hell, no. It's got to be *Buzzer,*" Buzzer snapped. "Everybody knows who Buzzer is. It's always got to be Buzzer LeBrand."

Carl took a sip of coffee and read: " 'Although it is not required, the State Board of Elections suggests that you immediately file with this board a Certificate of Candidate Qualification form for Member of the House of Representatives. A form will be forwarded to you upon receipt of your mailing address.' "

"Make it right here, your address," Marge said quickly. "This is your home for the rest of the campaign."

Under the table, she gave Buzzer's thigh a little squeeze.

"All right, that's enough of that, Carl," Buzzer said. "Fill in the forms and don't bother me with them. Take care of any mail addressed to me. Open it, answer it, unless it's something I should see. Got that? Just give me any papers I have to sign. I'll be getting mail forwarded from my house. Get Herman Throe on the phone, sometime today, and set up a meeting for me. Herman's got no horse now, so why shouldn't he back me? I'm as born-again as Joe Wholey ever was."

When Carl left the room, Marge, pressing her leg against his, said, "That was just *wonderful.* Last night, I mean. Since you've been saved, you're a new man. No more, er, problems, like you'd been having."

Buzzer, half listening, was scanning the documents Carl left on the table and didn't reply.

"I just felt last night that I was, well, I was *all* yours and—" she said.

"Damn it, Marge, why don't you just get on the damned television and tell the *world?* Keep your voice down, woman."

"Sorry. Like I said, you're a new man."

"A new man. Hey, wait a minute. I like that."

"So do I, honey."

"No, I mean I like the way it sounds. Buzzer LeBrand, a new man. A new man for . . . the country? That don't sound right."

He sat in silence for a moment and then smiled.

"Buzzer LeBrand—no, no, just Buzzer. Buzzer—'A New Man for New Times.' Damn it, that's *it.* That's my slogan. Got that religious angle—new . . . born-again, get it? Jot that down, Marge, so we don't forget it. And I really am a new man, you said so yourself."

"You sure are," she said, squeezing his arm. And then, in that damned annoying little-girl voice he hated: "Buzzer? Did you really mean what you said last night? That I could be head of Volunteers for Buzzer?"

"Did I say that? When?"

"Yes, honey, don't you remember, last night, when you wanted me to . . . you know, do that thing with the whipped cream and the—"

"Oh, yeah, that. Sure, sure, you can be head of volunteers. First thing you do is get in touch with Nurse Patsy Earlings. She's got all her Tabernacle morons all just dying to work for me, night and day. They all think I'm God's own candidate. Get them out there, ringing doorbells, putting up signs—when we get signs. Joe has to get on that right away. I still got my list of donors from the last campaign we need to get on the phone. Call the damned telephone company, have them install phones in the basement. I'm going to win this damned thing, Marge."

1:06 P.M., THE LEBRAND RESIDENCE, GRANGE CITY

Georgie, Bo, Russell, and Ida Mae were seated around Georgie's kitchen table, discussing whether Georgie should debate Bobby Ricky.

"I don't want to be the one to drag reality into this happy little gathering," Bo said, chewing on a mint, "seeing how you three are slobbering all over each other because Georgie squeaked by last night. But let me put it to you straight: there is no way in the world you can beat Bobby Ricky in a debate, Georgie. You didn't exactly cover yourself with glory in the debate with Holy Joe."

"Bo, we *have* to debate," Ida Mae said. "Yes, the debate didn't go very well in the primary, but—"

"It went lousy in fact."

"But Georgie's been improving since then, Dad," Russell said. "And I think—"

"There you go again, Russell, thinking. Thinking don't win in politics. If it did, we'd have all professors in Congress, and wouldn't that be just fine? Okay then, we're all agreed Georgie shouldn't debate? Ida Mae?"

"I know she can do well in a debate."

"Russell?"

Russell could sense Ida Mae looking at him, but he didn't return her glance.

"I can see your point, Dad. And you have a good point too, Ida Mae. I—"

"Another undecided precinct heard from," Bo said. "Georgie?"

"If I really don't have to debate, I guess . . ."

She averted her gaze so that she would not have to look at Ida Mae. She was ashamed to give in to Daddy Bo. But he was right. She couldn't beat Bobby Ricky in a debate. May as well face the facts.

"I'm not debating."

"Then it's settled," Bo said. "The message is, Georgie the Republican job builder, Bobby Ricky the liberal Democrat job destroyer. Keep it simple."

2:00 P.M., THE LITTLE BROWN CHURCH

"It's the Devil's work, Herman," Joe Wholey said. "I know the signs. I know how Satan works."

"Joe, our base is changing out here. Newcomers aren't like hill people. And Ida Mae got out Georgie's vote in the snow. The Devil didn't do it, she did."

Herman said it with great patience, but greater weariness. They had been at it for an hour now, sitting on the couch in Herman's office, looking through the big window at the snow-covered hills to the west. Joe looked awful, unshaven, red-eyed, haggard. He was nervous and distracted, unable to sit for any length of time. He prowled about the office, stopping to look at the Bosch reproduction.

"Joe, it was that folks felt sorry for Georgie," Herman said. "I thought the drunk driving would sink her. So did you. But it boomeranged on us, Joe. It used to be a scandal meant you were finished. Nowadays, folks want to show how forgiving they are. Look at how Buzzer is getting all this attention."

"You went to see Buzzer in the hospital, just when I needed you. Why did you do that?"

"He asked for me, Joe. What was I going to do, turn away from him? That's not Christian."

"*Buzzer's* not Christian."

"Now, now, Joe, hold on. I haven't made a commitment to Buzzer. He's a write-in after all, what chance does he have? You're just tired. Get some rest, you'll feel better."

Joe walked out of the office without a word or a glance, striding toward the parking lot.

The phone rang.

"Good to hear from you, Carl," he said, puzzled. Why was Carl Racksley, of all people, calling him?

9:18 P.M., THE RACKSLEY RESIDENCE, GRANGE CITY

Buzzer was sitting on the couch, scotch in hand, watching an old movie on AMC, when Carl came into the living room.

"Buzzer, I don't want to interrupt you. . . ."

"You already did, pardner," Buzzer said, annoyed, not taking his eyes off the screen. "Bob Mitchum picture. He's kickin' ass and takin' names, like always. What's your problem?"

"It's about Marge."

Buzzer didn't take his eyes from the TV screen. But he put his glass of scotch down on the table.

"Marge? What about Marge?"

"Buzzer, with me in so much trouble with the Little Guy, you're my only friend and—"

"And what? Marge been saying anything to you?"

"That's just it. She don't talk to me at all. It's . . . we're not . . . *close* anymore. You know what I mean? Close?"

"You mean you ain't having sex with her?"

"Yeah, we got no sex life at all," Carl said resignedly. "But it's not just that. Marge, if you want to know, just between us men, she ain't much for that part of married life. Never was. But these days she's distant and cold. So I have to ask you, Buzzer. I know this sounds crazy and all, but you had a lot of experience with women. Do you think maybe Marge is, you know, having an affair?"

"Why in hell are you asking me a question like that?"

"Buzzer, I know, I put you in a tough spot, asking a personal question like this, but I have no one else to talk to. I'm crazy about Marge, she's all I got. If she ever found somebody else, God, I don't know what I'd do. I'd go crazy. Tell me the God's honest truth, you don't believe she's seeing another man, do you?"

"Carl, Marge isn't seeing another man. Take my word for it."

"Oh God, thanks, Buzzer. That's a load off my mind. This money thing, it's driving me crazy. I just lie there at night, thinking about things, crazy things. It's great to have a friend I can talk to at a time like this."

"That's what friends are for, Carl," Buzzer said, returning to Bob Mitchum, who was just then punching some joker in the face.

8:00 A.M. THURSDAY, MARCH 4, GRANGE CITY

Georgie, pink-cheeked from the cold, stood near the park on Grange Square, wearing a big red, white, and blue GEORGIE! button on her dark blue coat, squinting in the bright morning sunlight, looking for a bus filled with commuters, still two blocks away. The road crews had not done a good job of clearing the streets of snow, and traffic was slow. Russell, bundled up in his black overcoat and scarf, was at her side, with handouts under his arm, distributing them to passersby. After a while there was a pause, no one to meet and greet, and Russell said, not looking at her, "Georgie, Ida Mae and I were talking about things last night and she thinks . . . and I think Dad might be wrong. About the debate, I mean. I didn't say anything at the meeting because I didn't want to have a big argument with him, and get you upset. But we think he's wrong. Georgie, you have to debate."

He tried to hand out leaflets to a black couple who brushed by him, indignantly.

Georgie saw a bus approaching. She was about to tease Russell, and tell him Ida Mae was having a bad influence on him, when she heard a car horn. She turned and there, stopped at a red light, was Buzzer, in an SUV being driven by Marge Racksley, who resolutely kept her eyes on the snowy street. But Buzzer, with a big Buzzer smile, rolled down his window.

"Hey, Georgie, honey," he yelled, his left hand still on the steering wheel after honking the horn. "I was proud of you winning. I been praying for you." He gave her a wink and a thumbs-up sign. "By the way, I need to talk to you about little Buzzer. I want to see him, soon. I think we got to talk about custody, you being a drunk and all that. Have a nice day."

As the SUV headed west along the Pike (the main roads were cleared) toward the Little Brown Church, Marge said, "Buzzer, honey, why did you do that? Honk the horn, I mean. We could just as easily have passed her by. It's embarrassing."

"Just getting inside her head," Buzzer said happily. "It don't take much to set Georgie off. Low self-esteem. She's got issues. I heard that on the TV once, people like her who drink a lot got low self-esteem and issues."

"But . . ."

"Marge, just drive. I got to deal with all three hundred-something pounds of Herman Throe, plus his bunch of do-gooders soon, and that won't be easy. I don't need your chattering. Just stay quiet, let me think."

An hour and a half later—Marge had taken the wrong exit off the pike, and Buzzer had given her all kinds of hell, leaving her weeping—Buzzer was waiting in an anteroom to Herman's office.

In the office, seated at the round table, there were a dozen or so coalition coordinators. After leading the group in prayer, Herman said, "My friends, without any introduction, let me just bring out here Buzzer LeBrand, who asked for a few words with us this morning."

Buzzer walked into the room and shook Herman's hand. He sat next to Herman. He bowed his head for a moment. Then he said, "I spent my years in politics fighting you. I said you wanted to destroy the Republican Party, which I used to belong to. I said you were busybodies, putting your noses into people's business. I'm here today to tell you one thing."

He paused for a beat and then said, "I don't apologize for those words."

Herman twisted in his oversize seat.

"I don't apologize because that was a different man who said those words. I can't apologize for him because that man died in a coma. I stand before you as a new man."

Buzzer looked down for a moment and then lifted his head, and he was smiling that new, born-again smile.

"Now don't get all nervous now. Ol' Buzzer's not going to bend your ear with his ten-step plan for world peace."

Laughter.

"But I think I should at least tell you why I'm running in an uphill fight as a write-in candidate and why I need your guidance and counsel and support. The families of this district need someone to help them. Too many hardworking folks on food stamps. Good folks, Christian families, out of work. That's not right. I got to tell you one thing, up front. I'm not Joe Wholey. I got no ideas about the Ten Commandments—except maybe politicians like me should read them once a day, just as a reminder."

A good laugh.

"I'm not going to make many speeches during this campaign. I plan to spend every day being with the families in this district who are out of work. What do I mean by that? I'm sleeping in the homes of ordinary folks. I'm eating what they do. I'm going to the stores with food stamps like they do. And if they're lucky enough to get a job, I'm going to work with them, every day for the rest of the campaign. Except Sunday, when I'm going to church. No politics on Sunday. That's my campaign. Not much talk, just a lot of being with folks, listening to them, living with them. Most of all, listening to them. I'm not asking you for a public endorsement. I don't deserve it and I haven't earned it. Yet. All I ask is that you watch what I do and listen to what I say, and if you think what I'm doing and what I'm saying meets your standards, then I ask you to tell your folks that ol' Buzzer is a new man."

He got up from his seat and started to walk toward the door, but then came back. He stood next to Herman and placed his hand on his shoulder.

"What I got to say now is more directed to you as ministers and preachers and those who give spiritual guidance. This ain't easy for me to say, not easy at all. So I ask each of you to understand that what I am about to say here stays here. My marriage is broke up. I take responsibility for my actions. But I also got to say this—my wife, that poor girl, with her uncontrollable drinking problem, has been dragged into this race by my father-in-law, Bo Beaumont, a man who is against you and all you believe. So she drinks. A lot. I've never told anyone what me and little Buzzer have had to put up with. I'm not a man to wash his dirty linen and things in public. But here I'm among friends. Georgie wants nothing to do with me. She threw me out of our house when I left the hospital. She's neglecting my little boy—I got that from a reliable source."

He lowered his eyes and then, slowly, lifted them, and they were glistening.

"My friends, I ask you now to bow your heads and say with me a silent prayer for my wife. She needs God's help."

After the moment of silence, Buzzer said, "Just remember: what

I have said in this room about Georgie stays in this room. That is all I ask. If this ever got out to the press, there would be a scandal, and I don't want that."

He turned and walked toward the office door in silence.

SUNDAY, MARCH 7

The *Bugle*, front page:

BUZZER: GEORGIE DRINKS, "NOT A GOOD MOM"

. . . the former congressman was reported to have asked the ministers to join with him in prayer for his wife, saying her drinking problem was uncontrollable. Rumors of Mrs. LeBrand's alleged drinking problem have long circulated in fashionable East Side circles. But her recent DUI charge and now her husband's statements have brought the issue to the forefront of the campaign.

A participant in the coalition meeting who asked not to be named described the majority of ministers at the gathering as "on Buzzer's side, but still not fully committed" to his write-in candidacy.

Reverend Herman Throe would not comment on the meeting, except to say that Mr. LeBrand did meet with coalition leaders and "covered a wide range of political and personal topics which I am not free to discuss."

10:06 A.M., LEXINGTON AVENUE METHODIST CHURCH, GRANGE CITY

Georgie sat in the first pew, with Russell on one side and Buzzer Jr. on the other, as Pastor Leonard Worthy spoke on "Jesus Died for *Us*, Why Can't We Live for *Him*?" Ida Mae had called her early about the story in the *Bugle* and told her not to comment.

"Buzzer leaked it himself," Ida Mae had said on the phone. "It's got his fingerprints all over it. I have no proof, but I can tell you exactly how it happened because it's classic Buzzer. First he goes to Herman's church to get the coalition support. He plays the loving father and husband who was kicked out by his drunken wife. Then he calls a reporter. The reporter then calls some of the ministers to corroborate what Buzzer told him, without telling them it was Buzzer who gave him the story. Some of the ministers talk to the reporter, and he's got another piece of the story. Watch what happens today. Buzzer will say he's shocked his accusations leaked. He'll say he's deeply hurt because someone leaked the story to the press. Pure Buzzer."

Reverend Worthy was talking about the need to put the gospel to work in our daily lives, but Georgie was only half listening. Tomorrow night, Bobby Ricky and she would be making appearances at the annual alumni-faculty charity basketball game at the high school. Bobby Ricky would be playing in the game, and the crowd would love him. Georgie had to do something to turn things around and get the spotlight off him. But what could she do? Challenge him to a slam-dunk contest?

Jack had not called. It had been great seeing him the other day. Maybe he'd call today. Or maybe he read the *Bugle* article and got scared off. Or maybe he has a girlfriend. Or maybe he just wants to be a friend. It's like being back in high school.

High school.

Georgie smiled. There *was* something she could do to match

Bobby Ricky. It was a long shot, but that's all she had anyhow. After church, she called Ida Mae.

"Use some of your influence with the school board and find some school gym I can go to this afternoon. I'll need it for about an hour or two."

"Gym? What do you need a gym for?"

"I've got to turn things around," Georgie said, and laughed because she had inadvertently made a joke.

10:34 A.M., GRANGE CITY

Bobby Ricky stood at the pulpit of Mount Nebo New Baptist Church and, to the quick and lively responses of the congregation, spoke in the rhythms and with the passion he recalled from sitting out there in the pews with his grandma, years ago.

"I believe public service should be about justice, not about power!"

"Yes!"

"I believe we are all on the same team, on *God's* team. On the team of the Lord, we work *together,* we help each *other,* care for each *other,* love each *other*—and we will win the final *victory!*"

"Yes!"

"I believe you help the needy by acting out the Lord's commands. [Yes!] *Feed* the hungry. *Clothe* the naked. [Yes!] Make government *work for all God's people!* [Amen!] Not just for the rich and powerful! For the needy and the elderly and the downtrodden!

"My grandmother sat right out there where you are, years ago. I can see us now—there she is in her best Sunday hat, and I'm sitting next to her, all neat and scrubbed clean and starched and in my Sunday best, sitting quietly—can you imagine *me* doing that? . . ."

Laughter, applause, cheers.

". . . and my attention wasn't always on the service. I was too busy thinking of sports. But Grandma would give me that special look of hers. I called it sharp eyes, and I'd start paying attention. Grandma wanted what was best for me. And this church, my brothers and sisters, this church, with its big heart, was the very best thing she could think of."

"Amen!"

"And today I see another lovely face out there in the pews. It is the face of Kalya, my wife, the mother of our children. I say to all of you, married or not, I say marriage is hard, love is hard, faith is hard, but marriage endures when faith and love endure. When you have a loving spouse, ready to forgive, with a heart that can forgive, you have a chance, you have a chance!"

He ended by praising Dr. George Edward Witherspoon, founder and pastor of the church for thirty-six years, "a man who has played such an important part in my life, my mentor, my guide, my inspiration."

In fact, Bobby Ricky, after he was thirteen years old, had never set foot in this or any other church unless it was for a funeral, wedding, or political event. But he had to have Reverend Witherspoon on his side, to politically energize his flock.

"And I say that this man of God, this man of the people, this church he founded decades ago, needs and deserves a friend in Washington, a friend who knows the needs of this church and this community, and a friend who will never forget his own people!"

Cheers, shouts of "amen," of "yes," and even one anachronistically "right on, mah bruvver." Bobby Ricky then embraced Reverend Witherspoon, and they stood arm in arm, as everyone sang:

What a friend we have in Jesus!
What a hope we have in the Lord!
What a home we have in heaven,
What a faith in his sweet Word!

As Reverend Witherspoon spoke, praising him, Bobby Ricky, seated behind him, tuned out. Lee came into his mind. He really shouldn't be thinking of her, sitting here in church, but he couldn't help it. Sometimes he didn't know if she got a bigger thrill out of making love with him or out of meeting some national reporter and schmoozing. But he couldn't get enough of her. He began to fantasize about her. That cool, almost haughty look in those green eyes when she began to strip, not with some stupid stripper's boom-ta-boom-ta-boom rhythm, but just as if she were by herself, taking her time, not looking at him, with that very slight grin on her face, as if she were thinking of something funny. And then there was her need—her demand—for them to take their time, allowing every kiss and every caress to bring things just one achingly sweet step forward so that by the time he reached orgasm, it was as if the sensation had begun billions of years ago and was making its way in a slow, tantalizing, maddening way, so that when it finally arrived it was as if his mind exploded into millions of fragments of stars, and . . .

He snapped out of the fantasy as he saw Kalya in the pew, just staring at him, no expression on her face. He gave a little smile but she just kept on staring at him.

11:06 A.M., THE LITTLE BROWN CHURCH

Buzzer sat in the third pew, center aisle, of the new Little Brown Church and smiled as Herman huffed and puffed as he climbed the seven (reinforced) steps to the pulpit. Herman, breathing heavily, silently looked over the congregation—every pew filled and fifty deep in the side aisles. He placed his Bible and a small towel on the edge of the pulpit. For a time he was silent, looking over the heads of the silent congregation.

"Hell," he said.

There was no response.

"Let me repeat, in case you missed it. Maybe you were dozing off. It's cold outside in the hills with all that beautiful snow, and so nice and warm in here, you might be nodding off, so here I go again: Hell. At the Little Brown Church we have always preached the reality of hell. I do. My daddy did. His daddy, my grampa, did. But no sophisticated person believes in hell anymore. Even some preachers have forgotten."

He rubbed his chubby hands together.

"Why, they say, there might be heaven, but there cannot be *hell*. Just can't be. God must be a liberal. Has to be. Liberals believe nobody is responsible. Murderers and rapists and thieves, why, they are just victims of society. All these folks, they run Washington, they run the media, they run Hollywood, they run the universities. All these folks say, We are the best, we are the elite, and if *we* don't think anybody is responsible, well, God must think the same way, right? I mean, God Almighty wouldn't disagree with the networks and *The New York Times* and all those college professors over in State, would he? God must be a liberal, he has to be.

"We are lucky around these parts. We are lucky to have a man who is not fooled by these doctrines, who is not afraid to say drug lords must pay the price for their crimes, not afraid to bring God's own Word into politics. I won't mention his name. I don't want to offend those folks in the media and politics who want to see this church separated not just from the state but from any influence in society. I'll leave it up to you to guess who he is. The liberals in Washington and in Grange City and Cap City tried to keep him out of politics, but despite personal problems, he just keeps coming back, a man who has turned his life around and been saved by the blood of the Lamb, a man who . . ."

As Herman spoke, Buzzer, bored almost beyond endurance, sat in silence, fantasizing about Marge in the various positions he had taught her. He wondered if it was possible to rent a trapeze. He had some ideas of how that could work with Marge, with the whipped cream. . . . From time to time, he nodded in assent, as if something that Herman had just said particularly struck him. Buzzer hated being in church. It reminded him of his childhood when Mom used to drag him to that damned storefront mission place on the West Side. Bible-thumping morons. Even when he was a kid he found all this talk about God to be stupid. If God is so great, how come He needs all this confounded praise and fuss? If Buzzer were God, he'd just enjoy being God. He wouldn't need a bunch of morons singing songs telling him how great he is.

Buzzer knew people were sneaking a look at him, trying to see what his response would be to Herman's words. Occasionally he would turn to his pew neighbor (she was one damned ugly old woman) and smile and nod vigorously, and she would smile back, so he seemed to be doing okay.

Things like this had to be done in politics. Nurse Patsy Earlings and her TMC people, all certifiable lunatics, looked on Buzzer in awe. He liked it, but they were crazy, looking for the Messenger, Nurse Patsy said. What Messenger? And what's the message? Crazy people, the TMC. But they were working for him now, outside the church, in the cold, ready to hand out flyers telling of Buzzer's program:

BUZZER!
A NEW MAN FOR NEW TIMES
HE'LL WORK FOR US—
WRITE IN FOR HIM!

The story in the *Bugle* had been better than he had hoped for. Georgie looked bad. He had set the reporter up real good, and she had done a fine job of ferreting out stuff from the preachers, confirming the story, adding details. The campaign was off to a good start. First he had to destroy Georgie and then take on Bobby Ricky. And here was Herman just about endorsing him. He thought about the basketball game tomorrow night. Bobby Ricky will be the star there, no doubt. Georgie can't outshine him, not at a basketball game. But he had to be there. Show up, let folks see him. But how would he outshine Bobby Ricky? There must be a way.

The congregation had arisen and was singing "The Little Brown Church." He got to his feet a bit late and joined in. He didn't know the words but he faked it with energy. After the service he joined Herman in the pastor's office.

"You were rolling right along there this morning, Herman."

"Was I? Tell you the truth, I didn't feel it, Buzzer. I can feel it when I have the Lord in me, giving me strength. I was trying, but I just felt it wasn't there."

"I was listening to every word and you sounded good, especially about the liberals."

"That's nice of you to say. Buzzer, I guess you saw the *Bugle* this morning?"

"Yeah, I did and I got to say I'm disappointed, Herman. I thought that part of the meeting was off the record. I begged your folks to keep that stuff in the family."

"I know, Buzzer. I'm sick about it. I'm real sorry about it. I know you didn't want all that stuff about Georgie drinking and being a bad mother in the *Bugle,* especially on the front page."

"Of course not, Herman. What kind of a man do you think I am?"

7:03 p.m. MONDAY, MARCH 8 (THE OFFICIAL START OF THE THIRTY-DAY GENERAL ELECTION CAMPAIGN), EDWARD KINGSBURY MEMORIAL GYMNASIUM, GRANGE CITY HIGH SCHOOL

The public-address system in the gym blared the driving music of Joe Momma, a local rock group that specialized in straight-ahead, oldie-but-goodie, you-can't-miss-the-beat versions of Chuck Berry classics. When they finished their set with "Johnny B. Goode," the crowd roared its approval and sang along with the lead singer, a skinny white kid who did a passable imitation of the great rock idol, even managing an almost, but not quite, duck walk.

Every seat in the gym was taken. Against the walls behind each basket, and below huge green and gold banners proclaiming RANGER POWER, scores of students and parents stood, packed together but happy to be there. The annual faculty-alumni basketball game was one of the highlights of the year for the Grange County community. Tickets had been sold out months in advance, proceeds going to charity. Tonight the gym was overflowing with a screaming, stomping, happy crowd of high school students, parents, adult Ranger fans, just about every politician of note in the county, a television crew from WGMR, and a reporter from the *Bugle*.

When the last whanging chord and drum thunder of the Berry classic reverberated though the gym, the crowd stomped and cheered. Mr. Hudson, who taught junior English, was the announcer, and his bass-baritone voice now boomed out over the microphone.

"And *nnnnnow,* it's time to introduce the Fighting Faculty. . . ."

The boos came first but then there was applause and scattered whoops for each faculty member as he was introduced. The teachers stood together on the basketball floor, giving one another high fives and slaps on the fanny. Then Mr. Hudson said, "And *nnnnnow,* those green and golden-oldies, the boys from the 'hood of yesteryear, the amazing, electrifying, dynamic . . . Alumni Rangers!"

The cheers erupted instantly and continued as each alumni team member took the floor, waving his arms to the crowd and going through the high five ritual.

Mr. Hudson was not faculty drama adviser for nothing. He waited for the noise to die down. Then he dramatically lowered his voice and spoke more slowly. "And *now* . . . the all-city, all-county, all-state, all-American, all-pro, all-everything . . . our very own"—big pause—"Bobby . . . *Rrrrrr*ickee . . . Diddie!"

One sudden roar followed by stomping whistling and clapping.

Bobby Ricky, dressed in Grange City High green and gold sweats, leaped up from the bench and ran toward center court as the noise increased. He turned to all sections of the gym and held up his arms in acknowledgment as the cheers went on. He high-fived not only his team members but members of the faculty team as well.

At the main entrance to the gym, in the crowd by the double doors leading to the central school hall, Gary Garafolo thought, *Jesus, this is going even better than I expected.* Gary's stubble was at a perfect two-day growth tonight. He was wearing a thrift-shop blue suede jacket, with a large dark stain on the front and a zipper that didn't work. His maroon corduroy pants were torn at the knees, and the soles of his sneakers were worn down unevenly.

"He looks good," Gary said to Lee, standing next to him. Lee was wearing a green and gold Rangers sweatshirt and jeans, looking casually elegant as usual.

"Good? He looks great," she said.

Ida Mae came up to them, smiled and said, "Bobby Ricky can always get a job teaching gym after Georgie beats him, Gary. He's very popular."

"Don't you worry about Bobby Ricky losing, Ida Mae," he said without bothering to look her way. "Just help Georgie through those twelve steps before it's too late."

"Gary?"

"What?"

"I just *adore* your earring."

Mr. Hudson's voice boomed out, "May I have your attention, please, for a very special announcement, before the game begins."

The roar subsided but the gym was still noisy, so he spoke slowly: "Grange City Rangers basketball games over the years have been opportunities for participation by all parts of our school community. Not least of these are our wonderful cheerleaders. And speaking of them, tonight we have with us a distinguished member of our cheerleading alumni. For three years she was a member of our cheerleading squad. For two of those years she was cheerleading captain. Let's give a rousing welcome for our current cheerleading squad and especially for tonight's honorary captain . . . Georrrgggg-eeeee . . . Beaumont . . . LeBrand!"

The double doors opened behind Gary and Lee. Shouting Grange City High cheerleaders made a path through the crowd as Georgie, in a Grange City cheerleader uniform, ran onto center court. The crowd began to applaud and then cheer. When Georgie held out her arms to the crowd, there were even some whistles. Facing the alumni side of the stands, she pointed to Bobby Ricky. Then, with the cheerleaders beside her, she shouted:

Bobby Ricky
He's our man
If he can't do it, Georgie can!

She stepped back and thought, *Well, here goes nothing. I had to do some quick alterations to the skirt, but I got into it. My legs aren't that bad. Now all I have to do is pull this off. God, just this one thing, please.*

Her heart was pounding, and at first she couldn't take the first step. The noise of the crowd died down. Somebody hooted from the stands. One of the cheerleaders said, "Go ahead, you can do it." Georgie closed her eyes, took a deep breath, and opened her eyes.

She took the first running step and then she was running along the court, running faster now, running . . . and then she left her feet . . . and she was upside down and . . . she did a cartwheel.

It wasn't pretty. She landed unsteadily, tottering, almost falling. But she did it.

The delighted cheerleaders ran to embrace her and lift her up as the crowd leaped to its feet and let out a sharp, sudden, and sustained blast of cheers and shouts and applause. For the next few seconds the gym belonged to Georgie. She smiled and continued waving to the crowd. Then she made a palms-down motion with her hands, waited, walked over to the mike, and said, "Thanks for this chance to be with you all tonight. I just have one thing to say to my old schoolmate and current opponent. Bobby Ricky, you've always been a great competitor. I just want to take this opportunity to say to you, tonight, we should have a debate pretty soon. I have just one condition—that I will not at any time during the debate be called upon to make another cartwheel."

Cheers and laughter.

Bobby Ricky walked over to the microphone, laughing. He shook hands with Georgie and said, "It's good to see my old high-school classmate," he said. "That debate sounds like a great idea. So I want to take this opportunity to ask Kalya, my wife, to stand. She's my unofficial debate coach and she's never lost a debate—to me, at least. Stand up, honey."

Kalya, in a Rangers sweatshirt and dark green pants, was sitting in the second row in back of the alumni bench. She stood, grinned, blew a kiss to Bobby Ricky, and got applause.

"And let me just say one more thing," Bobby Ricky said when Kalya sat. "I just hope when this election ends, Georgie got all the votes of folks who can do cartwheels, and I got all the rest!"

There were cheers as Georgie ran toward the double doors and out of the gym. In the hallway, Russell stood grim-faced.

"Now, don't get all serious on me," Georgie said. "I just thought it would be a good thing to do, challenge him, with the crowd here."

"But what about Dad?" Russell said. "He'll be livid. Maybe we should have prepared him first, that you'd challenge Bobby Ricky to a debate."

"I'll take care of Dad," Georgie said.

Near the end of the second period, Bobby Ricky had scored fourteen points and grabbed six rebounds, and was going for his seventh when he fell awkwardly and was taken out of the game. Hobbling but smiling, Bobby Ricky waved as he sat on the bench while the crowd cheered. Gary and Lee rushed over. Lee, crouching in front of him, said, "My God, Bobby Ricky, are you okay?"

"Yeah, no problem, Lee, I just twisted my ankle. Nothing broken."

The last few seconds of the second period ran out. Gary and Lee were so intent on attending to Bobby Ricky that they didn't realize the gym had suddenly burst into cheers, jeers, whistles, and scattered applause.

"What the hell . . . " Bobby Ricky said, getting up from the bench, leaning on Lee and looking to the double doors.

Buzzer LeBrand was standing there, in what looked like his old sheriff's uniform: immaculate, starched, pressed khakis, dark glasses, gleaming leather belt, trooper's hat, and an empty holster. He walked slowly to the center of the floor, limping noticeably. He held up his hand for silence—which he didn't get—and then walked over to the table, slowly removed his glasses, and took the mike.

"Good evening to y'all. I'm former Sheriff and Congressman Buzzer LeBrand. I just want to say to all of you, it's good to be back in my old school. Not that I did that good when I was here. But given the shape I was in recently, being back is all that matters. I just want to say how much I respect Bobby Ricky Diddie, who lost to me last time. Bobby Ricky, sorry you hurt your leg. A few years ago, I got my leg hurt, not in a kid's game but by drug lords who shot me. That's why I got this handicap, this limp. I just want to say, tonight I am in a new uniform because I am declaring war on unemployment and I am going to do to unemployment what I did to the drug lords. I am a new man for new times. God bless you all, enjoy the rest of the game."

There was scattered applause as he walked, limping, to the double doors. When he got there, he turned, took off his glasses, saluted, and went out, the limp suddenly not as noticeable.

Later, after a hot shower, Bobby Ricky joined Kalya in her rental car. For a few blocks they drove in silence. Then she said, "Bobby Ricky, tell me something, just a matter of minor interest. Are you fucking that blonde?"

"That's crazy, Kal."

"You're not answering the question."

"There's nothing to answer."

"See, Robert Richard, if I ever found out you've been fucking the help while you've been begging me to come down here and help you, why, there's no telling *what* I'd do. Probably something both of us would regret. So let me run this past you one more time. Are you and what's her name . . . what is that blond girl's name?"

"You mean Lee?"

"Yes, I mean Lee."

"Kal, this is crazy."

"I notice you haven't denied it yet."

"Where the hell do you get these crazy ideas?"

"Where? From her eyes when she was crouching in front of you like that, when you came out of the game. Looked to me she's been in that position before with you, she looked so comfortable. And when you stood up, you just sort of naturally leaned on her, not on Gary. And I saw the way she looked at you. There's three ways a woman looks at a man she wants. Before she gets him, she's got that sexy look in her eyes. When she gets him, she's got that *satisfied* look, we all have it, the 'I got him' look. But after she's *had* him and she begins to think that she *owns* him, she gets this *proprietary* look. That's what Miss Lee had."

"I'm not carrying on an affair with *anybody*. But you're reminding me of why I've had affairs."

"Oh damn. I thought we were going to get through this without you telling me it's *my* fault. You are so goddamn predictable."

They drove on in angry silence. When they reached his apartment, he got out quickly, slammed the door, and hobbled toward his car parked a few feet away. Thirty minutes later, he parked the car at a motel just south of the Cap City airport, where he had met Lee twice before. He walked up the outside staircase to the second floor and went directly to room 223. He knocked on the door and waited. The door opened to a darkened room. Lee was standing there. She embraced him. They kissed. He entered. The door closed.

In the parking lot, a tall thin white man in his fifties, chewing on the stub of an unlit cigar, sat behind the wheel of a nondescript Chevrolet, taking photographs of them. He had been tailing Lee

Simmons for four days. The man, a private detective, had done work for Jay Hollings in the past. He wondered how Jay had found out about Bobby Ricky and this blonde. Follow the blonde, Jay had said.

Half an hour passed. Then forty-five minutes. The door to 223 opened. Bobby Ricky stepped out. The man began shooting the roll he had been paid handsomely—in cash—to take.

Bobby Ricky is turning back to the door, and right there is the woman. She has her hand on his arm. He turns and she is kissing him, her arms around his neck. The angle is perfect for the camera, both of their faces clear, and Bobby Ricky is not moving away. They stay locked in the pose for five clicks of the shutter.

8:45 A.M. TUESDAY, MARCH 9, GRANGE CITY

Suddenly the door to Bo's office opened and Bo strode in. He stared coldly at Georgie, Ida Mae, and Russell. He went to his desk and held up the front page of the *Bugle*. There was a big picture of Georgie doing her cartwheel. The accompanying story was headlined:

GEORGIE LEAPS INTO DEBATE

"This was *settled*. No debate, we all agreed. But you went behind my back. The damage is done. Now you got Bobby Ricky and you got Buzzer, too. On the radio they're saying Bobby Ricky wants Buzzer to be part of the debate. Any of you geniuses know why? I'll tell you. Either Georgie says no to Buzzer debating, and then she looks afraid, or she says yes, and Bobby Ricky can just sit there and watch the two of you kill each other while he gives his Team Concept pep talk."

"Bo," Ida Mae said, "we needed something to get the campaign jump-started, quick."

"Jump-started? You think getting Georgie's ass thumped by

Bobby Ricky in a debate is going to get your campaign jump-started?"

"Now, Bo, hold on," Ida Mae said. "We can schedule it for late in the campaign. That will give Georgie a chance to get some practice. We can hire a debate coach, we can—"

"Russell? You still awake? I told you to keep an eye on Ida Mae. I told you to tell me what she's been doing."

Seeing the puzzled look on Ida Mae's face, Bo continued, "Yeah, Ida Mae, I hate to tell you, but Russell was spying on you. But he's working for you now, a traitor to his own father. I don't want to hear about what you did for him or to him to make Russell turn. But I can imagine. Anyhow, you're fired. Get out of my office, you're washed up anyhow."

"You can't just fire Ida Mae, Daddy," Georgie said. "We're in the middle of a campaign."

"Oh, can't I now? I did it once before and I'm doing it again."

"Daddy," Georgie said, but Bo cut her off and zeroed in on Russell.

"And what about you? I put you in this campaign to keep an eye on this woman, but—"

"Is that true, Russell?" Ida Mae asked.

Russell looked down and then said, "Yes. He put me in there to keep tabs on you. But I never told him anything."

"You should have told me about this, Russell," Ida Mae said coldly. "You should have told me what you'd been doing. You owed me that much."

"But, Ida Mae, I didn't do anything. I—"

"That's your trouble, Russell. You never do anything," Bo said. "It seems to me it's more than your eye you've been keeping on her. She's one of those dominant, independent women. I've read about them. Some men like that kind of thing. I always preferred womanly women myself. But I guess there's no accounting for taste."

He reached for a JumBo mint.

"Shut up! Shut the fuck up!"

Russell had leaped to his feet, his face red, the shouted words erupting from him quickly and violently. He slapped the open jar of JumBo mints off the desk, spilling them onto the rug, and, in the same quick motion, grabbed Bo by the lapels and lifted him in the air, knocking off his glasses.

"Don't you *ever* talk like that about Ida Mae again," Russell shouted, his voice raw with threat and danger. *"Never."*

"Russell!" Bo screeched, trying to wriggle away. "Goddamn you, boy, let go of me. You turn on your own father because I know she let you in her pants—"

Russell roared and pushed Bo away from the desk. They stumbled toward the mini-aisles. Bo broke Russell's grasp and ran down the condiments aisle, yelling, with Russell after him, knocking over JumBo-sized bottles of mustard, relish, and ketchup. Bo fled up the cereal aisle, but Russell had outsmarted him, and doubled back. He was standing at the end of the aisle, waiting. He grabbed Bo by the bow tie and pushed him against a row of on-sale SugarBOaTies, "The Oat Treat That Can't Be Beat."

"Don't . . . you . . . ever . . . " Russell started to say. He reached for a JumBo-sized SugarBoTies box and was about to hit Bo with it when he felt a restraining hand on his arm. He turned, ready to attack, and there was Ida Mae, looking at him in a sad, puzzled way.

"Russell, it's all right, it's all right," she said soothingly. "Don't let him do this to you. You're too good and he's not worth it. Russell, for me, just let him go. Please."

For a second Russell didn't move. But then he dropped the box of cereal and let go of Bo.

"Damn it, Russell," Bo began, adjusting his tie.

"Shut *up,*" Russell shouted in Bo's face, spittle flying, and Bo winced. "I want you to tell Ida Mae that I never said anything bad about her and that I never spied on her. *Tell her.*"

Bo said, in a flat, weary voice, "He never told me a damned thing, more's the pity. All he ever said was how good you are. And that's all he said."

Russell turned away from Bo and looked at the spilled jar of JumBo mints on the rug. He began laughing.

"And these *mints*. I hate these damned mints. I had to watch you popping them in your mouth, the goddamn most disgusting . . ."

Russell jumped up and down on the spilled mints, then bent to pick up the JumBo plastic jar. He flung it against the wall behind Bo's desk. The door opened and Bo's secretary rushed in.

"Mr. Beaumont, do you want me to call security?"

"My son and I are having a little business discussion. Get out."

She stared for a moment at the chaos and then closed the door behind her.

Russell was now standing by the window behind Bo's desk, breathing heavily, glassy-eyed, confused, as if he had just half awakened from a dream. Ida Mae put a hand on his arm and he turned to stare at her. Then he walked by her and left the office without a word.

Bo returned to his desk, looking at the mess. He picked up his glasses and put them on.

"Well, *there's* a bad case of campaign jitters if I ever saw one," he said, his voice still shaky. "Tell lover boy when you see him, Ida Mae, that he's finished. Not just in the campaign. In BigBo stores. And with me. Attacking his own father like that, after all I've done for that boy."

"You got what you deserved," Ida Mae said. "He should have done that a long time ago."

"Maybe," Bo said, feeling more like himself with every passing second. "But he didn't. See, Ida Mae, that's the point. He didn't ever fight me because he's weak and timid. He wants folks to like him. He was always that way. But you seem to inspire him to violence, against his father, who gave him everything he has. The two of you deserve each other. Anyhow, Georgie, from now on I'm calling the shots."

"No, you're not, Daddy," Georgie said quietly. "Ida Mae stays. So does Russell."

"It's either them or me, sugar."

"Then it's them."

For a half a beat Bo didn't say anything, and Georgie could see—she knew him well—she had taken him by surprise. Then he said, "Ida Mae, get the hell out of here, permanently, or I'll have you escorted out. I want to talk to my daughter alone."

Ida Mae looked at Georgie, who nodded. Ida Mae left the office.

"I'm going to try to talk sense to you one more time," Bo said to Georgie, "not because I think you deserve it, but because when you lose—and you will—it will reflect badly on me. I'm ordering you not to debate, Georgie."

"You can't order me. It's my campaign," Georgie said. "I'll run it the way I want. I decided to run and I'll decide how I campaign."

"*Your* campaign?" Bo said, and suddenly burst into laughter. He sat in his plastic chair and shook his head in wonderment.

"Your campaign?" he said again. "What a joke. Do you know *why* you're running? A simple question. You're the big debater, so answer it. Do you really believe running was your idea?"

Georgie could see something in his eyes, the cold look he had when he was going in for the kill. She had seen that look all her life, and it still frightened her. But she didn't back away.

"True, when you first tried to talk me into it, I resisted. But I changed my mind for my own reasons, not because of anything you said."

"You damned little fool. I *made* you change your mind. I played you like a fiddle."

"That's ridiculous, I—"

"Georgie, I sent you Marge Racksley's letter."

"You? *You?*"

"Yeah, me. I found it in your apartment in Washington. I knew once you read that letter, you'd want to hurt Buzzer. I knew it because that's what I would have done if I was in your place."

"You couldn't possibly know what I was going to do. I didn't know myself."

"Right, you didn't know, because you live in a goddamned dream world, almost as bad as your criminal brother. But I knew once you got the letter, I could work on you and you'd eventually give in. It was only a matter of time. You just did it sooner rather than later. The only thing that surprises me is that you didn't go to Grange Memorial and try to kill the son of a bitch."

He saw the quick, all but imperceptible, movement of her eyes away from his.

"Or did you? Congratulations. You got my black heart, Georgie, even if you've been hiding it all these years. It takes a cold heart to even think about killing your son's father. But that's all in the past. You can still win that seat. You can revenge yourself on Buzzer, but only with me. Is it a deal?"

"You're more despicable than even I ever thought. You use everybody. My God, you have no heart at all."

"True, but you can't win without me."

"I don't need you and I never will, ever again."

"Suit yourself. But when you lose, don't come crawling back to Daddy Bo. If you walk out that door, you're just like Russell to me."

"That's fine with me," Georgie said, arising from the plastic chair. "And by the way, get one of your flunkies in here to clean up the mess."

She pointed to the sign hanging from the ceiling and said, "A clean floor makes a great store."

As she was walking out, the BigBo Ol' Grampa Clock blasted out a bugle call. Nine o'clock.

When Georgie reached the Bronco, instead of getting in the backseat, she opened the driver's door.

"Russell, get out, I'm driving. Get in the back with Ida Mae. Are you two okay?"

"Yes, we've talked. We're fine," Ida Mae said, and took Russell's hand in hers.

"Don't worry about us," Russell said, smiling at Ida Mae.

"Good," Georgie said. "Now I have one more question. Are you still with me? Russell?"

"You know I am, Georgie."

"Ida Mae?"

"All the way. There's only one thing—"

"Let me finish. From now on, I'm in charge. I'm the one who decides where we go and what I say and how I act. If I'm going to lose this thing, at least I'll lose it on my own terms. Nobody is ever going to use me again. That's the way it has to be. Ida Mae, how are we fixed for money? Daddy won't do any more fund-raising."

"We'll squeak by. He did great fund-raising for us, you have to give him credit. It would be good to have more money flowing in during the last week. But we don't really need him now. If he had done this a few weeks ago, it would have cut us off from a lot of money. We'll probably wind up in the red, but we already have money for radio ads. We'll get by."

"Good. Now let's get moving."

"We're with you, Georgie," Ida Mae said. "But there's just one thing."

"What is it, Ida Mae?" Georgie said, annoyed, as she started the engine.

"Your license is suspended. Remember? I don't think it's wise to be driving."

George sat behind the wheel for another few seconds, sighed, and said, "Russell, damn it, get up here and drive. But I'll tell you where to go."

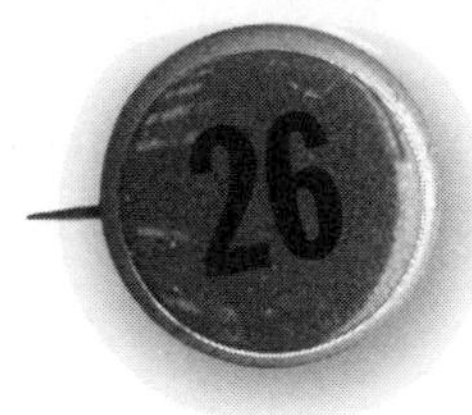

5:32 A.M. WEDNESDAY, MARCH 10

Telephone message from Georgie, at home, to Ida Mae at headquarters:

> *Ida Mae? Do you know those two volunteers, the married couple, Trader, Trialer, sounds something like that. Trainor? He's been out of work for a long time? They asked me a couple of times if I'd come visit them. They live on the West Side. Set it up. Maybe we'll get some press coverage. Georgie cares, that kind of thing.*

5:36 A.M.

Telephone message from Georgie, at home, to Ida Mae at headquarters:

> *Ida Mae, on that other thing, set up the debate, today. I don't care where or when, just set it up with Garafolo. If they want Buzzer, fine. Any format they want, any number of debates.*

THURSDAY, MARCH 11

The *Bugle*, headline:

GRUDGE MATCH: GEORGIE, BOBBY RICKY—AND BUZZER—TO DEBATE APRIL 1

. . . Former Congressman LeBrand said he was eager to participate in the debate, and was surprised and delighted that he had been included.

"I guess my wife is so desperate, she'll even appear on the same stage as ol' Buzzer, who knows so much more about government than she does. I am going to tell the truth to the people, like I've always done. I'm going to win that debate and the race."

11:06 A.M., THE TRAINOR RESIDENCE, GRANGE CITY

"John, how long has it been since you lost your welder's job at the Styler works?" Georgie asked.

"Year and a half," John Trainor said. His wife, Sally, nodded in agreement.

Georgie was sitting in the cramped kitchen of their home. Ida Mae was standing in the doorway to the living room, out of the way, and there were a television crew from WGMR and one young reporter from the *Bugle*.

"You politicians are all supposed to help us, but you don't," John said. "We're good people. We worked hard, when we had jobs. The folks down the block, the Pearsons, they got it worse than us, even. Martha Pearson has cancer. George Pearson got laid off down at the Farm n' Town last year. It's hell for them. But you know something? Ol' Buzzer's been staying with the Pearsons. That's ol' Buzzer for you, a man of the people. Why don't you do something like that?"

Ida Mae, who had been thinking about the next campaign stop, suddenly became alert. There was something about the way Trainor had spoken that made her political antenna quiver, a quality in his voice when he said "ol' Buzzer."

"You come here and talk to us," Trainor whined, looking at the camera, "you got this reporter here, TV camera, show how you care about folks. But then you go back to the East Side, sleep in a big nice house we could never afford. But ol' Buzzer, he's from West Side folks."

We've been set up. Oh my God. Even as the words formed in Ida Mae's mind, she was moving toward the kitchen table, beginning to say, "Well, guys, we have to move on," when there was a loud knock on the front door. In the instant before the front door opened, Ida Mae realized, too late, what was about to happen.

Buzzer stood in the doorway, resplendent in a brown leather jacket over his khaki uniform, and a blue baseball hat with an American flag design on it.

"Johnnie," he said in a booming voice, moving into the living room, reaching out and giving Trainor the two-hand grab, "good to *see* ya, buddy! I was passing by and I thought I'd just drop in. How's the best bowler on the West Side? How y'all doing? And where's the prettiest gal in five counties? Where's my gal Sally? There she is. Always good to see somebody so pretty."

The cameraman had turned his camera away from Georgie and toward Buzzer.

"Georgie!" Buzzer said suddenly, as if he had just discovered her presence. "Why, what a nice surprise, it's so *nice* to see you, honey. I hope someone's looking out for my little Buzzer while you're out playing politics. I'm real concerned about our boy, honey."

"Buzzer, what the—" Georgie began.

"See, my wife here, she won't return my calls, when I just want to ask about my little boy," he said to the camera. "I'm a dad, but she keeps me away from my own son."

"That's a shame," Sally Trainor said, shaking her head. "A boy should be able to see his daddy."

"Why are you wearing that stupid uniform?" Georgie said. "You're not allowed to wear it, you're not a sheriff anymore."

She knew it sounded petulant, but Buzzer's sudden entrance had totally erased any semblance of ordered argument from her brain. Buzzer seemed to fill every inch of the small room.

"Stupid, did you say, Georgie? If you think our good law enforcement folks are stupid, I'm sorry for you. Somebody with your driving record, I guess, must hate the police. Look close and you'll see it ain't a real police uniform. I wear it to remind folks we need to get back to basic values. Discipline, obeying the law, not endangering folks' lives by driving drunk, taking care of our children, not abandoning them. Wearing this uniform, I'll go hunting for unemployment the way I went after those drug dealers. I'll hunt it down, and then I'll kill it by creating jobs."

"Jobs?" Georgie shouted. "You never built any jobs when you were in Congress. You never even showed up at your damned committee hearings. You missed votes on the floor. You took junkets. What do you know about building jobs?"

"That's a good question, Georgie." He turned toward the camera. "How am I going to build jobs? I still got a lot of friends in Washington, both parties. I'm an independent now, so I can cross the aisle, not like you. I got friends in Washington."

"Friends? What you had were lobbyist friends, people who want something, fixers," Georgie said suddenly, her voice filled with anger. "You took their money and did them favors."

"Georgie, you got any proof of that? You want to name names? Give the press the names, honey. Right now, or apologize."

Georgie rushed across the small room to where he was standing, brushing aside John Trainor, and, looking up, put her face inches from Buzzer's.

"You bastard," she said, her voice shrill. "You *hit* me, you *drank,* you were carrying on with *women.* You were a terrible husband, a terrible congressman, and you have the nerve to accuse me—"

"Now, now, honey," Buzzer said gently, with his tolerant new smile. "Let me give you a piece of advice: a soft answer turns away wrath, Georgie. Forget Self, Georgie, it ain't worth it. Well, this has been real nice, being back on the West Side. Bye to y'all. John and Sally, God bless, and I'll be fighting for jobs for both of you."

As he left the room, smiling, he turned to the camera and saluted. Georgie rushed out after him and slammed the door behind her so the television camera wouldn't follow. Buzzer turned, grinned, and began to walk down the steps. She grabbed him by the arm.

"Forget to give your husband a kiss good-bye, honey?" he said.

"Either you drop out of the race now, or else I go public with your affair with Marge. I swear to God I will. I still have the letter she sent you. I kept it to remind myself what a bastard you are."

"Georgie, do you think I give a damn if you publish some letter—which I never seen, by the way—on the front page of the *Bugle*? That's a letter from her to *me,* not from me to her. I'm born again. I ain't responsible for what some fan of mine with hot pants said in a letter. Read it on TV for all I care. I'm a new man."

He gave her a snappy salute and strode away.

FRIDAY, MARCH 12

The *Bugle*, headline:

BATTLING LEBRANDS: BUZZER KO'S GEORGIE IN AMBUSH

11:18 P.M., THE LEBRAND RESIDENCE, GRANGE CITY

Georgie sat on the edge of her bed, exhausted. Ten events, five counties, a rush of faces and handshakes and questions and remarks.

Now she wanted a drink. She tiptoed downstairs. Mrs. Cummins, the baby-sitter, had left when Georgie came home fifteen minutes ago. Russell had gone over to Ida Mae's. Little Buzzer was asleep.

One drink. She had been good for what seemed forever, but enough was enough. All day, in every county, at every event, there were media questions about the ambush and about her drinking. Buzzer was going around saying he was going to seek some legal remedy to get Buzzer Jr. She was so angry at herself for walking into the trap. Walked right into it.

In one sense, the ambush had not turned out too badly. Ida Mae said there were dozens of phone calls to campaign headquarters from working moms, expressing sympathy for Georgie. Buzzer had gone too far, Ida Mae said, there would be a backlash from women just like Georgie, moms who had to be out of the house. But Georgie didn't want sympathy. She wanted a drink. She searched through the liquor cabinet and the hutch in the dining room and under the sink in the kitchen. There wasn't one bottle of alcohol in any form. Russell had done a good job, the bastard. The phone rang and she let the machine take it.

"Hi, it's Jack. Just calling to say hello, see how you're doing. I'll be at the debate. I can't openly root for you because I'll lose my subscription to *The Nation*. But I'll root for you in my heart. Good luck!"

She reached for the phone, but she knew she was too tired to make any sense. She went to the bedroom and began to undress, but she was so tired that she flopped onto the bed. I'll just rest my eyes. She fell asleep instantly. Ten minutes later she awoke with a start. She arose, groggy, aching, still bone-tired, but with the idea still vivid in her mind. She dragged out the security box from the closet and carried it to the dresser, where she kept the key. She opened the box, and there it was, amid important mortgage papers and old, outdated insurance polices. She took the letter out of the pink envelope.

My Dearest Darling Buzz-Boy,

By the time you read these words, my B-boy, we will have already been together once again. . . .

There were risks involved in what she planned to do. She wished she had someone to talk to. Jack. Ida Mae. Even Daddy. No, damn it. You make the call. You decide. You're the one.

MARCH 13 TO MARCH 27

TV ad:

Music: strings, lush harmonies.

On the screen: Bobby Ricky and Kalya, in sweaters and jeans, with their children, running and laughing in the hills of Freeman County; cut to Bobby Ricky running with a football—as his little boy tackles him, Bobby Ricky falls, laughing, as Kalya stands by, holding their daughter; cut to a serious Bobby Ricky listening to elderly people; cut to a smiling Bobby Ricky in a classroom with schoolchildren, cut to a solemn Bobby Ricky on the steps of the church, shaking hands with the pastor; cut to Bobby Ricky standing on the steps of the United States Capitol, looking serious and purposeful.

Woman's voice: Bobby Ricky Diddie is not only one *of* us. He's one *for* us. He cares about strengthening families. He knows that a team working together can get the tough jobs done—and create jobs for families. He is committed to creating jobs, protecting Social Security, and setting a good example for our children. He has a Team Concept that will get results in Congress. Join his team—it's our family team!

WEDNESDAY, MARCH 17

Radio ad:

Hi. I'm Georgie LeBrand. I care that my friends and neighbors are out of work. I care that we have not received the kind of representation we deserve in Washington. I will create jobs. I will put the interests of working folks first. And I will do everything I can to make this community a better place for the old and the young. I need your help. Working and caring together, we can build a new, stronger community.

SUNDAY, MARCH 21

The *Bugle*, headline:

BUZZER SAYS WIFE IS "SICK," "NEEDS HELP"

MONDAY, MARCH 22

The *Bugle*, headlines:

GEORGIE ANGRILY DENIES BUZZER'S CLAIMS

BUZZER CALLS BOBBY RICKY "LABOR'S BOY"

REV. THROE: BUZZER IS "TRYING"

. . . Emphasizing that he was not speaking as head of the Religious Coalition but only as "a simple preacher of the word," Reverend Throe said, "I have prayed with Buzzer. I have looked into his eyes and his soul. He will make mistakes. But he is trying to reform his life. I truly believe he wants what is best for this district."

8:09 P.M. FRIDAY, MARCH 26, THE LITTLE BROWN CHURCH

Seated at the round table in his office, Herman faced twelve members of the coalition.

"Well, friends, I got John's call yesterday"—he nodded and smiled toward Reverend John Reming—"and I'm glad to see you all. But I'm not too clear what this is all about. You got a problem with Buzzer, as I understand it."

"More than a problem, Herman," John Reming said. "A while back, Buzzer was here, telling us he was a new man. He said we should watch what he says and does. Well, we've been watching. A lot of us feel he used us, set us up, like they say. No one here leaked that story about his wife to the press. He did."

"We don't know that for a fact, John."

"You know it as well as I do, Herman. It was Buzzer. And you got to put a stop to these attacks he's making on his wife."

"I don't rightly see how I can," Herman said. "I consult with Buzzer some. We talk. He seeks my advice from time to time, but "

"Advice has nothing to do with it, Herman," said Reverend Tom Mooney heatedly. "You just about made Buzzer our candidate, in the public mind at least, with the things you've been saying in church. But he lied to us and he's going beyond any decent limit with his personal attacks on his wife."

"That's hardball politics, Tom."

"That ain't *Christian* politics, hardball, softball, or Wiffle ball. Just not Christian. There's a lot of folks, from the start, they had real doubts if his conversion was sincere."

"I think it's sincere, Tom."

"But you got a personal stake in this because he said your tapes converted him, Herman. You're blinded to the reality because you want to believe Buzzer's changed."

"Now just hold on a minute. . . ."

"Herman, we're just telling you what coalition folks think," said Tom Mooney. "So we're here to just ask you to back off."

"I thank you, my friends, for saying this to my face," Herman said, rising from his chair with a couple of grunts and a wheeze. "Now let me tell you some facts to your face. Bobby Ricky is a big-spending union-boss liberal. He tones down the social issues stuff, but we all know where he stands. Georgie broke with her daddy, but she's weak on our issues, a Republican pragmatist just like Bo. We have to make accommodations with political reality. Sure, Buzzer isn't perfect, but—"

"Now listen to me, Herman," Rooney said, his voice now harsh. "It hurts me to say this, but here goes. Some folks are saying you've become, well, too much a politician and not enough of a pastor and—"

Herman slapped his big right paw on the tabletop, the sudden, raw sound of it echoing throughout the room.

"My good friends," he said with just a little grin, "this meeting is over. If you want my resignation as head of the coalition, just say so. And I bid you good night and a safe trip home."

11:09 P.M. FRIDAY, MARCH 26, THE RACKSLEY RESIDENCE, GRANGE CITY

Marge was in bed, watching the TV news. She missed Buzzer. She hadn't seen him for days. She could understand that he had to stay at the homes of these poor people. Still, she really missed him. She hit the power button on the remote and fluffed up her three pillows, disconsolate. After a while she heard the garage door open, and a few minutes later there was a knock on her bedroom door.

"Marge, can I come in?"

"Can't it wait until morning?"

"No, honey, really, I got to talk."

"All right, come in."

Carl sat on the side of the bed. He looked like hell.

"What's the matter with you?" she said. "You've been drinking, I can smell it."

"Marge," he said, "I'm in big trouble. I been borrowing money from Jasper Huggins and now I can't pay it back."

"Jasper Huggins? That horrible little dwarf? He's a gangster. Are you crazy?"

"I couldn't help it, Marge. He's the only one who would lend me any, and now he wants me to pay. Marge, honey, please, I need some of the money your daddy left you. I need it quick."

"Absolutely not. Never. We've been over this. That money is for the children and for me. You agreed to that when we got married. You'll never get your hands on that money."

"But—"

"No means no. Now get out of here, you're drunk and you're very inconsiderate. I'll have a hard time falling asleep."

Carl went to his room and closed the door. In the darkness, he walked to the dresser, opened the third drawer from the top, reached under the pile of underwear, and pulled out a gun. He sat on his bed without moving. He could feel the gun. Small, hard, perfect, real. Everything else in the world was make-believe: his debts, the moonlight, Marge's scorn—only this was real. Cold and hard and very real. He gradually raised the gun to his head and gently placed the end of the barrel just in front of his right ear. He put his index finger lightly on the trigger.

He lowered the gun. No, not this way. He still had Marge. He had messed up everything. But as long as he had Marge, he had hope. She would help him in the end, when she knew how desperate things were. Maybe he'd talk to Buzzer about it, about the Little Guy. Buzzer had an optimistic way of looking at things.

10.00 A.M. SATURDAY, MARCH 27, BOBBY RICKY DIDDIE CAMPAIGN HEADQUARTERS, GRANGE CITY

Gary had thought it would be good to invite some of the local press for an informal but on-the-record chat. Coffee and doughnuts, just sitting around the office, comfortable and at ease. It would give Bobby Ricky a chance to show his human side, informal and relaxed. And it would give Gary a chance to show that he was still a Character, bellowing and profane, outrageous and, as always, confident and infallible.

When the meeting was breaking up, Will Parsons of the *Bugle* walked over to Gary.

"Gary, I need to talk to you and Bobby Ricky. And Lee. Right now."

"Jeez, we can't, Will. Bobby Ricky has to get right out to the West Side and catch up with that crew from CBS. They're doing a story on Bobby Ricky and his old neighborhood. Lee is out there with them."

"This is very important, Gary."

The three of them went into Gary's office.

"So, Will," Gary said, pointing to the battered leather couch, "what the fuck is so important that we got to sit here with you?"

"I'd like both of you to take a look at these," Parsons said. He opened a manila envelope and shuffled out a group of eight-by-ten black-and-white photos. He placed them one by one on the desk: Bobby Ricky, dressed in his leather jacket and a stocking cap, getting out of his car; Bobby Ricky on a flight of outside stairs to some building; five different photos of Bobby Ricky and Lee embracing and kissing in the doorway.

"So, Will," Bobby Ricky said easily, with the slightest smile, "I guess I missed the news. It looks like the *Bugle* got bought by the *National Enquirer*. When did that happen?"

"We didn't take these. They were sent to me yesterday."

"I bet."

"Do you want to make a statement?"

"A statement? What is this, an *NYPD Blue* rerun? Is Andy Sipowitz going to come through the door and beat me up? Are you going to read me my rights? A statement? Hell, the man in those pictures don't even look like me. I'm prettier than that."

"Are you denying—"

"There you go again. I don't even *acknowledge* that the pictures have anything to do with me, so how can I deny anything?"

"Look, Bobby Ricky, I don't like this kind of thing, either—"

"This kind of thing? It has a name, Will. It's called bullshit journalism."

"Have it your way. Like I said, I don't like it. But we have to go with this story."

"You throw some blurry pictures on a table. You ask me, Do I want to make a statement? You tell me I'm *denying* something. Who the hell do you think you're fooling with here? I've been dealing with guys like you since I was fourteen. Trying to put words in my mouth, ambush tactics, all the rest of it. Where the hell did you go to journalism school—J. Edgar Hoover Grad School?"

Gary was about to say something about cooling down and taking it easy when Parsons shouted to Bobby Ricky: "*You're* the one telling voters about family. You're the one says you're going to bring family values to Washington. All your TV ads are about family. And at the same time you're fucking your own press aide in a seedy motel up near Cap City, and you don't think that matters? The personal became the political when you—not the *Bugle*, not me, *you*—made family values into an issue. We're going with something on this. Now you can either just sit there and not say anything or you can tell me your side of the story."

"What story? All you have is some pictures."

"We sent people up to the motel with photographs of Lee and of you. Two of the employees have identified Lee Simmons as having taken a room on at least three occasions."

"That doesn't prove a damn thing about me," Bobby Ricky said.

"We have a picture of the registration form on which she used another name. We have the pictures I just showed you. I'm giving you the chance to—"

"Clear myself? My ass!" Bobby Ricky shouted, leaping out of his chair, fists clenched. "Don't give me that 'I'm giving you a chance' bullshit. You're trying to destroy me. Because I'm black and she's white. That's it, isn't it? If I were white, you'd throw those pictures away."

"Whoa, wait a minute, wait a minute, hold on," Gary said, moving Bobby Ricky behind the desk. "Let's keep our heads here. We can work this out. Will, give us time to think this through."

"No can do. Do you have any comment on this now? Whether you do or don't, we're going with it."

"Yeah, I have a comment," Bobby Ricky said. "Here's my comment. Shove these pictures up your ass. That's a quote. You're attacking my right to privacy."

"Privacy? You have your estranged wife come down here to campaign with you, you go to church with her, she's in your TV ad—

with your kids, for Christ's sake. *But all the while you're fucking one of your employees*. What the hell is private about that? Besides, we're running down other leads."

"What are you talking about? What leads?" Gary said, thinking, *My God, there's* more?

"I hate to break the news to you. But I think you have a spy in your campaign office. We got two calls from a woman who told us you've been banging Lee Simmons in your own apartment. People who live in your apartment building have been questioned. Have they ever seen Lee there, that kind of thing. The answers are yes, they've seen her. This story is running, Sunday," Parsons said, and left the room.

Bobby Ricky and Gary stood in silence. Then Gary said, "Let me ask you one thing. Do you think Lee set you up?"

"Why ask me? You're the one who hired her."

"Yeah, and she did a good job at what I hired her to do. Press work. But you were screwing her, which as I recall wasn't in her job description. Did it ever occur to you she might be setting you up?"

"No. That's impossible."

"Impossible? Suppose she was planted on me, although I can't see how. But you never can tell. I have to do something about this whole situation. But first, we have to get into some really creative lying. We have six days to do damage control before the debate."

29

10:09 A.M. SUNDAY, MARCH 28, THE RADKOLEY RESIDENCE, GRANGE CITY

Carl had gone to church with the children for the first time in years. Marge was drinking coffee and reading the Sunday *Bugle* when Buzzer pulled up in his car.

"All right, I already been to church over at First Baptist, let all those holy folks get a good look at me. How much time we got, Marge?"

"Carl won't be home until after three. He's taking the kids to his mother's after church."

They went directly to Marge's bedroom.

Twenty-three minutes later, Marge, trying to catch her breath, whispered, "Just . . . like Adam and . . . Eve."

"Yeah, sure. Now just get your ass downstairs and cook me up a big breakfast. After that, I got some more plans for you."

"Oh, Buzzer," she said as he gave her a playful but stinging slap on the ass, "you say the craziest things."

11:05 A.M., THE LITTLE BROWN CHURCH

At the end of the service, Herman was singing "The Little Brown Church" with the congregation when something extraordinary happened. He forgot the words.

" 'In my childhood . . .' " he sang, and then couldn't for the life of him remember the next words. He had been singing that song all his life. But the words were just gone. A few minutes later, the service over, he exited through the side door and walked to the original church. He squeezed into the last pew and, with difficulty, knelt there. His soul was dry, barren, no prayer coming from him, nothing, emptiness, abandonment, a kind of spiritual terror. All he could think of these days was the congressional race. Not about God, but about Buzzer.

And suddenly, with stunning, painful clarity, like a slap in the face, Herman saw what he had become. Just another self-deluded politician who believes that what he wants is what God wants—or what God would want if he had inside information. Satan had known his weak spot, the desire to do good on Herman's own terms. That was it.

He began to sob violently, his massive body shaking, kneeling in the church his grandfather built and in which his own daddy had preached to the hill people.

2:26 P.M., BOBBY RICKY DIDDIE CAMPAIGN HEADQUARTERS, GRANGE CITY

"Lee, believe me, I don't want to do this," Gary said into the phone, one finger idly playing with his earring. "It breaks my heart. But Bobby Ricky's mad as hell. He says it's all your fault. Yeah, his very words. What? Well, he said you weren't careful enough. Hey, that's not me talking, that's Bobby Ricky. No, he doesn't want to talk to you. I can't help it. Look, he told me last night you have to go. You know how stubborn he can be. I wish to God I didn't have to do this, but he's like a madman, blaming everybody but himself. Lee, for the good of the campaign, stay away from the press until this blows over. Yeah, sweetie, I know the bastards are trying to get a story out of you, but remember two golden words: no comment. Are you fired? Hell, no, of course not. Just go back to Washington and stay below the radar. I'll be in touch. You did a great job for Bobby Ricky, and if it were up to me, I'd keep you on. But my hands are tied."

Gary couldn't tell if Lee was buying any of this bullshit, but he wasn't going to be the bad guy in this little drama. She had to go, that much was certain. But let Bobby Ricky take the rap. The funny thing was, Bobby Ricky wanted her to stay on because he believed that if she was fired or resigned, it would look as though they were panicking. But the risk of keeping her was too great. The story Gary and Bobby Ricky had concocted wasn't exactly believable, but it was all they had. And Lee being around would mean either one more version of events or coaching her on the cover story. Gary always believed that in sex and in damage control there was only one rule: keep it simple. Bye-bye, Lee.

3:38 P.M., THE RACKSLEY RESIDENCE, GRANGE CITY

When Carl returned, the house was empty. The kids went upstairs to their rooms, and he went directly to the den, remembering how Marge had scolded him for not taking care of the mail as he had promised Buzzer. Maybe it'd get his mind off things for a while. He was about halfway though the pile of mail when he came across a manila envelope addressed to him. At first he wondered if he should open it. Jasper Huggins might be sending him one of those letter bombs. No, that was crazy. But just to be on the safe side, he gingerly opened the envelope and shook out the contents. A pink envelope, already opened, fell on the desk in front of him.

MONDAY, MARCH 29

The *Bugle*:

BOBBY RICKY—DID HE?

In a statement released by his campaign office, Mr. Diddier said:

"I visited Ms. Lee Simmons, my press aide, at a local motel. Exhausted and overworked, she had gone to the motel to be alone—a luxury in a political campaign—and I went there to consult with her, strictly on campaign business. I have a great professional and personal respect for Ms. Simmons. I am a demonstrative person and perhaps I made an error in judgment in kissing Ms. Simmons in a fashion that some might construe to be in an improper way. The real issue here is that someone has been using dirty tricks, spying on Ms. Simmons and me and trying to break up my marriage. The real issue is why those opposed to my agenda are engaging in the politics of personal destruction. That is the real story the *Bugle* should be pursuing."

9:38 A.M., THE RACKSLEY RESIDENCE, GRANGE CITY

Buzzer and Carl were sitting at the Racksley kitchen table, drinking coffee. Marge had left for her real estate office.

"Carl, the debate's coming up in three days and you haven't done one damned thing for me so far as I can tell. I been getting more help from Marge than from you."

"Has Marge been a big help to you, Buzzer?"

"Yeah, at least she drives me around. All you've been doing is looking gloomy and mooning around the house. You look like hell. Take a shower and shave, it will make you look better and feel better. It's not easy sitting across from someone looks so bad."

"I'm sorry, Buzzer."

"Sorry don't cut it, pardner. This last week of the campaign I need your special attention."

"I promise you, Buzzer. From now on, you'll be the only thing on my mind."

"That's more like it. Action is the best thing in the world for you. It gets you to stop thinking of Self. Well, well, just look at this in the *Bugle*—ol' Bobby Ricky stepped on his dick this time. Anybody believes his story, he was going there to *talk* to that blonde, anybody who believes that is crazy. They got him dead to rights. Cheating, that don't look too good, does it?"

"No, it really doesn't, Buzzer."

30

TUESDAY, MARCH 30

The *Bugle*, front page:

REV. THROE QUITS POLITICS
CITES NEED FOR "RENEWAL"

Reverend Herman Throe, pastor of the Little Brown Church in the Woods and founder of the Religious Coalition political action organization, last night announced his "irrevocable decision" to resign as head of the coalition.

"I have come to a point in my life where I must decide what my ministry means to me," he said in a talk to coalition members at the church, "and I have discovered that although God needs Christians to work in politics, I am no longer the man who should head that effort in our community. I will stay informed. I will vote. But from this moment forward, I will never participate in active politics again."

5:46 A.M. THURSDAY, APRIL 1, THE RACKSLEY RESIDENCE, GRANGE CITY

Marge was suddenly awake. For a few seconds she didn't know why. The room was dark. She turned and squinted at the digital clock.

"Marge."

She let out a yelp. There, in her bedroom doorway, was Carl. He was clean-shaven and dressed in a suit and tie, just standing there, quite still.

"Carl, my God, you scared me. Are you drunk or something? It's not even"—she looked at the clock—"six in the morning. What's the matter? Is it the children?"

"No. They're fine. I drove them to my mother's last night."

"What? Your mother's? Tell me the truth, is something wrong? Are they all right?"

"They're fine."

"Oh, *now* I see what you're up to," she said in her most scornful voice. "You send the children away and it's the maid's late day. So we're alone. Well, just get the thought out of your head, mister. I'm not in the mood for sex. And I don't plan to get in the mood. How dare you wake me up? You know I want to look my best at the debate tonight. I need my rest. I have to look good for Buzzer's sake."

She saw the gun in his hand. She screamed and tried to back away, but in the big bed there was nowhere to go.

"Marge? I want you to read something."

"Read? Put that thing away. I'll call the police. Help!"

He reached into the inside pocket of his suit jacket and withdrew a pink envelope. He threw it on the bed.

"Open it. Read it for me, Marge. Out loud. Every word, slow."

8:26 A.M., BOBBY RICKY DIDDIE CAMPAIGN HEADQUARTERS, GRANGE CITY

When Gary got to headquarters, Bobby Ricky, in his running clothes, with an angry look on his face, was sitting in Gary's chair. Gary hated it when anyone sat in his chair, and Bobby Ricky knew it. So it was deliberate, some kind of stupid macho challenge. Gary closed the door and stood in front of the desk.

"So, what's on your mind?" he said, unzipping his leather jacket.

"What disaster do you have for me this morning? You been banging any of the volunteers?"

"Gary, goddamn it, you fired Lee. When I tried to get in touch with her, I found out she's gone."

"I didn't fire her. I suggested she get far away from this campaign. That's all we need now is pictures of her in the newspapers. Where's Kalya?"

"Gone back to New York. She didn't even say good-bye."

"It figures. Will she keep quiet?"

"Yeah, I guess. What difference does it make now? Damn it, Gary, you had no right to get rid of Lee. Now it looks as if she had something to hide."

"It was a judgment call. If she stays here, she's the story for the next few days. Besides, what the hell do you care? You got what you wanted out of the bitch. Tell me something. Was she worth it? Was she that good?"

"Don't press your luck, Gary. Don't start on me. I'm not in the mood."

"What the hell do I care about your mood? Who do I look like, one of your stupid football coaches who had to kiss your ass? You should have won this race easy. But now you're finished. And remember, this is my fucking *reputation* we're talking about here. I'm involved in a losing campaign. Me, Gary Garafolo. What you did wasn't just wrong. It was dumb. I can't stand dumb. Crooked, I understand. Irresponsible, I can understand. But not dumb. No excuse for it in politics. All you had to do was keep that thing in your pants for sixty days. Your *wife* was down here, man, and you decide you need to knock off a piece with your fucking press aide. And do I have to remind you, she was a blonde? Down here? You must be crazy. Once you let your dick become your campaign manager, you don't need me anymore. I was going to stay until it's over, but I can see you still don't have a clue what you did."

"Fuck you."

"That's real eloquent. Did Lee write that line for you? I was crazy to come down here in the first place. You messed up the race against Buzzer, and now you've lost this one, too. But now it's over, all but the great debate of the century tonight, where they'll be asking questions about character. And while I'm at it, get the fuck out of my chair."

Bobby Ricky slowly rose to his feet, his eyes blazing, his fists clenched.

"You want me out of your chair? You want me out of your fucking *chair?* All right, I'm out of your chair. And now I'm going to do something I should have done a long time ago. I am going to kick your sorry ass."

Bobby Ricky leaped across the desk and just missed grabbing Gary, who had instinctively backed away. Gary, terrified, turned to run but his leg got tangled in the computer wires and he fell. He began to crawl toward the door, screaming. Still crawling, he reached his office door and opened it, but Bobby Ricky grabbed him by the leg and began to drag him back into the office. Volunteers in the outer office were standing at their desks, looking on, not knowing what to do.

"You're *dead,* motherfucker," Bobby Ricky bellowed. "I'm going to rip that fucking earring off and shove it—"

"Help me!" Gary shouted to the volunteers, holding on to the doorframe with both hands as Bobby Ricky tried to pull him back, inch by inch, into the office.

Bobby Ricky suddenly lost his grip and fell backward against the desk. Gary, in full-panic mode, screaming incoherently, crawled through the doorway, got up from the floor, and began to scramble toward the headquarters entrance, about twenty-five feet away. Bobby Ricky, with superior speed and agility, instantly shortened the gap between them. Gary ran around desks and copying machines and soft-drink-dispensing machines, but Bobby Ricky stayed with him. Just before Gary reached the entrance, Bobby Ricky tackled him. They knocked over a volunteer who was holding a big box of coffee and doughnuts. As the girl fell to the floor, yelling, coffee containers spilled steaming hot liquid over Gary and Bobby Ricky, and chocolate-covered cake flew one way, bear claws another, and jelly-filled doughnuts bounced off nearby desks.

Bobby Ricky struggled up from the floor and, reaching for the first thing at hand, threw a jelly doughnut at Gary, hitting him in the face. Gary yelped and then Bobby Ricky, laughing, threw every piece of pastry he could get his hands on, splattering Gary with custard, chocolate, and raspberry jam.

"I always knew I should have been a quarterback," Bobby Ricky shouted in delight as his pastry passes hit their target.

Gary, with the adrenaline-induced strength that only cold, gut-level fear can produce, crawled away, still screaming, to the doorway. He pulled open the door just as Bobby Ricky hit him in the ass with a cruller. Gary got up and raced blindly along East Eleventh Street, never looking back, screaming all the way.

Bobby Ricky watched Gary slip-slide his way through the crowd of people on their way to work.

"Yo, Gary," Bobby Ricky shouted, "you got a future as a broken-field runner. Twelve hundred yards your first year, I guarantee it."

Bobby Ricky, laughing, was out of breath, out of the race, out of his marriage, and out of hope. But he felt good inside for the first time in a long time. It wasn't that he had just used Gary for target practice, although that had been fun. It was that he felt like Bobby Ricky Diddie again, carefree, confident, loose, at ease with himself, and not this campaign automaton he had been for so long.

He went back into headquarters, closed the door, and faced the campaign workers, who were staring at him amid the chaos of doughnuts and coffee containers. One girl was crying. Bobby Ricky went over to her and put his arm around her shoulder.

"It's all over, honey. Just calm down. Nobody got hurt."

He turned to the rest of them.

"All right," Bobby Ricky shouted, "halftime entertainment is over. We got a debate to win tonight. And we got an election to win next Tuesday! Let's get back to work, goddamn it! Team Concept! And somebody go out and get some more doughnuts. Lots of them. On me!"

12:35 P.M., GEORGIE LEBRAND CAMPAIGN HEADQUARTERS, GRANGE CITY

Ida Mae and Russell were sitting in her office, prepared to put Georgie through a Q and A session at her house, when Billy Lemke, the volunteer who had dropped off debate briefing books to Georgie earlier, poked his head in the doorway.

"Just tell me when you're ready to go, Ida Mae," he said.

"How did Georgie look this morning? She feeling good?"

"Just great, real loose, smiling. I guess she's kind of glad her husband is finally being nice to her."

"What are you talking about?" Ida Mae said.

"Just as I was leaving, some delivery guy came with a case of wine, all wrapped in pink ribbon. He said it was a gift from Buzzer."

"Russell, call the house," Ida Mae shouted, leaping up from her chair. "Billy, start the car. You're going to drive us to Georgie's, now. Russell?

"Wait. It's ringing. No. The answering machine."

"Damn it!"

It took them seven minutes to get to the house. Ida Mae and Russell ran up the brick steps. Russell used his key and they entered the hallway.

"Georgie?" Ida Mae shouted. "Russell, look downstairs."

There was a case of Merlot on the kitchen table. Two of the bottles were missing. There was a card by the case, with a handwritten note:

Honey,

This is just to wish you good luck tonight. May the best LeBrand win,

Your husband,

Buzzer

"Georgie!" Ida Mae shouted again. "Russell, check upstairs. She's got to be around someplace."

Russell ran up the hallway steps two at a time and in a few seconds he was shouting, "Not here!"

"Check the garage, see if the car's there."

"I looked. It's there."

"Then where the hell is she? Oh my God, Russell, she's drunk, she's—"

"Who's drunk?"

Ida Mae turned, and there was Georgie in the doorway, smiling, looking great, red-cheeked from the cold, dressed in a zipped winter jacket and jeans. There was a man, dressed similarly, standing next to her.

"What's the matter, Ida Mae? You look like you just saw a ghost."

"I saw the wine and—"

"Hey, calm down," Georgie said, placing an arm around Ida Mae's shoulder. "I'm fine. This is Jack Danzig. I don't think you two have met. The wine? We dropped off two bottles with Fran Cummins next door and then we walked up to the park and I guess we lost all track of time. Everything's fine, Ida Mae. Russell, you remember Jack?"

"I sure do."

"Then why don't the two of you go into the living room and

talk sports or something while Ida Mae and I start the Q and A?"

When they were alone, Ida Mae said, "I thought you were . . ."

"Drunk? Not now, Ida Mae. Maybe after the race is over. Maybe never again. I don't know. But not now, so don't worry. I'm not going to let Buzzer beat me. But just to be on the safe side, take the case home with you, save it for the victory party. Now, come on, we have a lot of work to do."

When the Q and A session was over, Ida Mae closed the briefing book, reached for a cigarette, and said, "Buzzer wants to destroy you. He's going to pull out every trick to humiliate you and make you lose your cool. You know that, right?"

"I'm ready for him, Ida Mae. And I'm ready for Bobby Ricky. Just watch me."

6:36 P.M., THE TRAINOR RESIDENCE, GRANGE CITY

Buzzer stepped out of the shower, five minutes after banging Sally Trainor. Her husband, John, had been out all day, handing out leaflets for Buzzer and was now carrying Buzzer signs outside the Grange City Community College, along with Nurse Patsy Earlings's idiots.

Sally, it turned out, liked to talk dirty during sex. God almighty. Why didn't they all just shut up? It was enough to drive a man crazy, all the talk, talk, talk, as if they had something important to say. He had to admit that it had not been all *that* bad, she did just about everything he wanted. Sometimes a little persuasion was necessary, but mostly she was enthusiastic. Despite the talking, she excited him, considering she was sagging a bit here and there.

When he finished dressing, Buzzer admired himself in the dresser mirror. He pulled the baseball cap a little lower on his forehead. He stared at his reflection and pulled in his stomach a bit. He had gained some weight since coming out of the coma. He took off the cap and brushed his hair back with his hands. Great.

"Sally, get the hell out of the sack, get some damned clothes on, and make me coffee. And get me a big towel to put over my shirt so I don't spill anything. If Carl Racksley, my so-called manager, calls, tell him to get his ass down to the debate. I called his house early this morning, thinking he'd give me a ride tonight, but no one answered. He's probably out looking for money."

7:10 P.M., WASHINGTON, D.C.

Gus smiled. The Speaker smiled.

"It looks as if we're going to take this seat after all, Mr. Speaker," Gus said, beaming. "There's no way Bobby Ricky can get out of this scandal."

"Do you think it was Bo who had those pictures taken?"

"It had to be Bo or Buzzer. Who else would be that desperate?"

"Yeah, desperation can bring out the worst in some people. I've got to be direct with you here, Gus. If we lose that seat, I'll be getting a lot of pressure to ask you to step down from the campaign chairmanship. For the good of the party."

"That's what's most important to me," Gus said. "The good of the party."

31

7:08 P.M., APRIL 1, ORANGE CITY COMMUNITY COLLEGE

Georgie, Ida Mae, and Russell sat in one of the classrooms just off the auditorium. They had finished the final run-through of issues and answers. Georgie read aloud the opening remarks Ida Mae had prepared. Ida Mae made a few suggestions—slow down, hit that word—but generally she was satisfied with Georgie's delivery.

There was nothing more to say or do. The campaign was operating on autopilot. Plans for the last days had been prepared a week ago. Radio ads were finished and in the pipeline. There were no more big decisions to make. There would be no more journeys to the western part of the district, no more brunches or lunches, or pancakes. Just get the candidate before as many people as possible, energize your base one last time, and then get out the vote.

Ida Mae, seated at the teacher's desk, needed a smoke, but she didn't want to get caught smoking on school property and cause a fuss just before the debate. She felt tired but good. She knew she had done everything she was supposed to. Russell's management of day-to-day problems in the campaign office, his tact in handling the inevitable personal disputes as tension and sleeplessness brought nerves to a raw edge, had been invaluable. She caught his eye, and they smiled at each other.

Georgie was standing by the window, watching the lights of the cars as they drove into the parking lot. She wondered what kind of crowd they'd get. Ida Mae said it didn't matter. This debate was for the media. For a second or two, a thought about the letter she had sent to Carl Racksley leaped to Georgie's mind, but she quickly dismissed it. *Concentrate. Just do well tonight. Be confident. Just finish the campaign and win. That's what the whole campaign has come down to. Not jobs, not education, not even Buzzer or Daddy. Just getting it over with. And winning.*

8:02 P.M.

Bo Beaumont slipped into the back row of auditorium seats, took off his overcoat, and sat down. There were about fifty or sixty people scattered around the auditorium. Not much of a crowd, but there was still about twenty-five minutes to go. He knew the size of the crowd didn't make much difference. Tonight all that mattered to the three candidates was not making mistakes that the media could report going into the final weekend. Bo settled in his seat and popped a JumBo mint into his mouth. More mint, more flavor. But he still wasn't sure if he liked the size. It was awkward. Still, a mint is a mint.

He wiggled in his seat, trying to get comfortable and prepare himself for an evening of platitudes, cover-your-ass rhetoric, and campaign bullshit. He could have watched it on the cable access channel at home, but he had wanted to be present when Georgie got her comeuppance. He wanted her to discover that her daddy, as usual, had been right and that it had been a major mistake to debate Bobby Ricky. Sure, Georgie caught a break when Bobby Ricky gave himself that self-inflicted wound with the girl. But Bo felt that Bobby Ricky was still dangerous. Georgie was giving him a chance. But when you knock a man down—or, as in this case, the man knocks himself down—you don't extend a hand to lift him up. You jump on his ribs and kick him a few times.

There were three lecterns on the stage. Seeing them reminded Bo that Buzzer had been included in the debate. Well, that was only fair. Somebody had to represent the idiots of the district. Bo sighed and took another JumBo mint out of the box.

8:28 P.M.

The auditorium was about three-quarters filled. Offstage, in the wings, Ida Mae and Russell watched as the moderator, Bobby Ricky, and Georgie came onstage to brief applause. Georgie walked to the lectern on stage right, and Bobby Ricky took his center position.

Russell took Ida Mae's hand and gave it a squeeze.

"Georgie's finally teeing off at the eighteenth, Ida Mae," he whispered. "She's going to make birdie."

"I'll settle for par," Ida Mae said.

"Ladies and gentlemen, good evening. I'm Dr. Kelly Hollman Tyler, the moderator for tonight's debate. As you can see, Mr. LeBrand has not yet arrived. I have just conferred with members of our panel and with Mrs. LeBrand and Mr. Diddier, and we agree it is only fair to begin the proceedings on time. We hope that Mr. LeBrand will arrive in due course. Mrs. LeBrand, your opening statement, please."

"When I started this race," Georgie said in an assured, controlled voice, "my campaign manager asked me: Georgie, what do you believe? What is your philosophy? I couldn't answer those questions. Like a lot of people, I guess, I took my political views for granted. But when you become a congressional candidate, you better know what you stand for."

She paused and took a sip of water.

Ida Mae whispered to Russell, "What the hell is she doing? This isn't what I wrote."

"After traveling all over the Sixth District," Georgie continued, "and listening and talking—and talking and talking"—she got the laugh—"I came to believe that no one—not me, not my opponents, not the Republican or Democratic Party, not Independents, not the media, not even a good campaign manager—has all the answers. Don't get me wrong—I believe there are clear differences between the two major parties. I believe the Republicans, at their best, want a country in which voluntary associations and private businesses are strong and government is limited. I believe Democrats want not just strong government but expanded government. So we have different principles, and the differences are important. But as candidates, we have to pretend we have *all* the answers. But we don't. No matter who wins this race, he or she will go to Congress and be faced with a whole new bunch of questions that we're not even considering in this race, because we don't yet know what they are. Someone once told me that politics is always about something else. You're always surprised by new issues. I guess he was right, if I may judge from this campaign."

In the back of the auditorium—the only person in the last row—Bo smiled. At least Georgie remembered something he had taught her.

"So, what do I believe?" Georgie asked. "I believe that a candidate has to have a set of basic political principles and tell people what they are. I have done this throughout the campaign and I will do it again this evening. Then the people have to place their trust in the candidate. In that sense, politics is like a marriage. Big promises are made publicly. Trust is essential. You make a commitment. The rest, in marriage and in politics, is up to things like character, courage, and a sense of duty and honor and integrity and honesty, all those old words we've heard so often. Unless you have those qualities, it doesn't matter if you know every last issue or have great political instincts."

"Damn, it," Ida Mae said. "She shouldn't be talking about marriage. What's she *doing?*"

"She's telling us what she believes, Ida Mae," Russell said, beaming. "Isn't that what you've wanted all along?"

Georgie paused and looked at Bobby Ricky and then at the audience.

"Let me tell you: I don't have a surefire solution to unemployment in our district. I wish I did. But I don't. Of course, neither do my opponents. We can talk about government programs all we want, but the only way jobs will come to this district is if companies want to locate here. And the only way I know how to do that is to make it attractive for them to do so. I believe tax breaks can help. But I can't guarantee it. I'm ready to discuss my approaches tonight."

She was about to conclude when she heard shouting at the rear of the auditorium. The doors opened and there was Buzzer, wearing a starched and pressed uniform, a shining black leather belt, and glistening black boots. He was smiling broadly and carrying an American flag on a long pole. He strode down the aisle, followed by Nurse Patsy and twenty TMC members, clapping and cheering. When he got onstage, a few people booed, but Nurse Patsy and her people, standing in the center aisle, drowned them out, cheering and applauding some more.

"Mr. LeBrand, please," Dr. Tyler said. "This is out of order. This is highly irregular, sir."

Buzzer ignored her and, waving the flag, shouted over the hubbub: "I defended this flag against the drug lords. I got a bullet in my leg that qualifies me to hold this flag. Nobody is prying it from my hands, and nobody is going to shut me up. This ain't Russia or Nazi Germany! This ain't, uh, you know, one of those other countries in South America, Costa Rica or whatever. This is, by God, America! God bless America! God bless America!"

Dr. Tyler tried to regain order, but the TMC people had removed little flags on sticks from beneath their coats, and were waving them, chanting, "Buzz-*zer,* Buzz-*zer,* Buzz-*zer.*"

Two security guards were trying to get to the stage. Newspaper photographers and TV cameras were focused on Buzzer, who was waving the flag and shouting, "God shed his grace on *thee!* America! And crown thy good . . ."

Finally, the aisles were cleared. The guards came onstage and stood there, staring at Buzzer, not knowing what to do next.

Dr. Tyler said, "Mr. LeBrand, sir, you are out of order."

"Order? Whose orders? Bo Beaumont's orders? The labor union bosses, their orders?" Buzzer shouted. "The people want to hear ol' Buzzer! These two get all the publicity. They get all the media attention. So tonight, let's just hear what *I* got to say. I'm a new man for new times. A new man who rose from the dead to save this district. Give me a chance to speak. I seek closure! I seek closure! I been cheated out of my seat by that woman over there. But God raised me up again. God saved me, and he did it because I'm a new man for new times. Forget about party labels. Write in for the right man!"

Cheers, boos.

"Mr. LeBrand—"

"Hold on, I got the floor, honey. I got two questions to ask. One, how come a man from *New York*"—he pointed the flag at Bobby Ricky—"how come a rich athlete who lived in *New York* for so long says he's one of us? The fact is, he thinks just like those folks up there. He has no regard for family values, consorting with one of his own employees like that. Is this man fit for public office? Number two is, how come a woman"—he pointed the flag at Georgie—"how can a woman who drives under the influence, how can she says she *cares?* Cares? Cares about her own self, far as I can see. Look at them: one's unfaithful and the other's dangerous, driving drunk, endangering good folks and little tiny kids. Will someone tell me why they are qualified to take the seat they stole from me while I was with God?"

Dr. Tyler said, "Mr. LeBrand, we must ask you to leave the stage—"

"No! Let him stay!"

Everyone turned to Georgie, who left her lectern, walked swiftly downstage, and stood in front of Buzzer.

"You want to debate, Buzzer?" she said, waggling her finger in his face. "Then let's do it. Let the people see what kind of idiot you are. Name the issue."

"I agree," Bobby Ricky shouted. "Let him stay now that he's here. But since this has turned into a shambles, Madam Moderator, let me say something."

The auditorium gradually grew quiet. Buzzer, still carrying the flag, went to his lectern, as did Georgie.

"Let me say this about the charge just made against me by Buzzer LeBrand," Bobby Ricky said. "I don't think anyone's private life—mine or Buzzer's or Georgie's—should be used in a political campaign. I just don't think it's right. I never used any of the charges made by Georgie LeBrand or her husband against each other. I never stooped to the gutter. But let me address this issue head-on. First question: Did I go to that motel to see Ms. Simmons? Yes. I went to that motel to talk her out of quitting the campaign."

"Oh, come *on,*" Buzzer snarled, handing the flagpole to a security guard and walking over to Bobby Ricky. "Nobody believes that, not even you."

Dr. Tyler said, "Mr. LeBrand, *please,* return to your lectern. We must have regular order."

"Oh, shut up, Buzzer," Bobby Ricky said. "I'm not letting you—of all people—call me a liar. As I was saying, the young lady in question felt under tremendous pressure because of the campaign."

"You put some pressure on her, but it wasn't political, believe me," Buzzer said with a leer as he walked back to his lectern.

"With all this talk about morality," Bobby Ricky continued, "is anybody bothered that I was tailed by some secret political operatives and that clandestine pictures were taken of me? Who is responsible for that? Have the media investigated that? And here's an important question: Would the media have paid attention to this if I were white? Is there a double standard for black men who won't play by the old racist rules? Do my so-called moral opponents have an answer to these questions?"

"Well, I wouldn't put it past Bo Beaumont, who is still pulling the strings on my wife's campaign, to use dirty tricks," Buzzer shouted.

"Thank you, Mr. Diddier and Mr. LeBrand," Dr. Tyler said coldly. "Now, since we are hopelessly out of order, let me skip opening statements and turn to Shirley Hevling of WGMR."

"Mrs. LeBrand, I planned to ask you about incentives to companies that might relocate here. But I think you should get a chance now to say something, if you wish, about the charges made against you by Mr. LeBrand."

"Yes, Shirley, I do want to say a few things. I agree with Bobby Ricky on one thing—and maybe one thing only. My personal life, even when it is spread across the front pages and the TV news, is nobody's business. The differences between my husband and me are deep and real and lasting—and irreconcilable. But I'm not going to dignify his attacks on me and on my capabilities as a wife and mother. Instead, I want to make a confession."

The hall grew quiet again.

"Concerning the charges made by my husband, they hurt me, deeply. But one of them, I'm afraid, happens to be true. In the past I drank too much, too often. As I recently discovered, it is still a problem for me, one that I must confront every day. So, yes, Buzzer is right about that, although I'm taking it day by day, and I'm sober.

But please do me a favor now, everyone in the hall: take a good look at my husband. Just look at him."

Buzzer gave a wave and an old-fashioned Buzzer smile to the crowd, knowing he looked great.

"There he is, the Fighting Sheriff. He's a fighter all right. But the only person he's been kicking around in recent years is me. Buzzer LeBrand is a wife-beater."

"That's a damned lie! I never—"

"What you have seen from Buzzer LeBrand tonight," Georgie continued, "the arrogance, the meanness, I saw for all those years, every day of our marriage. What you have seen tonight is what he is: someone with complete contempt for me, for Bobby Ricky, for the rules, and for you and everybody else who gets in his way. Buzzer's a user. He uses people. Now he's using religion."

"That's a damned lie. I'm born again. Reverend Herman Throe, God bless him, can vouch for that. I'm a new man for—"

"For *yourself,* Buzzer," Georgie shouted, pointing at him. "For *yourself,* that's who you're for. You use everything and everybody. This is as good a time and place as any to tell you to your face. I'm divorcing you. If you want to know the grounds, they are repeated adultery and spousal abuse. I am going to name names and I am going to tell people how you hit me and beat me."

Buzzer swiftly came from behind his lectern and rushed across the stage toward Georgie, his face red. He came within inches of her and stopped, glaring at her. She didn't budge.

"What are you going to do, Buzzer? Hit me again? Go ahead, take your best shot! I'm not afraid of you anymore!"

There was a sudden burst of applause and shouts of approval from the audience. People were standing and cheering.

"All right, *Georgie!*" Ida Mae yelled, and hugged Russell.

Buzzer, looking down at Georgie, bellowed in her face: "You're on your way to *hell,* Georgie, lying like that about your son's daddy."

He turned and began to walk away when Georgie shouted, "Hell? You're on your way to divorce court, and if I were you, Buzzer, I'd choose hell. After I'm finished with you, hell is going to look like a resort in the hills. I'm beginning a new life, without you. If I'm elected, I'll divorce you and go to Washington and do my best. If Bobby Ricky wins, I'll just get my divorce and start over again. Either way, Buzzer, you've lost this race. Just as you lost me a long time ago."

Cheers and applause drowned out what she was going to say next, and she paused. Most of the audience, except for the TMC members, were standing, shouting and applauding.

In the last row, Bo jumped up, caught up in the excitement of the moment. As the crowd continued to cheer, he popped in a JumBo mint and started to cheer, and . . .

He couldn't breathe.

The JumBo mint had lodged in his throat. He tried to take a deep breath, but it only made things worse. He fell back into his seat, waving his arms, trying to get the attention of someone. But people in the rows in front of him were too busy cheering his daughter. He tried to get up, but when he got to his feet he was dizzy. He fell to the floor. There, as he lay facedown amid the gum wrappers and scraps of paper, the JumBo mint continued to cut off his breath.

Offstage, Russell and Ida Mae were waving and giving the thumbs-up sign. Georgie turned and was about to speak, but out of the corner of her eye she saw someone coming onstage. There, entering from stage right, was, of all people, Carl Racksley.

Then everything seems for Georgie to be happening in a strange kind of time: slower—she can make out every detail—but faster, too, with everything happening all at once. There is a shout: "Omigod, he's got a gun." Buzzer grabs Georgie by the arms and places her between Carl and himself. Carl has a small black gun in his right hand, pointed straight at them. Georgie struggles to get out of Buzzer's grasp, but he is too strong. Carl is shouting something, but Georgie can't make it out. Something or someone hits her, she is suddenly free of Buzzer, and she is falling to the floor. She hears crack crack. *Someone is on top of her. It's Bobby Ricky covering her with his body on the floor, his face near hers. Georgie looks up to see Carl backing up. He smiles, saying something to her. He puts the gun in his mouth.* Crack.

10:11 P.M., THE LITTLE BROWN CHURCH

Herman walked out of his office and smelled the smoke. He moved as fast as he could to the side door. When he got outside he saw the smoke and flames coming from the original Little Brown Church. He went back into the office and called the fire department, and by the time he was back outside, there were half a dozen church aides running around and yelling and not making much sense. He told them to calm down and to stay away from the fire, which was gathering intensity. Herman stood there in the cold, transfixed.

"It's Joe Wholey," someone behind him shouted. "He set fire to the church. I saw him. He had a gasoline can."

"Where is he?" Herman shouted. "Where's Joe? Oh my God, is he in there?"

Through the broken window, in a momentary gap in the wall of smoke and flames, Herman saw what could have been the figure of a man in the flames.

"Joe! My God, Joe!"

Then Herman heard singing coming from behind him.

He turned and there was Joe Wholey, holding a gasoline can in one hand and a Bible in the other.

" '*Oh,* the Little Brown Church,' " Joe sang. " 'Don't be left in the lurch . . .' "

Someone, Herman couldn't tell who, tackled Joe and knocked him to the ground, but Joe kept on singing. The fire was now through the roof. The little place wasn't that big, and it was all old wood. There was the distant wail of the fire engines, but by that time it was too late for the Little Brown Church. It was burning like hell.

Herman waddled over to where three aides had Joe Wholey pinned to the ground.

"Let him go," Herman said.

"But Herman . . ."

"Just do as I say."

The aides let go of Joe. Herman crouched and took the gasoline can from Joe's hand. Tears in his eyes, Herman lifted Joe's shoulders from the cold ground and then cradled him in his arms.

"It's all right, Joe. It's all right," Herman said soothingly as the fire engines pulled up. "You couldn't help it. God loves you, Joe. God loves you."

10:07 P.M., TYSONS CORNER, VIRGINIA

Jay Hollings and Candace Gilman, former volunteer in the campaign of Bobby Ricky Diddie, were sitting in the front seat of Jay's car, parked in the deserted open garage near the Macy's entrance of the Galleria Mall in Tysons Corner, Virginia. Her car, in which she had just arrived, was parked a few rows away. Jay, wearing gloves, handed her a manila envelope.

"Here," he said. "Count it."

She expected him to say something more, but he had his hand on the key, which was still in the ignition. She wanted the moment to last, being in the car with him, seeing him after all this time.

"I trust you, I don't have to count it."

"Suit yourself."

When they were in college, Candace, a poli sci major, had the biggest crush on Jay Hollings, although he never knew about it. He was the campus politician and he knew everybody, even plain old, chubby, dumpy Candace, because she distributed his flyers and helped in his campaign office. After graduation, she worked in an insurance company back home for a few years and then went to work as a receptionist in the Washington office of her congressman, an Illinois Democrat. Much to her surprise and delight, from time to time she would see Jay walking the halls of one of the House office buildings and she'd go out of her way to say hello. She never could figure out what he did.

Right out of the blue one night about six weeks earlier, Jay Hollings had called her, asking if she'd meet him for drinks the next evening after work. Jay said he was sorry that they hadn't known each other better at school. He thought this was a good chance to catch up.

The next evening, in a booth at the Hawk and Dove bar, they talked. It turned out that Candace's job as a receptionist hadn't worked out, so she was sort of between jobs. Jay commiserated with her and asked how she was fixed for cash. She said everything was fine, but he kept on coming back to the question and she finally admitted she was desperate—her savings were going fast, and there were no immediate job prospects. Then he asked her if she'd like to come back to an apartment he used—it belonged to a friend of his—and just have a nightcap and talk about her problem. There just might be something he could do to help her.

The apartment building was just a few blocks from the Capitol, on the House side, near the Folger Library. What happened when they got there was a bit of a blur because she had had four or five drinks at the bar. But she clearly remembered that Jay started kissing her and telling her how nice she was and then he had her sweater and bra off in about a minute and a half. It all happened so fast. They were on the bed and he was all over her. It was so *wonderful.* Actually, it was all over very quickly, he didn't want to hold her or cuddle afterward, and when he was finished and he rolled off, he had a strange look on his face, as if he were sick. But she could tell he really liked her. She was in love, just the way she had always dreamed about it.

Afterward, he said he might be able to help her get a job. It would involve a few weeks' work and he could guarantee that the job paid well.

Candace was delighted.

"What kind of job is it?" she asked.

"Before I tell you what it is, you have to promise me something."

"Anything."

"Everything I tell you is top-secret. This is a very sensitive job you'll be doing. I can't tell you everything, but I work for a certain agency I can't mention. I have highest-level, need-to-know, Q-clearance. But I think I can trust you enough to say this. The job you'll be doing involves national security. It is of very high importance for certain people—I can't name names—at the very top of the government. The very top, Candy. Do you get what I'm saying?"

"I think so."

"You have to promise me you'll never tell anybody about the job. Ever. Can you promise me that?"

"Sure. It sounds exciting."

"Oh, it's exciting all right. But you have to be willing to go under cover for a while. You'll use your own name, but you have to play a role. Can you play a role?"

"Yes, I think so."

She was beyond happiness. Jay Hollings had made love to her and now he was getting her an exciting national-security job. All in one night. Two days later, after the most romantic moments she had ever dreamed of, better than dreams, she was on her way to the Sixth District. She had only one order from Jay: find out all she could about Bobby Ricky's private life and, every evening at the same time, he'd get in touch. No, he didn't want to give her any of his phone numbers. National security.

When Candace got to the Sixth, it was easy. The Bobby Ricky campaign people checked out her Democratic credentials with the congressman she had been working for, and she told them how much she wanted to help Bobby Ricky, how he was such a star, how she had always admired him. She was taken on as a volunteer. In campaign headquarters, she saw the way Lee Simmons and Bobby Ricky looked at each other, and how, one day, Lee had taken papers over to Bobby Ricky's apartment and didn't come back for over an hour, and she passed it on. Jay told her to keep an eye on them, and she did. It was fun, like being a spy in one of those movies. Jay, during the phone calls, never said much, just brief questions, all business.

Now here she was, sitting next to Jay, after all these weeks.

"So, why don't we celebrate," she said with what she felt was a sexy smile. "We could go to the Ritz-Carlton right here, if you want. We can get a room."

"No," he said, reaching over to open her door. "I got to get back."

"Jay, will you tell me one thing?" she said as she got out.

"What?"

"Did my information reach that top-level official you mentioned? The one at the very top?"

He didn't say anything. He just shook his head, gave her a dirty look, and then slammed the door and hurriedly pulled out of the garage, leaving her, manila envelope in hand, to walk to her car alone.

He's busy. But he'll call.

FRIDAY, APRIL 2

The *Bugle,* front page:

**BUZZER LEBRAND SHOT AT DEBATE;
ASSAILANT KILLS WIFE, SELF**

. . . The former congressman was shot once in the back and once in the head by Carl Racksley, prominent local businessman and Mr. LeBrand's campaign manager. Police say that hours earlier, Mr. Racksley had killed his wife in their East Side home, shooting her five times.

Mr. LeBrand was rushed to Grange Memorial Hospital, where a team of surgeons operated on him for six hours.

A high-ranking hospital official, who asked not to be named, said, "I can't believe Mr. LeBrand is still alive, given the damage the bullets have done. One bullet missed his heart by a millimeter, and the shot to the head left the bullet lodged inside his skull. He should have died almost instantly. But the paramedics got to him in a hurry, he was given blood and operated on, and he is still somehow alive."

Police have not yet established a motive for the assault on Mr. LeBrand and the two deaths, but according to business associates, Mr.

Racksley was deeply concerned about a downturn in business, which led to severe financial problems for his company.

"Carl was a nice man in his own way, and he sure was crazy about Marge," one developer said. "But he got himself in over his head. His business was falling apart. He owed a lot of money to certain people. In recent weeks he just let himself go. He looked awful. I think he just snapped under the pressure. Poor Marge and Buzzer just happened to be in the wrong place at the wrong time. It's a real tragedy."

DIDDIER SAVES OPPONENT'S LIFE

Asked why he risked his life by covering Mrs. LeBrand with his own body, Mr. Diddier said, "I didn't think. I reacted. My grandmother had a saying. 'Just do,' she always said. That's the way it was. I didn't think, I just did. I'm glad Georgie is all right."

Police Chief Irwin Rhymer called Diddier's act "the bravest thing I have ever seen in twenty-six years as a law enforcement officer. Bobby Ricky deserves a medal."

The *Bugle,* front page, below the fold:

"BO" BEAUMONT CHOKES CONDITION "GRAVE"

. . . Physicians at Grange Memorial Hospital said that Mr. Beaumont ingested a nut mint, which lodged in his windpipe. It is not known when the superstore pioneer was stricken or how long he lay unattended.

"In a case like this," said Dr. Kevin Munson, "there is always the chance of permanent damage because of oxygen deprivation. He was found just in time for us to save him, but we don't yet know what damage has been done."

Mr. Beaumont has not regained consciousness, and his condition is described as "grave."

The *Bugle,* page four:

HISTORIC CHURCH BURNED IN APPARENT ARSON CASE

. . . Senator Wholey was handed over to Pritchard County police by Reverend Herman Throe, pastor of the Little Brown Church. Senator Wholey was reportedly distraught over his loss in the recent Republican primary race.

"The loss of the church is total," said Reverend Throe, speaking to reporters in his office in the new church building. "The Little Brown Church is irreplaceable. Yes, we have this fine new church, and thank the Lord it was spared. But I have to say my heart has always been in the original building. We knew it was vulnerable to fire. But we never thought of arson. Poor Joe Wholey, God help him, the poor man, he was sick and couldn't help himself. I'm praying for him."

When asked what his plans for restoration were, Reverend Throe replied, "I don't know. It's all in God's hands."

NINE MONTHS LATER, DECEMBER 10

The *Bugle*, front page:

JOBS INCREASE; CITY, REGION BEGIN COMEBACK

. . . The most optimistic forecast came from Russell Beaumont, chief executive officer of BigBo, the giant retail chain founded by his father, the stricken Beauregard "Bo" Beaumont.

From his vacation home in Florida, Mr. Beaumont said, "Our area is coming back strong and will continue to do so. We are by no means out of the woods yet. But we are doing well in every leading economic indicator. Tourism in the western part of the state is up. The central counties will benefit tremendously by the auto plant that's going to be built in Zellenborn County. There's a sense of optimism all over the region. Sales are strong at all our BigBo stores. We look forward to one of the best Christmas seasons in years. More and more people in our community are working again. That's what you need, good news and optimism."

The *Bugle*, page 6, the "Politics Today" column:

NO NEED TO TUSSLE WITH RUSSELL

. . . In less than a year, since his father fell victim to a tragic incident that has left the retail pioneer unable to communicate and confined to a wheelchair, Russell Beaumont has provided quiet, effective leadership to BigBo Inc., which is seeing daylight after a few bad years. He has also transformed Republican politics in the county and the state. Unlike his hard-driving, autocratic, often cantankerous father, who never stopped working, the easygoing Mr. Beaumont can be found on the golf course as much as he can in his office in the Beaumont Building on Grange Square. But don't be fooled by the casual approach. He gets things done—his way. Beaumont has met with leaders of the Religious Coalition—something his father would never do—in search of party unity.

"There remain a lot of questions to be answered about where the party is headed," said one member of the coalition, "but Russell Beaumont has the respect and I'd say the admiration of all our members for his sensitivity. There's not all this day-to-day fighting that characterized Bo's politics. Russell listens and when he speaks, he makes sense. He's not the most astute political technician I've ever seen, but he's improving. For years, Russell had to hide his light under a bushel, working for his father. Now he's his own man. He gets things done in his own quiet way."

11:38 A.M., RAYBURN BUILDING, WASHINGTON, D.C.

The representative of the Sixth District listened with half an ear as the committee witnesses droned on about the need for local control of schools. The representative looked around the committee room. Almost empty. A boring hearing on a rainy day. Well, anyhow, the breakfast meeting had gone well. The constituent wanted a special favor. Nothing new there. But the contribution would come, in good time. The representative sat there, trying to look interested until it came time to ask a question or two.

2:09 P.M., HEAVENLY HOPE MISSION, JERSEY CITY, NEW JERSEY

Herman Throe sat behind the battered, dented, secondhand desk with the wobbly left front leg and listened to the homeless, almost toothless black man in the ripped and dirty army jacket mumble and babble about ray guns and space aliens and the CIA and the FBI and the United Nations and how they were all trying to get him.

Two weeks after the fire, after much prayer (and fasting!), Herman knew he had to get back to evangelistic basics. Folks are saved one by one. Politics can be a good way to bring the Lord's message to people. But a real minister of the Word needs to deal with one soul at a time. Herman had forgotten that timeless truth. But now God had given him a chance to get back on track.

He had resigned his ministry, left control of the new church in the capable hands of Reverend John Reming, and drove away in his SUV, not sure where he was going or what he'd do when he got there. All he knew for certain was that he needed a fresh start, something completely different from what he had been doing, and the chance to save one soul at a time.

In a few days he found himself, still aimlessly driving nowhere, headed north on Route 95 in Virginia. Hours later, on the New Jersey Turnpike, he decided that the Lord was leading him to New York City. But he got off the turnpike at the wrong exit and found himself in Jersey City. He got lost trying to get back on the turnpike and decided to spend the night in his SUV. It was risky: this wasn't a part of Jersey City that had been gentrified and built up and renovated, with the old brownstones fixed up for young New York stockbrokers to live in. No, this was poor, old, worn-down Jersey City as it had been for decades. So it was a risk sleeping in the SUV, aside from being uncomfortable. Herman was still a considerable size despite the fact he had lost a lot of weight since the fire.

But when he awoke the next morning, he found that he was parked outside an empty store on Communipaw Avenue. And he decided that this was where God had led him. So he rented the store and put up a hand-painted sign saying HEAVENLY HOPE MISSION: WE PREACH LOVE AND HOPE. He bought some secondhand furniture. As one or two locals came in to help, he put in some kitchen appliances. The mission was open for any poor or hopeless or sick person who came in for a meal or a prayer or just to get out of the rain. Herman had not been happier in years.

And now he held the derelict's hand as the man babbled on.

"And with the CIA, they, with the FBI, all in my teeth, John Kennedy Jr. put it in my tooth right here"—the man pointed to his gums—"here where it was, they put it in, a radio wave, it shoot out those *rays*."

"You ever think about heaven, son?" Herman said gently.

"Heaven?"

Herman smiled.

"Yes, heaven. I used to preach hell. But now I preach heaven. Let me tell you about it."

6:14 P.M., WASHINGTON, D.C.

The Sixth District representative smiled and took a quick look at the clear plastic name badge pinned to the lapel of the man who had just extended his hand.

BOB JENKINS
DONNELLY ASSOCIATES

Who was Jenkins? For that matter, who was Donnelly and who were his associates? Why was Bob Jenkins smiling? The representative listened to him explain why the amendment to the telecommunications bill was not acceptable to the industry his firm represented. How could anyone support anything as bad as that?

Ridiculous. The representative had no idea what amendment Bob Jenkins was talking about. But the representative listened, nodded at strategic moments, and hoped Bob Jenkins would not ask an intelligent question.

6:45 P.M., RESTON, VIRGINIA

Lee Simmons was at a book signing at a megabookstore. Her book, *Political Erections: Hard Facts About Building Campaigns from the Bottom Up,* had just been listed as number twelve on the *New York Times* bestseller list. Her role as a political analyst for a cable talk show was moving along nicely.

There was a man, a bit older than she was, standing in front of her, his blond hair so light in color that it was almost white. He wore a blue suit, a white shirt, and a perfectly knotted dark blue tie. He was holding out a copy of her book.

"I enjoy you on the talk shows," he said. "I watch you all the time."

"Thank you. What would you like me to write?"

"Just write, 'To Jay.' "

She signed the book and handed it back.

"Are you in politics yourself?" she asked.

"You might say that," the man said, and walked away.

8:00 P.M., CAPITOL HILL HYATT REGENCY, WASHINGTON, D.C.

The Sixth District representative sat at one of the fifty-three tables that had been set up in the main ballroom, listening to speeches about the next election, how much it meant to the party and the country, and the world, how there was a big difference between the two parties and we represent the values of the American people and . . . and this . . . and that . . .

The speakers babbled on and on. The representative picked at the filet mignon medallion and wondered how long this was going to take. Tomorrow the representative would fly back home to begin a series of town meetings around the district. And then next week, there would be a series of votes on issues ranging from health care to foreign policy. When the dinner was over, the representative began to get up from the uncomfortable chair. There would be a big mob at the hotel garage. Perhaps it would be better to just sit and wait for fifteen minutes, let the crowd clear out. But a lobbyist waved and began to approach the table, and the representative decided it was better to get stuck in the garage than to listen to one more lobbyist present the case for justice, liberty, the American way, and, oh yes, the people. But it was too late, the lobbyist had made his way through the crowd and, smiling a lobbyist's big, friendly, warm, intimate, personal smile, said, "Glad to hear you're running again. We want to help."

"Well, that's very good to hear," the representative said. "Why not drop around next week, we'll talk."

"Sounds good. Anyhow, I want to discuss the trade bill. Good to see you."

The representative sat there, tired but happy to be alone for a few minutes. There would be two fund-raisers next week. The representative was in fairly good financial shape for the next election, and things looked all right. The district was recovering. The good economic news had nothing to do with anything the representative had done, however. The recovery had begun just as quickly and just as mysteriously as the recession that preceded it, and the representative was benefiting from the return to good economic times. Politics 101.

9:07 P.M., MARINER'S YACHT CLUB, WEST WHITE BEACH, FLORIDA

Russell looked at Ida Mae, reached across the table, and took her hand in his. She gave his hand a squeeze. They were dining alfresco on the patio of the club dining room, looking out on the beach and the Atlantic. They had finished dinner and now were just sitting there, sipping wine, enjoying the breeze.

"What am I doing wrong?" Russell said.

"I told you."

"Tell me again."

"You're turning your left shoulder out when you drive. And on the green you're trying to read every last blade of grass before you putt. Just take a look and then hit the damn ball. It works for me."

"Good advice," he said. "I don't know what I can do about that shoulder thing. I just can't get rid of it. I think about it. I break down my swing and go over it in my mind, but . . ."

"Don't think about it, Russell. Look at me. I'll never be able play golf as well as you can. But I don't worry about it. Just be happy that these things are all you have to worry about."

"Will you marry me?"

"No. Not until you improve your game. On the course, I mean."

"What an incentive!"

For a long time they sat without speaking, just taking in all the beauty of the night and the beach and the water.

"I'm so damned happy," Russell said. "Are you happy?"

"Happier than I ever dreamed I could be."

"Would getting married make you even happier?"

"I told you, Russell. Marriage is a big step. For both of us. We each have our own lives. We're not kids. This is great, what we have now. Let's not push it."

"You're right, as usual. Now, if only I could get my drives straightened out, things would be perfect."

"Have you talked to Georgie? About what we've been discussing?"

"No. I was thinking of giving her a call tonight," Russell said.

"Good idea."

10:06 P.M., GRANGE MEMORIAL HOSPITAL, GRANGE CITY

Nurse Patsy Earlings pushed Bo Beaumont's wheelchair out of the Helen Forrest Beaumont Suite, which was now his permanent home, and into the quiet hospital corridor.

"Now, Mr. Bo, we're going for our little ride."

She made the left-hand turn by the nurses' station and then a right by the elevators.

"I heard your doctors say so many times there's not much of a chance you can hear me and understand. But I think you can."

She wheeled him into room 856. Buzzer LeBrand lay in the hospital bed, pale, motionless, but technically alive, with tubes and wires and plastic bags and machines attached to or near him. Standing by the window were Elder Jimmy Tuckerhoe and two other members of the TMC. Nurse Patsy had sneaked them up to the eighth floor for their monthly vigil.

Nurse Patsy Earlings wheeled Bo to the side of Buzzer's bed. She smoothed the blanket across Bo's lap and wiped some drool from his mouth with a tissue. She placed the wheelchair so that Bo was close to the bed, facing Buzzer.

"There! Mr. Bo, I'm not one to leave a man to his own lonely self, sitting in that room all the time. A man in your condition needs to see folks he's used to, like Mr. LeBrand here. So you just sit there and make believe you're having a good old talk, like I bet the two of you did in the old days, him being your son-in-law. Yes, you had your differences, but all that's behind both of you now."

Nurse Patsy went over to Elder Jimmy Tuckerhoe and whispered, "Mr. LeBrand is the Messenger. I know it in my heart."

"Amen," said the other two TMC members softly but with great conviction.

"At first I didn't believe," said Elder Jimmy Tuckerhoe. "But when I'm here, I can feel it's him, I feel it stronger every day. When the time comes, this man will arise and smite sinners the way Joshua smote the inhabitants of the city of Jericho."

"Joshua, chapter six, verse twenty-one," Earle Gooch, one of the two TMC members, said. "I know the passage well."

"Amen," Nurse Patsy said.

"The first heart attack Mr. LeBrand had," Elder Jimmy Tuckerhoe continued, "would have killed another man. Then he was in his coma. And then he arose from the deep sleep and walked among us, telling the truth while they told lies about him. All lies. And then, after trying to save his wife there at the debate, trying to move her out of harm's way he was, he gets shot in the head by that evil Racksley man. But Mr. LeBrand is still alive. Oh, he's the instrument of the Lord all right."

"When's he coming back this time, Nurse Patsy?" Mrs. Jennie Yardway said. She had been a widow for the past fifty years, since the day her husband, Ezra, a good man but weak in the head, got run over by a steamroller. She was from Pritchard County, and her son had driven her all the way into Grange City just to get a look at the man the other TMC folks were all talking about.

"I don't rightly know, Mizz Yardway. He'll just get out of that bed one day and he'll walk among us again, just like he did before. When he's ready, he'll know the time. We got to be patient. And we can't tell nobody. He's all ours. I wheel Mr. Bo in here so both of them can kind of communicate in the spirit, even though the doctors—and they don't know everything—say both of them can't understand anything. Well, as long as I work here, every single night I'm wheeling Mr. Bo in here and let him stay the night, by the bedside of the Messenger to Come."

"Tell us about the last words the Messenger spoke to you, Nurse Patsy," Mrs. Yardway said.

"Well, I can remember like it was yesterday. There we were, ready to go through those doors into the auditorium where the debate was. He had that flag in his hands and I was just standing there by the door. And he pushed me out of the way and he said, 'Get out of my way, you idiot woman!' And those were the last words he said to me. I'll cherish them forever."

"Pushing you was his way of showing leadership," said Elder Jimmy Tuckerhoe. "And to a man with his gifts, we're all idiots."

"Ain't that the truth? It was just his way of talking."

Nurse Patsy continued to talk with her TMC friends. Had she gone over to Bo's wheelchair, she would have seen two tears running down his cheeks and a look of uncomprehending horror in his eyes as he fixedly stared at Buzzer's face.

10:22 P.M., NEW YORK CITY

Kalya walked quickly along Fifth Avenue, glad to be out in the fresh air after the long, long after-dinner meeting with the executive board of the proposed American Popular Music Museum. They didn't know what they wanted, and she—the public-relations expert—was supposed to tell them. Well, she did tell them, over and over: they needed a big, brash, splashy, in your-face image! Museum? Junk that word! Call it the Pop-Bebop-Doo-Wop-Hip-Hop House of Sounds. That reflected the nature of the music it celebrated: informal, brash, in-your-face exuberant. But half of the board wanted dignity, and the other half didn't know what it wanted. She was exhausted, but she needed the walk in the brisk—chilly, in fact—night air. Tomorrow, another meeting, this time with a group of black business executives looking for advice on how to project an image of black pride to black children failing in school.

Thank God her kids were doing well in their private school. The last time she had spoken to Bobby Ricky, he had been pleased about that. Her thoughts turned to him. We used to walk through the streets at night, just like this, young, happy, and . . . stupid. She smiled. Damn it, sometimes she missed him, the rotten, lying, cheating bastard. There had been times during the past few months, after the divorce, when she had, in moments of weakness, thought, *Damn it, maybe I should have hung in there.* But the proud, practical, prudent part of her mind said, *Honey, Bobby Ricky is who he is, you knew that all the time, he'll never change. It would be crazy to try to fix a marriage as broken as yours. Crazy.* She knew that was right.

As she approached Saint Patrick's Cathedral, she saw police cars with their lights flashing and, for this time of night, a pretty big crowd, even some TV camera crews. She asked a policeman what was happening.

"Some protesters, trying to camp out on the church steps."

Kalya walked through the crowd and saw one of the protesters, screaming obscenities and holding a placard with the words:

HEY, MR. POPE—LEAVE WOMEN'S BODIES ALONE!

About to walk away, Kalya stopped and saw that the screaming woman was Susan Weinstein. She recognized her from photographs in the *Bugle*. Still protesting. Kalya felt a grudging admiration for the woman. Two policemen were trying to hold her, but here she was, at night, in the cold, hoping the TV crews would find something useful for the morning news. A crazy woman, Gary Garafolo had called her. But she was one of those people who never stop fighting for what they want, never give up hope, never surrender, keep on believing when there is no longer any point in believing. As Kalya walked, the strangest thought occurred to her. *What the hell, why not call Bobby Ricky?* Just to see how he was doing.

11:00 P.M., RUSSELL BEAUMONT'S RESIDENCE, WEST WHITE BEACH, FLORIDA

Ida Mae and Russell were in bed. He was reading *Golf* magazine. She was reading the results of an opinion survey Russell had commissioned on voter attitudes in the Sixth District.

"Remember to call Georgie," Ida Mae said.

"I'll give her a call tomorrow."

"No, call her now. Just to see how she's doing."

11:03 P.M., THE REPRESENTATIVE'S RESIDENCE, WASHINGTON, D.C.

The representative was asleep and dreaming.

In the dream, the representative was sitting in a seat near the center aisle in the House Chamber, admiring the dark brown wood and cream-colored ceiling and the enormous, etched-in-glass eagle looking down on the different shades of blue on the rug and on the wall coverings. Here, the representative of the Sixth District was the equal of the other 434 members, possessed of equal dignity. There were no windows in the chamber, because once you were there, the rest of the world didn't matter. All that mattered was your judgment, your courage, and your ability to get things done. And so, in the dream, the representative was just sitting there, alone, taking in the quiet, majestic splendor of the scene before the legislative day began.

11:04:38 P.M., KALYA DIDDIER'S RESIDENCE, NEW YORK CITY

Kalya, sitting by her bed, picked up the phone to call Bobby Ricky.

11:04:38 P.M., RUSSELL BEAUMONT'S RESIDENCE, WEST WHITE BEACH, FLORIDA

Russell picked up the phone to call Georgie.

11:04:48 P.M., THE REPRESENTATIVE'S RESIDENCE, WASHINGTON, D.C.

The representative, awakened from the dream, picked up the phone.

"Hello?"

11:09 P.M., RUSSELL BEAUMONT'S RESIDENCE, WEST WHITE BEACH, FLORIDA

Ida Mae watched Russell as he talked to Georgie. He spoke softly, teased her a bit, and reminisced about the old days. Then he made his pitch.

He put the phone down. He was grinning.

"So, what did she say?" Ida Mae asked.

"You're going to be surprised."

"Damn it, Russell, don't keep me in suspense. What did Georgie say?"

"She said she isn't against the idea. She said she'll think about it and call me back tomorrow with her answer."

11:23 P.M., THE REPRESENTATIVE'S RESIDENCE, WASHINGTON D.C.

Since the moment the phone's ringing broke through the dream, the representative had been unable to get back to sleep. Some damn crank call. The caller had hung up. United States Congressman Robert Richard Diddier, Democrat, of the Sixth District, tossed and turned for fifteen minutes and then gave up and just lay there in the dark, thinking about tomorrow.

11:24 P.M., KALYA DIDDIER'S RESIDENCE, NEW YORK CITY

Kalya lay in the dark, smiling. She had almost given in to the temptation of talking with Bobby Ricky. But when she heard his voice on the phone, she knew she had absolutely nothing more to say to him. Now. Or ever. So she had put the phone back in the cradle.

11:25 P.M., GEORGIE BEAUMONT LEBRAND'S RESIDENCE, CAPITAL CITY

Georgie, lying in bed, test papers from her sixth-grade class spread on the blanket, was thinking of the conversation she just had with Russell. She had not given him a definitive answer. There was no use rushing into things. He had said that she should take her time but that he'd like to know just after the holidays, at the latest.

So there it was. She had to decide. Did she want to run against Bobby Ricky next year, or didn't she?

Russell had commissioned a public-opinion survey showing that Bobby Ricky, although popular, had vulnerabilities. He had missed some key votes, since, as a celebrity politician, he was busy making speeches around the country (not back home, where he belonged). He leaned over backward to be kind to the unions, which did not play well with the few businessmen who, last time, had found him attractive, a "doer," and someone who would be on their side, despite his rhetoric.

Oh, yes, Bobby Ricky Diddie could be beat. It would take an absolutely perfectly run campaign, a lot of money, and a candidate willing to bring the fight to him.

He was a congressman today not because he had won the debate or convinced voters he was the candidate who could get things done, but because instinctively he had saved Georgie's life the night of the debate. After the election, Shirley Hevling had told Georgie she believed his action had turned a few hundred voters toward him, exactly when he needed them. And he had turned out just about every black voter, all of them eager to vote for a man who had been criticized for doing what white politicians did all the time and got away with.

The entire campaign had been, in Daddy Bo's words, "about something else." First it had been about jobs. Then it was about drunk driving. Then it was about sex. Along the way it had been about cartwheels and rebounds in a charity basketball game or about Buzzer's uniform and even about a snowstorm. What it finally came down to was a few seconds of violence and one act of heroism. So much for sophisticated theories about what politics is "really" about. Politics is always about something else. The world keeps turning, and politicians and pundits try to make sense of events. But in the very act of trying to interpret events that have already happened, the experts misinterpret the events and trends that are happening now.

Damn it, she had been primed and ready for Bobby Ricky and Buzzer the night of the debate. She had been *pumped!* She would have surprised the both of them, surprised all the experts; she would have turned the whole thing around; she would have ripped them apart in a real debate. She had peaked at just the right time. *That seat should be her seat, damn it, not Bobby Ricky's. . . .*

Now, now, let's not get too excited.

She returned to correcting the history tests but found she couldn't concentrate. She got up, put on her robe and slippers, and went to the kitchen to make a cup of tea. She took the steaming cup into the living room and sat on the Revenge Decor sofa, one of the few pieces of furniture from the old house in Grange City.

She tried to watch TV. On a cable channel, Gary Garafolo, now clean-shaven with a buzz cut and wire-rimmed tinted eyeglasses and wearing an expensive navy blue blazer over a white turtleneck sweater, was shouting at former congressman Gus Gorham. Gus had resigned his seat in April, "to spend more time with my family," and was carving out a new career as a consultant for such business groups as the National Association of Mouse Pad Manufacturers and the Committee of Big Businessmen for Higher Profits Now. Gus could not get a word in as Gary fumed and fussed and talked down to him, sneering and sighing, showing contempt one minute and world-weary amusement the next. Gary's new persona was that of a revered liberal guru who understood in principle the idea of toleration of ideas dissenting from liberal orthodoxy but found actual disagreement with his views somewhat distasteful and quite possibly a sign of mental derangement.

"Your view is vintage Mussolini, circa 1927. It is preposterous," he shouted at Gus. "Truly outrageous!"

But Gus still had great hair, you had to hand him that, and from what Georgie had seen, his hair was more than holding up its end of the debate. She clicked off the TV.

Georgie let her mind wander. No need getting upset just when you want to fall asleep. She closed her eyes. Unbidden, her mind went back, as it had a habit of doing, to Marge and Carl Racksley. One part of her mind said what happened to Marge and Carl was not her fault. She had no way of knowing how he might react when she sent him the awful letter. But another part of her mind insisted she should have realized something awful would happen. Adultery. Lies. A letter like that. What did she *expect* would happen?

The letter had never been found. Poor Carl had probably destroyed it, trying to wipe out forever any evidence of Marge's betrayal. All that Georgie had wanted to do was get Carl angry at Buzzer, and put Buzzer on the defensive for once. But she should have been aware of the possibilities. She would have to live with what she had done for the rest of her life.

Georgie willed herself to stop thinking about the past, at least for tonight. She gave a little, rueful grin. This is exactly what Daddy would have done in a similar situation. Analyze the problem, face the facts, don't fool yourself about your motives or the consequences of your actions, but don't dwell on what can't be changed. He had been right about one more thing, too—she was more like him than she was willing to admit.

Her new apartment in Cap City was great—three bedrooms with a view of the Little Pinellas River—and it was in a nice neighborhood. She had sold the East Side house in Grange City and had not returned there, except for a few visits to see her father in the hospital, God help him. And, yes, she dropped in on Buzzer when she visited her father—they were down the hall from each other. But the real Buzzer was not there. It was just as it had been a year ago. There was only his body, not dead but not really alive.

The move to Cap City had been among the most difficult things she had done in years. But she knew she had to get out of Grange City. There were too many bad memories. There were a few days and especially a few nights after she had first moved that she wanted a drink more than anything in the world. But she hadn't touched a drop. Yet. In fact, she didn't even dare eat Cheez-Its! Too many bad associations.

But everything had turned out as well as could be expected. So far. Little Buzzer wasn't so little anymore. He had mellowed, just a bit. He was still a handful, but all in all, things were coming along pretty well. He was now into sports, especially football, and all that energy at last had a constructive (if too violent) outlet. Jack Danzig was a big help, kind and considerate and funny and supportive as always, and she could not imagine what life would be without him. They were taking it day by day—and night by night—and it was very, very nice. She had been lucky to be able to get back into teaching again. One of her former colleagues was now a principal, and she had helped Georgie get a job at the school.

So things were looking pretty good. She was not only content. She was happy. Except for one thing. Bobby Ricky. On election night, when it was clear she was going to lose by a slim margin (it turned out to be 497 votes), she swore she'd never run again. But after a few months she began to read about him in the *Bugle* (and, now, in the *Capital City Times*), and every time she read about him or saw him on the TV news, she became angry.

Just before Russell had called her from Florida, she had been watching a brief news segment in which Bobby Ricky talked about his interest in the balance of trade. There he was, handsome as ever, glibly spouting some statistics someone else had prepared for him. There was something about the way he spoke, a smugness, a condescension, as if he were an expert on arcane matters of international trade, when he was really just a freshman congressman with a pretty good staff.

So when Russell suggested that she think seriously about running for the seat next year, he had unwittingly caught her at a vulnerable moment. She had a good long conversation with Russell, and she had told him she was going to think about it.

Georgie was getting drowsy. She put the teacup and saucer in the dishwasher and went to her bedroom, being careful not to wake Buzzer Jr. She put out the light. In the darkness she thought: *I have campaign experience. I can speak to crowds or to a roomful of people. I can meet and greet. I know the issues. I know the district. I'll have Ida Mae and Russell. And I'm ready to debate Bobby Ricky, anywhere, anytime.*

I know the words, and now I know the tune.

I'm going to be one hell *of a candidate!*

And then she was asleep.